TELL-TA

CW01500522

A Detective Inspector F̶̶̶̶ ̶̶̶̶ ̶̶̶̶ ̶̶̶̶

NC LEWIS

ISBN: See back cover

Version: 2024.06.18

For news about new books in the series and other works by NC Lewis, please use the QR code to join the reader mailing list.

1

Later, Ann Crombie was to wonder what would have happened if she hadn't heard the noise.

If she'd taken an extra pill.

If she had fled from the village and booked a hotel room in town.

If the manic fury of the argument was not still spinning in her head so her dreams were shallow and sleep restless.

But she did hear the noise. In the bedroom of her two-room stone cottage on the edge of Borrans Wood. After midnight. As she slept alone. A tap like someone knocking to come in.

Ann sat up and blinked. She had felt a presence. Someone in the room. Sensed them fade into the shadows as her head rose from the pillow. She flipped on the bedside lamp, it's stark light harsh in the darkness.

It was a small room with bare brick walls where the faint tang of fresh paint clung in the still air. There was a dresser with a cracked mirror, a rush-seated chair and a huge oak wardrobe weathered with age and so deep you could hide a body in it. She kept a leather-bound bible next to her pillow and a pen inside *Northworder*, a puzzle magazine. An iron crucifix, five feet in length, hung on the wall above her head. The agony of Christ reminded her there were debts to pay in this life and eternal suffering for the unforgiven in the next.

Again she blinked and glanced around the spartan room, clean and tidy and clear of the hoard of junk others carried through their lives. A room for sleep and prayer and crossword puzzles and nothing else. The magic happened in the other room. Creation exploded onto the canvas in her studio.

Ann climbed from the bed, warm feet in cold slippers, and listened. Dim sounds of wildlife came from the garden. The wind rustled through the trees, carrying with it the ringing hoot of an owl; and with the haunting avian moan, the fug of sleep cleared from her head.

Was she dreaming? Did she imagine the tap on the door? The owl hooted again. Long and slow and mournful. The hollow wail of the graveyard. Why did she feel so uneasy?

She gazed at the crucifix. "Forgive me, Father, for I have sinned." Always the same words on waking alive in this room. Always said with her head bowed in shame at what she had done. "I'm sorry, Father, there was no other way."

A yowl caused her to turn to the curtainless window. She waited for the soft scutter and the low guttural call. When it came, she smiled. The fox that lived at the end of her garden was back from a killing spree. Had it been at the neighbour's hen coop again? *Good for it.*

Another huge argument with the locals in the morning, then. They'd glare at her. She'd glare back. She had forbidden them from her garden, telling them the fox had a family to feed. But sneering villagers threatened to dig the foxes out. Pitchforks and spades and a large cloth sack. Piano wire around the neck for the dog and vixen. Their limp bodies hung from high branches to twist in the breeze. A cold cloth sack and Lake Windermere for the cubs.

Ann shivered.

The lamp flickered out. Had the power failed again? Or had the bulb burnt out? There were no neighbours nearby to ask for help. She'd have to go to town to buy a replacement bulb. How much would it cost?

Everything was going up in price. At least she had her art to sell. Her latest works had sold fast, won prizes, turned heads. Soon she'd have an agent from London. Soon she'd make millions. The wildlife she adored and painted would be in safe hands. Next week she'd see a lawyer about her other dream—setting up a wildlife sanctuary. *Yes*, at last, she was on a winning streak. Did she deserve it? After a life of struggle and strife, was she ready for the big league?

An electric hum hissed. The lamp flicked on. Ann turned to the dresser mirror—a woman with grey hair and a lined face stared back. Her face. Each wrinkle etched deep from worry and guilt and shame. She smiled. Her brown eyes gleamed with razor-sharp brightness. *Yes*, she was ready. Mainstream success after all these years. Fame at sixty-five!

A soft thud echoed from the foot of the bed. Was it the same sound which stirred her from her dreams? Ann looked down and gaped at the field mouse lying on its side. *Must have run into the bedpost and knocked itself out.*

"Poor thing." She scooped its warm body into her cool hands and headed for the door. She'd release it deep in the woods and pray it didn't come back. "You poor little thing."

Ann closed the front door and leaned back to gaze at the night sky. A trail of glitter traced out the Milky Way. Ancient sailors used the stars to pick their way across raging seas, but she knew where she was going. No need for stars. She sniffed. Tonight the air smelled of rain. The treetops twitched in a soft mutter at the gentle hand of the breeze.

She hurried along the garden path, only feeling the chill cut through her pale nightdress as she passed from the gate onto the trail that led to the woods. Thunder rumbled in the distance. She wished for her coat and torch, but she'd walked this path many times, knew the way with her eyes closed. It would not take long. Memory guided her way.

The moon dipped behind a cloud and the land went dark. Ann slowed. It was easy to stumble on the tangle of roots, which snagged and snatched like claws.

Under the branches of a larch tree laden with vines, she squatted and released the mouse. It twitched to life and scurried into the undergrowth.

"Goodbye my friend."

She steadied herself to her feet. Why was it so quiet? Where were the animals? She listened. The wind howled with the soulless tone of a tomb.

A twig snapped.

A sharp, violent crack.

Something was off.

Ann scanned the dark foliage, homing in on a thicket of brambles. She didn't know why, but she had the uneasy feeling that she was being watched. Someone had their eyes on her. Someone in the thicket.

"Hello, is anyone there?"

She listened for a reply, for the sound of the animals, for anything. Only the low moan of the wind replied.

"Hello?"

A shadow moved. Dark against night. Ann's stomach flipped. The shadow moved again. Her throat tightened. She scanned the darkness again. The moon came out. Blood surged through her ears when she saw the face.

"Who's there?"

Rapid footsteps crunched in the undergrowth. A figure appeared less than five feet away, swaying toward her.

Ann placed her hands on her hips, a burst of nervous laughter escaping her lips. "If you think jumping out of the bushes and trying to scare me will make me change my mind, you are a bigger fool than me."

The figure continued to advance, swaying as though in a trance. A flash of steel glistened in a ray of moonlight. The figure lurched, slashing the knife through the dark air and shouting in a savage voice. "You and those bloody foxes. "

Ann Crombie ran.

Moonlight caught her pale nightdress as she fled. She dashed through the woods, hell for leather, slipping, sliding, clambering through the foliage and leaping over a stone wall the way no woman of sixty-five should.

At the edge of the woods now. Close to the path that led back to her stone cottage and her mobile phone. Breathing hard. Chest raw. Bile souring her mouth. Ahead, dense vegetation. Behind footsteps, the *clip-clop* of the figure half walking, half running.

The moon plunged behind dense clouds, colouring everything midnight blue. Ann ran on, gasping for breath, chest heaving in ragged jerks. Sixty seconds and she'd be out on the path, in the open. Memory guiding her way.

Another bolt of terror struck. Was she running the right way? Ann knew the woods like the back of her hand. Knew she was running toward her cottage and away from the shore. No way was she confused by the darkness and the fear fuelled panic driving her on. But what if she had made a mistake and was running toward the lake? Lapping waves ahead. Behind, the slash and cut of the attacker's blade. She'd be trapped.

She glanced at the sky to check her position. Dark clouds swirled like angry faces. Ann Crombie ran on.

A roar tore through the sky, shaking the trees. Thunder. The clouds burst. Rain lashed down in torrential waves. The hoot of an owl screamed through the dampness. Ann ran on, slipping, sliding, staggering homeward.

She had the edge.

She knew the woods.

She'd get away.

She made her way through the thicket using animal trails she knew well. Puffing hard now, chest heaving. Scrambling toward her cottage.

A vine.

It snagged her foot.

Ann stumbled against a tree trunk, tried to tug her foot loose, but the vine tightened with the clasp of a snare. She tugged again, yanking her leg with such violent force she tumbled to the weed-strewn earth, head first. A heavy wet smack.

As she lay immobile, wheezing, she wondered what

would have happened if she hadn't told the truth. If she'd fled the village and booked a room in a faraway city, taken an extra pill and fallen deep into the softness of dreams. And she thought of her secret buried as deep as tree roots.

From the foliage came the predatory shuffle of footsteps. A constant clip-clop. Like the cloven hoofs of the devil.

Clip-clop.

Cautious and calculated.

Clip-clop.

Steady and sure.

Ann held her breath. If she kept still and hid here, the figure might walk past her. She wriggled deeper into the foliage, trying to make herself small. Thorns and thistles and the sharp prick of brambles.

A crack of lightning streaked the sky. Another rumble of thunder shuddered the trees. Ann exhaled a slow breath. Why should she cower in the damp undergrowth waiting for fate to show its hand? She was a winner now. An artist on the threshold of fame.

This is not the end.

Shards of pain surged through her ankle. Could she even stand? To hell with it, she would get up and limp the last few yards to her stone cottage, bolt the door and call the police. She could do it. Yes, she would see this night through.

I've waited long enough. It is my time now. My shot. No one is going to snatch destiny from my grasp.

She thought of her art and she thought of the foxes and she thought of her animal sanctuary. She eased to her knees but fell back, gasping as the first blow landed. A clenched fist to the side of her head. Then came a grunt from the figure, cruel and bloodless and cold. "Why didn't you listen?"

Another blow landed. Dazed, Ann gasped and then screamed.

A cloth sack.

Over her head.

It's roughness scratching her face.

The bone-chilling stench of dead things flooded her nostrils. Her eyes adjusted to the new gloom, lungs thirsty for air, suffocating in the stench. Biting back pain, she tried once more to stand, swinging her arms in wild arcs to push the attacker away. A third blow landed, and a fourth. Blow upon blow smashed Ann Crombie's body to pieces, and with the thrust and cut of the blade, sent her world eternally black.

2

Fenella sensed trouble was coming.

She had not told anyone. The strange sensation, if it could be called that, came over her the moment she climbed out of the car in the village of Ambleside. A feeling that something wasn't quite right, that something awful was about to happen. She had kept silent, not wanting to spoil the joy of her family day out.

She strode along the narrow trail in her worn-out hiking boots. An early morning storm had washed in from Lake Windermere, leaving the path slick with rain. Now the sun was up over the treetops. The dark clouds had cleared from the mid-morning sky and the July heat was already rising. Swirls of mist hovered over the green fields. Bumblebees flitted about. After the storm, the day smelled hot and uneasy.

The wilderness reminded her of Uncle Glen. He loved the Cumbria countryside, marching across the trails in his giant hiking boots, head held high, naming the birds and foliage and sniffing the weather. She stopped by an orange flag, took off her green kagool jacket and tied it around her waist.

Time for a breather.

A fat man in an unfashionable green tracksuit jogged by, wheezing with heavy breaths. Back along the trail, her mam and a gaggle of tourists huffed their way up the incline. Her husband staggered at the back of the pack, stopping once in a while, hands on his knees.

The Ambleside Village Artists Walkabout was in its twenty-sixth year. Locals dressed in historical clothes. A man in a Victorian waist jacket swung a sword-tipped cane. A lass dressed as a milk maiden carried a steel pale. On the brow of a hill, a gaggle of people marched in Roman armour, complete with breastplates and spears.

Orange flags marked the spot that had inspired local artists to create objects of art. The number on each flag matched the tag on an art piece for sale in the Parish Centre. Fenella had her eye on a dazzling blown glass lamp. It was as smooth as water to touch, with a delirious riot of colours which scattered pearls of light—flag number twenty-three.

Earlier, she had watched a middle-aged couple in orange Roman togas eyeing the glass lamp. They'd stood very still, staring at it, their fingers touching the price tag. It was an expensive piece, not to be bought without careful reflection. Minutes passed and still they did not move. When Fenella approached, they nodded and walked away.

And now, like a lamp, the sun was brightening the morning gloom, splashing the hillside in glorious rays. Fenella inhaled and fancied she could taste the tang of Lake Windermere. She cocked an ear, listening for water lapping the shore, hearing nothing but the low moan of the wind.

Fifty yards ahead, a figure in a hooded cape clambered over a stile and dashed onto the trail. They moved with the easy glide of the Grim Reaper floating across the stage in a play. The Grim Reaper without his death crook and wearing a cape too large for their slight frame. The excess cloth billowed in the ceaseless breeze.

Normally, Fenella might have glanced away, back down the trail to see how her mam and husband were doing, but not today. There was nothing normal about today. She kept her gaze on the hooded figure who carried a brown cloth sack and sped up the incline at a smooth trot, away from the crowd. And, like the Grim Reaper, disappeared between a thicket of brambles and into the shadow of oak trees as suddenly as they had appeared.

Fenella watched the flicker of shadow between the oak trees. *Probably a local dressing up as part of the festivities. Nowt odd in that.* But still, she stared at the tangle of brambles and the branches shivering in the breeze. An irate bumblebee buzzed by her ear. She brushed it away, and her gaze fell to the view below. Ambleside Fort, built by the Romans.

"Is that it?" Fenella's mam, whom everyone called Nan, was by her side, huffing. "It's nowt but a heap of soddin' rocks. I've got a better-looking rock pile in our garden. Where are the turrets, flag poles and iron gates? And where are the walls?"

"You have to use your imagination." Eduardo, Fenella's husband, shielded his eyes as he took in the view. "The stone foundations are all that remain of the place. It served as a Roman defence against Scottish raiders. After two thousand years, I'm surprised there is anything left." He paused for a long moment, squinting hard at the rocks. "Yes, I can see it as it once was. A magnificent place. Can you see it, too?"

"Nah." Nan squinted at the remains of the fort. "All I can see is the gory chaos as the kilted men attack."

Eduardo placed a hand on Nan's elbow. "Bet you thought they'd still be a few of those Scottish chaps striding around in their kilts. Explains why you were walking so fast to get here."

"Cheeky sod." Nan slapped his hand away. "But those Morris dancers in the village were quite tasty. I suppose they'll have to do."

Fenella laughed. Earlier, they'd watched a group of Morris men folk dancing in the village. Bells and sticks and rhythmic stepping. Shouts and cries of laughter. Nan was picked out by one of the dancers and dragged into the fray.

"You've got some nice dance moves, Nan." Fenella wiped a teardrop from her eye. "Gave them a run for their money."

There was nothing better than striding the trails of Cumbria with Eduardo and Nan on a Saturday morning, then poking around a flea market. *Family time.*

Her five children and her grandbairns were due next weekend for a big family get-together. They would chat and eat while the bairns played. When the sun went down, she'd tell the bairns a bedtime story and tuck them into bed, then she'd gossip all night with her children and Nan and Eduardo, drinking wine and beer. *Yes*, she'd bring the grandbairns here next Saturday, let them run wild and wear themselves out.

For several minutes, they observed the ruins of the Roman fort and listened to the mumble of the breeze. A pair of buzzards soared. Something moved in the brambles. The leaves shimmered and shook. A red fox appeared, pulling itself onto the trail by its front paws, dragging its hind legs behind. It glanced in their direction and let out a pained howl, turned and crawled from where it had come.

Nan's face crumpled into a frown. "Poor mite, doesn't it have a family? I can't see it living long in that condition."

"I hope it doesn't have cubs to feed." Fenella's gaze remained on the brambles. "Probably lives deep in the woods."

"It'll be dead by nightfall." Nan spoke in a low voice. As if she didn't really want to say the words. "The others will turn on it to put it out of its misery. It won't have to suffer for much longer. Nature is quick to dispatch the sick."

They fell silent. Spots of rain fell from a passing cloud. Eduardo cleared his throat. "The woods are lovely, dark and deep, but I have promises to keep and miles to go before I sleep. And there are pancakes and honey and apple pie to eat."

Nan rolled her eyes. "Oh, so now you are a poet. Robert Frost must be spinning in his grave at the way you've butchered his poem."

Eduardo touched his chin. "I've added to Robert Frost as my pencil strokes add to a drawing." He winked. "Steal like an artist and the world thinks of you as a genius."

Eduardo drew comics for a living, his first passion. His second was food. It showed on his growing waistline. On Saturdays, he went for a jog with Fenella to fight the flab.

Nan shrugged off her jacket. "I thought a walk out here would give you inspiration for your cartoons, but all you can think about is food."

Eduardo twirled, arms out wide, spinning top style. "Feed me. Feed me now." He patted his stomach. "I've got to keep my gut muscles working in order to feed my creative brain."

Fenella smiled and rolled her shoulders to keep them loose. "Let's walk around the fort. Local legend says it is a portal for sheep."

Eduardo's mouth dropped. "What do you mean?"

Fenella waved the guidebook, laughing. "Like in Dr Who." She put on her spooky voice. "On the first full moon, spectral sheep appear. They shimmer with an otherworldly glow as they graze in the ruins. Are they echoes of the past or glimpses of a future flock?"

Nan jabbed a finger at Eduardo. "You'll be at home with all the weird goings-on, seeing as you draw cartoons for a living."

Eduardo opened his mouth to answer when a bee landed on his shoulder. It buzzed. He swished at it, turning his body and his ankle in the soft soil.

"My foot!" He grimaced. "Think I've twisted it."

"Lean on me for support," Fenella wrapped an arm around her husband. Something in his body always seemed to break when it was time for vigorous outdoor exercise. "Does it hurt?"

He stooped to rub his ankle. "Think it is swelling."

"Serve you right, you fat bugger." Nan wagged a finger. "If you hadn't eaten pancakes with honey for breakfast, it wouldn't have happened. You can't eat food like that and expect it to give you the necessary strength to walk in the countryside. Your breakfast was an accident waiting to happen. You need to binge on fresh air and exercise from now on."

"But you had pancakes too." Eduardo straightened. "In fact, if my memory still holds, you cooked and served them to me."

Nan's eyes twinkled, but she said nothing.

He loosened the laces on his boot. "If I was a suspicious man, I'd think you were trying to do me in with your fine cooking. Not that I am complaining. Next time I'll have seconds."

Nan laughed. "You devil. No wonder that bee buzzed you. It knows who ate half its hive. My God, I bet it has gone to get the others. Mark my words, it will be back to sting your hide."

Eduardo's eyes widened and his gaze darted about. "You really think so?"

Laughing, Fenella stepped away from him and looked at his foot. "Are you alright?"

"Yes, but I don't think I can go on. Do you mind if I limp back to the village and crash in that café by the river until you and Nan have finished?" He kissed Fenella on her lips. "Did you see the size of their scones?"

"I'll go with you." Fenella wanted to visit a few more orange flags, but her family came first. "We can have an early lunch, then look around the flea market."

"No, no, no." Eduardo cast a brief look at the Roman fort. "You two must go on. Don't you want to visit the spot that inspired that glass lamp you have your eye on? Flag twenty-three, isn't it? I'd blame myself if you didn't see the landscape that led to its creation. Take a photo, as I'd like to see it too."

Flag twenty-three was further along the trail. Fenella

glanced at the Roman fort and she glanced at the trail snaking off into the distance and she glanced back toward the village and its cafés. The couple in orange Roman togas climbed slowly up the incline. *They are definitely interested in buying that lamp and want to see the spot where it was created.*

"I'll go with him, Fen." Nan rolled her eyes again, but it was clear she liked the idea of sitting in a café eating scones. "Just to make sure the greedy sod doesn't eat out the entire shop. He's a fiend when it comes to cream cakes. The slob hoards them on his plate and gawks with an evil eye at anyone who gets close. I'll make sure he doesn't get out of control."

Fenella laughed. They would both pile their plates high with scones and spoon on jam and clotted cream. She fancied one or two herself. *I'll jog the next few orange flags, then back to the Parish Centre to buy that glass lamp.* She tightened the kagool around her waist. "I'll meet you at the café in one hour. Rescue a scone for me."

Eduardo kissed her again. He turned, and with Nan at his side, hobbled with remarkable speed for a man with a twisted ankle, down the trail toward the village and the café with the giant scones.

3

Fenella was fifteen minutes into her jog and breathing hard. She rounded a sweeping curve lined by ancient oak trees. The sun had risen higher and the warm breeze cleared the remaining clouds. The sky was crystal blue. She hadn't seen a living soul since she left the Roman fort, though the village swarmed with tourists visiting the Ambleside art show.

A familiar buzz settled in her chest, the gnawing sense she got whenever things were off. Had she taken a wrong turn? She slowed her pace, half wishing she had gone with Eduardo and Nan to the café to dine on giant scones with clotted cream and blackberry jam. Her mouth watered and a pang of hunger stabbed in her gut. *If I've got it wrong, I'll turn around, jog to the café, and gobble down a plate of scones.*

She'd just passed a hawthorn bush when she spotted what she was looking for. An orange flag. It fluttered in the breeze—number twenty-three. Delighted, she stopped and punched a fist in the air. Ahead of her snaked a narrow trail hedged on both sides by deep green foliage. It dipped and climbed through a stand of ash trees to a slatted gate set in a dry-stone wall. Beyond, she could make out a whitewashed stone cottage with a traditional slate roof and window frames made of dark wood.

Fenella pulled out the Ambleside Artists Guide from her pocket and ran a finger over the page. The cottage was built over a hundred years ago by a retired circus performer and known by locals as Bede Thatch. She looked again at the house. A tangle of brambles clawed above the dry-stone wall. The small windows were dark, watchful as eyes.

She took her time now, moving in a slow three-hundred-and-sixty-degree circle, taking it all in. Bushes shivered in the constant breeze. Damp rose in swirls of earthy aromas. And behind her lay Borrans wood. She stopped, facing the cottage and enjoyed the glorious view. A long line of dry-stone wall smeared by lichen as thick and green as on any tombstone. The slate roof of Bede Thatch rose above the tree line like a dark and permanent scar. It was mad how one thing led to another. How this landscape led to a glass lamp.

"A rather fantastic view, wouldn't you say?" A plump woman with wild white hair and a face flushed as though she'd been drinking stepped from behind the hawthorn bush. "I'm Bella. Bella Timbol."

She said the words as though Fenella should know who she was, with an upper-class lilt to her tone, her beady eyes staring down a long narrow nose. A lover of the country for sure, and a lover of its bloodthirsty ways. She was the type that chased foxes on horseback with hounds baying at her heels.

"Oh aye." Fenella folded her arms. "The name sounds familiar, but I can't place it."

"Chairwoman of the Ambleside Village Artists." Bella

smoothed a ring-bedecked hand down her skirt, straightened the pearl necklace around her neck and dusted leaves off her green tweed hunting jacket.

"Members of the committee are at various flags counting how many people show up. I've been here all morning. This cottage is a bit isolated. The only way here is via the trail." She smiled with a mouth full of white teeth. "Our art community is one big happy family. I'm pleased you made it."

Fenella extended her hand. "I'm Fenella. Nice day for it." She paused for a moment, trying to hide her keenness for the answer to her next question. "Have many visited this flag?"

"Other than Miss Fish, our local fire warden who stopped by for a quick chat, you are the third. A couple in orange Roman togas were here a short while ago. Interested in item twenty-three, eh?" Bella's beady eyes stared without blinking. "It's a wonderful lamp. I can't deny it would look just right on my coffee table. Expensive, though. If it doesn't sell, I will. . . "

She broke off as a gust whipped up twigs and leaves, throwing them in her face. Fenella closed her eyes and turned away from the salvo. It pelted down like rain. For several seconds the mini dust storm raged.

Bella continued. "Are you interested in joining the Ambleside Village Artists? Membership is very reasonable?"

"I live on the outskirts of Port St Giles."

"Our members come from across Cumbria."

"I've tried painting by numbers but couldn't get the swing of it."

"We take all levels, there are no boundaries, except a

love for creating art. I can tell you have a sharp eye; you'd be an excellent creative. Tell me, what is it you do for a living?"

Fenella turned to look at the cottage. "That lamp would look nice in that window of an evening, eh?"

Bella grimaced. "I used to own the cottage. Nasty business. One must always be prepared for a mele when one visits Bede Thatch. Ever since I can remember, locals have talked about a curse hanging over the place."

Fenella enjoyed gossip and sensed she had a fellow talker. "Oh aye, and what's that about?"

She expected to hear a tale about ghosts with hollow voices and women in grey dresses peering through fogged windows. Spooks were everywhere in Cumbria. But the story she was told was one she'd rather not know.

Bella looked at the cottage for a long while. "Locals say a church bell tolls at midnight when death is near, but it can only be heard from here, and there are no churches out this way."

Fenella glanced around, looking for a steeple. "A bell, you say?"

"A sullen metal thud to warn of death, brought by a monk who never speaks and whose face is never seen. Locals call it the curse of Borrans Wood."

Again, Fenella glanced around. The trees and bushes looked so peaceful. "The woods are haunted by a monk, eh?"

Bella picked a twig from her jacket and looked away. "This wind wreaks havoc with one's hair. Did you know the house was built by a circus performer who retired here with his monkey? A bit of a Dr Doolittle, I hear, liked to talk to the animals; sang to them too. It has been a favourite spot for creatives ever since. Only two rooms, mind you. Poky. Not suitable for a family."

Only then, as Bella continued to wipe away leaves, did Fenella notice the cuts and scrapes on the back of the woman's hands. Another blast of wind whipped up leaves into a demented whirl. And with it came a scream. Two figures, both wearing orange Roman togas, stumbled from the shadow between the trees. The woman was out in front, bare foot and running fast. Ten paces behind, the man staggered, his legs wobbling as though he'd lost control.

Another scream rang out. It came from the woman, her words a blur of hellish fear. But it was the man's voice, clear and crisp, which sent a shiver along Fenella's spine.

"A body. We've found a body in the woods."

4

Fenella had planned to spend the rest of the morning in the café that sold giant scones, plate piled high. Lashings of blackberry jam and clotted cream. Guilt-free calories since it was the weekend. Instead, she found herself on the edge of a crime scene about to view the body for a second time with no idea of what lay ahead. No idea of the hell to come.

She stood by the police tape under the shade of a broad-leafed oak tree, seeing the world through a detective's eye. A fierce sun bore down, its late-morning rays dappling the brambles and nettles. Moisture rose in loose swirls, bringing the earthy scent of the forest. Above the treetops, a raven flapped. It muttered and croaked, the sweep of its eye taking everything in. A sense of the graveyard hovered in the shadows. You couldn't see the crime scene tent but you could feel death was near.

The right thing to do was to go back to the station and wait for the official reports to come in. That was protocol these days. The detective came in after the crime scene officials had finished their work. But the first time she saw the body lying between the clods of soil, fat tendrilled vines and brambles, she knew something was off. And the pathologist, Dr MacKay, was on site now. She wanted his opinion. Sometimes protocol got in the way of what needed to be done. Sometimes you had to bend the rules. A little.

The crowd had grown. A fat man in an unfashionable green tracksuit watched with bright eyes, his lips turned up at the edges. But most stared with blank faces; a few crumpled in woe; others out for a jolly good gawk. Locals and tourists. The curious and the sad and the excited. Their chatter carried like prayers at Evensong. How could they have known today was the tip of the iceberg? No one could have foreseen the suffering to come.

A boom rang out as an arc light generator burst into life. Fenella's gaze followed the noise then flicked back to the crowd, scanning the faces. A habit picked up on her days on the beat. Criminals often returned to the scene of their crime to feast on the chaos and gloat over what they had done. What were the percentages? She couldn't recall, but they were high.

A stooped woman in a peach headscarf chewed hard on a stick of gum. A man in a bright orange shirt with punk-style hair rubbed a hand over his forty-something face. A twig-thin woman with wild honey eyes scratched her neck. She stood next to a young couple, him in a white t-shirt and blue shorts, her in a lime floral dress that clung to her curves.

The man in the unfashionable tracksuit pushed to the front, his bright eyes excited and watchful. Near the back, bathed in the strobe of police lights, Bella Timbol ran a plump hand through her white hair. It did nothing to tame the wildness. Next to her, a lean man with an oversized forehead rubbed his hands. He wore dark clothes, his dog collar gleaming bright white. He stood close to Bella. Too close.

Bella caught Fenella's eye, looked frightened for an instant, then waved. Tentative and timid. A tiny royal movement of the ring-bedecked hand. Fenella waved back, stepped across the police tape, and then cast one last glance at the crowd. This time she did not see the mass of humanity. Or the police officers now trying to drive the crowd back. Nor the man with the dog collar staring hard at her and whispering into Bella's ear. All she saw was the gruesome scene that awaited inside the billowing walls of the crime scene tent.

The dark soil.

The strong vines.

The sharp brambles.

The terrible state of the body.

Something was definitely off.

5

Fenella walked along a narrow dirt track which twisted away into a void of shadows. An ominous blanket of vegetation crowded in from both sides. Bushes with thorns. Nettles and thistles. Low tree branches which snagged and snared and clawed through clothes. If you weren't careful, they'd rake your skin and draw blood. She came out in a small clearing of trampled bushes and bindweed.

"Over here, guv." Detective Sergeant Robert Dexter, her right-hand man, waved from a table. It contained boxes of white coveralls, gloves and shoe protectors. "Ain't a trail most folk would walk, more a track for the animals with all those thistles and brambles. But we've got the ball rolling. The forensic search is well underway."

He pointed at two figures in white suits, one crawling on hands and knees, the other prodding a patch of nettles with a stick. Two uniformed officers fiddled with an arc lamp. And at the centre, the white walls of the crime scene tent shielded prying eyes from the horror inside.

Fenella approached the table and took a pair of gloves. "Mr and Mrs Grange found the body. Jon and Joan. They didn't touch anything. When they saw the state of the victim, they ran."

"Don't blame them, guv." Dexter squeezed his eyes. "If I weren't a copper, I'd have taken to my heels at the cruel sight. Finding a grave in the woods is one thing... but this... can't get my head around it. They will want to keep the lid on the coffin tight shut at the funeral. A crying bleedin' shame."

Fenella did not speak. A sudden gust lifted the earthy scents of the wood—soil, leaves, the faint tang from Lake Windermere. A refreshing blast if it were not for the sickly-sweet stench of death.

Pimples rose on her skin.

Arms.

Shoulders.

Back.

Legs.

She exhaled and her breath carried with it the promise to dig until she uncovered the truth.

Dexter rubbed his chin. "It's the artists me heart goes out for, guv. And with them having their festival today to raise funds for their passion. What a great shame. Did Mr and Mrs Grange see anyone?"

Fenella shook her head. "PC Beth Finn is with them, taking a statement. They are both very shocked. Mr Grange wept."

They fell silent.

The whirr of a generator echoed through the trees. The arc lamp flickered to life, illuminating a black cape slung on an oak branch. From inside the walls of the crime scene tent came the shout of a familiar voice; giddy with excitement; a joyous yell; half song, half poem mixed with nursery rhyme. "Because I could not stop for death. He kindly stopped for me. The carriage held but just ourselves, and immortality."

Freakish given the gloom of death which hovered over the place.

Fenella fiddled with the gloves. "Sounds like the doctor is having fun, didn't know he was a fan of Emily Dickinson's poetry."

Dr MacKay, the pathologist, adored his work with the dead. When they first met, enthusiasm oozed from him with such force it alarmed Fenella. That was when she was a green-faced rookie trembling in his studio as he sliced open a bare-chested corpse. He wore a Victorian black cape back then. He was still wearing it today.

"Aye, guv, the Doc's in his element." Dexter made no attempt to suit up. He'd already visited the inside of the crime scene tent. One look was enough. "Hope the Doc finds something useful in all that...mess."

Fenella tilted her neck to relieve a knot of tension. "Grab a couple of constables and get the names and addresses of everyone in the crowd. Anyone see or hear anything?" She paused as the wind picked up, shaking the leaves. Florid flashes of light shone through the canopy. "There is a cottage at the end of the trail, locals call it Bede Thatch. Ask PC Woods to have a poke about, see if anyone is at home."

Dexter nodded, then half turned, gaze fastened on the crime scene tent. "It's the work of a crazy sicko, guv. A lout who needs putting away."

Fenella said nothing for a moment. It took time to take in the terrible sight and she was still digesting what she'd already seen. "Did you notice anything off with the crime scene?"

"Aye, guv, but I can't put me finger on it." Dexter covered his eyes for a heartbeat. "It ain't right what happened in there. It just ain't right."

He strode off, shaking his head and muttering.

6

Lisa Levon, the crime-scene manager, greeted Fenella at the flap of the tent. "Dr MacKay is with the... remains."

Even though Lisa worked with the gruesome and grim, she had the body of a Paris fashion model, the voice of a Hollywood star, and the teeth of a Harley Street dentist. Youthful with vibrant skin and glowing everything even though she was close to forty.

Fenella's hair had long gone grey, and her body, despite the jogging, raced toward plum pudding. *How does Lisa do it? Must be her genes. Can't imagine her wolfing down giant scones stuffed with clotted cream and blackberry jam even though it is the weekend.*

Fenella chased the snatch of jealousy to the back of her mind. "Saw the doctor on his way in, cape flapping as he raced to the crime scene." She didn't let her gaze wander inside the tent flap. Not yet. "Never heard him so full of song."

Lisa laughed with the tinkle of a piano. "He was in the village when he got the call and came blowing in like a gale. He hasn't moved from the remains since he got here."

Dr MacKay had been in his job for more years than Fenella recalled. The man was happiest amongst the dead, decaying and rotting bones. She thought the gaseous stench of decomposing flesh gave him the vigour of youth, but she knew better than to mention it. He'd once told her that as a teen, he'd crept around graveyards at night, growing his private collection. She never asked what he was collecting.

That Dr MacKay was here so soon after the discovery meant he'd have plenty to tell her. He'd speculate until the cows came home and bet a bottle of Glenmorangie whisky on his best guess. Fenella liked that about him.

She suited up. A flutter stirred in her gut. It flitted like the buzz of bee wings. Always the same feeling of sadness when she entered a place where the Grim Reaper had struck. Now she must face what lay inside. Again.

7

A white-suited assistant eased through the flap and wandered off along the trail. A surge of heat flowed from inside the tent carrying with it the scent of death. Fenella swallowed. *Soon I'll be inside that sodden and putrid furnace.*

She turned her attention back to Lisa. "Anything you can tell me?"

She tried not to sound too hopeful, but she wanted to wrap this one up fast. A fingerprint or splatter of blood might lead them to the killer.

Lisa didn't sound optimistic. "The rain has not helped. I hope the earlier downpour hasn't washed all the evidence away." Her voice dropped to a whisper. "This one has shaken me. I'm taking a breather. I need some fresh air. Do you think I'm getting soft?"

"Nah, just practical." Fenella thought crime scene techs had the worst job in the world. She'd not do it, no matter how much it paid. "It must be an ordeal to crawl through all that... stuff and with such rigour."

Lisa sighed. "Thank you. Sometimes I think I'm a nutjob taking this on. Yes, it is an odious job to some, but most of the time I love, love, love it." She glanced at the tent flap. "Not this time, though."

8

It was hot inside the tent which had a high ceiling and thin walls and an arc lamp. Fenella's clothes clung to her, the dampness chilling her skin. The forensic coveralls didn't help. The harsh light exposed every corner.

Two white-suited assistants worked in respectful silence. The sharp click of a photographer's camera quickened Fenella's heartbeat. Blood pooled on the ground and a wet pink spray glistened in the bushes. The victim lay on her back amongst bindweed and brambles, bloodstained nightdress hitched up over her breasts. The left leg buckled the wrong way and vines snagged the right ankle. Her arms twisted above a gaping hole that was once her head.

Hell had come to Ambleside.

Dr MacKay crouched, his face almost touching the body. "I need the head. Can someone please find me the head?"

Deep sorrow seared Fenella's core at seeing the corpse in such an undignified pose. And it was a pose, she was sure of that. Death was difficult enough without this humiliation. She wanted to pull the nightdress down and cover the poor woman with a sheet. How would they fix the body for the woman's relatives? She prayed for the moment when she left this gruesome place and felt guilty for that thought. "Well, doctor?"

"Ah, Fenella, I wondered when my favourite detective might arrive." Dr MacKay turned, his eyes glittering through his face mask. "A horrid image. It doth unfix my hair and make my seated heart knock."

"Shakespeare?" She played the doctor's game. It was the best way to get information out of him. "A quote from Macbeth. Act 1, Scene 3. Have you got some good news for me?"

Dr MacKay chuckled. "Fun and games today, eh?" He turned back to the body. "Interesting serrations on the cervical spine. Come, take a look at the trachea, better known as the windpipe."

Fenella gritted her teeth, swallowed bile and leaned in. "What am I looking at?"

Dr MacKay poked at the weeping grey flesh. He spoke with the gusto of a child in a fairground, in awe of it all and eager to try every ride. "See that, it is the windpipe. It connects the larynx. . . oh, I'm getting technical. It connects the voice box to the bronchi which leads to the lungs." He prodded a gloved finger deep into the cavernous hollow. "Our killer did not make a clean cut, more a hack job. Savage."

A shout came from outside the tent. Muffled and unclear. The crime scene photographer's camera continued to click.

Dr MacKay lifted the victim's right hand, then her left. "Notice these lacerations on the back. Defensive wounds. She tried to fend off the attacker."

"And," Fenella began, staring at the left hand, "she was

single and lived alone."

"How can you be certain?"

"No wedding ring."

"Lots of women choose not to wear one."

"Aye, but if she were wed her hubby would have called the police by now. He'd be at the front of the crowd, fighting his way to get to the body. She lived alone, hands of an artist." She leaned closer, pointing at an ink-black tattoo on the left arm. "Looks like a castle. Not a local building, then. I don't think she was originally from around these parts."

"Ah, my favourite detective has made an interesting find. Yes, that tattoo looks familiar, can't recall why."

Fenella gazed around. "Why did the killer cut off her head and leave her chest exposed?"

"I'm no detective, Fenella, but I'd say you are dealing with a deranged sex maniac. Not that I'd put it in those terms in my report, and there are tests to be done and so forth." He dropped his voice to a whisper. "But if you'd like to bet a bottle of Glenmorangie on my theory, I'd be happy to take you up on your kind offer."

Fenella shook her head. The doctor had an uncanny habit of winning his bets, and Eduardo got upset when she gave away his good whisky. She refocused. "How did the body end up here?"

"I can't answer that." Dr MacKay was shaking his head, gloved fingers feeling inside the crevice of the corpse's neck. "Many of us like to wander at night."

Fenella ignored that. She knew he had a habit of exploring graveyards at night and skipped to her next question. "Was the body moved?"

"Not a chance." Dr MacKay snorted. "I'd bet a good bottle of Glenmorangie on that. Fancy taking the bet?"

"I don't like the odds." Fenella folded her arms. "You know something I don't and I want to know it too."

Dr MacKay laughed. "The crime scene assistants have found signs of a struggle right here. The lady died in this scenic spot. Why she was here in the dead of night in her nightdress is beyond my powers." He turned and held Fenella's gaze. "I fear the killer took her head as a sick trophy."

Sweat prickled Fenella's brow. "Time of death?"

Dr MacKay leaned close to the severed neck, sniffing. "Easier with the head on, isn't it, my darling? Oh yes, with the head we can be more precise." He eased from the body, staring at it like a psychic consulting a crystal ball. "The animals haven't been at her, can't vouch for the flies. She died late last night, around midnight. You'll have a written report as soon as I get her to my studio."

And that is when she saw them. Scattered near the body. Two, maybe three feet from where the victim lay. Four white rose petals curled in the flattened bindweed. She waved at a white-suited assistant. "Bag those petals, please."

The assistant nodded, produced a clear plastic bag and dropped them in.

"Has our eagle-eyed detective found a clue?" Dr MacKay turned from the body.

"Not sure. Rose petals."

"Ah, fair is the rose, but it is quickly gone."

Fenella couldn't help herself; she loved Shakespeare. "The Merchant of Venice, Act 1, Scene 1."

"Superb." Dr MacKay made a show of clapping. "Have you considered they may have blown in on the wind?"

"Aye, that is a possibility."

"Then you will also have considered the possibility they were placed here by the killer as a weird icon in the worship of some gory idol." Dr MacKay paused, warming to playing the detective. "Or they may have fallen from the killer's clothing as skin falls from the scalp. The thing is, what are they doing here?"

Fenella's mind had already raced over both possibilities and come to the same question. "You should have joined the force."

"With my nighttime record?"

Before Fenella responded, Lisa Levon burst into the tent. "We've found the head."

9

Within seconds, Fenella was outside in the clearing, hurrying behind Lisa. Dr MacKay was several paces in front, racing toward a tall larch tree. Two white-suited assistants were by the tree trunk, one kneeling on the damp earth.

"Mine." Dr MacKay's voice echoed through the trees. "Please take care. It is mine."

They approached at a trot, stopping several feet away. The assistant peeled back the sides of a brown cloth sack. Fenella held her breath as gloved hands lifted out a head, soaking wet and stained with dark blood. The brown eyes might have been alive, so clear and bright they stared. But the face was pale, with a bloated tongue poking through the teeth. It was the bruising which churned Fenella's stomach the most. Mottled splotches ran the length of both sides of the head.

Dr MacKay squatted next to the assistant and bent closer. "A vicious attack with many blows to the head." He stopped and let out a sharp gasp. "I'm guessing here, but the indentations suggest a fist and... yes, a big stick. Nasty."

Silence fell over the clearing. It seemed to Fenella that even the constant hiss of the breeze died away to nothing.

A vacuum-like stillness.

A hole in the air.

A moment later, Dr MacKay spoke in a strange and taut shrill. "The raging rocks and shivering shocks shall break the locks of prison gates." He lowered his head. When he glanced up, there were tears in his eyes. "That is from Midsummer Night Dream, Fenella."

She said nothing.

"Today has turned into a hellish nightmare before mine eyes." Dr MacKay's gloved hands trembled as he parted clods of bloodstained hair and stared at the face. "I know this woman. I bought one of her paintings to hang in my study last week. Her name is Ann Crombie."

10

It was hard to stay still, Liam Brampton found, even though she'd agreed to his request. He glanced at the door with a growing sense of excitement and wanted to pray it would go well. But he didn't believe in telling God his plans because when he did, the Lord snatched them away.

He spread his new smock, wheat-gold, on the pine table, smoothing it down with his hands. Next to it lay his French beret hat, once cream, now dyed blood-red. Next to the beret was the crystal bowl given to him by his gran. Soon, he'd cover his naked body in the sacred garments and dip his hands into the bowl. Not yet, though. He must wait until the downstairs door creaked its rusted hinges. Keep calm until her footsteps clattered up the stone stairs. Breathe easy until she was inside and he'd bolted shut the front door.

He'd placed his lucky rabbit paw next to the crystal bowl for safe keeping. Now he swept it into his palm, stroking it three times and muttering in a strange fox-like gurgle.

Today, he would not deny himself a full measure of pure pleasure.

Outside, the wind was singing. Golden rays burst forth from an orange sun in wide streaks of warming glitter. Inside, traces of stale booze and cigarette ash tinged the air. She wasn't due for a quarter of an hour so Liam sat on a wooden chair, wriggled his buttocks on the cool hard surface then stood up to pace.

He must not get nervous.

Must not tremble.

Must not stand naked on the landing by the sixty-three stone steps, listening for her footfall.

The last time he invited a lass to this place it ended in a howl of foul language. He'd worn an old mud-brown smock which stretched tight over his pot-belly, open-toed sandals for comfort and a cream beret for a touch of style.

He sensed doom the moment he opened the door.

The evil-eyed hag with blue-rinsed hair stepped in. All false teeth and demanding payment at twice the rate he had agreed. The bleedin' steps were worse than climbing a mountain she had said giving him a shove. If she had known she had to scale Ben Nevis for the peanuts he was paying she'd never have shuffled out of the house. Didn't he know she was missing her favourite soap on the telly? Sweet Jesus, her heart was knocking against her chest from the bleedin' climb. Did he have a bottle of gin?

It had been a huge mistake to invite a woman he didn't know to this sacred place.

Today he'd been more careful. Kate Owen pulled pints in the village pub. Kate was lovely. Childlike and plump. In her mid-forties with rumpled black hair. She wore tight jeans over her chicken drumstick legs and a short-sleeved white blouse which showed pearls of armpit fat. He'd counted the hairs growing from the wart on her chin—three; one grey.

But it was the splotches that first caught Liam's eye. They were smeared on the top buttonhole of her blouse which she kept clasped tight over her flat chest. He supposed they were grime stains from whatever the pub served for lunch. Brown gravy from steak and kidney pie and smudges of red ketchup. And then there were green smears he couldn't identify. *His Kate*, for that is how he thought of her now, was a working-class lass, gruff and cheap and cheerful.

He turned his head and looked around the single room. Afternoon sunlight shone through the vast window which he had pushed wide open. Stone walls and flagstone floors which came clean with soap and water. A dingy green sofa bed, two mismatched chairs and a pine table which wobbled if leaned on. The secluded top floor of the old mill house was a grand space to show his glory. He'd dreamt of this place since he was a child. His paradise. Forty-three wasn't too late to live his dream to the full, was it?

This was where Liam Brampton created his art.

He was a member of Ambleside Village Artists, invited to join by Bella Timbol. His workmates laughed when he told them he was leaving work to become an artist. Just like his school careers advisor had sneered, telling him he was bound for the factory floor with a broom. He'd believed them for so long.

And, yes, he'd worked in a factory sweeping the floors, as a toilet attendant in a public loo, and cleaning out animal cages before the zoo visitors arrived. And then there was the slaughterhouse. They said he was good at the job. A genius. They called him the Professor. And they said he'd be back when he told them he was leaving to follow his dream. He'd left before. Twice. But this was different. He'd found his passion. The artist's way was his path back to a meaningful life.

He put his motivational cassette into an old tape machine he'd bought in an antique store, bartering the owner down to five pounds. It crackled and hissed and then came the exciting strains of an American voice, rapid-fire quotes and uplifting words:

"The treasures of life are waiting for you if he would but pick up the key and open Fortune Chamber's door. The Chest of Wonders awaits your firm hand. A precious trove of jewels glistens inside. You can do it if you try. You must do it. You will do it. With a positive attitude, determination and grit, nothing can stop you now. You will win. Win. Win."

Liam punched a fist in the air and twirled. Kate Owen would pose for him today and tomorrow and the day after that. She would pose for him for the rest of the month if that's how long it took to get his creation right. Now Kate had agreed, there was no turning back.

11

Would she be on time?

Liam Brampton sniffed and turned off the tape. Maybe he should have another of his special smokes to calm his nerves? He brooded over the question. On the one hand, it would help with the tremble. They got frightened when he got the shakes.

He began to look for the brass tin with the swan on the lid.

Roll.

Light.

Inhale.

He found the tin under the sofa bed, picked it up and froze. Mummy would have a fit if she caught him sucking on a fag and she'd know what it contained by the smell.

"I'm a good boy, always do what Mummy wants."

The sound of his voice startled him so much that he looked around to see if anyone was there.

No one watched.

Not even Mummy.

He decided against a smoke.

His latest works leaned against the wall, covered by a great white sheet and unseen by the world. Except for Mummy. He'd shown them to Mummy. Portraits. Five. Images of *his women* created in a gust of lust which whirled him to paint through the night. He'd used photos, of course. He snapped them in secret—*his women* as they went about their daily lives. He toiled for nights to form their likeness on canvas, and for days after lingered as though in mourning, perfecting every detail.

It didn't matter how much Mummy cursed, for him this passion was normal.

At first, he found it easy to ignore Mummy's words. But as time went by, her disquiet wriggled into his brain. Now he was unsure if the five in his collection would ever sell because his brush strokes showed real faces. In great detail. Sagging wrinkles and craggy crow's feet and food stuck between crooked teeth. Giant images of local women. Their faces on supersized canvas. His homage to art.

Mummy yelled when he showed her the first painting, calling him a demon. She said women would find it creepy that he was taking their photo in secret; they would hate the image reflected back to them on canvas; hate him. He must see the priest, confess his sins, and stop watching women on the sly. She began to sob then, and Liam, although he did not know why, cried too.

He never showed Mummy his art again.

Anyway, he had a new project now. A better one. Yes, it had started on the wrong foot with the evil-eyed hag with blue-rinsed hair, but Kate Owen was different. The first time he really looked at her, his whole body shook like a spider on its web doing its death dance toward a trapped fly.

Now he watched her, followed her, knew her. Even chatted to her as his imaginary friend at night for his personal amusement.

And *his Kate* would soon be here. His first live portrait.

Any minute now the creak of the downstairs door would alert him to her arrival. He must contain his excitement. Suppress his eagerness. Must not tremble. He would say nothing to scare Kate. He would sit the lass down, toss her a can of ale and watch her until she relaxed. But it would be difficult to resist beginning at once with her so close, sipping ale and spreading herself on his sofa bed.

He closed his eyes imagining the tip of his brush sweeping across the canvas and the rub of the wheat-gold smock against his bare skin.

Did he have everything?

He readied his easel and palette then walked to the pine table, his naked body ablaze with excitement. He dipped a hand into the crystal bowl, caressing and stroking the contents. Next, he cracked open an ale, draining half the can in two gulps. He snuggled onto the sofa bed and closed his eyes. The soft lullaby of the breeze whistled through the window.

12

The squeal of the phone woke Liam Brampton. Stunned by its wail and astonished to find himself naked, he sat for a few moments in utter shock. How long had he slept? Was Kate calling to let him know she'd be here at any moment? He scrambled into the smock, placed the beret on his head, slanting it at an angle, and slipped on his sandals. Finally, he reached for the phone.

"Hello Kate... Doing well... Uh-huh... Oh, no... I'm sorry to hear that... How about this evening?" There was a little catch in his voice, a tightness which frightened him. "Or tomorrow or next week... I see... I know... I know... Okay... Bye."

Breathing hard, Liam slammed the phone on the table and tore the beret off his head. Blood thrummed in his ears. His body shook. Kate had told him a bunch of bloody lies. She said she couldn't pose for him; that she was a mother and it wouldn't be right. Not with a teenage daughter who was into women's rights.

Frustration twisted a tight fist in his gut, pounding and beating and squeezing up bile. Seething, a pained howl screeched from his thin lips.

Kate Owen would not get away with treating him like

this.

Nor would the rest of *his women*. He let loose a torrent of vexed cursing, thrust a hand into the crystal bowl, clutched a fistful of its content and threw them at the window. They climbed in the warm air, swirled back into the room and fluttered to the flagstone floor—a carpet of white rose petals.

13

A moment after Kate Owen clicked off her mobile phone she had the sinking feeling it wasn't over. She dropped the phone into her pocket, wiped moist palms over her tight-fitting blue jeans, and slumped into a chair at the kitchen table.

"You told him?" Ken Ashworth, her on-and-off boyfriend, stood behind her chair.

He was older than Kate by five years but wore the bright clothes they advertised to youngsters on the telly. His jet-black hair was spiked, punk style, and he wore a gold stud in his nose. He made her feel younger than her forty-four years, and Kate and Ken had a nice ring to it.

She didn't want to admit it, but she was deeply in love with him. Not in the swept-off-your-feet teenage romantic kind. Hers was a more practical love. Ken taught art in school which meant a regular wage, and her daughter got on well with him. It would be nice to be a teacher's wife. In a village like Ambleside, that brought with it status—tea with the vicar and judge at the summer fête cake bake-off. Maybe she'd pick up the pencil and draw again. She used to enjoy her time with the sketchbook.

Ken placed a broad hand on her shoulder and squeezed.

"Told him, no, not ever, never?"

"Oh God, I feel awful." Kate touched the wart on her chin, her gaze on the window. The sun was setting behind St Mary's, the shadow of its steeple pointing like an accusatory finger. On the kitchen table lay a closed sketchbook. "I thought it was a lark, I should never have led him on."

Ken removed his hand. He was a practical man. A man of routine despite his youthful clothes and spiked hair and gold nose stud. "Liam Brampton's a nutcase, Sweetmeat. No woman should be alone with him in his lair. No man, for that matter."

Kate toyed with her phone. "Oh come on, Liam is not that bad." She couldn't tear her gaze from Ken. He was dressing smarter these days, more to her tastes, and younger too. "Liam is a bit odd, but aren't we all a bit weird?"

She was thinking about herself. Five long years renting a two-bedroom cottage she could hardly afford. Living with her teenage daughter, Skye, who had made it clear she would flee the nest as soon as she was able.

I'm a single mum who'll soon be an empty nester, dating a man who finds it hard to commit.

Four years now. On and off. Ken filled her up in so many ways and emptied her in others. At least he was here for dinner which meant he'd stay the night. His favourite dish simmered in the oven—cottage pie. The rich meaty scent filled the air.

Ken took out a package from his pocket. "Got a gift for you."

Kate looked at the white butcher paper willing her stomach not to heave. "Kippers?"

Ken always brought kippers when he visited. She always cooked cottage pie. She didn't like either, not really. The thought of smoked fish for breakfast turned her stomach and the animal grease in cottage pie stuck in her throat. But she wanted to please him, keep him happy, after all, she had invested four years of her life into their relationship. Time she'd never get back.

"You are the one person who gets me." Kate touched the wart on her chin. "I feel connected."

Ken grinned. "You'll grill them in the morning, Sweetmeat?"

Kate put on *her smile*. She wanted to please him and appease him. She didn't want a fight over vile smoked fish. "They smell fresh."

"Got them from Sid Fenwick, not sure where he gets them from but they are tasty, aren't they?"

Kate swallowed, picked up her phone and showed him the screen. "Look at these."

Ken leaned forward then jerked back. "Rings?"

"Beautiful aren't they?"

"Expensive."

"Diamonds don't come cheap."

Ken sniffed. "That cottage pie ready?" He stepped from the table and went to the window. "If Skye hadn't told me about your plans to visit with Liam —"

"Don't start." Kate felt foul about dumping Liam at the last moment. He had looked so surprised and happy when she agreed to sit for him. His body literally trembled with joy. As an artist herself, she understood. And the wad of cash Liam had waved in her face would have helped pay next month's rent. "I feel sorry for him, he never knew his dad; never had a proper family."

Kate glanced at Ken then she glanced at her left hand and imagined the gleam of a diamond ring.

Ken ran a hand through his spiked hair. "A male figure wouldn't have helped Liam, might have made him worse. Anyway, family is an outdated concept, we don't need it anymore. We've done fine on our own, haven't we?"

"Oh, don't be so morbid, family is a good thing and Liam Brampton is a nice man. So what if he fits into a different slot?" Kate paused, watching for that flicker in his eyes which came with his temper. "That is normal for us creatives."

"You a creative!" Ken laughed. A speck of foam bubbled in the corner of his lips. "Stick men and stick women and stick cats and dogs. Come off it, Kate. Cavemen drew better blobs than the crap you scratch."

His belly laugh rang in her ears and heat rose in her cheeks. He was always going on about her childish sketches and putting her down whenever she told anyone she was an artist. He taught art and knew what art was and said her drawings were nothing more than monkey scribble, that he'd seen more creativity in the random brown smears at the bottom of a toilet bowl. Her job was to pull pints as a smiling barmaid, and that was the sum of her artistic talent. Pub work paid the bills, he reminded her all too often.

Kate kept her voice low. "Why can't you leave my art out of it?"

"I'm sorry, Chicken Drumsticks."

"Don't call me that." He had started to use the term after their first night together. He always said it with affection but it reminded Kate of her paunch and thick thighs. "It doesn't make me feel good."

"I'm sorry, Sweetmeat." He blew a kiss. "Forgive me?"

Kate didn't want to argue. Dinner would be ready soon and Skye back from her friend's house. This evening they'd eat as a family. After, she would shake off her tatty white blouse with its smears of food stains from serving in the pub, have a bath and slip into something sexy. Tonight she and Ken would share her bed.

Once again, she put on *her smile*. "Forgiven. But Liam needs our help, Ken." She paused, trying to find the right words. "Art is not just about what we create. It is also about what it gives. I want to help him. I want to give."

Ken shook his head. "This is not good. Something bad is going to happen. I wouldn't be surprised if Liam is in his hovel planning revenge. The man is a creep, a Peeping Tom who delights in watching girls from the shadows. Bet he's got a rag doll and a tin of steel pins. He's the type that doesn't take kindly to women saying no."

"Liam's not like that." Kate didn't know why but a sense of fear overcame her as she said the words. She'd stand by them now they had come out of her mouth. She was stubborn that way. "He is nice when you get to know him."

"How well do you know him?"

"What is that supposed to mean?"

"You accept an invitation to the weirdo's secret lair and now, all of a sudden, you are singing his praises." Ken paused, watching her with his keen school teacher eyes. "You've been to his place already, haven't you?"

"No."

"Don't lie to me."

"We have to help each other, Ken. That's what village folk do." Kate liked the ring to her words. "Please don't judge me, and don't judge Liam, either. The world needs more kindness. More understanding. Less judgment."

"Yeah, well someone ought to pass the message on to Bella Timbol."

"Oh Ken, you haven't applied to join the Ambleside Village Artists again, have you?"

"Rejected for the eleventh time by the cow."

Kate didn't want his mood to turn sour. Tonight she wanted the happy Ken. The Ken who wooed her with white roses and Belgian chocolates. "You are a fantastic art critic, Ken, but the collective was formed as a safe place for creators, a sacred place." She tried to step around her membership. Bella Timbol approached her the first day she moved to the village and she signed up on the spot. "Ambleside Village Artists is a home where the likes of Liam Brampton can create what is in his mind unfettered by prying eyes. We encourage each other, isn't that a positive thing?"

"What is it with you and your bleeding heart?" Ken's voice dropped an octave; the tone he used to control the classroom. "Liam Brampton is as mad as they come; a real nutjob; a slice short of a full loaf; call it what you like. If I were a vet, I'd say the dog must be put down."

"Liam's not a dog and you are not a vet."

"The man's a sicko. They should carve a tattoo into his forehead warning folks away."

"Don't be so nasty." Kate thought of the cottage pie in the oven and she thought of dinner and she thought of the night ahead with Ken in her bed. Again, she put on *her smile*. "Can we change the subject?"

"I'm trying to warn you away, Kate. Stay well clear of the pervert."

"I'm not a bloody child, Ken." She regretted the words as soon as they came out. All she wanted was dinner, a hot bath and the touch of him in her warm bed. It had been a long day. Her voice softened. "Liam's had a hell of a rough life. You'd be a maimed wreck if you suffered what he went through. He needs our support, not sticks and stones thrown by a wild mob of misguided villagers. Do you fancy a glass of red wine? I've got a bottle I've been saving for tonight."

But Ken was on his high horse now. He'd never commit to her but was quick to tell her what she should think and do. "You will never go to his home again, got that? It'd be for the best if they locked up the evil fool." He stared, challenging her to disagree. "Most folks around here would vote for that. So would you, Sweetmeat."

Kate dabbed at a smear on her blouse and she dabbed at the sketchbook and she dabbed at the tear forming in the corner of her left eye. She clenched her jaw. "At least Liam Brampton treats me like I'm a woman. His woman." She wanted to stop, but she couldn't. "That's more than I get from you these days."

Silence.

The shadow of St Mary's steeple stretched across the table covering her sketchbook in dark. A faint smell of charcoal seemed to fill her nose and the soft scrape of pencil on paper thrummed with quiet contentment in her ears. This was the table where she sketched when she was alone;

each tick of the clock stretching to eternity as she lost herself in black and white. But the smells and the sounds were just memories now. It had been a long while since she picked up the pencil. She glanced at the closed sketchbook, a hollow pang rising inside. A thick layer of dust had settled on the cover.

Ken cleared his throat. "That man is a menace, we both agree on that, Sweetmeat." He spoke each word with emphasis. "Heck, this morning I saw him behind the bushes on Nook Lane watching the children's playground."

Kate's mouth went dry. "What were you doing on Nook Lane?"

That was where the other woman lived. Twiggy, big-breasted Millie with her husky voice, swinging hips and twenty-eight-year-old body. Called herself an actress but didn't have a job. A leach that attached itself to men with jingle in their pockets until she'd sucked their cash dry. Ken had promised he wasn't seeing that woman anymore. That she was nowt but a loose tart. A fling. A stupid mistake. Yes, he wanted to settle down eventually, only loved one woman, just had to get his mind right before he was fully committed. He said all of those things in this kitchen as the shadow from St Mary's steeple fell across his face.

14

"Well?" Kate folded her arms. She would not move on until she had an answer. "Why were you on Nook Lane?"

Ken just stared. When at last he spoke, he did so with an unnaturally pleasant lilt. "Let's not argue, Sweetmeat. Pour a glass of wine. Is dinner almost ready?"

"I'm not arguing." Kate was, but she wouldn't let him score that point. "I just want to know what you were doing on Nook Lane this morning. Where did you sleep last night?"

"Look, Kate..."

"Don't look Kate me!"

Faint sounds from outside came through the closed window—the squeal of the rusted gate followed by light skipping footsteps; a car rumbled along the street, its engine gruff and raw. From the far side of the village came the ring of Market Hall clock.

Ken opened his mouth but closed it and took a deep breath. He blew air between his lips forming tiny bubbles of white foam. "Kate, you and me. It's over. I'm marrying Millie in September. I planned to tell you after tonight."

The words fell from his lips like a steel blade and twisted between Kate's ribs. He was dumping her for a twig-thin woman whose breasts were so large she looked deformed. The front door slammed.

"Mum, I'm home."

And Skye was in the kitchen with her scruffy peach jacket and blue streaked hair.

"Yuck! Not cottage pie again." Skye wriggled her nose in disgust. "Steph wants me to go back to finish our homework. I know school is out but we have to get ready for next term. Then we'll watch a film. Oh, and did you—"

Ken raised his right hand, finger pointing to the ceiling. "Your mum has something to tell you." He smirked. "I'll leave it to you then, Kate."

He winked at Skye the way he used to wink at her, turned and slammed through the door. His quick footsteps echoed on the garden path. The rusted gate squealed.

Kate squeezed breath through her teeth, heart hammering. It was depressing, and there was going to be a lot more of it to come. At least she had the company of her daughter to help her through the long night of worry and self-doubt ahead.

Kate cleared her throat. *Best get it over with.* "Skye, me and—"

"Don't mum." Skye rolled her eyes. "If Ken didn't stay for his cottage pie, it must have been a huge row. Can I stay over at Steph's tonight?"

That was the thing about teens, their entire world revolved around their needs. Kate wanted to blast her daughter for being so thoughtless, but what was the point? A brawl would make her day even worse. "Only one night, got that? Tomorrow you sleep in your bed."

"Thanks, mum. Oh, and the police were over at Borrans

Wood. They found a body. Ann Crombie, the old crow who lived in Bede Thatch, has died. I won't stay for cottage pie, can't stand it."

And with that, Skye was gone.

On automatic and dazed, Kate scraped the cottage pie into the bin, washed up the dish, dried it and put it away. Only then did the weight of it all strike her so hard that her stomach lurched. She staggered to the sink and threw up. Again and again, until her stomach was empty and her throat raw. Then she crawled to the chair, slumped down, and resting her elbows on the table placed her head in her hands.

No. I will not cry.

It wasn't that life was unfair, Kate had accepted that long ago. It was that it was unfair in so many ways.

She sat for so long in the growing dusk that Market Hall clock struck again. Melancholy settled like grime on an unswept floor. Ken marry Millie! It was Millie who was to be the teacher's wife. Millie who would move into his cottage. Millie who would sleep under black silk sheets in his queen-sized waterbed while she was left pulling pints as an ageing barmaid. Big boobed Millie in a tight white dress at the altar! Kate touched the wart on her chin and glanced down at her flat chest. Why did Millie get triple rations when she got hardly any rations at all? Oh God, if she didn't stop thinking like this she was going to scream.

The shadow of St Mary's steeple edged out the last slither of daylight.

At last, Kate raised her eyes. "If he can move on without a backward glance, so can I."

She rose and went to the kitchen counter, flipped the

kettle on and stared through the window. Beyond the garden gate, the bushes shimmered casting spidery shadows across Vicarage Road. All around, darkness was continuing its creep. Soon it would settle over the trees to cloak the village in night. She dropped the tea bag into the mug, poured on hot water and suddenly shivered.

Is someone watching me?

It was the same feeling she got when she was with Ken. How many times had she awoke in the dead of night to find the quilt dragged off her naked body and him staring at her with those greedy eyes? She found it comforting and disturbing at the same time. She liked the idea of her man looking at her but not watching all she did.

She turned to the window, straining to see through the dusk. The gate was shut. Leaves skittered along the path to her front door. It was impossible to tell if anyone hid in the shadow of the trees or crouched in the bushes, but why would anyone do that?

Then she heard footsteps.

Slow and steady and careful.

Coming from the lane.

A fat man in an unfashionable green tracksuit jogged slowly by. His head turned so he was looking straight at Kate. She moved away from the window, felt foolish, and went back to look.

The man in the green tracksuit was gone.

She pressed her face against the glass, hoping to see which way he went. And that is when the hairs went up on the back of her neck.

It was the huge forehead she saw first. Above the hedge and bushes. Bobbing up and down. Then she saw the second head, full of wild white hair. Vicar Bill Kemp and Bella Timbol, walking side by side along the lane in intense conversation. A discussion about something important. Their words were too distant to penetrate the closed kitchen window.

Curious, Kate eased the glass open, willing the dusk to carry their voices to her ears.

The click of the latch hovered in the air.

Vicar Kemp's head turned; his eyes, the colour of dried peas, stared at the window. Bella Timbol followed his gaze. A primordial instinct caused Kate to duck. She waited a full five minutes before looking again. Vicar Kemp stood alone, running a hand over his dog collar, his eyes fixed on her window.

15

Exactly twenty-one minutes before all hell broke loose, Fenella stood at the front of the briefing room in Port St Giles hopeful of a quick breakthrough but still upset and nauseous with shock.

"Ann Crombie. Killed late Friday night or Saturday morning in Borrans Wood." She paused for a moment, scanning the faces of her team and suddenly feeling pleased. Seven a.m. on Sunday morning and everyone wide awake. Dexter paced at the back of the room. Detective Constable Zack Jones sat on the front row with his laptop balanced on his knees. "No witnesses and with all that rain, forensics haven't offered much hope."

"They don't never offer up much hope, guv." Dexter stopped pacing. "Not even if they have a mega amount of yuck filled with the killer's fingerprints and DNA. It is always 'we don't know' or 'we're not sure' or 'we have to wait for what the lab says'. Can't get a straight answer out of the sods. Especially the youngsters who've been through forensic school. What do they teach them? The only thing they seem to learn is *no*."

"We must be fair, give them time." Jones opened his laptop. Thirty-five, he joined the team straight from the

National Detective School. He'd worked in industry before signing up for the police and had an artist's passion for photography. "Most of their tests can take weeks. They are right to be cautious."

Dexter snorted. "Teach you that in detective school, did they, lad?" He had little time for the classroom, said you learned your best tricks on the job. "Maybe I should sign up to learn a thing or two I already know."

"They have a spot waiting for you." Jones kept a straight face. "And they told me to let you know they have a special class for unlearning bad tricks. Not sure it would do any good."

Dexter laughed. "Aye, lad. I've a thick skull. One point to you."

Fenella said nothing. Her team needed time to blow off steam after the grisly death in the village of Ambleside. Crackle and spit eased the tension and kept them on their toes. Anyway, she needed space to clear the foul smog of the crime scene from her mind. No one wanted to talk about death on what should have been a lazy Sunday morning.

Jones folded his arms. "We need to find out what happened and fast, boss."

"State the bleedin' obvious, why don't you, lad?" Dexter paced to the front row and sat next to Jones. "I'm pleased they taught you something useful in detective school." He put on the mock voice of a professor, jabbing a finger in the air. "The first thing we must do is find out what happened. The second is to catch the killer. Oh, and by the way, if a hard-working detective asks you a question, say *no*."

Jones laughed. "Now you put it like that, it all makes

sense."

Dexter's phone buzzed. He stared at if for a long while, shaking his head and muttering.

Fenella couldn't help herself. "Are you going to share the good news with the rest of us?"

"It's Superintendent Jeffery, guv."

"Oh aye?"

"She's been banging on about the number of search warrants. Ain't nowt going down without her say-so from now on. Apparently, the station is at the top of some list. Lots of bigwigs watching us. And she is on a tear about pop-up voluntary training."

"What's that when it is at home?" Fenella tilted her neck, sensing his reply would not please her.

"Instead of scheduling training ahead of time to give folks a decent chance to come up with an excuse not to attend, they have events on dates no one knows about. Random. They round up whoever they catch for the day's medicine."

Jones looked up. "It worked wonders with the Met Police in London, boss. Guaranteed packed lecture rooms for all the speakers."

Fenella said nothing.

Dexter was still shaking his head. "Word on the street is they have video cameras pointed at the audience in the lecture room and tell you the Chief Constable will show up. Designed to keep you in your seats. Right crafty."

The tea urn gurgled at the back of the room. The box of doughnuts Fenella had brought from the Grainbowl Café, remained unopened. The moist Battenburg cake baked by Nan untouched. A good sign, she thought. They were here to focus on the job. She sensed they were ready. "What are we dealing with?"

"Don't know but it is nasty, guv." Dexter flashed a sad smile. "Real nasty."

Jones rubbed his hands. "Ann Crombie must have stepped on someone's toes. A big shot." He rocked back and forth in his chair, eyes bright, warming to his idea. "It is like a gangland killing, boss. We must check her place for drugs and gather a list of her associates. There may be more execution-style killings."

Dexter grunted. "Don't be daft, lad. This ain't the East End of London."

"I know Ambleside looks like a quaint village." Jones tapped a finger on his laptop. "But it is the sort of place where drug overlords go to relax. I think there might be a gangland connection. They arranged her body in a pose as a warning."

He had a thing about organised crime. Fenella wondered if it was because he studied in London or because he watched too many American crime shows on the telly.

"Aye, keep that one brewing." She didn't want to rule anything out at this stage. "We'll have to dig deeper, yank up the roots and we'll need to be quick about it. Actions for today—speak with the faces from the crowd and anyone who knew Ann." She looked at Dexter. "How many names did you get?"

"Thirty-one, guv, excluding a couple from Texas staying at the Ambleside Inn. They came here for the art festival; said they spent Friday night in the pub and retired early due to it being their wedding anniversary. I've checked with the inn and they confirmed their story."

Jones glanced from Fenella to Dexter. "That will take us all week, boss."

"Or more." Dexter rubbed the back of his neck. "Village folk are like family; they stick together to guard each other secrets."

A knock thudded at the door. It burst open. For an instant Fenella thought she was seeing a ghost. PC Woods, unshaved and shabby, staggered into the room. He was an office cop who sneaked off for a quick smoke when no one was looking. He preferred the warmth and comfort of the desk to the exertion of pounding the beat. He paused at the table to pour a mug of tea and tore open the box of doughnuts. Carrying the mug in one hand and four doughnuts in the other, he made his way to the front and squeezed next to Jones.

"Me eyes must be fooling me, guv." Dexter made a show of widening his eyes. "It can't be so. Never seen ought like it first thing on a Sunday morning."

Fenella laughed. Despite the misery of the job, her team found humour between the cracks of the grim and gruesome. "PC Woods, what cruel hand of fate shook you from your bed to bring you here on this fine morning?"

PC Woods snatched a bite of doughnut followed by a mouthful of tea. "Orders of Superintendent Jeffery, ma'am. She said you were short-staffed with Detective Sergeant Ria Leigh out on medical leave and to report for the first briefing. I only found out an hour ago." He scowled. "My wife woke me; said I had a message from the big boss and shoved me out of the house."

Another knock thudded the door. PC Beth Finn hurried in, her face wild with frustration. "Sorry I'm late, ma'am.

Car trouble." She glanced at the doughnuts and passed. "Superintendent Jeffery asked me to report."

Fenella smiled. For once, the superintendent's hand brought good news. Two additions to the team. "Right, PC Finn and PC Woods are to work with Jones. We have thirty-one names to get through. Focus on Ann's relationships—friends, enemies, lovers. I'm interested in everything, including village gossip."

This was the part she relished—poking her nose into other people's secrets and bingeing on what they wanted to keep quiet. Her unique skill she supposed, although Nan called her a nosy parker, said she was like a pig in a trough.

PC Woods slurped his tea and let out a sharp burp. "Sorry, ma'am, a bit of doughnut went down the wrong way."

16

Fenella bounced on the tips of her toes. "What do we know about Ann Crombie?"

PC Beth Finn raised her hand. "She was a recluse and an artist, ma'am. Not famous or anything like that, but her paintings of foxes have sold quite well in recent months."

"Do you have a photo of her art to share?" Fenella was thinking about the glass lamp. She'd not bought it as the sale was called off. "I like landscape paintings."

"No, ma'am." PC Beth Finn shook her head. "I tried, but they are listed as a private sale, for the eyes of the buyers only."

Jones scowled.

"You have something for us?" Fenella nodded at Jones.

His lips curved into a smug smile. He had news for sure, and he wanted centre stage and he wanted it now and he wanted their total attention. A peacock about to spread its plume.

A hush fell over the room. Everyone waited. PC Woods licked his fingers and turned to gaze at the Battenburg cake. The tea urn hissed.

Jones cleared his throat, making the most of his moment in the limelight. "Ann Crombie has no living relatives in England. She moved to Ambleside seven years ago from London, Ealing. Sold her flat on Madeley Road near Ealing Broadway tube station for a life in the countryside." He paused, glancing from face to face. There was more. "Like PC Beth Finn said, she was a recluse. No relatives in Scotland, Wales or Northern Ireland and not often seen in the village."

That meant they'd have to find someone other than a relative to identify the body. Fenella wondered whether the man with the huge forehead and dog collar might do. What was his name? "Anyone spoke with the vicar?"

Dexter glanced at his notebook. "Reverend William Kemp, guv. Everyone calls him Bill. He was in the crowd on Saturday and was very upset when the name of the victim leaked out." Again he glanced at his notebook. "He said Ann Crombie was one of his women. Thought he was going to cry, guv. He was choking back tears as he spoke."

A good start, Fenella thought and pointed at PC Woods. "You had a poke around Bede Thatch on Saturday, find anything?"

"I visited before we knew the victim, Ann Crombie, lived there, so I didn't go inside the cottage, ma'am." PC Woods sounded defensive. "Didn't want to break any rules, ma'am."

Fenella thought he had a quick look around then went in search of a quiet corner for a smoke.

PC Woods continued. "I looked around the garden and found an old shed." His nose wrinkled. "The stink of the place, like someone was dossing down. I didn't see anyone, though."

"Nothing else unusual?" Fenella wanted to double-check. "What was in the shed?"

"Junk, ma'am. Lots of straw in one corner, boxes and tins and the like." PC Woods realised that wasn't enough. "Only odd thing was a red fox, dragging itself by its front legs. It let out a yowl and darted into the bushes when it saw me."

Dexter was speaking. "Me grandfather said red foxes ain't half crafty. Used to tell me a story about a cunning fox who outwitted a crow."

This could not possibly have anything to do with the case, but Fenella wanted to hear the story. Her nosy gene led her down rabbit trails. *A pig in a trough.* "Go on, and don't drag it out, this isn't bedtime."

Dexter's eyes glazed. He was in the past. She could see him sitting around the fireplace with his grandad in an armchair with a plumped pillow at his back. He spoke in the voice of memories. "This old fox sees this crow, guv. You know how crafty crows are, always snatching at things that glitter. You have to keep an eye on the buggers else they are in the window and off with your jewellery box."

PC Beth Finn spoke as if to herself. "Happened to me with a brooch. Gold. Given to me by a boyfriend." She snatched a glance at Jones. "Never saw it again."

"Aye, lass, them crows don't give a damn. Break your heart, they will." Dexter turned to scowl at Jones, then closed his eyes. He was in his element. He loved talking about the past, Cumbria's myths and legends. "This crow had a chunk of Crofton cheese in its beak. Right tasty is Crofton. Soft and creamy and goes down a treat with a glass of wine." He opened his eyes and caught Fenella's sharp gaze. He was supposed to be on the wagon. Booze almost cost him his life. "Not that I'm drinking these days. No, no, no. But that Crofton tastes so good you can eat it on its own."

Fenella loved Crofton cheese. Her mouth watered with memories of its creamy richness. "From Thornby Moor Dairy?"

"Aye guv, and the old fox wanted some of it. Foxes love cheese, just like dogs. So the fox flatters the bird, tells it what a great singing voice it has, how much he'd love to hear it sing. Crows are vain and this crow liked praise. It opened its beak and began to squawk. A terrible noise; nowt like a nightingale. Quick as a flash, the fox snatches the cheese and is gone. Damn crafty, them foxes."

Jones raised a hand, dragging them back on track. "I spoke with big cheese Lisa Levon; forensics will start their work at the cottage around noon, with it being Sunday."

"Aye." Fenella thought she'd nip in ahead of them, and have a poke around. Once the forensic team arrived, they'd take charge, and she'd have to wait or else only be granted limited access. She'd take Dexter with her; Jones would complain about breaking the rules.

A fist knocked on the door. Fenella half expected Superintendent Jeffery, arms swinging, to march in. Instead, Len Moreland, the duty sergeant, hustled through the door, out of breath.

"Ma'am, there is a fire at Bede Thatch. Plumes of black smoke. The fire service is on the way but I'm hearing there is nowt but ashes left. The place has burnt to the ground."

17

It took an hour to get to the village of Ambleside.

Fenella dashed along a narrow trail with Dexter at her side. It was nine, and the sun blazed red as an eye from hell. Bad news was coming her way, but she wasn't in the mood to back down. Not today.

"Guv, must have gone up like a bonfire." Dexter caught his breath, bending over at the knees. "Some of them old houses ain't nowt but wattle and daub."

They were on the brow of a hill, the landscape sweeping down to woodland. Fenella mulled over what they'd find. She conjured up vivid images of flames lashing blackened wood and the air filled with choking ash. She tilted her neck from side to side to ease the growing tension. She'd wanted to visit Bede Thatch and have a poke around before the forensics team arrived. What was the point if the house had been reduced to ashes?

They passed through a stand of trees and came out by a hawthorn bush where a crowd had gathered.

A fat man in an unfashionable green tracksuit watched near the front, his hands on his hips. A pregnant woman in a floral dress stood next to a narrow-faced man with a baby in a sling across his chest; the wide-eyed faces of two children stared from either side of a stooped woman carrying a brown sack; and a mob of dog walkers stood in a semicircle talking in excited tones, their pets tugging on the leash.

Near the back of the throng, hidden by the shade of the trees, a solitary figure watched. It was the domed forehead which sparked a flicker of recognition in Fenella's mind—Reverend Bill Kemp, the vicar, watching as if he didn't want to be seen.

"Everyone's talking about it, guv." Dexter cocked his head, listening to the mutter of the crowd. "How Ann Crombie was murdered in the woods and now her place is burning down. The curse of Borrans Wood, they say, and it has come to dish out revenge."

18

They made their way through the crowd to a gate in a dry-stone wall.

"Sorry folks, you can't come any closer." The uniformed officer held up his hand, eyes staring through hooded slits. "The fire crew are still at work."

Fenella showed her warrant card. "Where is the fire? Thought there'd be a few plumes of smoke."

"Sorry, ma'am, I didn't realise you were with the police. I'm a volunteer constable, Sid Fenwick. You'd best speak with the fire warden; she asked me to stand guard and can give you all the details."

He was an odd-looking police officer. A broad face covered in a heavy black beard which matched the dark circles around his hooded eyes. They did not blink. More of a local than a regular bobby, Fenella thought. She wondered what he did when he wasn't volunteering for the police. But that wasn't what caused her to pause for a long moment to take him in. There was something else about the man, something about his challenging stare as though to say she'd never get to the bottom of this one. She imagined him skulking around the countryside at night. Not as a police officer. As a poacher.

"Lead the way." Fenella nodded in the direction of the activity.

"Aye, ma'am." The words came out slow as if PC Sid Fenwick didn't want to lead the way, as if he wished all this bother hadn't come to his patch. "Not too far from here."

As they walked, a question popped into Fenella's mind. "Tell me about the vicar."

PC Sid Fenwick turned to look at her through his hooded eyes. "Reverend Kemp?"

"Aye."

"He's a good man."

Fenella waited, expecting more. When he said no more, she asked another question. "Is there anything else you can tell me about him?"

"He's one of us, ma'am. A local." PC Sid Fenwick stopped, his hooded eyes watching Fenella closely. "People around here have a lot of time for the vicar, listen to what he has to say. He's good at organising folk, getting them to do things. Things they wouldn't normally do."

19

The miracle happened as Fenella, Dexter and PC Sid Fenwick picked their way along the garden path through the bindweed, brambles and ghosts of flowerbeds. She expected to see the blackened ruins of Bede Thatch. Nowt but timbers and ash. That is not what she saw.

She placed her hands on her hips, mouth wide. No foul fumes were pouring through the slate roof of the cottage. No crash and crack of timber. No squeal of shattered windows. Not even the acrid stench of smoke billowing through the front door. Bede Thatch was untouched by flames. The two-room cottage squatted, shabby and content, like the life of the artist who once lived in it.

"It ain't what I was expecting, guv." Dexter sounded confused. He usually had his ear so close to the ground he'd hear rain before the clouds burst. "No doubt about where the fire started, though."

"And where it stopped." Fenella too, felt the hand of confusion, her eyes darting for the flicker of a flame. "Are we really talking about a shed fire?"

Four grey-haired men and a woman with blue-rinsed hair clustered around the doorway of a blackened shed.

"Yoo-hoo!" The blue-rinsed haired woman waved them

over. "Are you with the police? The vicar said two detectives were on the way. I'm the fire warden, Miss May Fish."

Miss Fish had a touch of the tropical sea creature about her face—rouge on her cheeks, pink lipstick and coin-flat eyes. Fenella judged her to be close to seventy and gazed at the shed. The fire had ravaged one side, and the roof sagged where the flames had burst through. She made the introductions. "Tell me about the fire. What's happened here?"

"Oh, this is a shock." Miss Fish spoke with such a shriek it was clear she was excited more than shocked. She had a clownfish way of smiling, upturned lips and flat eyes. "A murder in the woods and now a fire at Bede Thatch." She paused and looked around to make sure everyone was listening. "We broke down the door to get inside." Miss Fish pointed at the shattered wood. "Fortunately, we got to it before there was wider damage. I called it in as a precaution. I fear I rather over-egged the pudding in my description, told them the whole house was ablaze, but you can't be too careful, can you?" She pointed at each man clustered by her side. "These kind gentlemen are my helpers."

They were all seventy if they were a day, with one propped up by two walking sticks.

"Can someone tell me what happened from the start?" Fenella smiled at each man, then turned her gaze back to May Fish. "I'm rather perplexed."

Miss Fish pushed the men back three steps, then thrust herself forward. She and she alone would tell the detectives the tale. *A gossip, eh?* Fenella was already warming to the woman.

"You see," Miss Fish began, "it being Sunday, most of the fire team were out on the trails, getting fresh air or walking their dogs. A dog does so need exercise, and the younger they are, the more you have to wear them out. We have a new—"

"I see." Fenella interrupted, sensing Miss Fish would go off tangent if she didn't keep her on the straight and narrow. "The fire?"

Miss Fish blinked. "When the alarm was raised, we were all nearby. Curiosity, I suppose, given recent events in the woods. And I have a unique gift. I'm rather sensitive to the universe's vibrations and sensed trouble in the air." She half turned to stare at the darkened windows of Bede Thatch. "Such a terrible and wicked thing to happen. Murder! Here in Ambleside. Ann Crombie butchered like a slaughterhouse pig."

Mutterings of outrage came from the men, their voices a chorus of shock. Except they were all grinning. The men stepped closer, each looking eager to join in. Each one was a feisty gossiper who wanted to have their say. And they'd have plenty to say about the way the victim was sliced and diced. Gossip galore. Tall tales and fantasies were part of the Cumbria way of life. The murder of Ann Crombie had entered village lore.

Fenella glanced at the men and she glanced at Miss Fish and she glanced at the blackened shed. Tension drained from her neck. She would find out what happened. The forensic team were not due until noon so there was plenty of time to poke around the cottage, and plenty of time to listen to Miss Fish's gossip.

She turned to Dexter. "Would you be so kind as to

speak with these gentlemen while I get Miss Fish's account?"

She nodded at each of the four men. Eight eyes glittered back. They had tales to tell and a detective to listen. *Oh, glory be!* Dexter let out a moan drowned out by happy murmurs. Two of the men took his arms, and they shuffled off out of earshot already yapping in his ears.

Fenella turned to PC Sid Fenwick. "You can go back to your duties."

He frowned and then ambled back along the garden path.

"Now, Miss Fish." Fenella fixed the woman with her friendliest gaze. "Shall we continue?"

Miss Fish clapped. "Oh, I'd be delighted. You are speaking to the right person because I arrived here just ahead of the men and saw smoke coming from the shed. As the first fire official on the scene, my words must carry the greatest weight. I expect they'll be part of the official record and properly attributed—Miss May Jezebel Fish of Old Lake Road."

Fenella murmured an encouraging reply without using actual words.

Miss Fish continued. "There is a well at the side of the garden with a pump and a hose. I grabbed that, and with the help of the others, we soon put the fire out."

"I see." Fenella paused for a long moment, staring into the darkness of the shed. "And who raised the alarm about the fire?"

Miss Fish cast an anxious glance at Dexter who was nodding as one of the men spoke. Dexter took out his phone. Miss Fish huffed, puffing her cheeks and blowing air between her lips. "Your detective colleague is taking notes on his phone." There was a long pause which implied a question. "You do have your phone on you, don't you, Inspector Sallow?"

Fenella grabbed her phone and held it out.

That encouraged Miss Fish. "You asked who raised the alarm. Why the vicar, of course. I am one of his women. He called me and stayed to help until we put the fire out. Not that he was much help, all thumbs and more of a hindrance. If it wasn't for my quick wits, he'd have let the blaze get out of control. The whole place might have been nothing but ashes." She glanced around. "Where is the vicar? Oh my, he seems to have gone."

"Guv." Dexter was running toward them. "Just got word the forensic team are coming early. They'll be here in ten minutes."

20

Everything seemed to happen slowly, except the *tick-tock* of the clock. Ten minutes didn't leave much time to look around. Nine minutes now they were outside the front door. The old cottage had settled over the years so the threshold tilted at a slight angle. Fenella flipped the knocker and then thumped on the wood panel. She waited for a count of ten.

"Nobody home."

"Ain't going to be an easy open, guv." Dexter stepped back and eyed the frame and the solid oak door.

"Yoo-hoo!" Miss Fish scurried toward them waving a hand. Behind, three of her helpers raced. The man with two walking sticks trailed at the back. "I say, yoo-hoo!"

Miss Fish held a metal object in her skeletal hand, a look of triumph on her clownfish face.

"Trouble, guv. I know it."

Dexter's whispered words matched the acid gurgle in Fenella's gut.

Miss Fish was at the door now and slightly out of breath. "Are you going inside? Ann Crombie kept her work a closely guarded secret. She displayed her art only when it was complete. But I have a key, inspector. I've always had a key."

She handed it to Fenella all clownfish grin and flat eyes. It was a long, thick bolt of a key with a heaviness that matched the solid oak door. The type of key you'd expect to open the bolted gate to some macabre dungeon.

Miss Fish continued. "Goodness me, I just remembered I had it. Ann gave it to me years ago as a backup if she should fall ill. Murder wasn't on the radar back then. Oh my, what a terrible way to go. Stabbed and butchered with your head taken off!"

Miss Fish trembled in rather a dramatic fashion and let out a tortured cry. All the while her flat eyes were on the door, peering like X-ray. She wanted to see what was inside and she wanted to see it now. She might even poke her head in when the detectives went in.

That comforted Fenella. She was confident the idea of snooping hadn't crossed May Fish's mind until now. "Does anyone else have a key?"

Miss Fish flashed a puzzled look. "I have a rather privileged position in our community as the fire warden. But, yes, others may have a key to Bede Thatch."

A chill ran along Fenella's neck. This was not good. Not good at all. "Help me out with some names, please, Miss Fish."

Miss Fish gave a petulant pout of her lips. "Bella Timbol has her own key. She is chairwoman of the Ambleside Village Artists and used to own Bede Thatch. And Vicar Kemp must have a key. Not that I've asked him. He takes an interest in the old place. I suppose Ann may have given her key to other people, neighbours and friends. That is what we do out here. I can't tell you the number of times

I've forgotten my key and had to ask a friend who kept my spare." She began to count on her fingers. "Twelve. I've got twelve friends who have a spare key to my place, I'm sure Ann Crombie had more. She was the type who outdid herself. Not that anyone ever needed a key, she always kept the door unlocked."

A red-hot ache pounded between Fenella's temples. Half the village might have trampled through the doors to drown their ghoulish curiosity. Or the killer might have returned to clean up the place. The intense throb kicked into a headache.

Eight minutes. The countdown clock hurtled toward zero. Miss Fish's male helpers were at the door now, jostling for position. Fenella needed a new plan and she needed it now and she needed to be quick about it.

She raised both hands, palms out. "We are expecting our forensic unit to arrive at any moment. Miss Fish, can you go back to the shed and tell them about the fire? They'll want to start there. I'm sure they will have questions, so please be ready to answer. You may have to repeat yourself several times for clarity. It may take some time."

Miss Fish looked as if she'd been swindled, but after a moment, flashed her clownfish smile. "Very well, if you feel it will help."

She turned and trudged back to the shed.

Fenella watched her go, then turned to the men. "Gentlemen, please hurry to the garden gate and give PC Sid Fenwick a hand with the crowd. The numbers are growing and until help arrives you are all the support we have. Thank you."

The men nodded and murmured and shuffled away, engulfed in the electric euphoria of being asked to help the police. *Murder and fire!* More tales and fantasies and village lore were in the making.

Dexter cleared his throat. "Nice one, guv."

"If I didn't give them something to do, they'd have jostled until they were inside." Fenella put on shoe protectors and a pair of gloves. "Imagine what Lisa Levon would say if she caught half the village inside the cottage."

"Ain't going to think about it, guv. The more you think about those things, the more they happen."

Fenella pressed the door handle. She panicked when nothing happened and was about to try the key but instead yanked the handle hard and then shoved.

The door swung inward on silent hinges.

21

They stood on the threshold for a heartbeat, blinking into the gloom as though they had broken the hermetic seal to a long-forsaken tomb.

An instant later, a horrible smell hurtled toward them. Rotted flesh, for sure. It curled in their nostrils like some godawful bout of foul flatulence blasted from the bowels of a beast in hell.

"Ain't the sweet scent of roses, guv." Dexter placed a hand over his nose. "Ain't the smell of anything living, neither."

They remained on the threshold, peering inside. It was a square box of a room with bare brick walls and a curtainless window with views of the garden. A clutter of brushes, paint tins, cans of solvents, and palettes lay scattered around an easel. Shoved against one wall crouched a worn green canvas sofa. Against another wall were a round pine table and a single chair. On the far side was a door. From somewhere came the buzz of flies.

"Looks like the studio of a starving artist, guv." Dexter made no move to cross the threshold. "Hard to imagine a thing of beauty created amongst this grime. Suppose it is like the swan. Serene on the surface and frantic leg kicks below."

Somehow, Fenella stepped through the door.

Engulfed in the rotting aroma, she scanned the room and found the source. On the pine table, a swarm of black flies, shiny as fresh tarmac, feasted on a plate of kippers. They rose in a buzzing cloud as she approached, leaving a fistful of white maggots crawling over the flesh. A festering tub of yoghurt stood next to the plate.

"I thought there was a body in this hellhole, guv." Dexter was looking around. "Ann Crombie must have had a bit of supper before she went out. This heat caused her food to go bad fast. At least the flies enjoyed it. Look at the size of them."

Fenella swatted at fat flies dancing around her face and wandered to the easel. She stared at the canvas for several long moments, the buzz drowned out by the beat of her heart. Dexter joined her.

"God Almighty, guv. Never seen anything like it."

Neither had Fenella. "What on earth have we got here?"

The painting, partially complete, was of the beautiful landscape around the village. It captured the trail near the Roman fort. There were foxes. Some blissful. Some grinning. Some with bitter frowns on their narrow faces. All on horseback with hounds at their heels. And they were galloping—crashing through hedges and jumping over ditches.

"Jesus, Mary and Joseph!" Dexter raised his hand to point although it wasn't necessary. "Look."

Fenella blinked and swallowed, her throat burning hot. "The terror of it is so convincing."

"It is demented, guv." Dexter's voice cracked. "Deranged. Devilish. Like it were painted by the hand of... a bitter crackpot."

For several more moments, they stood and watched foxes hunting down prey. Naked people fled across the countryside. Foxes on horseback followed. Men and women; boys and girls; all running from the foxes; all with fear in their eyes.

Fenella tilted her neck from side to side. "I think there is a message in it."

"Aye guv, but I can't figure out what. It is awful, though. Boggles the mind. How'd she eat making these? No wonder half them artists are starving."

Details began to emerge. The head of one figure was covered by a brown cloth sack, but you couldn't tell whether it was male or female. A plump woman with drumstick legs pelted through a stream chased by a fox with an extra-long snout and eyes that glittered like daggers. From between the hawthorn bushes, a frightened face peered.

With dread, Fenella leaned closer, gaze fastened on the terrible sight. "Isn't that Miss Fish?"

Dexter leaned in. "Aye, guv. A remarkable likeness, even captured her clownfish smile. And look, ain't that the vicar?"

It was him all right, squatting beneath the branches of a larch tree. Behind him, a plump woman with a narrow nose and wild white hair watched through wide eyes. Something furry was attached to her neckline.

Dexter let out a gasp of disgust. "Her neck! The fox has her neck in its jaws."

Fenella spoke without realising her lips had moved. "That's Bella Timbol, the chairwoman of the Ambleside

Village Artists."

They both looked again, recognising faces and putting names to them where they could. A fat man wearing only a ragged green tracksuit top waddled along a trail with three hounds snapping at his bare bottom. An elderly woman wearing nothing but a peach headscarf clambered up a larch tree and a naked young couple holding hands fled a snarling fox on horseback. Carnage everywhere you looked.

Soon, the squalid images sneered their ugly truth. Ann Crombie's triumphant foxes hunted the entire population of Ambleside village.

Dexter squeezed his eyes. "No wonder they say great artists are half mad. Everyone we speak with will have a bleedin' strong motive."

Fenella was thinking along the same lines and wondering how wide they would have to throw their net. "It is obvious now why the chatter of the crowd mentioned revenge. I'd not want to be painted running naked through fields chased by horse-riding foxes. How about you?"

"I ain't a lunatic, guv. If they paint me running, it better be in me clothes."

Fenella stepped away from the grizzly painting, over-whelmed with revulsion. She placed her hands on her hips and glanced at the canvas and she glanced at Dexter and she glanced at the closed door to the other room. They were yet to go into that room, God only knew what they would find. A new thought struck. "We might be searching for two individuals."

Dexter continued to stare at the canvas. "What do you mean?"

"The person who killed Ann Crombie and the person

who found the body and cut off her head. We've nothing to say they are one and the same person or persons. We've nothing to say she wasn't attacked by a mob."

Dexter let out a low whistle, nodding.

Fenella became suddenly aware of the passage of time. *Six minutes left.* And there was the other room to search. "Take as many photos as you can with your phone."

She padded to the other side of the room and stopped by the closed door. Ann Crombie's art studio had been a shock. Now, as she clutched the handle, she wondered what awaited her on the other side.

22

Fenella saw the giant crucifix first.

It hung on the wall above the bed, with Christ's face twisted in anguish. Next came the silence, as still and deep as a pond. A second later, she saw the oak wardrobe. Broad and tall, it loomed with an ominous presence. You could hide a body inside and have room for one or two more.

From the other room came the click of Dexter's mobile phone. He zapped photos, all-out. A zealot who wasted no time. "Found a bathroom, guv. Toilet, sink, shower, nowt else."

Fenella scanned the room. Bare brick walls, a dresser with a cracked mirror, a rush-seated chair and a leather-bound bible on the pillow of the unmade iron-framed bed. Next to the bible was a puzzle magazine, *Northworder*. The room was much smaller and even more spartan than the art studio. And it had the peaceful air of a prayer chapel.

That wardrobe!

She hurried over and yanked open the doors. Clothes hung on hangers—dresses and skirts and blouses and trousers. All neat and organised by colour. A gradient of light to dark. It was obsessive, with no item out of place.

The neat row of women's shoes at the bottom filled Fenella with melancholy.

Walking to the bed, she surveyed the room again. Sounds drifted from the garden—the gentle rustle of the breeze through the trees, the caw of a crow, and a yowl she knew well. Had this been a regular Sunday at home, she'd have dashed out the door with the grandbairns, trying to spot the fox. She touched the leather-bound bible, then picked up the puzzle magazine. A pen dropped out. There were sections for crosswords, sudoku, word searches, anagrams and mazes.

She turned to the first page. A crossword puzzle: *Four across. Four letters, first letter beginning with 'F'. Disco, CB radio and beanbag chairs, once.*

She turned to the second page. Another crossword puzzle, blank. She moved forward to another page. Another blank puzzle. She flipped through the crossword and sudoku sections. All blank. Only the word searches, anagrams and mazes were partially complete.

She closed the magazine. A scrap of paper fluttered out. She stooped and picked it up with gloved hands. A till receipt. On one side was a list of items purchased from Giles Rare Books, a second-hand bookshop in Port St Giles. On the other side, a handwritten note:

Mail Benny Label. Okay?

She read it slowly, snapped a photo with her phone, and slipped it back between the pages.

"Reminds me of a monk's prayer chamber." Dexter stood in the doorway. "Find anything interesting?"

Fenella looked at him and smiled. "Fads."

"Eh, guv?"

"Four across. Four letters. Disco, CB radio and bean-bag chairs, once. The answer is fads."

Dexter stepped into the room. "Ain't got a clue what you are on about, guv, but we best leave, sharpish. Our time is up."

"Aye, happen you're right, and I want a word with the vicar."

"It's Sunday, guv. He'll be in church."

"Then I'll know where to find him."

Dexter gazed at her as though she were mad. "Are you going to tell him about the painting?"

"I've a feeling he already knows."

23

Someone had to identify the remains of Ann Crombie. Fenella thought the vicar was her best bet. Until she saw the landscape painting hanging on the study wall. At that point, everything changed.

The vicarage clock rang the noon hour, its tide of chimes disquieting in the stiff air. Two worn leather armchairs faced the bare fireplace with a coffee table in between. A small window overlooked the graveyard. A sparkle of sunlight lit the room in an eerie glow. It smelled of cigars with a faint whiff of sherry. There were tiny pinholes in the fabric of the armchairs.

The landscape painting hung above the mantelshelf.

"Interesting room you've got here." Fenella could hardly believe her eyes.

Books were crammed in every corner, each covered in brown butcher paper and tied with a loose thread of string. They were stacked in uneven rows on bookshelves' which ran the entire length of one wall. Piles tottered in almost every place. Books leaned, Tower of Pisa style, on the narrow mantelshelf. Her head spun with the volume of tomes. There was almost nowhere to stand. She counted fifteen stacks, knee-deep on the floor as they picked their way to the armchairs. And, of course, there was that landscape painting.

Only the coffee table was devoid of books. A teapot and two bone China teacups were laid out next to a plate of custard creams.

The vicar expected her call.

Reverend William Kemp leaned back in his armchair, placed a hand on his domed forehead and sighed. "Tea?" He poured without waiting for a reply. "I haven't had time to clear up, too busy. You wouldn't believe the number of blessings a vicar has to perform. Baptism, confirmation, marriage, house blessings, blessing of the sick, of the animals and even graves on All Soul's Day. Funerals, too. Help yourself to biscuits. I believe you are partial to custard creams."

Up close, he was a cave-chested man with an anxious stare and a slit of a mouth with thin lips that didn't evoke trust. Not the face you'd expect for a vicar. Not with that massive forehead and secretive, pea-sized eyes.

"You expected me?" Fenella eyed the plate.

"A man of the cloth knows many secrets."

"Oh aye, and can you reveal how you knew custard creams are my favourite?"

"A priest must be on alert to the needs of their flock." He picked up a biscuit, nibbled and placed it in his saucer, mouth turned down. "Quite delightful."

Fenella eyed the piles of books covered in brown butcher paper and she eyed the landscape painting above the mantelshelf and she eyed the custard creams on the plate. She guessed, in quick succession—avid reader, collected books for a jumble sale, book reviewer for a blog. Her mind drifted back to the plate of biscuits. *Nowt like a carb top-up before I get to work.*

She reached for a custard cream, wanted to cram it into her mouth, but took a dainty nibble. "Nowt as tasty as a custard cream when the mood strikes, wouldn't you agree, Vicar Kemp?"

"Bill, please. Everyone calls me Bill." He smiled with perfect teeth so white he might have painted them. "I must compliment you on your taste."

It was ridiculous, but Fenella smiled back. A big broad toothy grin. She was partial to a complement, and had a blind spot to them, especially from men. "I see you are quite a reader."

"Indeed." He gazed around with a cheerful glow. "I've read each one, some many times. I read until my pupils burn and still keep going to the joyful end. A small pleasure for the vicar, eh? My secret sin."

"Not so secret, you can't move for the books." Again, Fenella gazed at the piles of novels. "All carefully wrapped in brown butcher paper."

He flashed a dazzling smile. "What you see is what you get. I'm neither pious nor a hypocrite. I became a vicar *because* of my earthly desires. I restrain my carnal inclinations through daily penitence, prayer and reading. Lots of reading."

Fenella felt herself slipping down a rabbit hole. She came here to ask him about Ann Crombie; how well he knew her; if he would identify the body. But now she was eager to know more about the books, peep behind the brown butcher paper and have a good look. "How do you tell the books apart?"

He winked and, for the first time, she saw a handsome edge to his sly face. In the natural light of the study, he looked much younger than his forty-seven years. He tapped his domed forehead. "Excellent memory."

"I'd never remember which book I put where." She tried not to stare at his huge forehead. *Must be filled with brains.* "I'd be a mess."

"Yes, it can be a challenge." He turned away. "I prefer to keep them covered and under lock and key. They are rather... sensitive."

Fenella wondered how to get him to leave the room so she could take a quick peep beneath the brown covers. "You must be a busy man, parishioners calling all the time?"

"I've asked not to be disturbed."

"Ah, very wise." She strained to look at the nearest pile and thought she saw the faint outline of a bare-chested man beneath the brown paper. She blinked. "I won't take up much of your time. Are you sure we won't be disturbed?"

"Quite sure."

"Hadn't you better check the front door, just to be certain, with it being Sunday?"

He waved a hand. "No need."

"But what if someone is there?"

"They will knock."

"Ah!" What lay under the brown covers of the books was none of her business. She was here on other matters. Her detective's brain told her to move on but her nosy parker genes wanted to know more. *Like a pig in a trough.* "So many books and me, I have hardly any time to read. And here you are surrounded by paperbacks."

He raised a hand and squeezed his domed forehead.

"I'm an author in my spare time and read to keep up with the latest trends."

For the first time, Fenella noticed his wedding ring. "Mystery books?"

"Romance."

"Eh?"

"Sweet romance, with a long burn." His gaze lingered on the pile tottering on the mantelshelf. "These are romance books, some with rather salacious covers. I wrap them all with brown paper to be discreet."

Fenella tried not to sound flabbergasted. "Reverend William Kemp, eh? I've not read any of your works. I love romance books and watch them on the telly. You write sweet romance, eh?"

"I'm not published yet, not for want of trying. This writing business is taxing. My latest work feels... flat. Not enough emotion for a publisher to pick it up. I've been told I need reader feedback." His eyes darted around the room as if searching for something. They settled on a tall stack of yellowed papers on the cherry wood desk. "I've twelve unsold manuscripts. Since you enjoy romance books, I'll give you a copy of each. Would next week be agreeable for your feedback?"

Fenella changed the subject sharpish. "Is Mrs Kemp a reader?"

His expression changed from hope to surprise to sadness. "Mrs Kemp is not with me at the moment."

"I'm sorry to hear that." Fenella couldn't tear her eyes from his wedding ring. It was as thick as a bracelet. Solid gold. Expensive. "Is the wife about?"

"Which one?"

"Eh?"

"I've been married three times, Inspector Sallow." He made a soft gurgling sound. "Three beautiful women. God has been good to me. I've been spoiled for choice. Even had a stint in a rock band. I played keyboards and sang a little."

Fenella stared, dumbstruck. When she was a child, a vicar married once, might strum the acoustic guitar and sing a hymn or two. Now they were like the stars on the telly—played in touring bands with two and three marriages, all ending in divorce. She'd been married to Eduardo for donkey's years and was all the happier for it. Were the wives attracted by the vicar's huge forehead and those secretive, dried pea eyes?

The vicar repeated the gurgling sound. "The first wife died in a fire." He closed his eyes. "I ran from the house and was saved, but she... her body... it is terrible what fire does to flesh."

Fenella waited a respectful length of time. "And your second wife?"

He squeezed his eyes tighter. "My second wife lost her life in a horrifying car accident. I was driving. Ice and snow and late at night. Not my fault. The other driver swerved into my lane after a night of drinking in town. Gin and ale and rum and vodka; the driver had drunk the lot. It was a head-on crash." He fell silent for a while, the gurgling noise like a quiet prayer. "I had to identify the body. Her skull... it was... crushed. I couldn't do it again."

Fenella took a gulp of tea. She shouldn't pry. It had nothing to do with the case. "And your third wife... is she well?"

His eyes snapped open. He picked up the teacup, held it high in front of his face and peered at her over the rim. She wondered if he would speak, and why, in the end, he just stared at her through those pea-sized eyes.

They remained silent for some time, but Fenella couldn't get the third wife out of her mind. She had to know what happened to the woman and prodded him with a question. "How is the third Mrs Kemp these days?"

The vicar slurped from his teacup and placed it down. "There is no Mrs Kemp. My third wife and I are. . . no longer one. But I'm an old romantic fool and hope to marry again. If God commands it, I must obey."

Fenella's matchmaking brain kicked on, but she had her doubts and wondered if she ought to warn women away. "Do you have a lass in mind?"

"It is in the hands of the Lord."

"Nice. I. . . suppose you and your last wife divorced because you were incompatible?"

"That is a rather personal question."

"I'm a detective, can't help it." Fenella smiled. "You were telling me about your third wife."

He answered in such a soft voice that, at first, she didn't recognise his words. She expected him to say something about a disagreement; that they went their separate ways, and the bishop would give a blessing when he found his fourth wife.

"She drowned, Inspector Sallow." Vicar Kemp gazed at the landscape painting above the mantelshelf. "A terrible boating accident in Lake Windermere. I was thrown clear of the sinking vessel but my third wife went down with it and perished. A tragic accident, nothing more, but I'm blessed to be alive."

24

A deluge of rain burst from the heavens and pounded against the vicarage. A sudden and violent July storm. It raged across the graveyard and swept in great sheets across tombstones, drenching the trees and pooling in puddles on the ancient soil.

Fenella gazed at the window. A streak of lightning forked. Thunder roared. She turned back to the vicar. "You've not been at the clergy thing long, then?"

"Long enough." He looked at the window with deep thought etched into his face. "I came to the calling late in life. Nine years now and counting. Seven years in this parish."

"Ann Crombie's death must have come as a real shock." Fenella waited for a heartbeat. "It came right out of the blue, didn't it? "

He picked up his teacup, pressed it to his lips but did not drink. "We all feel helpless. I dreaded today, tried to buoy my flock but with the police everywhere they are panicked." He flashed a white-toothed smile. "You and the other officers will leave soon, I take it? The villagers love the police but we don't want them hanging about on every corner. Not a long investigation, we all hope. Am I correct in that?"

Fenella ignored the question and pointed at the landscape painting. "Interesting bit of art you have on the wall."

Foxhunters in blood-red jackets on horseback chased a fox through the green fields. A pack of hounds with snapping teeth raced alongside. Fenella recognised the Roman fort and the trail in the background.

The vicar followed her gaze and gave a little start. "I should have put it away."

"Where did you get it?"

"God in his goodness gave it to me." The vicar stood for a moment, his gaze on the landscape painting, and then he slid back into the armchair. "That scene is quite stunning, don't you think?"

Fenella did not reply. The storm passed and a weak sun glinted through the study window. Vicar Kemp glanced at Fenella and he glanced at the painting and he rubbed his forehead. He opened his mouth and closed it and looked like he was kicking himself for leaving it on the wall. He sighed but did not speak.

Fenella stuffed another biscuit into her mouth and munched, thinking. "Not often I have tea with the vicar. I've got to make the most of it."

He laughed. A warm, genuine belly laugh. "I'm not a fan of custard creams. Why don't you take the lot?"

"Aye, think I will." She scooped the remaining biscuits into a handkerchief and dropped them in her handbag. "Tell me about that landscape painting."

"You're an intelligent woman. Make them laugh, then get them to talk." He flashed his bright white teeth. "The painting was given to me by. . ." The smile faded from his face. ". . . a friend."

"A woman, eh?"

"You are very perceptive. I can't keep secrets from you, can I? It was gifted to me by Mrs Bella Timbol, the chairwoman of the Ambleside Village Artists. Have you met her?"

He asked as though he already knew the answer.

"Aye, I've met her. I saw you standing next to her in the crowd on Saturday."

He pressed a hand on his oversized forehead. "The entire village must have been at Bede Thatch, and you notice me?"

"That's what I'm paid to do. Notice things."

Again he glanced at the landscape painting. "I can see you are rather good at it."

"So, that painting is Mrs Timbol's handy work?"

"Oh no, her artworks are more. . . abstract." The vicar smiled in the same way as when he took his first bite of custard cream. "That landscape was painted over thirty years ago by Ann Crombie. On her very first visit to Ambleside. A three-week artist's retreat. I believe Ann gave it to Bella as a gift. Ann was taken by the beauty of the village and came back to settle some twenty-four or so years later. Alas, the painting has no commercial value. I've checked. Three independent art dealers have told me it is worthless."

Fenella glanced at the landscape again, then focused on her next question. "Tell me about Ann Crombie. What was she like?"

It took vicar Bill Kemp half a minute to think about it.

Then his gaze shifted to the landscape painting. "A warm, motherly woman. She knew everyone and gave herself to her art." The words fell from his mouth with the softness of a eulogy. Like he was practising, getting ready for the part; condensing as many good traits into as few words as possible. "A woman who will never be forgotten."

Fenella tapped her handbag. "Oh, come off it. We both know she wasn't an angel. Was she well-liked?"

"It is not for me to judge." He paused for a moment, eyes blinking. "I have access to confidential information as a vicar, and there are times when I want to share with others who might be touched by what I learn. Alas, I cannot. My vow of trust is sacred. I'm a priest, not a gossip monger."

Fenella changed direction. "Do you have a key to Bede Thatch?"

"A key?"

"Yes."

"To the front door?":

"To any door."

He blinked. "I do not have a key to that cottage."

"Did you ever have a key?"

"Haven't I made myself clear?"

Fenella tried a different question. "Who would want to do Ann Crombie harm?"

"Really, inspector, it is not for me to point fingers."

Again, Fenella changed the subject. "Have you seen Ann's recent art?"

"I have. . ." He looked around the study, his gaze falling on the window and lingering on the graveyard beyond. ". . . heard of it."

"What have you heard?"

"Just rumours. Pure gossip."

Fenella felt her heart thud and touched a lock of stray hair. "That is how we catch half the criminals, rumours. And today, in this room, you and I are just having a little chat. Sharing information."

The vicar sighed; a blue vein pulsed in his forehead. "Look, there is real fury in the village about Ann's latest work."

"Why?"

"She had some minor success with her humanised fox paintings and decided they might sell even better if she depicted real people rather than figments of her imagination. Naked images of Ambleside people, especially those who hold prominent positions. Myself included. Hunted down by red foxes. Running naked and terrified through the fields. Men and women. Boys and girls. Of course, this is all hearsay and gossip. I've not actually seen any such painting and hope it does not exist. It would be a shame to learn that Ann Crombie abandoned all morals in a desperate dash for fame." His pea-sized eyes shrunk to pinheads. "The flock will not tolerate being humiliated. When the body ingests a foreign object, it spews it out. We are a small village. We stick together."

It disturbed Fenella that his face had become red, nostrils flared and the speed at which the blue vein in his forehead thumped. *He is under a lot of pressure, holding back on some big secrets.* "We need your help, the help of the villagers. Did anyone see anything, hear anything, or say anything that might help me catch the person who did this to Ann?"

His gaze went to the window, and he spoke as if to

himself. "The police have so little time these days. A week of intense questions and then you'll be on to the next thing. Two weeks at most and then it will calm down and we'll draw a curtain over it. Forget about it." He pondered for a moment longer, and then his gaze drifted back to the window which looked out onto the silent graveyard. "I heard from one of your police colleagues that unsolved cases end up in the cold case files."

That was all there was to it, the vicar seemed certain of that. His reply was nothing, and it was everything.

Fenella rubbed her hands. She wanted a list of gossip mongers in the village. "And your source for this rumour?"

He shook his head. "I'm a priest, we pride ourselves in keeping secrets." He touched his dog collar. "People are frightened, they look to me to tell them what to do. Do you have news about the killer?" His lips stretched into a white-toothed smile. "Do you have any idea where they might be? Is there anything you can tell me to set the flock at ease?"

The wind slammed the window pitching twigs and leaves against the glass. Fenella looked helplessly at the swirl and the quiet graveyard beyond. She turned back to the vicar and hated to admit the cruel truth. "We have no leads. We don't know who the killer is. I've no idea where they are hiding, whether they will strike again, and if they do, who the next victim will be."

25

Kate Owen was running late for work in the pub and felt rotten, still hurting from the news her long-time boyfriend, Ken Ashworth, was to wed a young lass called Millie. And she was annoyed at agreeing to pose in Liam Brampton's studio and annoyed at breaking her promise at the last moment. Ken was right, she shouldn't be alone with the man, and that annoyed her even more.

The July afternoon had turned hot under a cloudless blue sky. Kate's white blouse clung to her with clammy dampness. Tourists and locals ambled in and out of shops. They ate ice creams and snapped photos. Only the church shop on the corner, for which the street got its name, remained closed to the wallets of Sunday shoppers.

Kate raced through the crowd, sweating in the heat, out of breath and thinking about the past. Soon after moving to Ambleside, she visited a mystic in Whitehaven. She wanted to know what her future held. In the flickering glow of candles, they sat at a round table in a room steeped in the aroma of incense. The mystic's amber eyes fixed on Kate's face for a long while then slid to a blue velvet pouch on the table. At first, Kate thought it held coins. Gold coins. She leaned forward, eager, holding her breath. Her past had been dark streaks of grime, she hoped her future glistened.

The mystic spoke, voice low and misty. "What is your greatest desire?"

Kate didn't hesitate, eyeing the blue velvet pouch and wondering how many gold coins were inside. "I want a man with a big bank balance and a future, not a drunk without a penny to his name. I want my daughter to grow up in a happy family."

The mystic's hand hovered over the velvet pouch but did not dip inside. "You have been fishing with bad bait in shallow waters. Such places only yield minnows. You must fish with good bait in deep waters. You must sling your hook further."

Kate remembered the words as though it were yesterday, remembered the sad gleam in the mystic's eyes. And she remembered crossing the outstretched palm with a fifty pound note to get a deeper look at her fate.

She'd expected a crystal ball, but that cost a hundred and Kate didn't have that sort of cash. Instead, the mystic dipped a bejewelled hand into the blue velvet pouch. Kate's heart skittered against her chest. Her future lay in the palm of those jewel-encrusted fingers. How many gold coins did the mystic hold in her closed fist?

A clock chimed from some distant room announcing the top of the hour. It seemed an eternity before the mystic's hand opened.

Kate shrank back, away from the hideous sight.

Bones.

Bleached salt white with strange blood-red characters scrawled on each one.

The mystic muttered an incantation and threw them across the tabletop. They clattered, spreading out in an elongated oval.

It was the dust motes floating in the dim air that Kate would always remember. And the stillness. And the sharp intake of the mystic's breath.

A moment later the mystic began screaming, finger pointing at the door, stuffing the money back in Kate's hands, telling her to get the hell out.

Kate no longer believed in mystics. She didn't believe in the casting of bones. Whatever the future held, she didn't want to know. Even if this was her last day on Earth.

26

They sat in silence in the vicarage study for some time.

Then Fenella opened her handbag, riffled around and took out a custard cream. She took her time eating. She planned to ask the vicar to identify the remains of Ann Crombie. Not a pleasant task in the grim, dim morgue. At least, as a vicar, he was used to death, even if not so brutal. First, though, she had to get him to agree to help.

The *tick, tick, ticking* of the vicarage clock counted down the seconds to the next doleful chimes. The storm had long passed, with the sun blazing hot. When, at last, Fenella spoke, it was in a whisper of hope.

"I've news about the case, for your ears only."

The vicar's hand moved to his dog collar, removing it. "Go on, Inspector Sallow."

Ah, so he enjoys a bit of tittle-tattle like me! Fenella wondered if that was why he took his dog collar off. He'd be more willing to trade gossip without the reminder of God watching around his neck. "Did you know Ann Crombie well?"

His eyes rolled toward the ceiling. "I will pray without ceasing."

"For Ann Crombie's soul?"

"That you catch the killer before the fiend strikes again."

"What makes you certain there will be more deaths?"

"Once a wolf gets a taste for human blood only a bullet will stop it from taking more."

Fenella said nothing.

He sighed. "You were asking about Ann Crombie, well, I'm a shepherd. I make it my job to recognise my flock."

Fenella thought about Ann Crombie's bedroom with its giant crucifix of Christ. "Was she a regular in church?"

The vicar let out a bitter laugh. "Before I came to the parish, she wrote me an encouraging letter. She told me that she, too, was moving to Ambleside and made mention of her willingness to offer substantial financial support for the new vicar." He leaned back and shut his eyes. "When I arrived in the village, I invited her to tea that first Sunday. I was still unpacking and had an eager expectation she might write a cheque right there and then. She had lived in America, and you know how they enjoy waving their wallets at good causes. And I had my eye on a rather nice Ford. I never expected..."

His words fell away. Silence ballooned. The sun dipped behind a cloud and it became dark. In the shadows, the vicar's face seemed aged.

Fenella coughed. "You were saying?"

Red splotches rose in the vicar's face. "It came as a biting blow when Ann Crombie refused to join me for tea. On that Sunday or any other. She offered no explanation, and it proved impossible for me to find out exactly why she turned down my many offers. I all but dropped to my knees and begged her to show up. I was left in a difficult position

as I had put a nonrefundable down payment on the Ford."
He snorted. "I'm riding a bicycle at the moment. Keeps
me fit, I suppose."

"Can't be easy." Fenella thought the room had the
touch of the lush about it, and his teeth were so white
he had to have an expensive dentist. "Money that tight,
eh?"

"The church does not pay well. I have to beg and
barter and plead for help. It's a wonder most clergy aren't
dressed in rags." His gaze flicked to the landscape painting
above the mantelshelf. "It was reckless of me to accept a
position in the hopes her financial support would make life
here a touch more comfortable. Man makes plans and God
laughs."

Fenella didn't know what to say, so she said nothing.

The vicar's eyes were suddenly bloodshot. The blue
vein pulsed in his forehead. When he spoke it was with a
harsh, furious bark. "Ann Crombie never set foot in this
church. Never!"

The vicar was upset and in danger of becoming enraged.
Shocked, Fenella scrabbled for the right words to calm him
down. Someone had to identify the body. She tried again,
keeping her voice soft. "But you would know Ann Crombie
if you met her?"

"I would."

"Are you sure?"

"Certain."

"You could identify her on sight?"

"I'll never forget that woman." He stared through angry
eyes. "Her face is etched so deep in my brain cells that I
can draw her mugshot with a blunt pencil in a dark room.

Sweet Jesus forgive me, but that is one smirk-filled face I shall remember to my dying breath."

There was no point beating about the bush now. Fenella sucked in a shallow breath. "I need your help."

He became instantly alert. "What type of help?"

"With the investigation."

"Like an amateur sleuth?"

"Aye, in a way."

He thought about the idea and seemed to like it. "I lay myself at your service."

"It won't be easy."

"You can depend on me. I'm up for the task."

Fenella's lips quirked at the edges. "We have not been able to track down any of Ann Crombie's relatives. Her parents are both dead. No siblings. We have reached a dead end and are stuck. This is where you come in."

He leaned back in his chair, a majestic smile creeping across his lips. "Yes, yes, I can see that."

Fenella was about to continue when she noticed his lips were still moving. There was more. When it came she could have kissed him.

"Dear me, Inspector." He paused for a heartbeat. "Have you spoken with Helen?"

"Who?"

"Mrs Helen Grimes, Ann Crombie's niece. She lives in Greenport, Long Island."

Fenella had visited the town once, on an extended trip to New York City. A friend drove her and Eduardo to a country house for a lazy weekend. A land of vineyards and farms and beautiful landscapes. "That is an expensive area to live, eh?"

The vicar nodded. "I contacted Mrs Grimes and told her what happened. She is on her way to England and will arrive on Wednesday. One can only hope she is more generous with her financial resources than her deceased aunt."

27

Kate Owen didn't want to be late for her shift in the pub.

She dodged an old couple moving at a snail's pace and caught her reflection in a shop window. A terrible brown stain streaked from the top button of her blouse, radiating out in thin veins. Why didn't she put on a fresh top and do something with her hair? And that wart on her chin, she'd swear the hairs on it grew an inch overnight.

She drifted to the other side of the street where the tourists were fewer, picking up her pace. The stooped woman in the peach headscarf, head bent, carrying a shopping bag in each hand, wasn't watching where she was going, but it was Kate who ended up with her backside on the pavement.

"I'm so sorry." The stooped woman placed her shopping bags on the path and peered down at Kate. "My fault."

Kate hated to blame a feeble old woman for her fall. "I should have paid more attention. Stupid of me. I was in a rush for work."

"On a Sunday?" The old woman sighed. "I suppose every day is a work day for you youngsters these days. No day of rest anymore."

She leaned forward, offered Kate a hand and helped her

to her feet. Only then did Kate catch a whiff of alcohol on the woman's breath.

Kate touched the wart on her chin. "Are you okay?"

"Never better."

"Then I'd best be on my way."

"Where'd you work?" The woman had her hands on her hips, her chest heaving as if catching her breath. "Hope it ain't too far."

Kate pointed along the road. "The pub. Only a part-time job, but it helps pay the bills."

"Thought I'd seen you before." The old woman squinted. "It is my regular drinking hole. Once a month on a Sunday I treat myself to a steak and kidney pie and half a pint of ale."

Kate recalled her now. The old woman with sad eyes who shuffled in at lunchtime and sat in a dark corner, ordered food and ate it slowly over four or five hours as she knitted with steel needles and read from a giant bible. And for the first time, Kate realised the woman only came in once a month. She'd never have guessed. She chided herself for never taking the time to ask. "I remember you. Next time I'll bring you dessert, on the house."

The woman tightened her peach headscarf. "Can't do much on a pension these days, and I have to keep a few pennies back for the heating when the winter comes. It gets lonely when you are old and on your own. Most of my friends have died and it is hard to make new ones. Youngsters leave you alone, and old folk don't want to hang around old people." She turned and gazed at Kate with sad eyes. "It is just me and the Lord now."

Old age terrified Kate. She watched in helpless fear as

the years ticked by. In her forties already. And now Ken had chosen a younger woman. A twig-thin lass with giant boobs and a fertile womb.

The old woman glanced both ways along the street, lowering her voice. "When you are old, you realise it don't matter what they show on the telly, family is the family you get. You remember the small moments of joy. Unexpected moments that only matter to you. It ain't easy living on your own. These days everyone is too busy for a chat." Again she glanced both ways along the street, then back at Kate. "What you got on your mind, apart from dusting yourself down and dashing off to work?"

Kate sighed. She needed to talk, just a few minutes, to get things off her mind, and the woman seemed friendly. "I was thinking about my boyfriend. My ex-boyfriend."

"Kicked him to the curb, did you? Is that why you look so sad?" The old woman looked at her with sharp eyes. "I heard that phrase on one of those American soaps they show on the telly."

Kate laughed but her heart ached. "I'm not sure."

"Only keep the fruit you are certain of, honey. That's what I do in my weekly shop. I can't afford tasteless plums on my pension; they've got to be super sweet."

"You've got a point."

"I mean it, honey. If the lad ain't sweet then he is poison. Throw him back and sling your hook again."

Kate took in the lined face of the woman and decided. *I will not let Ken ruin my day.* The end of the relationship brought the promise of positive change. And it started right here and now. What would the pub landlord think if she showed up in fresh clothes with her hair done up and wearing bright red lipstick? *I just have to get through the ordeal of the next few days. My best life is still to come. From now on I'll get to work early, rather than always showing up late with a boatload of excuses. A small change, but I've got to start somewhere.*

A man in a tweed jacket patched at the elbows hurried along the opposite side of the street toward them. He stopped, his egg-shaped hairless head turning to watch them and his red shirt open at the collars. He waved, giving the thumbs-up. The woman in the peach headscarf waved back. Then, with large strides, he was gone.

"Let me help you with your bags." Kate dusted off her jeans. "How far are you going?"

"Corner of St Mary's Lane."

That was the opposite direction from the pub. Kate hesitated. It would cost her an extra ten minutes and she would be late for her shift. She picked up both bags and shuffled alongside the woman.

They walked much slower than Kate expected and the woman talked nonstop. "Terrible news from Borrans Wood. Ann Crombie murdered! I can't believe it. They always said Bede Thatch was cursed ever since that circus man built the place and moved in with his monkey." She stopped and turned to Kate, eyes glittering with excitement, mouth open exposing false teeth. "The curse of Borrans Wood is one thing, but murder. My God. And they say the police don't have a clue."

Kate didn't want to talk about it. She knew Ann through the Ambleside Village Artists group although they rarely talked at the meetings. A sudden pang of loss gripped her. Never again would she see Ann's face or chat with her over a steaming mug of tea. What happened in the woods was too appalling to discuss.

"Head chopped off like she was some wicked French queen." The woman was enjoying herself, fascinated by the details. "The police found the head hanging in a tree with the body tossed into the brambles for the animals to eat. A man in the pub told me the eyes were pecked out by ravens. Another lass said rats gnawed off her toes. It's a wonder the foxes didn't get at her, they do so love slurping up the internal organs."

Kate had heard enough. "Please, let's not speculate on the details. It doesn't do any good."

But the old woman wanted to speculate, wanted to pick over the bones. "The killing isn't over yet, mark my words." She turned and held Kate's gaze. "Oooh, do you think it has to do with witchcraft?"

"I have no idea."

"Do you know the police are looking for two different people? The one who killed her and another person who chopped off her head and fiddled with her body. Might even be a crowd of the buggers involved. Sweet Jesus, it makes me tremble and I'm an old lady living all on my own. What if those monsters take a fancy to my head? Oooh, I feel like they are watching me, following me and might pounce during the night, don't you?"

"Ambleside is one of the safest villages in the country."

The old woman stopped walking and again held Kate's gaze. "But what if today was your last day on earth, would you repent?"

"What?"

"I'd run to church and ask Vicar Kemp to say a special

118

blessing. He is such a kind man, don't you think?"

Kate sighed. She didn't want to be drawn into a conversation about church or the death in Borrans Wood or anything else for that matter. She just wanted to help the lady and get to work. "I'm sure it is a one-off and the police will keep us safe."

"You really think so because I heard..." And so it went on until they reached St Mary's Lane and Kate waved a weary goodbye.

As Kate turned to head back to Church Street, she suddenly sensed she was being followed. She glanced along both sides of the street. Two children and a young woman ambled from an ice-cream parlour. A fat man in an unfashionable green tracksuit leaned on a lamppost, a large coffee cup in one hand and a doughnut in the other. Cars and buses and vans trundled along either side of the road. She looked at the man in the green tracksuit. She'd seen him before but didn't know him.

She continued her walk, fretting that she was going to be very late for work. Out of the corner of her eye, she thought she glimpsed a familiar figure in the doorway of a gift shop—Liam Brampton. The weirdo who had asked her to pose for him in his art studio. She'd agreed then changed her mind and now regretted both decisions. Was Liam following her? She shivered, stopped and slowly turned.

If it was him in the shop doorway, he was gone.

28

Sweating and tired, Kate arrived half an hour late for her shift. As she approached the pub doors a sense of foreboding overcame her. Something bad was going to happen and it was going to happen soon and it was going to happen to her.

She stopped and stared at the pub doors. She had worked there since she arrived in the village. It was supposed to be a temporary job until she found something better.

She never did.

Five endless years. Now she dreaded six and saw seven coming as surely as the dawn. A pitiful, unbearable existence on a barmaid's wage. And now Ken, her salaried saviour, was off the cards, years nine and ten were on the horizon. She could hardly believe how the time had flown and didn't like where it was going.

I must stop thinking like this. Stop thinking about Ken. Stay positive. Pub work pays the bills. It is a start. I'll do better now Ken is gone.

A young couple ambled through the pub doors, arm in arm. The man wore a white t-shirt, and the woman wore a lime floral dress. They paused in front of her to kiss. Long and sensuous and slow.

Kate almost cried but her mobile phone pinged with a message from Skye:

Mam, I'm staying at Steph's tonight.

Kate's fingers flew across the keyboard of her phone:

No! You are to be home by seven. We are having a mother-and-daughter night in. Bonding time. I've picked a tear-jerker. You'll love it.

Kate's phone pinged a few seconds later:

Don't you want me to succeed? We've got a massive amount of study to do to get to university. Me and Steph must work half the night to get it done. Please can I stay over?

Kate sighed as she typed her reply:

Okay. See you Monday evening and don't go at it too hard. No all-nighters. Study needs rest.

It was as the swing doors of the pub opened again that a fresh wave of discomfort washed over Kate. Like a bad smell in the air. It hovered and clung and intensified to a stink.

Something was wrong.

She'd passed through the doors hundreds of times, most of the while on the run, arriving late and dashing behind the bar to pull pints. It was not a posh pub—locals and a few hardy tourists. Ale and pies and chips.

But today she sensed something was different.

The landlord appeared in the doorway with his hands on his hips. She stopped, at first to raise a hand of greeting, an instant later to stare at him in shock. For a moment there was only the two of them, eyes locked with the smell of warm ale wafting through the doors. And what was that gleam in his eyes? Anger at her arriving late? Fury at the lack of tourists? The quickness of the businessman looking to see if all was clear before doing an underhand deal in the back of the pub? Or was it like the time she forgot to put the prime steak in the fridge and found it days later covered in flies?

"You are late." He wasn't one to beat about the bush. "Always late and leaving early."

She'd heard it a hundred times before, but this time it was different. This time she didn't nod and flash *her smile* and take his gruff tone on the chin. "Look, I've had a rough night, personal problems and won't take any crap from you today. Yes, I'm late. I'm sorry. Now, I want to do my job without your creepy hands trying to touch me, go home to spend time with my daughter and then sleep. Got it?"

"I get it." He bared his teeth. "And you get this. You are fired. Oh, and tell your daughter to keep away. I'm not losing my licence over a fifteen-year-old tart."

The pub doors swung wide open. Music and laughter flowed out. A barmaid pulled pints behind the bar. A new woman, twig thin with a broad smile. Millie! Grey-haired men clustered around her, laughing like school boys in the playground. Sitting at the corner of the bar in a pink shirt with broad collars, drinking slowly was Ken. The gold stud in his nose caught a glint of light and his spiked black hair shone with grease.

For a moment there was silence, but then came another sound. A happy joyous booming Irish voice. A man in a flat cap with a red face and a double chin slapped Ken on the back. "Here's to a long and happy marriage. To Ken and Millie. May they have a schoolhouse full of beautiful children and a wallet always overflowing with cash. The next round is on Ken Ashworth."

Kate stumbled back, turned and fled pursued by a roar of drunken cheers. She didn't see the figure following her at a trot.

29

Dusk crept over the village of Ambleside. Another dark night loomed. Pimples of light trembled in the cloudless heavens; stars blinking like frightened eyes.

Liam Brampton turned his gaze from the darkening sky to the front door of Kate Owen's cottage. He flicked the stub of his special cigarette to the ground, crushed it with his boot and reached into the cloth sack for his lucky rabbit paw, fondling it between his fingers, his throat vibrating with soft fox-like barks.

He wanted to be a good boy tonight, told Mummy he'd do nothing wrong. He'd also told Mummy he no longer needed to paint women, told her he preferred landscapes—bushes and foxes and trees.

Liam wriggled from the bushes where he'd squatted until sunset watching the house through the crevice of leaves. He hesitated, keeping in a crouch low to the ground. The police were on the hunt for a maniac killer. A grey-haired woman detective seemed to be in charge. He'd seen her but didn't like the sharp look in her eyes. A mixture of X-ray and laser that penetrated all that it saw. He'd stay well clear of her and her probing questions. Fly low under the radar.

He glanced at the sky.
It was dark enough now.
No one would see.
Just like when I was a kid.

He was six when he first ran away from home as dusk turned to night, keeping to the shadows so the adults wouldn't see him. Three days later the village policeman found him in the woods, burrowed in a hole. When he told Mummy he'd dug the hole so he could live with the foxes and catch rabbits with his sharp teeth, she took him to see the doctor with the narrow mouth and brown nose hair. The doctor said it wasn't his fault, said he couldn't help it because he was not wired like a normal boy. Something was off in the brain cells. Something that would never be right. Mummy cried. Liam cried too because he wanted to live with the foxes and tear flesh from rabbit bones with his teeth.

When they got home, he made up his mind to keep quiet about his plans. He didn't tell Mummy he wanted to live with the foxes again. He told her he wanted to keep rabbits as pets, that Fluffy escaped with her friends and never came back, leaving only the babies; that rabbits were crafty that way. He didn't tell her that he planned to feed the babies until they were big and fat and that one day he'd tell her that they ran away too. Again he fondled the rabbit paw. He didn't like to lie, but sometimes there was no other choice.

A gust shook the trees rustling the leaves so they chattered like teeth. From somewhere came the howl of a dog, long and slow and mournful.

Liam fingered the brass tin with the swan on the lid,

toying with whether to light up again. His *special smokes* gave him more confidence than his motivational cassette tapes. And he'd need a full measure of confidence tonight.

Roll.

Light.

Inhale.

No.

He would wait until he was inside with the door locked.

He shook off his boots and his socks and wriggled his toes in the soft soil. He stood, took off his black trousers then he took off his white underpants and smoothed down his wheat-gold smock so it hung over his bare knees. Next, he reached into the brown cloth sack for his blood-red beret, placing it on his head so it shaded his eyes.

Kate Owen had said yes, and Mummy always told him when you agree to a thing you must see it through.

He stepped onto the garden path throwing his cloth sack over his shoulder. It slapped with a dull thud against his strong back.

30

Liam gazed at Kate Owen's front door. From this distance, it reminded him of a black eye. Dark and unblinking with a worried glare that whatever had caused the bruising might strike again.

Liam smiled.

Despite his pot-belly which bulged and stretched the smock, his legs were strong. Climbing sixty-three stone steps to his studio every day made them mule stout. Once, when he'd forgotten his key and found himself locked out of his studio, he kicked the door down with his bare feet. The entire door frame came off along with part of the wall.

And now, as the onset of night blurred his vision and darkness crawled deeper, Liam glanced around the silent garden and peered both ways along Vicarage Road.

Stillness.

Unnatural quiet.

A pale moon glowed above the rooftops, faded lemon growing in strength as it climbed. Hedges lined both sides of the road with a footpath on either side. Most of the cottage windows were dark. No one walked their dog. The complete stillness excited him. Thoughts of what lay ahead made him giddy.

"I'm a good boy, always do what Mummy says." He lowered his voice, grinning. "When she is watching."

The longer he lingered in the garden, the greater the chance someone would see him. He turned back to look at Kate's cottage. A warm welcoming glow shone through the kitchen window and he saw her moving about with her back to him. Her movements struck him as odd, jerky, like she was lost in the Sahara Desert and staggering toward a water hole.

And there was something else that was unusual.

The window was flung open, which was a first since he'd been watching Kate's home. It seemed significant but Liam didn't know why.

Until Kate turned.

She had a rum bottle in one hand and a giant spliff in the other. She took a long swig and then sucked hard on the spliff, puffing out a giant plume. She whirled around, staggered to the window and snapped it shut.

Liam ducked.

Kate remained at the window, hand on the latch, looking into the dark garden, swaying.

Liam crouched to a dot.

She opened the window and leaned out, peering in his direction. He held his breath and sensed her eyes scanning the darkness. It was the ring of a phone that distracted her. She retreated inside, still swaying and vanished into another room.

Liam exhaled, nausea curdling up from his gut. Mummy told him he mustn't watch women through their windows at night. "That is what strangers do, and the police put strange men in prison."

TELL-TALE BONES

On the surface, he didn't know Kate well, but he was hardly a stranger. She'd served him pints of ale and chips with peas and steak pies oozing with brown gravy. He had made a mental note of each stain on her white blouse. They clustered around the top button which she kept clasped shut. He was sure she had three work blouses that she rotated through the week. She washed them on Saturday nights in a boil wash with a few drops of bleach. He knew this because when she worked the Sunday afternoon shift in the pub he noticed the stains from the week were gone, and when she leaned forward to serve him, he sniffed the lemony scent of detergent with a faint trace of chlorine on her white blouse.

Liam smiled.

Whatever else they said about him, he was unfailing in his eye for detail. That's what they admired about him in the slaughterhouse. His eye for detail. He was quick and quiet and got the job done. He thought of another detail. Was *his* Kate all alone tonight? His eyes darted to her daughter's bedroom.

The window was dark. Skye was out, probably sleeping over at her friend, Steph's, house. He made it his business to find out the details. And he'd heard Kate had split from Ken Ashworth.

His smile swelled into a grin.

Excited, he placed a hand into the cloth sack, fingers caressing his lucky rabbit paw. Kate Owen agreed to pose for him. When he agreed to a thing, he did it. Tonight, he'd give her one last chance to do what she said she would. He'd give her mercy. Mummy would be pleased. She always gave him one last chance and made him beg for mercy.

A dog barked, and another responded. A third joined in with a strained howl. Liam adored animals but picked up his pace to a trot. Yowling dogs brought out their owners to see what all the fuss was about.

As he stood before the front door, sticky droplets of sweat formed at his temples despite the coolness of the breeze around his bare legs. He raised his fist to knock but stopped. What if it went wrong?

He thought about Ann Crombie and wanted to throw up.

Again he glanced at Skye's darkened bedroom window. It wouldn't go wrong. He'd thought about it, planned it, knew every detail. Still, he considered the possibility of failure. If it went wrong, he'd find another woman. A woman who wouldn't resist. He was a member of Ambleside Village Artists with plenty of women to choose from.

He knocked with an urgent fist.

The door opened at once.

Wide.

From the radio came the excited voice of the newsreader. "The body of a local artist was found in Borrans Wood near the village of Ambleside on Saturday morning. The police are asking for anyone who saw anything to contact them..."

Kate Owen stood on the threshold bathed in a halo of light, swaying, eyes glazed and shrouded in the perfume of cheap rum and strong marijuana. She glared in Liam's direction but wasn't actually looking at him.

It was as if he was invisible.

People did that to him all the time. He was there but they didn't see him. But he saw the stains on her blouse, some from last week, others from the rum which dribbled down her chin. Why hadn't she washed her top? It distressed him. He wanted her in a clean white blouse so he could sniff the lemony scent. And her face, oh God, it was ghostly with a greasy sheen. She looked exhausted and distressed and in horrific torment. A car wreck rather than the divine image he held in his mind.

She ruffled her hair, eyes red and spoke in a slur. "Forgot something?"

"Kate." Liam started strong but descended into babble. "I... I... we had an—"

It happened in a fraction of a second. A hand gripped his shoulder. Liam squealed as he spun around and saw a tall man in his late forties with jet-black spiked hair, a gold stud in his nose and wearing a pink shirt with broad collars. He knew Ken Ashworth was a teacher and could be perfectly reasonable if he wasn't drunk.

Liam blinked, and he caught a whiff of strong booze. Alcoholic fumes spewed on Ken's sour breath. He'd been at the ale, the liquor and the wine too. Red, judging by the blush streaks on his crooked front teeth. Ken didn't look reasonable, he looked like an unhappy hound dog. Liam blinked again and decided Ken looked more like a snarling Dobermann looking for a fight.

Ken glared, eyes bloodshot, nostrils flared, teeth jutting from his mouth in a Neanderthal snarl. "Beat it weirdo before I squash your bug-eyed face to mush."

But he was too drunk to see Liam. Or remember him. In the morning, Ken would have a throbbing migraine and an upset stomach and shadows of what happened tonight. Liam knew this. He knew details.

The dogs were barking again. A chorus of howls and yaps. Liam twisted and yanked and spun from Ken's grip. With his cloth sack over his shoulder, he ran.

As he reached the garden gate, he heard Ken's drunken voice. "Sweetmeat, can we talk?"

When Liam was on Vicarage Road, he looked back. Kate's arms were around Ken. She was kissing him and dragging him inside.

31

An hour before the unspeakable happened, Fenella wasn't paying attention. Which turned out to be a fortunate mistake.

It was 7 a.m. on Tuesday morning. Superintendent Veronica Jeffery leaned on the lectern, surveying her audience. She seemed pleased at the attendance for her lips twisted into a wolfish grin. "Thank you all for volunteering for this popup day of management training. I know you will find each one of our thirty-five speakers rewarding. The video will be available for your review. Chief Constable Rae may show up at some point today."

Fenella had arrived at the Port St Giles police station hoping for news of a breakthrough in the Ann Crombie case. Monday had brought nothing new. At least the news media hadn't picked up on the full horror of it yet and no reporters were snooping. So, this Tuesday morning she'd planned to review the files on the case. Not that there was much to look at, the docket was thin.

But Mrs Soper, Jeffery's assistant, corralled her and a gaggle of unfortunates into a meeting room with the promise of a free fried breakfast and pastries from the Grainbowl Café. There was only one door, at the front, behind the lectern where Jeffery stood. And the breakfast turned out to be cheese and onion sandwiches curled at the edges and bitter coffee.

Jeffery was still speaking. ". . . focus today is on a stark and glaring gap in our community policing. I was saying to Chief Constable Rae only last week that I have taken a personal interest in his idea that. . . "

The first two rows of hard plastic chairs were empty. Most people clustered at the back, near the toilets and as far away from Jeffery as possible. The boss took great delight in pointing her finger and asking impossible questions. The nearer to the front you sat, the greater the chance of being 'boss bombed'.

Fenella sat on the front row because she wanted to be near the door. When the opportunity struck, she'd be through it and away. Her only problem was the tide of rising boredom which threatened to close her eyes.

Why didn't I have a double shot of coffee?

Jeffery moved in front of the lectern, mouth still working. ". . . critical and, I must stress this to each of you as much as I stressed it to Chief Constable Rae. Absolutely critical we have a plan in. . . "

Fenella yawned and wondered which row Dexter and Jones sat in. They'd come in early too. She had waved at them in the canteen but didn't stop to chat in her hurry to get to her office. Now, as she snatched a sly look behind, she expected to see Dexter prowling the length of the back wall and Jones with his laptop balanced on his knees. She didn't see either of them.

She spun all the way around and scanned the back rows. A split second later she groaned. *How did they escape the net?* She felt a crushing sense of somehow being tricked and sent an acid text message to Dexter.

Jeffery was pacing now, swinging her arms military style as she spoke. "Our station does not issue search warrants willy-nilly. I take personal responsibility for each one. On the rare occasions when they are necessary, I keep a tight rein on. . ."

Fenella closed her eyes. Just for a few seconds to clear her mind. Two minutes later she pitched forward, tried to steady herself but tumbled off her chair. She glanced around, nodding and smiling and hoping no one saw. No one noticed, but she thought she heard a snore rise up from somewhere at the back.

Jeffery continued her speech. ". . . . evident that we accept the situation and work with things as they are. Chief Constable Rae agreed with every word, declaring me in charge of the operation. Our elderly care homes are my top priority. Chief Rae is determined, as am I, to stamp. . ."

It was then Fenella noticed the camerawoman and the sound engineer and a slender lass she'd seen on the telly—Dawn Margot, the documentary reporter. A big shot from the BBC.

Only then did Jeffery's words come into focus. ". . . filming a documentary about my role as a leading woman in the Cumbria Constabulary. Janet and her team will be following me about and recording everything. A fly on the wall documentary which will air on. . ."

Fenella's mobile phone pinged with such force it shuddered in her hand. As she stared at the smirking icon on the screen sent by Dexter, she became aware of the sudden quiet. She glanced up. Jeffery glared, and it seemed the entire room was looking at her.

Oh crap!

Jeffery's voice exploded. "All phones off during the presentations and that includes text messages. No rings. No pings. No buzzes. Have I made myself crystal clear?"

"Sorry about that, ma'am." Fenella raised her phone and made a show of turning it off. Only she didn't. She left it on with the volume down low.

The door opened. A group of dark-suited people came in. Men and women. All grey-haired, some stooped. Fenella counted thirty-five. A groan rose up from the back of the room. *Did Jeffery actually say there were thirty-five speakers?*

They filed in, muttering and happily looking around as they took their seats. A man with an egg-shaped head and no hair sat next to Fenella. His clothes were different from the others. He wore a tweed jacket patched at the elbows, a red shirt open at the collar and brown corded trousers. A musty shroud carried from his garments—a mix of cigars, pine and hard drink. Fenella recognised Professor Lee Coben.

He was known by all as Robot Drone because of his monotonous voice. The last time she heard him speak, Dexter was with her. Something to do with fraudulent billing in elderly care homes. She fell asleep halfway through. Dexter's snores woke her.

"Ah, our speakers are here." Jeffery's shrill voice only deepened the torment. "I, like Chief Rae, will review the video. We have two cameras today. Now, please welcome our special guest Professor Lee Coben. He is the..."

Fenella's mind wandered to the death of Ann Crombie in Borrans Wood. She wondered whether Dexter had dug up anything new and she wondered when she'd get Dr MacKay's report and she wondered if she missed something important when she searched Bede Thatch.

"Isn't that so, Detective Inspector Sallow?"

The question hung in the air for two heartbeats. Only then did Fenella become aware that the room had once again fallen into silence. It reminded her of the quiet hiss of tension in an old black and white film where nervous prisoners lined up and guards pointed at those assigned to rock-breaking duty. She snatched a glance over her shoulder. The audience in the back rows had definitely shrunk back in their seats.

What did Jeffery ask me?

Professor Lee Coben, now standing next to Jeffery, was nodding, his face ablaze with delight.

Fenella tilted her neck and tried to work out the question. *Best to agree if you don't know what they are saying. You can always disagree later.* "Yes, ma'am. One hundred per cent, ma'am."

Jeffery beamed. "Very well, I accept. You are in charge of the Elders Care Home Safe Spaces Plan. Professor Coben will work with you as a civilian advisor. We must keep our elderly community safe and that includes fraudulent accounting. Mrs Soper will send you the required reading. I'll expect you to meet with Professor Coben later today and have your strategic plan to me by Thursday."

"Eh?" Fenella didn't like the sound of that. "Strategic plan?"

Jeffery licked her wolfish lips. "I have a breakfast meeting with Chief Constable Rae on Friday. I will share my...our ideas with him." Jeffery turned to Professor Coben. "Okay with you?"

"Oh yes. Yes, yes, yes. Payment at the standard hourly rate?" Even with enthusiasm, the professor's voice sounded dull. He smiled at Fenella, rubbing his hands. "I welcome the chance to chew the cud with you. Should we aim for three or four hours this evening?"

Fenella jumped to her feet. "Ma'am, I'm at a critical point in a murder investigation."

"Then it is even more impressive for you to raise your hand." Jeffery turned to face the nearest video camera, smiling. "Detective Inspector Sallow is a shining example of the selfless culture I have nurtured in my station." She turned back to the audience. "Give her a hand."

A roar went up from the back of the room, a thunderstorm of clapping hands. Someone cheered from the last row and another person stamped their feet.

Fenella slumped in her chair, mind working. It was then that the door opened a crack and Len Moreland, the duty sergeant, waved a wild hand at Fenella. She had no idea what he wanted and waved for him to come in. A distraction would give her time to think.

But he didn't come in. His eyes darted to Jeffery, and he closed the door with a soft click.

A moment later Fenella's phone buzzed. She sneaked a sly glance at the screen. A message from Len Moreland. She devoured it with growing excitement, shouldered her handbag, stood and walked past the lectern to the door.

She turned, hand twitching on the handle, to face the startled crowd, video cameras and narrow-eyed Jeffery. "Ma'am, I'm getting a head start on the Elders Care Home

Safe Spaces Plan." Fenella's lips quirked. "The manager at Grange Hall Care Home has discovered a body. The constable who called it in said it looks like foul play."

32

Fenella stepped out of her car at Grange Hall Care Home unaware of the horror to come.

It was a grand Victorian mansion in the well-to-do area of Westpond on the outskirts of Port St Giles. Leafy oak trees and mature gardens. Wooden benches and flowerbeds in full bloom. The elderly residents were well-to-do—retired doctors, lawyers and business tycoons.

A pleasant place for your sunset days.

As she entered the ornate front doors, the smell of fried breakfast wafted in from an unseen kitchen. She'd had a cup of coffee and nowt else. All that training with Jeffery put her off food, but the breakfast smells made her feel hungry and she'd heard Grange Hall had a High Tea as posh as anything in a London Hotel. Better, as they made their own cakes and scones and used local fruit for their jams.

If this is a quick call, I'll pop into the dining room, grab a bite to eat and have a natter with the residents. Fenella's lips tugged into a grin. *Call it research for the Elders Care Home Safe Spaces Plan.*

She walked through a broad lobby with fancy furniture and peacock-patterned wallpaper. A walnut panel ran the length of one wall and a huge no-smoking sign rested on the empty reception desk. From the ceiling, a giant chandelier glittered. Not that it was turned on. It wasn't needed because sparkles of morning sunlight splashed through two huge windows and danced on the shined hardwood floor. Fenella wondered if she should take off her shoes, the place was all so polished and clean.

A stooped woman in a peach headscarf hurried through the lobby. At the front doors, she stopped, half turned, popped a stick of gum in her mouth then hurried outside. An official-looking woman in a brown cardigan sprang from out of nowhere. Her pale face, bulging red eyes and frizzy black hair gave her the look of a ghost. "So sorry but no visitors today. There has been an incident and the police are here."

Her breath smelled of cigarettes and fear.

"I'm with the police, pet." Fenella showed her warrant card.

"Thank God, I'm Miss Kim Jennings the general manager." Her trembling hand reached into her cardigan pocket. She snatched out a cigarette and placed it between her lips. "Sweet Jesus, the day has taken a horrible turn. To think I moved from Dublin to face this."

Fenella waited for a heartbeat. "What happened?"

"Look, this is my second day on the job. I have no idea how such a distressing accident occurred on my watch. I'm not God, can't be everywhere at once and it is a long shift, I've got to get some sleep for goodness' sake. Tell them I'm not to blame; you'll put that in your report, won't you?"

The woman's mangled words were unfathomable to Fenella. She was about to ask another question when a loud voice carried through the lobby.

"Come back here you old fool!"

The shout came from behind a swing door with a key-hole lock. A male voice. Unhappy.

Interest rose in Fenella. *Whatever is happening on the other side is none of my concern; I'm here on urgent business.* Then the door burst open and curiosity leapt up inside of her, the nosy gene wanting to know what was going on.

A gaunt old man in red pyjamas fled through the door, a chain of keys in one hand and a walking stick in the other. A male orderly, cricket ball round, shuffled after him.

"Mr Kuck, you are not allowed to have those keys." The orderly, puffing hard, was losing ground. "Come back here."

But Mr Kuck did not stop and go back. He kept moving, and with surprising speed toward the exit.

As he scurried by Fenella, she touched his arm. "Where are you going, pet?"

He stopped. "I'm hungry. They feed us nowt but packet mashed potatoes and gravy behind those locked doors."

"Fancy a custard cream?" Fenella reached into her handbag, unwrapped the handkerchief and gave him one she'd stashed from her meeting with Vicar Kemp. "Was saving them for my supper."

He munched and sucked with toothless gums and chewed and sucked some more. "I want to pick a rose for my Val. See, I pick a rose for her every morning."

"That's nice, luv." Fenella kept a tight grip on his arm. "Why don't I help you?"

He peered at her. "You with the police? I can always tell. It's in the eyes."

"Aye, pet. I'm a detective."

"Well, I saw her, and she was very keen to chat with me." He winked. "She told me her big secret. I liked her."

"Who are you talking about, pet?"

"The new nurse. I told her I used to be a detective inspector in the police. Would you care to join me for High Tea this Friday and I'll tell you how it was in the old days?"

Fenella, still holding his arm, smiled. "Aye, how'd you know what I was thinking? I'd like that. It's a date."

The orderly had caught up now, gasping and coughing and sucking in deep breaths. "Mr Kuck, your Val has been gone these past twenty years." He took Mr Kuck by the arm and led him toward the swing door. "Tell you what, how about we plan a visit to the florists today and we can spend the afternoon at the cemetery?"

The swing door closed. The lock clicked.

Fenella turned to Miss Jennings. "Tell me what has happened?"

Miss Jennings chewed on the cigarette. She opened her mouth and pointed behind Fenella.

"Ma'am." PC Jon Phoebe's screeching voice scattered the momentary silence. He was sweating and wiped his face with his sleeve.

A sickening explosion rumbled in Fenella's stomach. She'd never seen PC Phoebe's eyes so wide or his skin so pale and she had known him for donkey's years. She went out with his wife and a gang of other women when she got the chance. A fun night of meals and bingo topped up with lashings of gossip.

Fenella exhaled a breath through her teeth. "What happened?"

"One of the nurses. . . you'd better come and see." He turned and began walking away. "It's this way, ma'am."

It was noticeable that Miss Jennings did not follow.

33

They left the lobby through a side door, moved along a dim corridor and down a double flight of stairs to a solid oak door—broad with thick metal strips running from left to right. It looked like it was made in the Middle Ages and belonged at the entrance to a crypt.

"Behind here, ma'am." PC Jon Phoebe's voice echoed with a hollow ring and there was a shake in it, like his vocal cords were trembling.

Fenella stared at the door. "You'd best open it."

He shoved. It didn't move.

He turned to Fenella. His pale eyes sent sickening bolts of dread along her spine. He'd seen whatever lay beyond that door and looked the worse for it.

"Give it some shoulder, man." The nerves of it were getting to Fenella. "Let's see what all the fuss is about."

PC Phoebe rushed the door, shoulder first. He crashed against it and staggered back dazzled at the inevitable. It didn't budge. He tried again, then, exhausted, collapsed forward, bending over his knees. "Don't understand it, ma'am. Last time it opened easy and now it won't move."

That's when Fenella saw the latch. With shaking hands, which she blamed on the state of PC Phoebe, she pressed and shoved. The door screeched. It opened to a windowless corridor which smelled of damp and laundry. They scurried along the passageway for several moments and stopped.

"In there, ma'am." PC Phoebe pointed to a narrow white door. "They store the dirty sheets inside ahead of washing. Miss Jennings discovered the body. You spoke with her a moment ago."

"A frightening shock for her, eh?" Fenella glanced at the door. "To go inside that room and find a corpse."

PC Phoebe said nothing.

His silence told her all she needed to know.

She gazed back the way they had come. Dry mouth. Burning eyes. Nagging pain tightening both sides of her neck. She inhaled the damp air and mildew and the scent of something rotting. She listened but heard only the wheeze of her breath. She stepped back a pace, into the shadows, her footfalls silent on the stone floor.

It took a full minute to put on gloves and shoe protectors, and another minute as she surveyed the door. Taking a deep breath, she turned the handle and stepped inside.

34

Fenella imagined it would be bad; what she found was much worse.

It was the unmistakable stench which assaulted her first. The thick choking stink of an open sewer left to fester under the July sun. There was no light switch on the wall. A shaft of dull grey sunlight penetrated the grime of a letter-sized window. It took a full ten seconds for her eyes to adjust. Ten more to take in what she saw.

It was a narrow brick chamber with a high ceiling and crowded with soiled bedsheets, many stained with horrible brown streaks. A vast sea of brown and white sludge oozing with the stink of long evacuated bowels. She counted twenty piles jammed in the tight space but might have missed some.

Next came the terrific heat. Sauna hot. Sweltering. Lifting the odious odours in damp mists of compressed stink. Blasts of boiling air flowed through a giant air vent which echoed with the rumble of tumble dryers. A constant moan and wail and thud as though some hideous beast were trapped inside and fighting to get out.

Fenella stepped deeper into the room and stopped.

Stretched along the brick wall at the back lay the sprawling figure of a woman in a blue nurse's uniform. She was on her left side, back to Fenella. It was immediately clear that something about the body didn't look right.

She snatched out her mobile phone for more light. The woman's dress was hitched up over her bare buttocks and ripped across the top, exposing sagging breasts. She moved the phone from left to right, picking out four white rose petals.

Fenella moved closer, gazing down at the body. Bile leapt to her throat. The head was a good twelve inches from the torso; the blank eyes staring into the phone's beam. She didn't have to step any closer to recognise the wild shock of white hair. There was no doubt about it. The woman in the blue nurse's uniform was Mrs Bella Timbol.

35

By the time Fenella arrived back at the Port St Giles police station, she could barely breathe.

It was after one o'clock as she scrambled her team for an emergency briefing. She stood by the whiteboard. The death of Bella Timbol squatted in her mind. Had she missed something important in her search of Bede Thatch? The question chomped with unrelenting teeth, dragging an icy cold finger of depression along her spine. And with it the hellish fear that Bella Timbol might be alive if she knew the answer.

Dexter paced at the back of the room. Jones sat at the front with his laptop balanced on his knees. PC Beth Finn sat at his side. PC Woods hovered by the tea urn, eyeing the ginger biscuits.

"Ain't got no idea what this is about, guv." Dexter stopped pacing and sensed Fenella was too distraught to talk. He always got things started when she was frantic. "It was like a scene from a horror movie. Swamp hot with them tumble dryers howling like wolves. God Almighty, who beheads a nurse at an old people's home and leaves the corpse half naked in the sweltering heat?"

Disgust echoed in the hollow silence. The tea urn gurgled, spluttering out a high-pitched scream of steam. An internal fault that had yet to be fixed and made it spit out hot vapour.

Fenella took an enormous breath, and let the air out slow. The nightmarish scenes of the past few days were driving her hysterical. She missed something at Bede Thatch; she knew it. This tragedy was her fault.

She turned to the empty whiteboard. She wanted the killer's name and she wanted it bad and she wanted it right there and then. But the whiteboard gave a blank stare, from the wide wall under bright lights; and as the void glowered, malicious fingertips of dread whipped up a storm of heartbroken pain; because another death meant another life gone with the killer still on the run.

Infuriated, Fenella turned to face her team. It was up to them to make sense of the demented madness. "Theories about what Bella Timbol was doing at Grange Hall Care Home. What do we think?"

Silence.

They still seemed astonished at the tragic events. The initial shock of the gruesome scene was now past, but still seeping into their bones. A kind of delayed trauma. Even Dexter crouched forward like a boxer who'd gone one round too many. The demands of the case gnawed nerves raw, shooting bursts of impossible pain at the inhumanity of it all.

Fenella waited.

Jones closed the lid of his laptop. "Her husband is a wealthy businessman and she works as a nurse? Boss, it makes no sense. She doesn't need the money unless it is her way of doing good works. But I don't see it."

"Aye, lad, that's the point." Dexter shook his head. "Ain't no nursing agency in Port St Giles has ever heard of the woman. I've checked. She ain't with any of the national agencies, either. If she was ever registered as a nurse, it must have been a long time ago. And she weren't on the books of Grange Hall Care Home. They had no idea who she was and said she shouldn't have been there."

"So what was she doing in a nurse's uniform?" This was Fenella. "And why was she there in the first place?"

Silence again.

PC Woods snatched a handful of ginger biscuits, waddled to the first row and slumped next to Jones. "Whoa, it's a puzzle, like one of those mystery shows on the telly. Can't see how we stop it from going viral. The news media will crawl over this like ants."

"I want to stay in front of that scuffle." There was an urgency to Fenella's voice. "I want to know everything about the Timbol family and Bella's movements over the last month. We need to build a picture of her relationship with Ann Crombie. The killer or killers went after both of them, why?"

Dexter was at the front of the room, shaking his head, still crouched, boxer style. "It's got to do with that painting we found in Ann Crombie's studio, guv. The naked people running from them foxes."

"Aye, happen it has." Fenella closed her eyes for a moment. "What is the connection?"

"Both Bella Timbol and Ann Crombie were artists, guv." Dexter rocked on his heels. "Members of the Ambleside Village Artists. Bella Timbol was the chairwoman. There are twenty-five members, I've checked."

He stopped, his face turning a ghastly shade.

Fenella was with him and two steps ahead. The unthinkable was hurtling toward them—more deaths. Twenty-three more if the pattern continued. But was it a pattern? Panic chewed her nerves to the raw. The tea urn gurgled, coughing out a hiss of boiling steam.

"No more suffering." Fenella's voice came out in a fierce shriek. She glared at her team. "We speak to every member of the Ambleside Village Artists today. Find out the gossip. Prod and poke until you get an outburst or a secret. Like pigs in a trough. It sounds horrible, but we are trying to avert a disaster. I want every minuscule detail."

The helplessness which battered her and held her in its steely grip began to ebb. The sense of overwhelm receded. Now a visceral urge to catch the killer before they struck again took hold. And they would strike again, she was certain of that.

Jones was on his feet. "You want us to head to Ambleside now, boss?"

For a moment Fenella felt foolish as though asked a trick question. "Well." She considered for a heartbeat and looked at Dexter. "That note."

"Note, guv?"

"On that scrap of paper I found in Ann Crombie's bedroom. A Giles Rare Books store till receipt." Fenella paused, realising she hadn't mentioned it to him. She jerked out her phone and read the screen. "Mail Benny Label. Okay?"

"That's it, guv?" Dexter rubbed the back of his neck.

PC Woods raised a timid hand. "Did you know 'Okay' is the most used word in the world?" He stuffed a ginger biscuit into his mouth and munched. "Every language on the planet knows what it means. Even the French."

The room fell silent.

PC Woods shifted in his seat. "Thought it might help, ma'am."

"Aye, well I'll keep it in mind." Fenella gazed at her phone. "Track down anyone called Benny in Ann Crombie's network. Is there a Benny in the Ambleside Village Artists? Is there a Benny in the village or in Grange Hall Care Home? Not a common name, it should be easy to spot."

The door flew open. It slapped against the back wall. Superintendent Jeffery marched in with Mrs Soper, her assistant, on her heels. Tess Allen, the press communications officer, trailed three paces behind.

Fenella watched the gaggle make their way to where she stood. Jeffery's eyes were two dark dots, her mouth a straight slash. A red bloom streaked Mrs Soper's face as though she were about to burst into tears. Tess Allen stared with frightened eyes.

Superintendent Jeffery faced the room and gave a frosty smile. "Anyone worth knowing in Port St Giles has a relative in Grange Hall Care Home. Criminal activity in elderly care homes is the top priority of Chief Constable Rae. This death will be dynamite if it leaks out before we clear up this mess."

Tess Allen raised a hand. "No sign the press has got a whiff yet, ma'am. We are good for another twenty-four hours."

She sounded euphoric as if she were breaking the news of a massive lottery win to a woman who never gambled. Every word, every syllable, every sound came out dazzling bright, even the gaps when she drew breath. *Toss out a*

nugget of good news early when everything else is bad, eh?
Fenella felt sorry for the lass. The unremitting pressure of
Tess's job would drive her mad.

And then another thought struck. And it struck hard.
*Once news gets to Chief Constable Rae's ears, there will
be instantaneous hell for anyone touching the case.*

Jeffery's neck was on the line.

So was Fenella's.

They were supposed to be a team but when the blame
got dished out, it was the boss who became the pigeon and
everyone else the statue. Doom had spun its spider web
and Fenella could do nothing to avoid the snare.

Jeffery's next few words came out low and slow. Like a
hiss of steam escaping a sewer pipe. And they hung in the
air like a bad stink.

"I have a call with Chief Constable Rae directly after
this meeting. I will inform him of your situation and assure
him that the exact details of this killing will be on his desk
within the hour. I shall also tell him..." She paused, her
lips twitching into a wolfish grin. "... that I have every
confidence in Detective Inspector Sallow. I expect her team
to bring this to a speedy resolution. Of course, I reserve
the right to change things if progress is not as swift as we
expect."

Fenella opened her mouth to argue but decided to let
it pass. A dismal day would only slide to a hellish low with
a blowout argument with the boss. And she wanted the
case because she wanted to nail the killer. But if there was
another death and if it came soon, Jeffery would rip the
case from her grip and toss her to the wolves.

The tea urn bubbled and hissed, spitting out a giant

boiling plume.

Fenella massaged the knot of tension in her neck and made a snap decision. "Permission to step aside from the case, ma'am."

Jeffery's face became a block of ice. Only her eyes moved. With the quickness of a rat. "Step aside?"

"That's right, ma'am."

"Me too, ma'am." This was Dexter.

Jones raised a hand. "I'd like to step—"

"Now just a minute." Jeffery raised both hands. "If this is about my support, you have it in full. This is a team effort. I shall mention that to Chief Constable Rae personally."

There was no question Fenella had taken a risk. But her goal was to clear the deck by steering the conversation in a particular direction. "I'm glad to hear that, ma'am. Will Mrs Soper be there to take minutes?"

Fenella waited for a heartbeat as Mrs Soper gave a quick nod and then she continued. "I'm not worried about the Chief, ma'am. It's the Elders Care Home Safe Spaces Plan that bothers me."

"What about it?"

"You want it delivered by Thursday?"

Jeffery took two steps back, her eyes as frozen as her face. Then the quickness returned. "I'll assign that task to someone else."

"And Professor Lee Coben? I am to meet with him tonight. Four or five hours, at your request, ma'am."

"Not your problem, Sallow." Jeffery nodded at Mrs Soper. "Sort it."

Jeffery sniffed, and with arms swinging at her side,

marched from the room. Mrs Soper and Tess Allen raced behind.

Fenella clapped her hands. "We'd best get a move on before she changes her mind and comes back. Let's go."

And that is exactly what should have happened if it weren't for the door flying open and Len Moreland, the duty sergeant, racing in.

His red face and panting breath provoked in Fenella an instant of immeasurable fear. *Oh God, not another morbid death of an artist from Ambleside.* She jerked her neck from side to side to loosen the sudden bolts of tightening sinew.

But Len Moreland didn't mention murder. What he did say, however, changed the entire case.

36

It was Tuesday lunchtime. Liam Brampton squatted on a stool in his usual spot in the deepest recesses of the pub.

The usual smell of pie and chips.

The usual smell of ale.

The usual handful of locals.

A man in a flat cap with a red face and double chin leaned against the bar in his usual spot, chatting to anyone who'd listen in his boozy Irish brogue. He prided himself on being the first person in the bar and the last one to stagger home. The slot machine rattled and flashed. A woman in a peach polyester top with streaks of blue in her limp hair dropped coins into the slot, bellowing with anger or laughing with delight. She drank lager and lime, running up a tab which she paid at the end of the month from her disability cheque. The telly above the bar was on with the sound on mute. The landlord dragged a rag over the counter, humming a popular tune.

Liam knew details. Knew faces. Nothing had changed in years.

And he wore his usual green floral jumper knitted by Mummy and stretched tight over his wheat cream smock. His Tuesday wear. He was a straightforward man and

Mummy had always given him a second chance when he was naughty. Kate Owen would have a second chance. Not like the other women.

"Today's special is steak and kidney pie with chips and peas, honey." The woman leaned forward. "Fancy some? I'm Millie, the new barmaid."

Her tiger-striped blouse was perfect. Not a stain in sight, with the top three buttons undone, each one a brass dome with a twirl on top. Her face was made up, fashion-model style—pouting lips, long eyelashes with a shaggy mane of brunette hair swept back into a bun. Her dangling gold earrings, two giant hoops in each ear, clinked.

Liam's mouth dropped.

Full open.

Horrified.

This twig-thin woman was an imposter. He watched for changes. Prided himself in his skill. His stealth. He noticed details others missed, but Millie serving grub in the pub came as a bloody big shock. The way she looked at him made him tremble inside. With rage. Where was *his* Kate? Today was her final chance.

Liam's hand darted to his jacket pocket, fingers grasping the brass tin with the swan on the lid. He needed a special smoke to calm his nerves, and he needed it right now.

Roll.

Light.

Inhale.

But Mummy's voice rang in his ears warning him against it. She was right, the pub landlord would throw him out. He cursed under his breath, wishing for his lucky rabbit paw but he'd left it at home. He'd never do that again. He must carry it with him at all times. Now he tried to ignore the odd sensation that doom lay ahead.

The slot machine blasted a merry tune. The woman with streaks of blue in her limp hair howled with frustration and blew her nose on her sleeve. The flat-capped man with the red face and double chin shook his head, from left to right. Slow motion. A dire warning of trouble to come.

The barmaid continued to lean over Liam's table.

Stupefied, Liam looked to one side to avoid Millie's vast chest. He opened his mouth, words coming out in a dry streak. "Aye, I'll have the special with a pint of milk stout."

Millie leaned even further forward. Effervescent. French scent. Blue vein pulsing in her neck. "Will that be all, honey?"

"Where's Kate?"

"Who?"

"Kate Owen, the barmaid."

Millie straightened, her face turning severe. "Want anything else with your order?"

Liam wanted to be a good boy as Mummy had requested but Millie's tone licked up an internal firestorm of fury. "I asked you a question. Where is Kate?"

"What do you want with that tart?" Millie placed her hands on her hips.

"Where is she?"

Liam spoke with a fierceness he'd been warned never to use again. Mummy told him not to talk to women like that. It frightened them.

Millie took a step back. "You a regular?"

"Aye."

"Didn't see you yesterday."

"I took the day off." Liam's voice shook. He glanced at the man in the flat cap with the red face and double chin. The man stared back, watching. Liam lowered his voice. "Can't drink my life away in a bar, like some."

"Name?"

The question inflicted a puncture in Liam's pride. How many years had he drunk here? Decades, but he could count on one hand the number of times he'd engaged in conversation with the other locals. Did anyone know his name?

Bewildered, he blinked. "Liam Brampton."

"Brampton?" Millie's hand flew to her blouse, doing up the top three buttons. "Oh my God, I've heard of you."

And her eyes did that funny thing Liam had seen before. They went wide then turned grave then looked as if they didn't see him at all.

Millie stepped back two paces, whirled around and hurried behind the bar and through the swing doors to the kitchen. The smirking landlord followed her.

Panic-stricken, Liam blinked four times to make sure this wasn't some hideous dream. He had them. Dozens of times. On bad nights the dream would come to him twice. The second time in slow motion. A shadow floated toward his bed. A woman, her face a blank. No eyes. No nose. No mouth. Just a strange darkness covering her face. She'd admonish him for his wickedness. Her words echoed from where her head should have been. Then in his bewilderment, he'd recognise the voice. Mummy. Headless and naked with her arms open and racing toward him.

Vivid and visceral and traumatic.

He'd wake in terror unable to fathom what it meant. But he wasn't dreaming now. This lunchtime Millie served in place of Kate Owen. At least he now knew Millie's face, but where was *his* Kate?

The slot machine thrilled another merry jingle. Grunting and giggles came from behind the swing doors to the kitchen. Liam's head drooped. He'd been tossed into a sterile desert with the sun beating down and miles of sand dunes to overcome before the next neglected waterhole. And there was only one person to blame. Kate Owen.

The kitchen swing door flew open and the landlord hustled over, adjusting his belt. He slapped Liam on the back. A hearty thick-handed thud. "Getting along with Millie? An undeniable beauty, ain't she? Bet you wouldn't mind being in Ken Ashworth's pyjamas of a night, eh?"

Normally Liam would have smiled. Normally he'd have nodded. But this wasn't normal. "Is Kate sick?"

"Fired." The landlord slapped him on the back again and hustled back to the bar. "And banned from the pub."

A sad jingle sounded from the slot machine. The woman with streaks of blue in her limp hair laughed. The man in the flat cap with the red face and double chin drained his pint and stared morosely at the empty glass. Liam slumped to one side, a shipwreck battered by atrocious weather and scalding seas. *Kate Owen fired.*

"You alright, there Liam?"

The man with the flat cap, red face and double chin stood at his side. He pronounced Liam's name with a tipsy Irish twang. Liam didn't rouse himself at first. The man continued to talk and only as meaning sunk in did Liam jerk upright, stunned at what the man said.

"You're a right scallywag, ain't you?" Double Chin watched Liam through narrowed eyes. "My niece saw you at Grange Hall Care Home. I said to her, Liam Brampton is a dark horse. He has a rich aunt, to be sure. Why else would he be there? You've been holding out on us for all these years. How much is Aunty worth?"

The slot machine pounded out a merry tune.

Double Chin was still talking. "You pulled a fast one. Everyone thought you were worth peanuts like the rest of your starving artist friends. A rich aunt, eh? Well I never."

Liam didn't have a plan for this. What came next just happened. He roused himself, pulled his woollen jumper over his protruding gut and answered with a brilliant lie. "You are the fifth person to say that to me today and the fifth person to get it wrong. I haven't got a twin, but someone is wandering around who looks like me." Thrilled with his brilliance he went on. "As for a rich aunt at Grange Hall. Nope. Don't even have a poor one. What is your niece's name?"

"Gloria, a fine lass."

"Lives in the village, does she?"

"Port St Giles."

Liam licked his lips. "Gloria is a nice name. I know a Gloria from Port St Giles. What is her surname?"

"That's a lot of questions."

Liam's mistake was raising his voice. "I want her surname and her address and when I can find her at home alone."

"What's the argument about?" The woman with the streaks of blue in her limp hair pulled up a stool, squatting next to Liam. She jabbed a finger at Double Chin. "Don't be picking on Liam, he doesn't mean no harm."

"He is lying and I don't like lies." Double Chin jabbed a fat finger in Liam's face. "Watch his nose, see how it grows."

"You ought to pat him on the back." The woman's breath reeked with booze and she tugged at a lock of her limp hair. "You're the king of lying toads, ain't that right Liam?"

Liam said nothing.

"Who you calling a liar?" Double Chin's voice rose to a boozy shout.

Limp Hair laughed. Rowdy. "To think you came all the way from Ireland to sit here and tell a pack of lies. Have you no shame?"

Double Chin swore. "I tell you; he's been holding out on us. The lad's full of blarney. He ain't no pauper."

"What are you on about?" Limp Hair looked from Double Chin to Liam and back to Double Chin. "Look at him. He don't speak enough to lie and is always dressed in those ragged garments. He's a helpless mental cripple and as penniless as the rest of us."

"He has a millionaire aunty living in Grange Hall Care Home. My own niece saw him visiting."

Limp Hair's eyes glittered. "Buy me a drink, Liam?"

She ran her fingers through her greasy locks, smoothed her peach top and yanked it down. Wrinkles as deep as baked earth scrawled across her loose chest. They reminded Liam of ripples. Ripples on Lake Windermere, and the gasping last breath of the drowning.

"Get away from him." Double Chin waved his hands and shoved her away. "He's my friend and you ain't cheating him out of coins to waste in that slot machine. He's buying me a pint, aren't you Liam?"

Limp Hair swung a fist.

A wild flying claw.

Moving fast.

Alley cat fast.

Scratch out your eyes fast.

Double Chin swayed to his left.

Limp Hair's clenched claw whistled past his ear.

A moment of silence punctuated by the merry jingle of the slot machine.

Limp Hair giggled.

Double Chin giggled.

They turned to Liam, watchful.

He shrank back on the stool. He should have left the pub the moment he saw Kate Owen wasn't here. While there was still time. Now it was too late. Now they'd natter about seeing him in Grange Hall. They'd prod until they broke through his impenetrable defence. They'd soon discover other things. And now it was too late to turn back.

Millie arrived with pie and ale on a tray. "What's the fuss about?"

"It's my Liam." Limp Hair was back squatting on the stool and placed an arm around Liam's shoulder. "His aunty is very sick in the old people's home in Port St Giles. Not long left to live. And he is buying me pie and chips and ale, ain't you Liam?"

Millie turned to Liam. "Which care home?"

"Grange Hall." This was Double Chin. "The old folks care home in Westpond, Port St Giles. The rich toff's place."

Millie leaned forward and placed the tray on the table. "If there is anything else you need, Liam." The top three buttons were undone; the middle button missing. She flashed a sexy smile. "Anything at all, you know where I am."

She slowly straightened. With swaying hips, she returned to the bar, disappearing into the kitchen.

Liam looked at the pie and ale but did not eat or drink. His hunger fled, pursued by a new mission.

I must see Kate Owen today. I must offer her one more chance. I must offer her mercy. Mummy's mercy. The mercy I had to beg for.

He closed his eyes and began to think how it would be.

No, he mustn't think about that.

Mustn't think about what he intended to do.

Mustn't let God know about his plans because the Lord would snatch them away.

Limp Hair wrapped both arms around him and kissed his cheek. "It is you and me now, babe. When can we go to see Aunty?"

Double Chin's face darkened for a heartbeat then he sighed and tilted his head back. "Next round is on our Liam. May he live to be one hundred years and his wallet always overflow with Aunty's cash."

Limp Hair and Double Chin laughed. It was a big joke. But what Liam Brampton planned to do next was deadly serious.

37

What Len Moreland, the duty sergeant, told Fenella in the briefing room sent her scuttling to the Port St Giles Hospital.

Now she paced the low-ceilinged room, from one white tiled wall to the other. Five paces. No windows. Closed door. The cold air heavy with the scent of antiseptic. A chrome table stood in the centre of the room; its legs bolted to the floor. Three matching chrome chairs. Three plastic bottles of water, frosted with cloud. Nothing else. Except her sure knowledge of the horror to come.

Dexter leaned against the wall, eyeing the door. "Mind if I grab one of those bottles, it's sweltering in here?"

It was cold enough to chill raw meat. But heat rose in Fenella too. Anguish curdled in her throat. Helen Grimes, Ann Crombie's niece from America was due in the room at any moment.

"A day early, eh, guv?"

"Aye." Fenella would have preferred another day. More time to fit things together. More time to offer answers. "It was good of Mrs Grimes to travel here at short notice."

Dexter snatched up a bottle, cracked the lid off and drained half in two gulps. "Feel sorry for the heartbroken lass, hope she don't poke for too many details. A quick identification and we whip her out, eh, guv?"

Fenella wondered if it would be that quick. "We'll go easy on the questions today, dig deeper tomorrow, once she has had a chance to rest."

"I'll stay behind her, guv. Catch her if she faints."

Fenella grabbed a bottle, took a sip and swallowed. Then another. Footsteps clattered from the hallway. Full and heavy and in a great hurry. The door squealed, and they turned to see Dr MacKay.

There was a terrible silence in which the air seemed to shiver.

"Got word the niece is here, Fenella." Dr MacKay's normal boisterous demeanour was gone. Even his voice trembled. "My ladies have done their best, given the limited notice. Was Mrs Grimes a devoted niece?"

"She flew here from America." The acid whirling in Fenella's stomach climbed up her throat. *To come from the States to this. Oh God.* She exhaled. "I'd say they must be close."

Dr MacKay glanced from Fenella to Dexter, a helpless expression creased on his face. "Beastly business. The body was kicked about a bit. The monster had mule legs. This is a part of the job I wished they kept me far from— relatives of the deceased. But I've done as you requested, Fenella. I've overseen this one myself."

"How good a job, Doc?" This was Dexter. "I mean, with the battered head and the body and all that. You've made her look... nice, right?"

"I don't have a magic wand."

Dexter snorted. "If she were my aunt, Doc, I'd make

her look like a million dollars. Better than them stars on the telly. You made her look that nice, right, Doc?"

"My job is to find out the cause of death and I'll do a damn good job of it. And that requires the use of the knife. We've done our best."

The two men glared at each other. A confrontation in the midst of crisis. And each man charged with the same heart-wrenching emotion of wanting to put right something that was forever broken.

From the corner of her eye, Fenella saw Jones outside the door. In the shadows. His entire body looked stiff and his hands flapped in a small gesture. He moved to the entrance and his eyes rolled to one side; a signal of some sort.

He stepped into the room.

Behind him came a short woman—late fifties, ballerina thin in a pink floral sundress with black boots which gave her an inch or two, still less than five feet tall. Her frizzy brown hair was thick and shining. She took in the room with wide-apart hazel eyes. Her oval face had the look of the devout and the familiar look of an old friend.

It was the stillness that Fenella would remember most. Mrs Helen Grimes did not scream or shout or fall about in a crazy fit of grief. She did not cry or sniff or touch her eyes. But the room swelled with quiet sadness.

Dr MacKay broke the spell. He bowed. "Your aunt will be ready for you in a few moments." He turned to Fenella. "We are having a little problem with the lights in the viewing room, I hope they are not too dim."

He bowed again and withdrew.

Fenella's heart pounded. Furious beats. She introduced

herself and Dexter. Helen Grimes replied with a soft New England accent which reminded Fenella of Boston. They spoke of Long Island and New York City and Boston where Helen grew up. Within a short while Helen relaxed, the well of sadness retreating. Fenella asked her about her flight and her hotel and told her the best places to have breakfast in Port St Giles. They chatted about the town of Greenport, nestled on the coast of Long Island, and the cost of housing and of local wines and baking cookies and traded recipes for blackberry pie. Fenella listened and nodded and encouraged her to share.

"When I was a kid, we lived in Boston. In a triple-decker—a three-floor apartment with a balcony." Helen's voice glowed with the merriness of a meadow in summer. "Spent many hot days in July on The Cape—sea and sand and ice cream with jimmies. That's sprinkles or hundreds and thousands to you. Oh, and Aunt Ann made the best fluffernutter sandwich on the planet. Good times."

On Fenella's many visits to New England, she had tasted maple syrup with pancakes, clam chowder, lobster rolls and even Boston baked beans, but she'd never heard of fluffernutter. "A type of cheese sandwich, is it?"

Helen closed her eyes. "Two slices of white bread spread with equal parts peanut butter and marshmallow fluff. Only on the first day of the school holidays, though. That stuff will kill you." Her eyes opened, and she flashed a sad smile. "It's the little things I remember, like the time when I came home from school crying, and Aunt Ann wanted to know why. I told her it was because I failed a history test but she knew me too well to fall for that. She made me a bagel with cream cheese, told me I was beautiful inside and out, and waited for the truth."

The muted clip-clop of footsteps carried from the hallway. It was not a loud noise, a soft scuttle as if the person on the other side was walking on their tiptoes. It was enough for Helen to pause as they all looked at the door. Five seconds passed, then twenty. No one knocked and their gaze fell back on Helen Grimes.

She brushed a strand of hair from her eyes. "The problem wasn't with the history test. It was with my teacher, Mrs Jones. She was great and all the kids loved her, including me. But I was struggling in everything, even reading, and worried Mrs Jones wouldn't like me because I couldn't keep up. What teacher wants a child that can't learn in their class? Aunt Ann told me Mrs Jones would love me anyway because I did my best. I tried." She wiped her eyes with a tissue. "It's the small moments in family life from which we take the greatest joy. And now Aunt Ann is gone. I should have tried harder."

Fenella wished she could turn back the clock to give Helen more time with her aunt, but there was nothing she could do about the past. Her mind turned to the future and the grim task which lay ahead for Helen. A task she wished she could do herself to save the woman from more grief.

Jones sniffed and left the room. Dexter cleared his throat. Fenella waited.

Helen talked about her life as a nun; her marriage to the man of her dreams; his death and drawing on her inner resources to find self-resilience. She talked of her aunt and their life together and about how her aunt loved England and had settled in Cumbria after years in London to dabble in landscape paintings.

"The love affair of her life." Helen smiled, sad. "I was not able to have children, neither was Aunt Ann. I'm her only living relative. As a child, she'd take me to see shows on Broadway. Aunt Ann and I were the Dynamic Duo. Now we're not."

Dexter turned away. Fenella said nothing. The antiseptic smell intensified. The coldness in the room deepened.

Helen Grimes blinked. "I wish I'd been better about keeping in touch. I haven't visited her in ten years. Six since we last spoke. Life takes so much time and it passes so fast, isn't that so, Inspector Sallow?"

"Fenella, please."

Helen turned away, her face out of sight. They waited. They would have waited all day for Helen Grimes to ready herself. For her to say the words they knew she would say.

Helen faced them, the sad smile back on her face. "I'm ready to see Aunt Ann. But, before we go, Vicar Kemp said she died in a terrible tragedy. He didn't give any details. What happened?"

Fenella thought about how to respond and decided to be direct. "Helen, I'm so sorry but we are talking about a murder investigation."

"No, please sweet Lord, no. Please not this." Helen staggered to the table, resting an arm on the back of the chair. "Lord, please not this."

Fenella was at her side, Dexter a pace behind. Helen seemed to have shrunk so small. Her innocent face creased with the confusion of a child. And when at last she spoke, her words were as silent as steam.

"Aunt Ann was a sweet, gentle woman. She loved people and nature and life. What kind of cold-hearted monster did this?"

"Please sit down." Fenella touched her arm. "Have a sip of water."

"I don't want a drink. How can I sit? I want to know what evil devil did this?"

"I don't know." Fenella tried her best to sound confident; despite the devastation in her heart; despite the desperate lack of clues. "All my team are working on it; the entire Port St Giles police force want this one solved."

The room went silent. Screams of unanswered questions rattled with merciless force around Fenella's mind.

Helen's eyebrows gathered, and she spoke as if to herself. "You said murder?"

"Borrans Wood, late Friday night or early Saturday morning." Fenella massaged her neck. "A couple walking the trail found your aunt. They called for help. I happened to be nearby and came to assist."

"You tried to save her?" Helen faced her full-on, eyes glittering in admiration. "Thank Jesus, you tried. Thank God for you."

Fenella couldn't stand it. Those trusting eyes looking at her like some saviour. *I'm an imposter.* "Helen, please. . . I did nothing to save her. When I arrived your aunt was already dead."

Helen choked back a sob. "Was it quick?"

"Yes."

"Was Aunt Ann. . . touched?"

"We are waiting for the pathologist's report."

"But you found Aunt Ann. Please, I beg, tell me what you think."

Fenella studied Helen for a moment. She seemed so fragile and doll-like. There'd been enough suffering already. An eternity of it. And to be direct would cause more pain. *Not today. No more pain today.* She said nothing.

Helen spoke again, her voice harsh. "Did the monster violate my aunt?"

Dexter coughed. "They are ready for us, guv. This way Mrs Grimes."

38

They waited for the curtain to twitch.

No furniture.

No place to sit.

No piped organ music.

There was nothing in the dim viewing room but the glass wall and the brown curtain which covered it. Nothing but the heavy smell of antiseptic masking the vile scent of death.

After two minutes, Fenella pulled out her mobile phone to check for messages from Dr MacKay. There were none. She looked at the rail from which the curtain hung, wondering if it was in working order. Once, it hadn't worked—a viewing of a child. A wizened man in gumboots and a white coat stained with blood came into the viewing room. He grunted as he heaved the curtains with his strong arms. *Never again.* She dropped her phone back into her handbag and tried to think about something else.

A low-pitched whine grew in the nothingness. An electric click and whirr.

"Are you ready, Helen?" Fenella placed an arm around her shoulder.

Helen stared straight ahead, her head bobbing in acknowledgement. Dexter, quiet as a cat, moved behind her.

"We need you to identify your aunt, Ann Crombie." Fenella paused a heartbeat to let the words sink in. "Please speak clearly so we can confirm your response."

The curtain twitched. It shimmered and began to move.

Animal-like sounds rose from Helen's throat—anguish at what had happened; terror at what was to come. Helen bowed her head and leaned into Fenella. Dexter stepped closer.

The curtain continued to twitch and shudder and crawl. A chink of grey light was now visible. A growing crack of bleakness. Helen's breathing was audible.

In and out.

Rapid breaths.

A mutter of words from Helen. "Our Father, who art in heaven. . ." Fenella knew the rest. Old style and new. And so did Dexter.

Waiting now.

For the curtain to complete its slow creep.

For the end of the Lord's Prayer.

For Helen to look up, step forward, turn and nod, for Fenella to wrap her arms tight around the lass, for Dexter to move closer to catch Helen in a faint; and, later, for Fenella to ask question upon question until she found a chink, some new clue, as she wept inside at Helen's brave sacrifice, and mad, mad as hell at the endless wreck of misery that no justice in this realm could put right.

They were open now.

The curtains.

And the final "Amen," said.

Now they waited.

Breathless.
Helen moved forward.
A small step.
Tentative.
And another.

Then, closer to the glass wall, hands pressed against the panel, forehead touching, peering at the horror inside. White-tiled walls. Brown floor. A chrome wall of steel drawers. Row upon row. All chilled. With cold bodies inside. And in the centre on a trolley lay the corpse. A little old woman covered in a rubber blanket showing only her head.

Fenella wasn't prepared for the full-throated scream.

Neither was Dexter.

For a moment they stood there. The blood thrumming in their ears as Helen's voice echoed off the walls. Fenella dashed to the glass panel, her hand on Helen's shoulder, spinning her around. Dexter was there too, peering through the glass at the little old lady inside.

"What did you say?" Everything Fenella thought had started to fall apart. "What did you say?"

"Sweet Jesus, poor creature." Helen shook, her words erupting in bursts. "That woman is not my Aunt Ann. She is not Ann Crombie."

39

Before Kate Owen discovered the horrid truth, she said a silent prayer of thanks and wrapped her arms around Ken Ashworth. She snuggled against his bare back. The thick curtains of her bedroom blocked out daylight. Murk filled the room with the fine grains of an old sepia photo. A faint lemon scent of detergent hung in the air.

Ken turned and kissed her on the lips. "What time is it?"

"Almost two."

"Crap." He sat up, head turned to the bedside clock and scrambled from the covers.

"Don't go." Kate was warm and glowing and wanted more. She flashed *her smile.* "Come back to bed."

But he didn't come back to bed. He snatched up his underpants from the floor, then perched on the edge of the bed to put them on. Next, he slipped into his jeans. "I've got to go, Sweetmeat. My God, is that the time?"

"You weren't in such a rush to leave two hours ago." She sat up, letting the washed-out cover fall from her chest. "Come back to bed."

He put on his orange shirt printed with leaping foxes and adjusted the broad collars, buttons undone, exposing his chest. "They'll be a huge fight if I'm late."

Kate yawned. "Thought you had the week off."

"I'm meeting Millie after work. Her shift in the pub ends at three. Dinner tonight in Carlisle to celebrate our. . . " His voice fell away, and he began doing up his shirt buttons.

Kate flicked a strand of hair from her eyes, then tugged at the wart on her chin. "Oh, pardon me."

"Don't, Kate."

"You never take me out for dinner."

"We had lunch together, didn't we?"

Kate gazed around the bedroom, the furniture worn and faded by time. An empty fish and chip wrapper lay on the dresser. He'd brought lunch with a four-pack of ale. They scoffed the food, guzzled the booze, and then scrambled between the covers. How many cans did she drink? Two, no three. Ken only downed the one.

"Why do you keep me hidden away?" Kate's left hand covered her chin. "Aren't I beautiful?"

"Don't be daft." Ken was looking at himself in the mirror, running a hand through his spiked hair. He blew a kiss. "There is no other in the world like you."

"Do you mean that?"

"Oh yes."

Kate watched him, thinking, mind still in a dreamlike state. "We could get married, Ken." She kept her voice low, letting her words spread out like an ink blot. On marrying the teacher she'd get plastic surgery to remove the wart, lift her cheeks and widen her eyes. She and Skye would look like sisters. Again she flashed *her smile.* "You are the one person who gets me. I'll be a better wife than I am a mother. I'll always stand by my man."

Ken turned to face her. "How much beer did you drink?"

"Not much."

"Come off it, you are drunk again."

"I'm not."

He turned back to the mirror and blew another kiss. "Do you love me, Chicken Drumsticks?"

"Yes."

"What about Bart?"

Bart Owen, her first husband, had broken her heart and ruined her life. "You know how I feel about that man."

"Then tell me."

"I hate him."

"Louder."

"I hate him. He's poison."

Ken smiled. Big and broad with the corners of his lips stretched up. "Do you mean it, Sweetmeat, about you and me getting wed?"

"I do."

"That you'd like to be my wife?"

"Yes."

"Me and you getting old as a couple?"

"Please."

"Then say it."

"I want to be your wife."

"Crawl out of bed on all fours and come here."

She sidled out of bed, hands and knees, moving across the worn carpet, crab-like and naked. Dust particles hung in the air, tiny specs of nothingness, silent and still. The stale smell of fish and chips and ale curdled in her nostrils. He wanted her to beg. She'd done it before.

At his feet, she rolled over. "I love you, Ken."

He flashed his impish grin and blew a kiss at himself in the mirror, then staggered back laughing. "That's what I like about you, Kate. You are such a good sport. No time to play, though. I don't want to be late."

An emptiness crept from the pit of Kate's stomach hollowing out her throat. She swallowed down the bile of disappointment and rocked back on her heels. She would not cry.

Ken looked down, a frown creasing his forehead. "Hey Kate, what's wrong?"

"Nothing."

"Come on, Sweetmeat, I can tell."

"I'm fine."

"We were having a lark, and you suddenly changed. What's going on?"

"It is nothing." She flashed *her smile.* "I've been thinking."

"About what?"

"My sketchbook."

"Jesus, Kate, we've talked about that. We agreed to close that door for good."

"It's on the kitchen table, I might pick up the pencil again, take some lessons. Try to improve."

"Don't be daft, you're crap at drawing. I'll drop off a copy of *A Handbook of the Renaissance: The Age of the Great Masters* by Walter Pater. I use it with the school kids. It will teach you how to appreciate great art. Once you've read it, you will never attempt to draw again."

"I don't want to read about art, I want to create it."

"You are no good at it, Kate. Crap is too kind a word."

"But I'm a member of the Ambleside Village Artists, don't you think I've got some potential?"

Ken twiddled with the gold stud in his nose and snorted. "They'd take a baboon if it paid the dues. Look, I'm not trying to put you down but you'll never create anything worth hanging in a museum, so why bother? Why don't you take a cooking class, up your cottage pie game?"

Kate crawled back to the bed and wrapped the bedsheet around her. If she was his wife, she'd hire a cook and take art classes galore. "You still going to marry her?"

"Leave it, won't you?" Foam bubbled from the corner of his mouth and dribbled down his chin. "Just leave it."

"She doesn't love you, Ken."

He looked away and fiddled with his buttons.

Kate sighed. He'd visited her twice since announcing the wedding. Each time seeking the comfort of her body. Sunday night, when they were both drunk and today. He didn't love Millie, just lusted after her deformed figure.

Kate closed her eyes. "The hateful cow is after your cash. Don't you see? Millie is a gold digger. She will drain your wallet quicker than a blood-sucking vampire. She doesn't love you. The witch would never stand by her man."

The silence from Ken was so deep she wanted to scream. A car backfired in the street. From a treetop in the garden, a rook cawed.

Ken shrugged; voice robotic. "Please don't let your wrath at the hand of fate blind you to the truth, Sweet-meat."

"What is that supposed to mean?"

"I'm committed to you."

"But you are marrying her."

"My God, don't you understand?" He turned to the mirror on the dresser, wiped the dribble from his chin and pattered down his collars. "I want a child. I have to have one, and Millie's womb is fertile."

"Not withered and dried up like mine?"

"That's not what I mean." He smoothed a hand over his shirt and flicked at his spiked black hair. "One must work with time and not against it. Your season for childbearing is over. Biologically you are of no more use to Mother Nature."

"You make me feel cheap."

"I'm dealing with fact; you are too old a hen to have my child. Forty-five your next birthday."

"You will be fifty."

"Yeah, and my sperm is still dancing."

"I'm fertile."

"We can't take that risk, Sweetmeat. What if the child is born—"

Kate waved a hand, swatting his words away. "What about Skye? You are like a father to her."

"Yeah, we are real close." He flashed a sly grin. "She'll fly the nest soon and won't look back."

Kate tugged the sheet tighter. Her childbearing years were all but over which thrilled her in so many ways. But she was out of work, her only skill pulling pints with a bleak future serving in a café or pub awaiting. On Ken's pay, she'd stay at home. They'd hire a cleaner and a cook and travel everywhere, teachers had a lot of time off. And he didn't love Millie, just wanted to rent her womb. Her mind spun in desperation, brain cells thrashing for an answer.

And then it came.

The ideal solution.

Kate flashed *her smile*. "We can adopt."

Ken blinked and touched his collar and blinked again. A fleck of foam formed on the edge of his lip. "Don't you think I've already thought of that?" He sneered in the same way he did when he talked about her art. "Look, how many men take up teaching as a profession?"

Kate said nothing.

"How many?" Ken sounded hostile. Disturbed. A thin wisp of froth sprayed from the corner of his lips. "Tell me, Kate?"

She didn't like it when he got like this. She feared he'd turn violent. Again, she flashed *her smile*. It soothed him, made him feel important, in charge. "I don't know."

"I hauled myself up from an apprentice locksmith to become a full-time teacher. Seven long years. A prison sentence. And I did it, not for me, but for the children. Very few men teach art. Why? Because we lay our heart and soul on the line every day for pennies."

His pay was much better than a barmaid's peanuts but Kate said nothing. Ken was on his high horse now. He'd totally lose it if she interrupted.

Ken snorted, puffing out his chest. "Art teachers serve in hostile seas. We do it because we are true students of aesthetics. But what parent wants their child to be an artist when they could be a doctor or lawyer? The world has forgotten that we need art as much as we need air. It is essential to our true being." The words were oozing out of him now. All slick and shined. "I don't want a child for me, but for our community. You see, serving is in the genes. It would be a disservice to the next generation for me not to pass on my bloodline. If Millie has twins, heck, that's two more art teachers for the future, and she is young enough to have half a dozen more. And I've always wanted a—"

"Is she pregnant?"

That stopped him. He blinked. "How'd you know?"

"When is the baby due?"

"January. Twins."

And it struck Kate then—the times when she worked in the pub and Skye was studying at her friend's house. "Did you bring Millie here?"

"Millie wanted to... look around."

"In my bedroom?"

"That's not fair."

"Fair?" Kate laughed. "You bring that bimbo to my house, my bedroom and sleep with her in my bed and I'm not being fair?"

Ken pressed his fingernails into the palms of his hands. "Everything is such a mess, Sweetmeat. Life is throwing problem after problem at me."

"Well, guess what? I've got my own problems. No job, rent to pay, electric and gas bills." Even though she was light-headed from shock, she wasn't going to cry. "I just wanted better for my life. Why are you doing this to me?"

Ken wiped his lips with the back of his hand and his voice became very small. "I've been such a fool. Can you forgive me?" He stepped away from the mirror. "I can't believe how much I've missed you. Last Sunday, you and me together, it was precious. Today, too. I needed it... needed you."

"Oh, so now I'm your sex lifesaver?"

He flashed an impish grin. The grin she found irresistible. "You are my raft to paradise, Sweetmeat." He was at the bed now, pulling the bedsheet off her, holding her naked body in his arms and whispering in her ear. "We'll be fine, Chicken Drumsticks. What we have is genuine. Marrying Millie won't break that. Nothing will change."

"I don't understand."

"After the honeymoon, you and me, Sweetmeat, we'll continue to meet. Twice a week. More if I need it." He ran a hand through his hair, spiking it up, punk style. "I'll help pay your bills. Our secret."

She shoved him away, snatched up the bedsheet and wrapped it tight around her body. "What do you think I am?"

Ken ambled back to the dresser. She watched his tall sepia shadow and the way he adjusted his collars to perfection while looking into the mirror.

And his grin.

Ken had a big grin running from ear to ear.

"Think about it, Sweetmeat." He turned, and she saw the full flash of his smile. "Me and you together with all your bills paid."

"Get out."

He tucked his shirt in his skinny blue jeans and danced to the bedroom door. "You don't have a job and your pay as a barmaid is peanuts. You need some extra cash and I can help." His lips twisted into an impish grin then extended into a smirk. "The bones have been cast, Sweetmeat. I'll be back Thursday lunchtime. Make a cottage pie and this time wear something sexy."

40

It was early afternoon and nothing was going right.

Fenella was in her office with her core team. Dexter leaned against a radiator; Jones slouched in a chair with his laptop resting on his knees. PC Beth Finn sat next to him and PC Woods perched on the window ledge. Condensation dribbled down the clouded window even though it was open two notches. A thin breeze slipped in, warm and humid, adding to the damp air.

The case had turned complex. It reminded Fenella of wildfire. Wild flames, and the ashes left behind. This morning they had a body with a name and a niece ready to identify the corpse. Now they had a body and a missing person and a wild-eyed niece asking what had happened to her aunt. They were stumbling in the dark, going backwards. A single question hovered—what to do now the body in the morgue wasn't Ann Crombie?

Fenella paced behind her desk, trying to make sense of the extraordinary turn of events. "So, the woman in the morgue. Thoughts?"

"Ain't got a clue, guv." Dexter shook his head. "It has me dumbfounded. The labs are working on the dental and blood work of the woman. Might get a match. Might not.

We've got nowt."

Fenella tucked a stray strand of hair behind her ear. "Once Helen Grimes sends us some photos of her aunt, we'll have something to go with."

Jones raised a hand. "Everyone in Ambleside knew the woman as Ann Crombie, boss. Even the vicar. How'd she live in the village for that long without being detected? Everyone knows everyone in a village. Everyone knows everyone's secrets." He paused, frowning. "Unless the entire village is in on it, like a conspiracy. But that is too far-fetched, isn't it?"

Fenella sensed his disappointment. He'd studied in London where your neighbours were unknown. In the country, people were supposed to be more neighbourly. "One possibility is the real Ann Crombie never moved in."

"From day one, ma'am?" This was PC Beth Finn.

"Aye." Fenella didn't like where her thoughts were leading. Soon she'd be knee-deep in a thicket of poison ivy. She went on. "The woman in the morgue took on Ann Crombie's identity from the start."

"That's sinister." PC Woods shifted on the window ledge, but couldn't get comfortable and eased to his feet. "And all this time she's been living under a fake identity?"

Fenella thought about it. "That's my best guess. Anyone else?"

No one spoke. Not even Jones who always came up with weird theories.

Fenella waited thirty seconds more. "So, the fake woman moves in and lives the life of a reclusive artist. She keeps out of trouble and paints landscapes which start to sell. Word spreads her latest creation will mock the villagers." She stopped, backed up. There was a question which came before all that. "What happened to Ann Crombie?"

Jones raised his hand. "Kidnapped and killed, boss. Or killed straight away."

"Un-huh, lad." Dexter frowned. "Hate to agree, but the real Ann Crombie ain't alive no more. Not after all this time. That little old lady in the morgue was the killer or knew the killer. Ain't no doubt her hands are stained with blood."

PC Woods rocked from foot to foot. "They'll be a feeding frenzy when news of this gets out, ma'am. Heads will roll."

Fenella massaged her neck. Right now, there was nothing to be done about the press. There will soon be a flock of crows outside the station, squawking and clawing for news. The thought of them crawling all over the case before they got a good lead filled her with rage. Because she knew exactly how they'd spin the story and she couldn't do anything about it except focus on moving forward.

From outside came the wail of a police siren. Screeches, high and low, faded as a patrol car sped from the station. Exhaust fumes wafted from the courtyard below.

Then came quiet. Stifling.

Fenella kept things moving. "We kick off a proof of life inquiry for Ann Crombie. Jones, you run with it. You've got the next three days to find evidence that she is alive. Start with financials—banks, bills and the rest, then move on to gathering any medical records. PC Beth Finn, you assist. If Ann Crombie is alive, she'll have left some trace."

"And what about the woman in the morgue, guv?" Dexter gestured to the window and the general direction of the hospital. "I reckon someone found out she was a fraud and blackmailed her."

Fenella was struck again by the oddness of the two murders. It niggled at the back of her mind. Chimes of the town hall clock rang out with the sharp tugs of the hangman's noose. "Why kill the person you are blackmailing?"

Dexter leaned back against the wall. "It don't make sense, guv. I ain't got a clue what it means. Anyone?"

No one answered.

Fenella tried to put the puzzle pieces together, but couldn't get them to fit. "Any progress on Benny?" She glanced at her phone. "Mail Benny Label. Okay?"

Again nothing.

They faced a killer who was complex and crafty. And although they did not speak of it yet, there was a chance the person would strike again. If they did, Fenella was certain the horror would take them by surprise. She waited ten more seconds before another rapid-fire question. "Why cut off their heads?"

Jones was the first to respond. "I agree, the blackmail angle doesn't work. Do you think it might be mob-related, boss? The woman in the morgue might have been hiding from thugs in London. A village is good cover but her identity was blown."

For a moment Fenella didn't speak. "And Bella Timbol's death?"

Jones stole a look at PC Beth Finn. She shook her head. He sighed. "Don't know, boss. But forensics have completed their search of Bede Thatch. Now comes the wait for what they have found."

Dexter took two steps away from the wall. "Guv, suppose the killer didn't know Ann Crombie was a fake and had some other motive." He paused, rubbing a hand over the back of his neck. "It sounds ridiculous but the killer might have a grudge against women artists, wants to humiliate them because he don't like their art."

A knock sounded on the door. Mrs Soper, Superintendent Jeffery's assistant poked her head into the room. She glanced at Dexter and smiled. "The boss and camera crew will be coming this way in fifteen minutes. Make yourself scarce."

The door eased closed.

"You heard her." Fenella waved her hands. "Scarper."

"What about you, guv?" Dexter glanced at the door. "Want to come with me to have another chat with Helen Grimes?"

"Nah, I'm going back to Ambleside. Fancy another poke about Bede Thatch."

41

Fenella should have sensed trouble the moment she opened the gate at Bede Thatch.

The first darkening streaks of rain clouds stretched fingers of shadow across the garden path. Wind blew through the trees lifting leaves in loose swirls. The air smelled of burnt wood. She strode by a strip of blue and white police tape. It flapped with loud cracks.

At the edge of the overgrown pond, she stopped and studied the ghost of flowerbeds, bindweed and brambles and what she could see of the ruins of the shed. A gaping hole in the roof, like a deformed mouth, stretched in a hideous smile against the darkening sky. She stared at it suddenly remembering there was one thing she had been planning to do all day. She picked up her phone and dialled Helen Grimes.

"Hello, this is... yes, Fenella... I'm pleased to hear you have settled into your hotel... You are staying here until September? Wonderful... No news at the present... Un-huh... Un-huh... A quick question, did your aunt have a friend called Benny?" Fenella listened, stared at the phone and placed it back against her ear. "That's what she called you? Short for your middle name, Benedicta... I see. . . Have you received any mail from Bede Thatch, an envelope or package or anything with a label? Nothing in years. It might be waiting for you back home in Greenport. . . . I see. . . so, you get an electronic notification of mail and nothing has been delivered since you arrived in England. . . I see. . . If you do receive a package from Bede Thatch please contact me straight away. Okay. . . I will. . . Bye."

Fenella turned to the cottage half expecting lights to shine from the front windows and the black shadow of a woman to flit across the glass—Ann Crombie working with fury on her landscape painting of foxes chasing humans. But not this evening. Not ever. Not even in the past, really. But at least she knew who Benny was. She wished she could say the same for the woman in the morgue—the dead woman who'd lived in this house and pretended to be Ann Crombie.

"Who are you, pet?"

Her question was answered by the mumble and sigh of the breeze.

Fenella thought of the glass lamp that brought her to this place on Saturday and she thought of the body in the woods and she thought of the burnt-out shed. How had local artists created their masterpieces in this forlorn place?

Now Bede Thatch felt wrong. A godforsaken tangle of thorns and stinging nettles and grasses with razor-sharp edges. More the rot and cold decay of an abandoned graveyard than a bright landscape of inspiration. And the stone cottage with its slate roof looked bizarre against the backdrop of the unkempt garden. She massaged her neck.

The wildness seemed significant.

For some time she worked her fingers into the knot of tension only aware of the whispering leaves; taunts rising on the growling breeze. Her neck relaxed a notch and the words of Bella Timbol came to her. *"I used to own the cottage... one must always be prepared for a mele when one visits Bede Thatch."*

What did she mean?

Bright forks of light exploded across the dull sky. A thunderclap sounded in the distance. Something moved to her left.

Deep in the brambles.

A scratching sound.

Shaking the branches.

A pair of yellow eyes.

The fox hissed and retreated into the darkness.

Fenella watched to see if it was dragging its hind legs but it was gone before she got the chance.

With care, she picked her way around a patch of nettles spreading across the path and had the feeling the fox still watched. She stopped and turned in a slow three-hundred-and-sixty-degree circle. Brambles and thorns and bindweed and long grasses and the stone wall and gate and the shed. Other than the wind, the garden was still.

Except for the soft crunch of footsteps on twigs.

A light, cautious tread.

From behind.

Beyond the garden gate.

She spun and saw the man, head bent, picking his way along the length of the wall. She recognised him at once but didn't know his name. He was an onlooker in the crowd on the day she found the woman in the morgue.

"Come here often?" Fenella shouted the question, hurrying back along the path to the garden gate.

He looked up, startled, and thrust a hand through his jet-black spiked hair. Close to fifty, Fenella guessed, although he had a gold nose stud and dressed like a teen.

"I'm with the police, pet." Fenella waved her warrant card.

"Thought you lot were done here." He flattened the collars of his shirt with both hands. A kind of caress, soft strokes. "I'm Ken Ashworth, live in the village but teach at the school in Troutbeck Bridge. It's peaceful here, isn't it?"

"Aye, pet. Makes you feel one with nature." Fenella eyed the leaping foxes on his shirt. He was dressed for a telly advert not a walk in the countryside. "Come this way often?"

"When I need to think."

Fenella didn't want to sound too eager, but he'd piqued her interest and she fancied a dig. "Problems, eh?"

"Don't we all?"

"Is that why you were here on Saturday, to think about your big problem? I saw you in the crowd."

He stepped back, his eyes unreadable. "Not really, I like to visit the places where local artists are inspired." He glanced over her shoulder. "I'm an art teacher."

Fenella raised her eyebrows. "Let me guess, you are a landscape painter, one of Ann Crombie's lot?"

"Me? God forbid."

"Sculpture? No, no, don't tell me, you blow glass lamps?"

He sniffed. "I'm not an artist per se, but I understand artistic aesthetic, and appreciate the brilliance of the maestros—Michelangelo, Van Gogh, Picasso. They are—"

"So you don't pick up the paintbrush or pencil, luv?"

"Do film critics make movies?"

"Thought you might dabble seeing as you teach the subject. Thought you might be a member of Ambleside Village Artists."

He touched the gold nose stud, eyes shrinking to dots. "Look here, a maestro adds a thin layer of paint to the canvas. Light brush strokes. Heavy brush strokes. Layer by layer, the image becomes richer, the scene deeper, and it all comes together to become an interconnected whole. The so-called artists in this village are fat-handed clods, incapable baboons. My God, there are even those who paint by numbers amongst their throng. Do you seriously think I'd join an organisation like that?"

Fenella said nothing.

He made a small grimace and snatched another furtive glance over her shoulder. "That is half the problem. We are told the works of Monet are easy. We can create such wonders ourselves if we only pick up a paintbrush and follow the seven simple steps. It can't be done. A genius is born and shaped. A hobby painter will never create anything great."

Fenella thought there was a wild, almost frantic look about him. "Is that what you teach the kids?"

"I am an expert in critique."

"Eh?"

"Critique of good form. That is what I pass on to the children. I do not deem myself worthy to create it. Nor are any of my students skilled creators. True genius is hard to find and I can assure you it does not exist in Ambleside." A speck of foam bubbled at the corner of his lips. "But we can all appreciate great art even if we do not have the talent to create it. That is the message the world needs to hear. It is the message I drum into my students."

Fenella decided Ken Ashworth had a short temper, and she liked the idea of prodding his balloon to see if it popped. She pointed at the cottage. "Ann Crombie created her art in there, you liked it really, eh?" She held his gaze. "That's why you are here, isn't it, to have a peep at the Master's workplace, get inspiration for your next critique?"

Ken dragged the back of his hand across his mouth, glancing over her shoulder. "I despise Ann's work. Cheap, crass, everything painted with the loose hand of a monkey." He stopped, his face crimsoning at the sharpness of his words. "Not a reflection of the woman, of course. I'm sure she was adorable, but to call what she did 'art' is to spit on the meaning of the word."

A blackbird screamed from the bushes. A warning call for other birds not to get too close.

Fenella adjusted the strap on her handbag. "So, you didn't get on with the lass who lived here?"

Ken raised both palms. "Look, the entire village is shattered by what has happened. A shocking firestorm of hell has exploded amid our peaceful community. No one in the village likes what has happened here. No one understands it, either. I even went to church and spoke with the vicar. The man, like the rest of us, is in total shock."

"Are you a regular?" He didn't strike Fenella as the type. Too mean-spirited and too short a temper. But then again, that was the type that benefited the most.

Ken let his hands fall to his side. "At a time like this, our community comes together. The church is a natural gathering place. I try to go when I can because I want to be a better man."

Fenella thought he had something to hide. "Lots of sins to confess?"

A ghost of a smile flickered across his face. "A real shame what happened to Ann. To be beaten and left exposed to the beasts of the fields to do as they pleased. Shocking. Leaves me with a desolate sense of pain. Not as extreme as the suffering of Ann, of course, but pain nonetheless. Father Kemp is a beacon of hope."

Fenella's attention was caught by a second bubble of foam dribbling down his chin. She almost missed his words. "Father?"

"Eh?"

"You said Father Kemp like you are one of his faithful."

He looked at her thoughtfully. "Vicar, Reverend, Father, it is all the same to me." Once again he rubbed the back of his hand across his mouth. "Vicar Kemp was saddened by Ann Crombie's death. Very much so. We are a village. We are all in this together."

Fenella listened to the blackbird screaming from the bushes, then turned back to Ken Ashworth. He had a way of speaking that filled her with mistrust. And his forty-something face, punk-style hair and teenage clothes came across as seedy. Mutton dressed as lamb never sold well in the butcher shop.

She held his gaze, watchful for another flicker of temper. "How well did you know Ann?"

"To look at." Again came the ghost of a smile. "As well

as most, I suppose, and before you get excited, that simply means I didn't know her well at all. She was a recluse."

"Do you know about her latest painting?"

"I'm only interested in maestros and Ann's work was not in that league." His tongue licked a bubble of foam from the side of his lip. "I've no idea what she was working on but can guarantee it was a triumph to the hideous."

"I hear they are selling well."

His voice rose in indignation. "She had no genuine skill, no matter how much an ignorant baboon of a collector pays for her crap. Look, Ambleside is full of people who create atrocities to the artistic aesthetic. You mentioned glass lamps earlier. Ha! My God, there is even a woman in the village blowing such disfigured nonsense which she sells for ludicrous prices to fools who lack taste. Not art. At best, mere baubles to adorn a garish parlour."

Fenella waited as though giving his comments some thought. "When was the last time you saw Ann Crombie?"

"To speak with?"

"Aye."

"Years ago, three at least. Like I said, I knew her to look at but the woman was a recluse." His face fixed in a thin-lipped smile, eyes moving to look over her shoulder.

She turned to follow his gaze—the blackened shed.

When she turned back, he was staring at her, left hand clutching his throat. "Got a date, don't want to be late. Carlisle is a bit of a drive. Going to be a late one."

Another bolt of white light smeared the sky followed by a long blast of thunder. Ken Ashworth waved and hurried away with huge steps, almost a run.

42

Fenella returned her gaze to the shed and the towering slate roof of the cottage. Bede Thatch contained secrets and she wanted them now and she wanted them all. She thought once more of the miracle the place didn't burn to the ground leaving only blackened ashes. The forensics team had gone over the shed and the house and were crawling over their findings. Reports would come her way. But that might take weeks.

Rain began to fall. Steady dark sheets creeping across the landscape. Splashing. Splattering. A cold drenching spray forming puddles on the uneven soil. She opened her umbrella. It hit her then. She had it earlier and almost missed it.

The garden reminded her of a church graveyard.

Once again she surveyed the brambles, bindweed and nettles. An idea formed but could she take the risk? The killer might be watching now. Even if they were not, they'd keep a keen eye out for what the police were doing. Anything the police did might trigger another attack.

No more blood.

No more killing.

But therein lay the problem—what she had in mind

would send a giant signal the police were on the killer's tail. What to do?

Thunder rolled across the treetops, shaking loose more icy cold pellets of rain. The blackbirds were screaming from the bushes; the trees moaning in the breeze.

Fenella grabbed her mobile phone and dialled Dexter. "Gather a team to search the grounds of Bede Thatch. Sort out a search warrant for the garden. We'll start at daybreak. PC Woods knows the place, invite him to help. Plenty of shovels and spades."

"What are we looking for, guv?"

"The body of Ann Crombie."

43

It was six at night. A shroud of rain swept over Ambleside. Kate Owen slouched at the kitchen table in the dim with a shot glass at her side. She'd downed booze all evening, as though it were her last day on earth.

A six-pack of ale first, to drown the hell of the day. When she tossed the last can into the dustbin, she turned to the gin she kept for celebrations. It had never been opened.

She took bird sips, glaring through the window at the miserable storm. Gin dulled the world but turned her mood foul and gave her strange visions and a monstrous headache in the morning. What did she have to look forward to, anyway? When daylight came, she'd get the bus to Port St Giles and begin the search for another dead-end job. One of hundreds of grim faces looking for work. How could she show them she was the best person for the job?

She chewed over that question until a flash of hope flared, bright and hot. A resume, that's what she needed to stand out from the pack. But she'd left school with no qualifications and worked as a shop assistant (got fired by the wife of the red-bloodied owner); on a maggot farm with writhing vats of grubs raised for fishing bait (gross); Only

God knew how many cleaning jobs she'd done before she found work in a butcher shop (nine months before the hell of it turned her into a temporary vegan).

The low point came when, as a single mother and desperate for cash, she landed a job as a restaurant grease trap cleaner. Six days a week she cleared thick, putrid grease from restaurant collection traps. On the seventh day, she'd lie in a hot lemon-scented bubble bath trying to erase the stink. When she moved to Ambleside, she landed a job as a barmaid.

What the hell could she put on a resume? The flash of hope flickered and died.

She touched the wart on her chin and cursed. "Marvellous. Bloody magnificent."

Tonight she would not think about the mounting pile of debts. Her health insurance policy was the only bill she wasn't behind with. She'd never let that slip. Not since the time she fell ill. Three weeks in a public hospital ward left a scar that would last a lifetime. If she fell sick again, she'd at least have the comfort of her own private room. She wished she had a little more cash to pay the premiums for Skye.

A flourish of raindrops burst from a low cloud and smashed against the window. A tap-tapping like fingers drumming on the glass and demanding to come in. Kate took another sip, this time in exasperation. Skye was at Steph's house again, leaving her all alone. And Ken was in Carlisle with Millie. And she needed the company of people. After all she'd been through, she didn't want to be alone. If only she were better at making friends.

Rain continued to beat against the window, rattling the

glass like thrown stones.

She jerked to her feet, stumbled to the cupboard and downed a mouthful of baked beans straight from the can. *Best line my stomach.* Tonight she'd hit the booze hard.

Her life had gone to hell, and not just because of Ken Ashworth. She hadn't dreamt it would turn out like this when she moved to the village as a single mum with Skye all those years ago. Yet here she was in a living nightmare. Ambleside had inflicted blow upon blow ruining her dreams and rotting all hope. She ran a finger around the inside of the can and licked it. Why did she feel doom was pointing its finger at her and at any moment might strike?

I'm not helpless. I'll have a word with the pub landlord, make him see sense.

Kate belched, wiped a dribble of bean juice on her blouse and cursed. This week's wash would be by hand to save on the electric. She'd put the clothes to soak, ask Skye to scrub and hang them on the line. They were a team now, more so than ever before.

The rain continued to fall. A cold steady beat against the kitchen window. Thinking about other ways to save money, Kate staggered back to the table. After three sips of gin, her mind shifted. What was the best way to approach the pub landlord? He'd always had his ugly eye on her, his greasy hands touching her as if by mistake. If she went back to grovel, he'd want much more than a quick touch.

She swallowed a mouthful of gin.

It would be disgusting but what choice did she have? When he took her back, she'd squeeze more hours out of the tight-fisted pig.

44

Kate hadn't meant to fall asleep. It was the slam of the door knocker that woke her. Stunned by the loudness breaking into her dreams, she blinked in the darkness, bewildered and dizzy with gin. Eight o'clock and the storm filled sky as dark as night. No one knocked on her door at that time. Who? Skye had a key and always called on the phone when she was on the way home.

Alarm seeped into her bones.

Another clatter of the door knocker. Insistent. Someone wanted her to come to the door and they wanted her to come now and they wanted her to let them in.

It's Ken, he's back.

For several more seconds she remained still, one hand on the glass tumbler the other on her phone. Wasn't he in Carlisle with Millie? Maybe their celebration had gone wrong. She grinned imagining a dinner from hell where they'd argued over the main course and broke up over dessert.

Yes, that was it.

She knew he'd never last with the witch. But Millie was pregnant with his twins. That complicated things. It didn't matter. They'd cross that bridge later.

Kate laughed and for the first time in days felt the shiver of paranoia lift. She'd give Ken hell; tell him she tried to warn him and drag him inside. After, they'd talk and she'd encourage him to apply for a headmaster's post. He'd need the money to pay for Millie's babies. And, Kate thought, to allow her to give up bar work. No way would she squander this chance to grab him. Even if a judge gave Millie's brats a vast chunk of his cash, it would be worth it. What came after headteacher? She was sure it paid more money. When they were wed, she'd nag him to go after that. Make him a career man and point him at the top.

Another knock on the door. A pounding fist this time.

Excited, she staggered to the window and peeped out the edge. The dark outline of a cadaverous figure leaned against the doorframe. Kate could not see the face but sensed the head turn and look directly at her. She stumbled away from the window.

No way in hell is that Ken.

For days she'd had the unshakeable sensation of being watched. Someone had their eyes on her, following her. It was now she remembered seeing Liam Brampton in the shop doorway on Sunday as she made her way to her shift in the pub. He wore a wheat-gold top which stretched over his gut, and he carried a brown sack over his shoulder. Ken had warned her. *"Liam Brampton's a nutcase, Sweetmeat. No woman should be alone with him in his lair. No man, for that matter."* Now Ken's words came back to haunt her.

But was it Liam she saw in the shop doorway on Sunday? Because when she looked again, the shop doorway was empty with only tourists ambling up and down the street.

Kate's gaze fell to the gin bottle then bounced to the dark window. It stared back like an empty eye socket. A fresh chill shivered along her spine. When Ken came to her door on Sunday night, she had a memory of someone else on the doorstep. Who? She tried to think, but the fug of booze blocked full recall.

She listened for another knock and noticed the rain had stopped and the sky was midnight blue. It was very quiet here in the stone cottage. No cars rumbled along the street. No one walked their dog. She might as well be on an isolated island. An island where your screams were drowned by the sea.

Another knock blasted from the door. Hard and fast and insistent.

Kate touched her phone, wondering whether to call the police. They'd take forever to get here. The last time she called, they didn't show up at all. And anyway, what would she tell them? That someone was knocking on her front door? That didn't sound like an emergency. She guessed they'd tell her to answer it and hang up.

More pounding on the door. Fast and furious and not giving up.

Darkness grew deeper. Kate's breathing increased. Dry mouth. Watchful eyes. The tart tang from the open baked bean can crawled up her nostrils. *Thank God I didn't have the lights on.* Whoever was on her doorstep could not see her inside. How long had they been standing there, watching, waiting?

Bam. Bam. Bam.

Something stirred in Kate's memory. A horrible recollection from the past. She'd buried it so deep and for so long the vividness of the flashback made her gasp. The gin in her gut turned to shards of glass and a thousand pinpricks prickled her skin. It couldn't happen again, could it?

Like that awful time when Skye was two, and they'd been living alone in a single room in Carlisle. Dark and damp and dismal. The air smelled of mould and the single-bar electric heater spat venomous sparks when first turned on. Skye's dad, Bart Owen, turned up, pounding the door in a drunken rage. There was no time to hide. No place, either. No one to hear her screams.

He kicked down the door, the devil in his smiling eyes.

Hell had come back into her life.

Bart smashed up the room, taking his time, swinging a cricket bat with precision and all the while laughing. Satisfied, he cornered her on the sofa bed, unbuckling his belt. She was his wife and he'd do as he damn well pleased. He told her to smile. He liked *her smile*. Even now Kate trembled at that night and the desperate way it ended.

The door knocker clattered.

Kate was too drunk and frightened to run. Where would she hide? She tiptoed to the hall; thankful Skye wasn't at home. With a trembling hand, she flipped on the light, ran fingers through her hair, pasted on *her smile*, opened the door and stepped aside.

45

A second after Kate Owen opened the door, the figure stepped into the hallway. "It's about your daughter, Skye."

Nowhere could those words from a stranger strike more fear than in a mother's heart. Kate must have fallen because a cold hand pulled her to her feet. Helpless, she regained her balance and leaned against the wall. Only then did her brain begin to take things in. Slow, because of the gin and ale and fear which curdled in the depths of her stomach.

The figure was a woman, skeletal thin and smelling of expensive perfume. Middle-aged with sly brown eyes and an excited gleam to her wrinkled prune-shaped face. A vague sense of recognition dawned. Kate knew the woman. Not a stranger, then. But from where?

"Have you been drinking, again?" The woman sniffed.

"Me? No, no, no." Kate mumbled the words, still thinking. It wasn't like she was some old maid who knocked back booze on her own because she had no friends. "Just a tipple with dinner to help me relax."

The woman's gaze fell to the orange smudge on Kate's blouse. "Beans on toast, again?"

Kate's stomach lurched. She ate beans on toast for

dinner three or four times a week. How did this woman know that? "Beans are nutritious."

The woman glanced around the hallway, sniffing. "Are you on your own tonight?"

Kate remembered her now—Mrs Penelope Fowler. Steph's mum. *Oh Christ.* She fell back against the wall.

Mrs Fowler took her by the arm, steadying her to the kitchen. "We'd best get the kettle on. We both need a strong cuppa."

Mrs Fowler bustled around the kitchen, tossing the open baked bean can into the dustbin, wiping down surfaces with a cloth soaked in disinfectant and filling the kettle with water, and a few minutes later, poured tea into two large mugs.

Kate watched her work with a growing sense of shame. Mrs Fowler's husband, Stan, had a fantastic job which paid oodles of money. Kate's six-week fling with the lush man seared deep in her memory. Flowers and French perfume and expensive Belgium chocolates. It ended when she got greedy and demanded he divorce his stuck-up wife and buy a new house for them to settle. He told her it was a mistake; he hadn't done it before, that she'd hunted him and trapped him in her claws. He loved his wife and would never leave her. He waved Kate away like a king dismissing a disloyal subject.

Kate fumed for three days drinking ale and gin and smoking giant spliffs fortified with extra strong weed. On the fourth day, the plan came to her.

She knocked on the Fowler's front door. After midnight. Wearing a scanty negligée. In a drunken stupor. Telling the world what she thought of prune-faced Penelope Fowler and her chipolata-hung husband. Top of her voice. Spitting lurid words like ice-cold raindrops. All the neighbours' houselights flicking on. Yelling louder about what Mr Fowler was missing and dancing the striptease with boozy delight as a crowd gathered. Big mistake. The only person who would employ her in the village after the fiasco was the sleazy pub landlord.

Mrs Fowler added the milk and sugar. "It's your Skye, Kate." She sniffed, took a gulp of tea, cleared her throat, eyes as bright as new pennies. "You sure no one else is here?"

Kate was incapable of silence, despite the ale and the gin and her words coming out slow. "What's Skye done now?"

Mrs Fowler lowered her cup. "Is your new fancy man upstairs? It might be best if he came to sit with you."

Kate wished Ken was at her side and Skye doing her homework at the kitchen table. She wanted to be like the happy mother in the advert on the telly raising the pot lid on the stew as the family sniffed in delight.

Oh God, she wanted to scream. But she did not scream. She'd made a drunken fool of herself in front of Mrs Fowler before. *Never again.* She took a sip of tea wishing it was fortified with brandy. "I'm home alone tonight. What's going on?"

Mrs Fowler glanced up at the ceiling as if she didn't quite believe the reply. "No one upstairs, then?"

Kate swallowed. "Why are you here?"

"I asked Steph what happened between her and Skye." Mrs Fowler crossed her arms. "Teens are always making and breaking friends, it is so difficult to keep up, don't you agree?"

Kate said nothing.

Mrs Fowler licked her lips. "And Skye is almost sixteen and no bother at all. Her birthday is next month, isn't it?"

Kate nodded. She wanted the woman to leave. If Skye's friendship with Steph was over, Kate wouldn't shed any tears. Even better, Skye would soon be home. She relished a few hours of mother-daughter time. They'd watch that weepy movie.

Mrs Fowler was still speaking. "A nice teen when so many of them push you to the limit." She put a strange emphasis on the word *nice* and sniffed. "She must have come as a surprise to you, really, given the circumstances of her upbringing."

Kate kept her voice steady. "What is that supposed to mean?"

Mrs Fowler leaned forward and smirked. "It's Skye my heart goes out for. No dad in the house and her drunken, pot-smoking mam throwing herself at unsuspecting married men while working all hours in a..." She sniffed."... cheap tavern."

Kate pushed to her feet but her legs were jelly and she slumped back down. Ale and booze and a mouthful of baked beans were not enough to stand on. For the first time, she realised the fug which hovered around her head meant she was drunk. She became suddenly self-conscious. Her breath must reek and she was aware she could not put two words together without slurring. Did she even wash today?

Mrs Fowler raised a hand. "Let's not argue. Not tonight." Her lips creased into a know-it-all smile. "You'll need your strength."

"Pardon?"

Mrs Fowler shook her head, her wrinkled prune face shining. "Steph is going to university and wants to be a lawyer. I suppose Skye will find a job as a barmaid or wait tables in a café. The servant class are always in such short supply."

Kate bristled. Her daughter was every bit as good as Steph. "Skye is as brainy as they come, top of her class. Wants to be a doctor."

"Really?" Mrs Fowler raised an eyebrow. "Doctors need to attend to their classwork, don't they? I haven't seen your daughter since last week."

"But..." Kate's head spun. "...she is staying at your place to get her homework done, right?"

Mrs Fowler gazed around the grubby kitchen and sniffed. "It's incredible it didn't happen sooner. That's what I told my Stan. We've been happily married for twenty-five years. He's a good provider, would never let me live like...this." She was enjoying herself, gloating with bright button eyes. "Women of our age shouldn't be pulling pints in a pub and flinging themselves at married men. My Stan saw right through you, and it is not my place to tell you—"

"Where the hell is Skye?" Somehow Kate was on her feet, her right hand clutching the edge of the table, her body trembling. "Where is my daughter?"

Mrs Fowler rose slowly to her feet, nose in the air. "My Steph tells me Skye has left Ambleside with her fancy man. She is shacked up with him in Carlisle. I popped around to find out if it was true. Had to see it for myself."

Acid burnt in Kate's stomach. "What!"

Mrs Fowler was grinning, skin taut over her skull and showing a full mouth of polished white teeth. "Your daughter is living with a used car salesman; an older chap with thinning hair and a paunch. Your Skye will no doubt be only too eager to please him. The cheap tart." She strode to the kitchen door. "Like mother like daughter, isn't that what they say?"

46

Kate waited for the front door to slam before she fumbled her mobile phone and dialled Skye. Ten times she called. Ten times she left a voice message. In the gaps between dialling and waiting, she sent text after text.

No reply.

Frustrated, she teetered to the window and gazed out at the garden. The moonlit path snaked across the lawn to the gate. Beyond, Vicarage Road was barely visible in the cloak of night.

Something moved in the shadows.

Kate froze, watching.

A fat man in an unfashionable green tracksuit limped along the lane, he turned to look at her window and she saw he was eating from a packet of fish and chips. Wolfing it down. He paused by her garden gate, took a long slow swig from a beer can then limped on. He vanished into the dark.

Kate watched and waited.

An owl hoot echoed over the treetops. She studied the darkness of the lane looking for anything moving. Any trace of Skye. She hoped her daughter would come hustling through the gate and along the garden path.

Five minutes.

Fifteen.

Twenty.

The moon dipped behind a cloud and her hope faded.

With an immense sigh, Kate wobbled back to the kitchen table and slumped in a chair. She sipped from the mug of cold tea. Her child was living with a car salesman! It came as an utter shock. Again she snatched up her phone and again she dialled and again she left a voice message. Then she sent a text. Whatever Skye was up to with that grubby man, she'd turned her phone off so as not to be disturbed.

Kate shoved the mug away, reached for the gin bottle and swigged a mouthful from the thick neck. She hated the whirl of tumult spinning in her head. A perpetual sense of foreboding. Was there no end to her misery while she lived and breathed on this Earth?

She took another swig of gin.

In the morning Skye would text her with another pack of lies, but at least she'd know her daughter was safe. She'd deal with the scoundrel car salesman later. Give him a shock by setting the police after him. She wondered if he was married and decided he was. Well, she'd have a word with each of his kids. Tell them what she thought of Daddy.

Bloody gin's made me moody.

She was restless and flipped on the radio to the local talk station. The host, in her upbeat voice, introduced the night's topic with gusto—how can people be lonely when millions are living in the country?

Kate turned it off and picked up her phone. Her hollow-eyed reflection stared back from the blank screen. Dead battery.

She had to get out of the house. Do something. An idea emerged through the drunken fug. *Yes, I'll visit the pub landlord, reason with him, give him what he wants and get my job back.*

It was madness.

A foolish decision.

She made it anyway.

Kate toddled to the bedroom, slipped into her French negligée, sprayed cheap perfume under her armpits and between her legs then wrapped herself in a thin blue coat and opened the front door.

A glimmer of silver moonlight pierced the low clouds. The breeze held its breath. By the time she tottered to the garden gate and turned the wrong way on Vicarage Road toward Borrans Wood, a gang of dark clouds had overpowered the light of the moon, smothering it in night.

47

Fenella arrived at Bede Thatch the next morning with high hopes the search team would find a trace of Ann Crombie somewhere in the overgrown garden. It was seven, and the sun was up; a threatening ball of blaze. Everything pulsated in its orange glare. The brambles, bindweed and grasses glistened from the overnight rain. A rook cawed with a torrent of thrashing clacks. Another responded with a ghastly scream.

Where is everyone?

She expected the team to be setting up, a few uniformed officers digging here and there. She opened the gate in the stone wall and studied the brambles and long grass and bindweed. The rooks were howling now, each answering the other with a primal scream. She recalled Dexter's story about the fox that wanted the cheese in the beak of a crow. How could she get the unknown dead woman in the morgue to sing?

She walked several steps along the overgrown path and surveyed the ruins of the shed. Who set it on fire? Why? Was it related to the death of the unknown woman in the morgue and Bella Timbol? Where did the real Ann Crombie fit in? A moment before she dipped a hand into her handbag to retrieve her phone, Dexter came hustling along the path waving his arms and shouting.

"Guv ain't nowt happening here today." He was at her side now, doubled over, breathing hard.

Fenella waited, letting the phone plop back into her handbag and taking in the front of the cottage. It sat squat and venerable, a Cumbrian stone house looking out over a wild garden. A garden with secrets hidden from view.

"Problem with the search warrant, guv." Dexter straightened. "Jeffery is holding it up, double-checking it is only to search the garden."

"But it is." Fenella had excluded a search of the house having already looked around, hoping it was an easier sell with Jeffery on the warpath about the number of search warrants issued. "We have requested permission to only search the grounds."

"Aye, guv."

"So what's the deal?"

"That film crew, guv. They want in on the show and Jeffery is buying their idea."

"Which is what?"

"They shoot the start of the search and if anything shows up, Jeffery will take the stage. Reckon she's hoping for a commendation from Chief Constable Rae, and is going at it like some artistic masterpiece."

Fenella massaged her neck sickened by the delay. "I'll call to tell her she is holding up my investigation."

"Ain't no point, guv." Dexter rubbed his chin. "Word is the boss has run her idea past Chief Rae and got the nod, but there are some forms that need to be signed. You know how that is."

"Tomorrow, then?"

"Aye, guv. That's what I'm hearing."

Fenella stared at the garden but then remembered Ken Ashworth, the man with the bright clothes from the telly, and his strange preoccupation with the shed. A flutter of trepidation stirred in her stomach. "We'll start by the ruins of the shed and work our way back to the house."

The howling rooks stopped screaming leaving the whoosh of the breeze through the trees. Moisture swirled in loose clouds under the warmth of the rising sun. The charred scent of burnt wood hovered over the place.

Their phones pinged a second apart.

Fenella was quickest to the screen. Slowly, her lips quirked at the edges. A single photo from Helen Grimes. A picture of her aunt, Ann Crombie. It was a tourist snapshot of two women. Helen Grimes, much younger, wore a pink t-shirt and blue jeans. She had an arm around a dark-haired woman in her fifties in a simple pink floral dress and high-heeled boots. Both women laughed, heads thrown back. In the background, the gates of Buckingham Palace loomed.

"That's her then, guv." Dexter studied the photo on his phone. "Ann Crombie, and she don't look a lick like the woman in the morgue."

Fenella's eye was drawn to the boots. "How tall do you reckon Helen Grimes is?"

"Less than five feet, guv."

"And look how she towers over her aunt. That makes Aunt Ann tiny, child-sized."

"Like a China doll." Dexter gave a little laugh. "With a face any Paris model would kill for. Any man, for that matter, too."

Fenella continued to study the photo. Ann Crombie had a thin gold chain around her neck, her left hand touching it. What a smile! It captured the essence of life.

Fenella smiled too. They were no nearer to a solution but at least she had a sense of Ann Crombie. They had her face. It flooded Fenella with sorrow and gave her a surge of strength. "Not the face of a recluse, more a woman filled with the joy of life."

Dexter stared at the image with a strange reverence in his eyes. "You sure this photo ain't been touched up? I mean, wow, imagine what she looked like when she was younger. Takes a vulgar hand to terminate the life of such a beauty. A frantic beast; a lusty looser."

He spoke in a sorrowful whisper, poetic, almost to himself.

Fenella, too, whispered her own question. "What did they do to you, pet?" She scanned the garden, perplexed, gaze settling on the pond. "Where did they put you?"

48

"Yoo-hoo." The blue-rinsed haired woman waved from the garden gate—Miss May Fish with her rouge cheeks, pink lipstick and flat coin eyes. PC Sid Fenwick was at her side. He turned to see who she was waving at and his bearded face crumpled into a horrified expression.

Odd, Fenella thought and hurried over to find out what the fuss was about.

PC Sid Fenwick hopped from foot to foot, the dark circles around his hooded eyes deepening. "No need to worry the detectives with your. . . stories."

"Stories?" Fenella hoped it had to do with the case, but knowing Miss Fish she doubted it. "Have you got something for us, Miss Fish?"

Miss Fish pointed at the cottage. "That place is cursed."

"Please, Miss Fish." PC Sid Fenwick stepped forward, waved a hand, his hooded eyes narrowed to slits. "This isn't the place for tittle-tattle, so we'll hear no more."

Miss Fish did not stop, she continued to speak. "The curse of Boron's Wood will not be denied. Once the monk with no face rings the bell, death is nigh."

PC Sid Fenwick took her arm. "Come along now, I'm

sure the detectives have important work to see to."

Miss Fish shook her arm free. "I am the chief fire warden and will not be silenced."

PC Sid Fenwick ran a hand across his beard and let out a groan. He wanted Miss Fish to be silent and he wanted her silent now and he wanted to be anywhere but in front of two detectives from Port St Giles.

Fenella sensed his discomfort but couldn't help herself. "I've always got time for you, Miss Fish. What is going on?"

That is all it took. Miss Fish threw her head back. "At last a police officer who will listen."

"Oh God." PC Fenwick mouthed the words, but Fenella read his lips.

Dexter joined them. "What's all the fuss about?"

Miss Fish's eyes shone. Two detectives were much better than the local part-time volunteer police constable. She drew a breath. "I'm a woman devoted to good causes. Fire warden, worship at the church and steadfast in my duty."

"Aye, luv." Fenella wanted her to hurry up and get to the meat. "I've not heard anyone say otherwise."

"Thank you Inspector Sallow, you are so kind." Miss Fish turned and gave PC Fenwick a withering look. "Women understand these things so much better than men."

"Tell me what happened?" Fenella tried to sound encouraging. "I'm listening, pet."

Miss Fish's eyes squeezed shut. "Last night I thought I heard a church bell ringing —"

PC Fenwick touched his heavy black beard. "The detectives don't need to hear about this."

"But I heard a bell tolling and there is no church out this way." Miss Fish jabbed a finger. "Locals say it is a warning of death."

"Are you sure you heard a church bell?" This was Fenella.

Miss Fish looked down at her hands. "It was around midnight. I looked out of my window and a mysterious man was walking along the trail and stopped at my garden gate."

Fenella glanced at Dexter who rocked back on his heels. PC Fenwick took a step back and shook his head.

"Go on, luv." Fenella had to hear it all now. "And leave nothing out."

Miss Fish gave PC Fenwick a triumphant look. "My house is less than a mile from Borrans Wood. Indeed, as I have mentioned, the trail passes my garden gate. And he was standing there, staring at my bedroom window."

"Did you get a good look at him?" Fenella nodded at Dexter who took out his notebook. "I want you to think and tell us."

"Oh yes, he was a monster of a man, all evil and shadowy."

"Can you be a bit more precise?" Fenella flashed a friendly smile.

"It was dark because of the storm and I'd had rather a heavy bedtime tipple, but he wore a. . . " Miss Fish glanced at PC Fenwick. ". . . well, robes is the only way I can describe it. With cowboy boots. The type of boots the hero wears in a Western movie. Strong and sturdy and solid and pointy at the toe. Oh, I do so love a Charles Bronson film, don't you?"

Dexter grunted.

Fenella nodded at PC Fenwick.

PC Fenwick got the message and touched Miss Fish's arm. "You were in your bedroom, right?"

"Yes."

"Getting undressed?"

"My bedroom is where I disrobe."

"In front of the window with the lights on." PC Fenwick emphasised each word.

"I live in the country and can do as I please in front of my window."

PC Fenwick sighed, rubbing the dark circles around his hooded eyes. "How many times, Miss Fish?"

"I don't know what you are talking about." Miss Fish looked as if she knew exactly what he was talking about. "Really, the detectives want to know about last night. What happened before is of no one's concern."

"Five times in the last month, Miss Fish." PC Fenwick spoke in a soft voice. "Five times you have complained about a man watching you from the bottom of your garden at night as you take your clothes off in full view of your bedroom window with the lights on. A great beast of a man feasting his eyes on your naked form. Big and beefy and broad with eyes as wide as melons. And every time he is wearing cowboy boots and strange robes." He paused and looked from Fenella to Dexter. "Your exact words, Miss Fish. I've logged them in the report."

"Really, PC Fenwick you make me sound—"

Fenella raised her hand to quell an argument and noticed a movement out of the corner of her eye. She turned, scanning the trail that snaked deep into Borrans Wood.

She had taken the path earlier. A brisk walk across the hills where the expansive view spread out toward Lake Windermere. Then down through the growing thicket until you were in the woods and dappled sunlight shimmered on the dirt trail. In her hurry to get to Bede Thatch, she must have missed it.

A thin blue coat, caught in the brambles, flapped in the warming breeze.

She ran toward the thicket, slipping on the slick soil, steadying herself, arms pumping, rounding a tall larch tree, slowing as the path dipped away. Dexter saw where she was going and sprinted after her. His footfalls pounded on the soft earth with a steady thud.

At that moment the rooks cawed, but Fenella did not have time to think about that because of the skimpy negligée and the woman sprawled on a blanket of bindweed, arm outstretched, hand pointing to nowhere.

49

"You are safe now, pet."

Kate Owen opened her eyes unsure where she was, or how long the woman with the sharp eyes and shoulder-length grey hair had been speaking.

"I'm Fenella, luv. Help is on its way."

Kate's body boiled with a heat she'd never known before. She tried to concentrate. Shards of pain prickled in her left hand. Her neck throbbed and her eyes were clouded with a foggy gloom. She let her eyelids droop.

"Stay with me, pet." There was a pause. "Tell me what happened?"

Kate fought a frantic battle to open her eyes and let the kind woman know she was fine. But with the heat and the excruciating pain which pummelled her body all she managed was to move her dry lips.

Once.

Open and closed.

"What was that luv? I didn't catch it."

Something warm touched Kate's skin. Someone held her hand. And something pressed against her neck, another hand, she thought, taking her pulse.

"Can you try again, pet? I'm with the police and will

help."

The hand which held her was strong and warm, it reminded her of Ken's roses. White roses, and the promise of married life. Still, Kate could not move her eyelids. She tried to work her lips. They did not move. She wanted to think about Skye and her two-bedroom cottage and the things she loved about life. But hellish agony suffocated all thought other than she didn't want to die.

"Don't go to sleep, luv. Stay awake."

A wave of guilt joined the fire raging along Kate's spine. Death would cloak Skye in grief. Mother and daughter separated by a distance that could never be crossed. And what type of mother had she been? More guilt. More pain. *No more, please.*

Someone was screaming. The birds. The birds were screaming in the trees; and there was a male voice now, gruff and furious, giving the time an ambulance was due to arrive. Shouting for them to get a bloody move on or he'd. . .

The world paled into a swirling murk of sickening agony and staggering heat. An intense headache throbbed. It pounded in Kate's skull until she was floating in pure light, overjoyed and released into numbness. Soaring now, to an unseen summit where the bitter clamshells of life fell away.

"I'm Fenella. Stay with me, pet."

Kate struggled with gallant force. Her brain cells howled that she must conquer the ailments that ravaged her body. *Must stay with the woman with the shoulder-length grey hair. Must live.*

A fantastic light pulsed.

One.

And brighter.

"I won't let you go. You will not leave us."

Two.

Brighter still.

"Stay with me, luv. I'm with the police. I'm ordering you to stay with me."

Three.

A constant of unwavering light, pure and without blemish.

Kate was running in Borrans Wood, her feet floating above the ground. The trail twisted around a sharp bend and somehow she knew she would be safe there. Eternally safe. Three men danced in drunken revelry a few paces behind, one in skinny blue jeans. They sang nursery rhymes with words familiar yet impossible to hear. Every time she turned to see if they were gaining, they vanished between the trees. Only their faces were visible. Blank and without form.

Three men.

One woman.

Deep in the woods.

The odds were stacked against her. No way could she win. Overwhelmed by terror at what was to come, Kate clattered through a bramble bush, apologising to the prickles and thorns. But the three men were in front of her, waiting by the bend. "Forget everything." They sang the words. "Forget what you saw."

Kate shivered and willed her eyes open. The woman with the shoulder-length grey hair had a mother's smile. Kate opened her mouth to speak, to tell all that had happened, and blacked out.

50

An hour after the ambulance pulled up at the Port St Giles Cottage Hospital, Fenella found herself outside Giles Rare Books Store. She couldn't settle, even after learning the woman's name from PC Sid Fenwick—Kate Owen, a single mam who lived in Ambleside. There was nothing more to be done but wait. PC Woods volunteered for that task. He'd call at the first flash of news.

Giles Rare Books squatted in a cobbled yard near the town market. The shrieks of the enthusiastic stallholders merged with the chatter of shoppers. It was a picturesque brown brick Victorian building which backed up to the towpath that ran along the canal. A place of ideas and dreams and practical *how-to tips.* The woman in the morgue had bought her puzzle magazine, *Northworder,* here. Fenella had visited many times and found it impossible to leave empty-handed.

She stared at her reflection in the glass pane of the door, adjusted her face into a smile and pushed.

Weak orange lights from flickering lamps lit specs of dust floating in the gloom. It was a cavern of a room with brick walls, stone slab floors and a ceiling which stretched up two levels. The scent of coffee beans mingled with the tang of mould and dust and a faint odour of something festering that Fenella could not identify. There were rows of bookcases filled with leather-bound tomes, and on the walls a movable ladder for reaching the topmost shelves. First editions. Signed copies. Illustrated books. Antique bibles. Maps and atlases and historical newspapers. Smaller bookcases formed alleyways, swollen with books of all sizes; magazines and pamphlets and tomes from great thinkers of the past.

Enchanted, Fenella's eyes strained for the comic section. Her husband, Eduardo, devoured vintage comics.

"Hello." Fenella stepped toward the cash register.

A woman sprawled in a recliner with her feet on a footstool, her nose in a book. She did not look up.

Fenella moved closer and coughed.

Nothing.

She tapped the woman's shoulder. "Hello, luv. I've a question."

The woman's head jerked, face bone white, eyes wide with terror. She held the book in a deathlike grip.

"Are you okay, luv?" Fenella wondered if there'd be another trip to the hospital and felt for her phone.

The woman's mouth dropped. Turnip wide. And then she giggled. "So sorry, was lost in a novel about a wild axeman in Alaska. Scary. Killed people by the dozens. I want to know whether the hopeless sheriff is next." She blinked. "How can I help you?"

"I'm with the police and have a few questions." Fenella showed her warrant card.

The woman stared at the card, mouth once again dropping turnip wide, still clutching the book. "If this is about

—"

Fenella raised a hand. "No, luv. I'm not here about that."

"But—"

"Not my department."

The woman's face relaxed, although her hands still clutched the book. "I'm Sandra Cole, part owner with my hubby, Mark. How can I help you?"

"*Northworder*, sell many?"

Sandra shrugged. "They went out of business years ago. We bought their stock as a job lot." She pointed to a bookshelf in the far corner. "That's all we have. It'll be some time yet before they are all gone. We sell one or two each month."

Fenella debated whether to show her a picture of the woman in the morgue. Maybe they'd struck up a conversation and shared details of their lives. It wasn't exactly busy and she could tell Sandra liked a good natter. One problem—the picture only showed the head, but it was clear the woman was dead and she didn't want to spook Sandra. She glanced at the bookcase with the puzzle magazines. "Don't suppose you have regular customers who buy *Northworder*?"

Sandra's next words sent a fizz of excitement through Fenella. "Only one person, alas. A woman from the village of Ambleside." She dropped her book on the counter. "Ann Crombie. She visits the shop once a month to buy *Northworder* and a few other books. Exactly twenty-five pounds each time. She has been coming here for years. I offered to send them to her home in Ambleside—Bede Thatch. Isn't that a lovely name? But Ann refused. She enjoyed her day trip to Port St Giles and said it got her away from the pressure cooker of village life."

Fenella kept her voice level, hiding the growing swell of excitement. "Do you know her well?"

"We have become close friends over the years; meet for tea three or four times a year at Grainbowl Café."

Fenella's heart pounded. Questions crowded in a hysterical throng. Everyone she'd spoken to so far knew little about the woman who claimed to be Ann Crombie. She was an artist and a recluse. And no one seemed to know anything else. Now, at last, there was a chink in the nothingness.

Fenella massaged her neck. "You got along well?"

Sandra nodded. "Very. She is so easy to get on with. It's like we have known each other all our lives, know what I mean?"

"Aye, luv. I get the picture. Like a sister, eh?"

Again Sandra nodded. A shadow crossed her face. "Why are you asking about Ann?"

Fenella waited a heartbeat and decided to be direct. "I'm afraid the woman you knew as Ann Crombie has died. I'm investigating her death."

"Oh my God." The turnip mouth returned along with the eyes filled with terror. "If the police are investigating, it means—"

"Let's not speculate, luv."

Sandra's features sharpened. "What happened?"

"We are still putting the pieces together. Tell me about Ann."

"What sort of thing are you looking for?"

"What was she like, family local? Friends nearby?"

Sandra cocked her head toward the puzzle magazines. "I used to tease her. Those magazines. One per month as regular as clockwork and a few religious books. Like I said, it always came to twenty-five pounds exactly." Sandra was quiet for a moment. "I said. . . used to say Ann was like one of her puzzle magazines. Do you know what I mean?"

Fenella shook her head. "Can you explain?"

"We must have met in the Grainbowl Café dozens of times over the past few years but I knew nothing more about her than her name and address. And I only found out her home address because she ordered a book we did not have in stock and I needed a forwarding address." She flashed a sad smile. "Bede Thatch, a lovely name."

"But you said you were like sisters."

"Oh yes, that is how Ann made me feel." She paused for a long moment. "Although I felt close to Ann I also sensed I was on the first line of a crossword and didn't have the brain power to go deeper. Now I think about it, I hardly knew her at all."

The reply sent a terrible spasm of disappointment through Fenella. She rubbed her neck. Yet another person whose knowledge of the woman in the morgue was surface-deep. The hope of a useful lead had turned into a dry well of despair. There had to be a crack somewhere. Was there a clue in the books Ann Crombie had bought? She tried not to sound too hopeful. "Do you recall the title of the book you forwarded to Bede Thatch?"

"Not exactly, but it was about St Catherine of Bologna, the patron saint of the arts. Would you like me to look up the exact title?"

"Nah." Fenella puffed up her cheeks and then fished out

a business card. "Can you think of anything else?"

Sandra shook her head. "Nothing."

"Are you sure?"

Something flashed in Sandra's eyes. "It is probably nothing."

"Tell me anyway."

"Once, Ann came in flustered, said she was being followed."

"When was this?"

"Oh, I don't know. . . months ago. She was in a terrible state. I calmed her down and went to look outside. I didn't see anyone, so I walked to the street."

"And?"

"There wasn't anyone about."

"Are you sure?"

Sandra blinked. "Well, only a policeman talking to a woman in a peach headscarf; an older lady. They waved when they saw me and walked away together. Other than that, the street was empty. I thought it was in Ann's mind. Who'd want to follow her?"

Fenella didn't have an answer. "Anything else?"

"I'm no gossip, but she always left the impression she was meeting someone after her visit here."

"Why do you think that?"

"Once or twice she let it slip that she had to leave because she wanted to be on time at the café."

"Which?"

Sandra shrugged. "No idea, but I reckon she was meeting a man because once when I asked her if it was a date, she flushed. I tried to avoid her personal life after that, she didn't like me prying."

"If you think of anything else, please call." Fenella handed over her business card and crossed to the bookshelf of puzzle magazines and stood there—*Crossworder, Countdown Magazine, KrossWord, Best Brain Workouts, Griddler Monthly, Enigmatist, Mind Benders Monthly, Northworder, Puzzler's Almanack.*

She ran a finger along the spines of *Northworder* and peered at the thick layer of dust. She picked up a copy and opened it to a crossword puzzle. She read aloud. "Five across, eight letters. The first letter begins with 'A': Steamed marmalade pudding is twice as nice for Napier's gran."

The answer didn't come, so she decided to buy the magazine and figure it out later. But before she took another step, the shop doorbell tinkled, and some sixth sense told Fenella it was trouble.

51

Fenella half turned, watching the door. A rat-faced man in a scruffy pea green duffle coat scurried into the bookshop. He paused, nose twitching, eyes darting around. She held her breath and counted to three, hoping he wouldn't see her. She wasn't surprised when he waved and scuttled to her side.

Rodney Rawlings was a reporter for the *Westmorland News*. An old-school, raw-boned rascal who boozed with the vigour of a teen, counted his female conquests by the dozens and proclaimed himself the voice of the people. Invaluable when Fenella needed his help. Poison when she didn't.

Rodney gazed over his shoulder, his eyes darting around. This was a man who didn't want to be followed. A man who didn't want anyone to know he was here. His gaze fixed on Sandra. She had her head down, knuckles white, reading her book.

His nose twitched. "You've been holding out on me, Fenella."

"How did you know I was here?"

"Please tell me what I can do to turn that scowl into a beautiful smile."

Fenella swallowed a frustrated gasp. "Turn around and walk out of that door and don't look back. Then I'll be very happy."

"Charming, I must say." Rodney reached into his duffle coat and took out a large brown envelope. "And after all the trouble I've gone to prepare this."

Fenella touched a copy of *Northworder*. "Does it tell me something I don't know?"

"Yes."

"About?"

"Bella Timbol."

The horror of the press already on her tail caused a jolt of tension in her neck. A headache began to form. "What do you know about Mrs Timbol?"

"That she is dead." Rodney's nose twitched. "What I don't have right now are the details, and we journalists make our reputation on the details." He waved the envelope. "How about we trade?"

Fenella glanced at Sandra. She held the book in front of her face, hands trembling. "What's in the envelope?"

"Everything you want to know about Bella Timbol and her husband. I've done it as a favour." His eyes moved from left to right like he was double-checking no one overheard. "I'm writing an exclusive, don't want the rat pack to sniff what I've got because they'll snatch my cheese."

A wave of exhaustion washed over Fenella. How long did she have before the rest of the press rat pack showed up? She stifled the urge to scream and flashed a half smile. "When are you going to press?"

"Sunday paper, but an early edition goes online Saturday evening at nine. I need off-the-record confirmation

237

Bella Timbol was found dead in Grange Hall Care Home."
He smiled. "And it wasn't natural."

Fenella thought for a moment. They'd traded information many times and always argued about who went first. She decided. "Okay, but no details from your pen until Saturday, and no sooner. I've got her husband and family to think about." She lowered her voice. "Miss Kim Jennings, the general manager, discovered Bella Timbol's body in the laundry room. The responding officer, PC Jon Phoebe, reported a suspicious death. I attended the scene and confirmed his findings."

"Gawd this is juicy." Rodney whistled. "I can see the headline—*Posh Lass Topped in Rich Folks Care Home. Is Grandad the Deadly Killer?*" He rocked from side to side, unable to control his excitement. "Was she found spinning in a washing machine?"

"No."

"Thrashing in the tumble dryer?"

"Nah."

"Shame." His eyes narrowed. "Poison?"

"The labs are still running tests."

"What do you think?"

"Not poison."

He rocked sideways and rubbed his hands. "Don't suppose any of the old codgers are suspects?"

"We are not ruling anyone out at this stage."

His eyes lit. "Anyone in particular?"

"Too early."

He sighed and handed over the brown envelope.

Fenella opened it and began to read. When she finished she looked up, blinking. "Are you telling me Bella worked as a journalist?"

"She was hired back in the day when print newspapers were king. Got in through her connections. Not like me, I had to fight my way in and got tossed into the sewer where you have to run fast to keep ahead of the bleedin' rats."

"It must have been horrible for you." Fenella kept her face straight. "But you've outlasted the others and made it to King Rat."

"Trying to be funny?"

"You brought up the sewer."

"King Rat, eh?" He shrugged. "Intelligent animals. Sniff things out."

"You were talking about Bella Timbol."

"A wannabe journalist."

"What do you mean?"

"Fancy pants with connections. Makes me want to puke. I've got to work my fingers to the bone for a few scraps of meat and the likes of Bella Timbol dance into—"

"Spare me the lecture. Tell me about Bella."

Rodney pointed at the envelope. "Bella came on board as a food columnist. She wrote recipes made from local ingredients. Got quite a following and was promoted to lifestyle columnist which morphed into writing about local history and art." He shook his head. "Know how many times I've tried to get a gig like that?"

"You've kept count?"

He frowned. "And after all these years I'm still running, trying to keep one step ahead of the bleedin' pack. Think about it, I have to sniff out news for a living when the likes of Bella Timbol get to dine on fine food, play historian, visit art shows and then write about them at her leisure. I should be more bitter."

Rodney Rawlings could talk all day about the miseries of being a print journalist, getting more irate with each sentence. Fenella changed the subject. "Did you meet with Bella often at the newspaper?"

He blasted a wretched sound between his lips. "I'm not in her circle." Again he pointed at the brown envelope. "It is all in there. She left the *Westmorland News* a year ago. Cutbacks."

Fenella was beginning to question the usefulness of his information. "When was the last time you spoke with her?"

"That's the funny thing. She called a month ago and said she was working on something."

"Something?"

"Sensational." His lips curled in disgust. "I'd have fallen for it except she used the same trick on me before. When I snatched the bait, she said we could co-write a story about artists in Ambleside. Where the hell is the news in that?"

Fenella understood his frustration. She pulled out a copy of *Northworder*, flipping through the pages. "And what was the sensational story this time?"

He gave a nasty laugh. "I'm not that dumb, didn't bother to return her call. Waste of bleedin' time."

52

It was six in the evening and Fenella sensed the lack of energy the moment she entered the briefing room. It didn't help the cradle of doubt brewing in her stomach. She'd missed something but didn't know what.

A faint whiff of chemical air freshener mingled with the grilled onions, burgers and pizza from an earlier user of the room. The Victoria sponge cake on a tray by the tea urn was untouched. Dexter paced at the back of the room, head down. A relentless back and forth. Jones slumped against the wall sipping from an oversized mug of black coffee. His laptop, on the first row, waited with the lid shut. PC Beth Finn sat next to the laptop with her eyes half closed. PC Woods lolled in a chair on the back row and sipped from a mug of tea.

They look worn out.

And Fenella, too, felt the case weighing down her limbs. She turned her gaze to the enlarged photograph of Ann Crombie and her niece, Helen Grimes, at the gates of Buckingham Palace. The more she took in the details, the more she saw beyond the faded colours paling away into nothingness and glimpsed a joyful day now vanished in the past. They were aunt and niece, two friends, women, posing outside the Palace. Smiling, spirited and unaware of what the future held.

She turned from the whiteboard, disgusted by what had happened and pierced by a plague of self-doubt, but when she spoke she kept it upbeat. "PC Woods, any news on Kate Owen?"

He sat up straight. "We can't speak with her yet, ma'am. Doctor's orders. Tomorrow afternoon at the earliest."

"She is our priority." Fenella's gaze went back to the whiteboard. "Kate has a daughter, Skye. Any news on her whereabouts?"

Blank faces.

Fenella pinched the bridge of her nose. "Who is with Kate now?"

"PC Jake Kent took over from me, ma'am." PC Woods took a gulp of tea and belched. "When she wakes, we'll have answers."

The team murmured their agreement.

Fenella wasn't so sure and wanted to keep things moving. "We'll not wait for her to wake up. Any visitors?"

PC Woods shook his head. "Didn't see anyone."

"Anything unusual happen?"

Again he shook his head. "Quiet as a graveyard."

"Have a word with PC Jake Kent, see if he has anything to report. And find out if Kate Owen is in a relationship. If so, I want to speak with her partner."

Dexter spoke. "I've done a bit of background checking, guv. Kate Owen married a Mr Bart Owen. He's a nasty bit of work, got a record longer than my arm, mostly for stealing jewellery from widowers. When they didn't give it freely, he used force. The lout lives in Carlisle, but I haven't been able to track him down yet."

Fenella felt some of the weight lift from her shoulders. "Bring him in, put out an All-Points-Bulletin." Her gaze drifted to Jones. "What is the latest on the woman in the morgue?"

"Still waiting for a medical match of the blood and DNA, boss."

Fenella considered. "Ask around the village, see if you can get any video footage of the woman in the morgue." She had a niggling suspicion seeing the woman on the screen might shake something loose about her real identity. "Anything unusual turn up in her finances?"

Jones picked up his mug and took a quick sip. "She banked at the Port St Giles Building Society and paid most of her bills electronically. I've requested the last five years of statements along with those from the electric, gas and phone companies. Hope the data will be in my hands in a few days." He paused as though checking everyone in the room was listening. "There is one thing I've noticed about her building society statement."

"Go on, don't keep us in suspense." Fenella thought he was enjoying his moment in the spotlight, dragging out what he'd found so he'd get full credit. Still, she encouraged her team to talk while she took a background seat.

Dexter spoke before Jones continued. "Found strange payments going in, eh? Large dollops of cash? Ain't no surprise in that lad. Ain't no shock in that at all."

Jones blew air between his lips, deflated. "How'd you guess? She had a regular payment into her account of twenty-five thousand pounds every quarter. Like clockwork."

Dexter whistled. "Cash?"

Jones shook his head. "Electronic, from an investment bank in America, and here is the thing—most of the money was withdrawn in lump sums of two thousand three hundred and sixty-five pounds over the following two weeks. Cash."

Dexter whistled again. "What did she spend two grand a day on?"

Silence.

"That's a lot of doughnuts." This was PC Woods. Talk of money or food and he became instantly alert. "Can't see how she could spend that much on groceries so it must have been placed on the dogs or the horses. Wonder what she did with her winnings?"

Jones reviewed his notes. "No signs of cash being paid in by bookies. Only money being withdrawn but I've only got a year of data, she might have been on a losing streak."

Dexter shook his head. "She was an artist, lad, and I've seen what she painted. Must have been into them psychedelic drugs like that Belgian bloke, Henri Michaux. Saw one of his creations years ago in New York City, couldn't make head nor tail of it. Read one of his poems, too. Didn't have a clue what he was on about. They say he took some powerful pills."

Fenella had tried to pick her way through an anthology of Michaux's writings but gave up on page two. "Jones, ask around the pushers, see if our lady in the morgue was known, and scramble up some CCTV footage from the building society."

Jones drained the dregs from his mug and placed it on the tray next to the tea urn. "Boss, it is not a coincidence the unknown woman in the morgue and Kate Owen were wearing a nightdress. I've an idea or two I'm playing with." He waited a moment, looking around. "What if both women were members of some devilish cult? We should speak with the vicar. Satanic groups will be on his radar."

Silence.

Fenella expected Dexter to object, but at this stage, they were grasping at straws. "Follow up with the reverend and while you are at it, have a word with Miss Fish. She reported a stalker. A beefy man looking into her bedroom window. She'll respond well to you."

Dexter laughed. "Be careful, lad. I hear she's a handful."

"I'll go with him if you like, ma'am." This was PC Beth Finn.

Fenella smiled. "Aye, Miss Fish will like that." There was one other thing on her mind. She turned to Dexter. "Have another word with Helen Grimes, see what else you can find out."

Dexter had a way with women.

The ceiling lights hissed, flickered off then came back on with a soft hum. Fenella decided it was time to break the bad news. "The press has picked up on Bella Timbol's death."

Dexter groaned and trotted to the front of the room, sinking into a chair on the first row. PC Woods glanced around with a *told you so* smirk. "It'll be hell from here on in, ma'am. Sheer bleedin' hell."

PC Beth Finn scowled. "I didn't see any reporters hanging around outside the station."

Jones hustled to the front row, opened the lid of his laptop and began typing. After a few seconds, he looked up. "Nothing on social media or news sites, boss."

It was only Wednesday and Fenella was certain Rodney Rawlings would keep his word. "Our friend Mr Rodney Rawlings contacted me today while I was at Giles Rare Books Store. He is writing a story about Bella Timbol's murder. It breaks Saturday night and will be in the Sunday paper. An exclusive."

Another groan.

Fenella took out the brown envelope and waved it. "Rodney's done his research on Bella. This is quite a docket, seems she worked for the *Westmorland News*."

"As a journalist, guv?" This was Dexter.

"Aye, she joined as a food columnist and was promoted to the lifestyle column, then she moved to writing about local history and art. Bella left the newspaper a year ago due to cutbacks, but phoned Rodney Rawlings last month with a new story."

"About what, guv?" Dexter was back on his feet, rocking back and forth. Eager.

Fenella shrugged. "He never took her call. But I suspect it was why she was at Grange Hall Care Home dressed in a nurse's uniform. Any ideas?"

PC Beth Finn raised a hand. "Could it be to do with fraud? Professor Lee Coben was at the station recently, Bella might have spoken with him. Want me to check?"

Fenella thought it was a long shot, but wanted to be encouraging. "Aye, but drink two mugs of strong coffee first, they don't call him Robot Drone for nothing."

Everyone laughed.

The hiss of the tea urn lifted PC Woods to his feet. He tiptoed to the table at the back of the room, refilled his mug and stuffed two slices of Victoria sponge into his mouth, sighing in delight and then realising the entire room watched.

"Sorry, ma'am. Missed my lunch." He eyed another slice of cake. "These days they say butter and cream are very healthy."

He shuffled back to his chair and slumped into the seat. His face burnt bright with shame.

Fenella waited for thirty more seconds, watching him. "Now I have everyone's attention, we've got the green light to search the garden of Bede Thatch."

A cheer went up.

It was a decent request, from a small hunch and a gut feel, but the agonising wait had whipped up a storm of doubt because of the lack of evidence to go on. *Haste and enthusiasm are no way to run a case.* But she wanted to search Bede Thatch's garden, and she wanted news of any finds, and she wanted to know if it was the resting place of Ann Crombie. That was her motivation. So she could put the lass to rest and let Helen Grimes know they'd found Aunt Ann.

Fenella pointed at PC Woods. "I want you on the search team since you are familiar with the grounds. Roll call is at six tomorrow morning. Sergeant Waller's team."

Waller was a no-nonsense officer who'd served in the army.

"Thanks, ma'am." PC Woods didn't look thankful.

Dexter, grinning, slapped PC Woods on the back. "I ain't one for haunted houses, but if I was, I'd not want to dig with me shovel in Bede Thatch in case something nastier than Sergeant Waller leaps out."

Everyone laughed, including PC Woods. The merriment lifted the mood. Fenella encouraged laughter, even in the darkest days of an investigation.

"Have I missed anything?" Fenella scanned the room, every face bright. She waited ten seconds more, mind already on the evening at home with Eduardo and Nan. "Okay, I'll see you—"

The tea urn screeched with an enormous hiss then gurgled with an ungodly *plop-plop*. The door flew open. Superintendent Jeffery marched in. Mrs Soper, her assistant, hurried a pace behind. Next came Tess Allen, press communications officer, looking worried and harassed. Then came Dawn Margot followed by the camera woman and the sound engineer. It was the gleam on Jeffery's face that finally convinced Fenella of news. Bad news.

Jeffery stepped to the front of the room, arms swinging at her side. "Forgive the interruption, I hope I'm not disturbing things?"

"We were just leaving, ma'am." Fenella made a shooing motion to get the team to split. "On our way home."

Dexter was first to the door, but Jeffery raised both hands and turned to face the camera. "Wait a moment, please. I have some exciting news. Please take a seat."

They shuffled back to their seats.

Jeffery smiled. "We'll get to the good news in a moment. First, our press communications officer has an important message for your ears only."

Tess Allen stepped forward. "I'm getting soundings the news media are on the trail of Bella Timbol. I've also fielded a few questions on Ann Crombie's death. Nothing definite as yet, but both stories and their link are bound to break soon. Please keep your eyes open and your lips sealed until told otherwise. We must manage these deaths with care. If the press makes contact with you, pass them to me."

Fenella said nothing.

Jeffery moved in front of Tess. "I hope everyone got that message. Now for the good news. You may not have heard but I shall be involved in the filming of a documentary over the next few days, so Sunday best clothes around the station. I. . . we have an image to keep up. Questions?"

Dexter cleared his throat. "Any truth to the rumours Chief Constable Rae will visit the station tomorrow?"

Jeffery grinned, bearing wolfish teeth. "If he does so, I must be informed immediately. I will show him around. Anything else?"

No one spoke.

Jeffery turned to the camera and smiled. "You are dismissed."

53

Looking back, Fenella should have seen disaster coming. It was eight at night and the first scream of thunder echoed across the countryside. She pulled her car to a stop in the driveway outside her cottage on Cleaton Bluff.

In the summer months, she often spent a moment enjoying the majesty of the rolling hills, resplendent in foliage and bloom. A thrill she never tired of. A chance to *flip her switch* from work to family life.

She lowered the driver's side window. The breeze blustered inside carrying the tang of the sea. Faint against the rumbling thunder came the clatter of waves against the shore. Questions about Ann Crombie and Bella Timbol clattered too. A sorrowful tragedy of cruel horror which burrowed deep under her skin.

She took a deep breath, listening to the sounds of the countryside as dusk settled—a couple of bees flitting between the bushes, the cry of a gull overhead on its way back to the beach, the distant bleat of sheep; and as the shadows lengthened, the hoot of a barn owl and the chirp of swallows preparing to roost. All the while thunder grumbled, low and slow in the background.

Fenella was glad the day was drawing to a close, but

she sensed more bad things coming. All kinds of them. A flash of movement out of the corner of her eye caused her to turn. A fox morphed from the gloom. It remained perfectly still, watching the car. The amber eyes were bright and fiery, reminding her of embers. Campfire embers, and the brightness they emit at night.

If only she could see the link between Bella Timbol, Ann Crombie and the woman in the morgue. Clarity was what she needed. Then, at least, her fear of another death might recede. The fox scampered across the yard, low to the ground and disappeared into the bushes.

Fenella tapped a finger on the steering wheel. Tomorrow, early, she'd go for a jog along the beach. Right now, though, she needed to clear her mind. She never took work home. Rule number one of married life.

She opened her handbag, took out *Northworder* and flicked to the crossword puzzle she attempted earlier. *Five across, eight letters. The first letter begins with 'A': Steamed marmalade pudding is twice as nice for Napier's gran.* She puzzled over the answer without success.

It began to rain. She watched raindrops splatter against the car windows and pool on the gravel. The wind picked up, and she closed the driver-side window as a great sheet of soaking spray passed over the vehicle.

Finally, as the sky cleared, her mind emptied of all that had happened at work that day. She exited the car and hurried home.

54

Eduardo opened the door before Fenella was halfway across the yard. He stepped onto the porch, still limping from his twisted ankle and looking up at the thundering sky. "Here comes the love of my life." He held a pint mug of ale in each hand. "Poured and ready for you to devour."

Fenella took the mug and downed a long slug. "Whew, didn't know I needed that."

"Tough day?"

Murder wasn't a topic Fenella let cross the family threshold. She never discussed the job at home. Whatever hell tomorrow brought wasn't going to cast its shadow over tonight. "It is easy to forget about work when your hubby shows up on the doorstep with two mugs of ale."

At the mention of beer, Eduardo glanced over his shoulder back into the house. He gulped down a mouthful and then another, looking pleased with himself.

"Cheeky monkey." Nan came out onto the porch, an apron around her waist. "I asked the greedy bugger to pour me a drink, and he's out here with two."

Eduardo flashed a broad smile, and the rain stopped. He sniffed. "What you got cooking in the pot, smells great?"

"You won't get around me with that cheap trick." Nan

wagged a finger. "I'm wise to your sly charm. Ale is off the cards for you, doctor's orders."

Eduardo had visited a private practice run by Dr Frederic Jonas, who'd claimed to have worked on Harley Street and specialised in weight loss. Why Dr Jonas came to Cumbria to set up practice remained a mystery. And why he set up shop in Port St Giles was an even deeper mystery.

"The man's a quack." Eduardo took another gulp of ale. "I'm not convinced he even went to medical school in England. He sounds German."

Nan sniffed. "Oh, and so the man who draws comics for a living is also an expert on medical practice?"

"I knew he didn't like me the moment I stepped into his plush office and asked for a custard cream and he offered me a carrot instead." Eduardo's eyes went wide in mock horror. "That wild celery soup diet the medic has me on is a form of barbarism."

Nan looked out at the clearing skies. "Thank your lucky stars it is celery because it might have been the Breatharian diet. Nowt but sunlight and fresh air."

"Good God is that a thing?" Eduardo sounded astounded. "Nothing but fresh air?"

"Dr Jonas has written several books on its health benefits." Nan's eyes flashed with laughter only visible to Fenella. "He is a world expert. Guess what's next if celery soup doesn't shift the flab?"

Eduardo limped out into the yard and splashed through a puddle before turning to face Nan. "I renounce that quack as my medicine man and will seek another practitioner. In the meantime, I have to keep my energy levels up for the search." He took a long and joyful slug of ale. "I ought to expose the rascal for medical malpractice."

Nan grinned. "Telling a man with a pudding belly to eat less isn't medical malpractice. Especially when the pudding-bellied man asked the doctor how to lose weight in the first place. Don't come crying to me when the grandbairns call you Mr Dumpling."

Eduardo staggered in a circle, splashing rain water and grinning between gulps of ale. "They will be here this week-end. A crowd of pure mayhem."

Fenella burst out laughing. "Come on, let's get inside before the neighbours think all those lead pencils you use to draw have turned you mad."

She was looking forward to seeing the grandbairns and her children at the weekend, and catching up on family gossip.

After a shower, Fenella sat at the scrubbed pine table in the kitchen. "What's for dinner?"

"Think it is fish and chips." Eduardo sniffed, drained the last of his ale and looked at the stove. "Can't beat battered haddock."

"Well, you can't have any." Nan turned down the stove and moved to the sink. "I'll make a wild celery and olive oil salad for you. Might throw in a few sunflower seeds for protein and half a sliced onion. How does that sound?"

Eduardo scowled. "Think I'd rather have a bowl of fresh air. What are you having?"

"Me and Fen are having sweet and sour crispy cod with egg fried rice and steamed broccoli. Blackberry and apple cobbler with custard for pudding."

She went back to the stove and lifted the lid on a pot. A surge of sumptuous smells curled in the steam. She spooned out rice into a large bowl, then another for the broccoli and finally, a large dish for the sweet and sour. She placed the dishes of steaming food on a tray and came to the table.

"Serve yourself." Nan put the tray down. "And go easy, Mr Dumpling."

But Fenella wasn't sure Eduardo heard. He was already spooning food on his plate. Fenella joined him. They ate in silence, save for the slurping of ale and soft crunch of broccoli.

55

Some hours later, in the exact same place, Fenella's neck muscles would tighten in shock. It was eight in the morning and she stood by the gate of Bede Thatch watching the search team at work.

A silky sun splashed glitter across the wild garden—bindweed, nettles, brambles and thistles streaked in a fairy-tale glow. Sunshine glittered across the murk of the pond, dripping dabbles of light on the still water. A thin wind blew in a ceaseless whistle. At times it screeched with menace. At others, it cooed an apologetic lullaby.

And again Fenella was reminded of her Uncle Glen and his love for being outdoors. The breeze from the lake, he had told her years ago, carried the future with it, and if you paid attention, you'd see it before it arrived. But she didn't foresee his future. Her heart wept at what happened to him.

Shovels clattered against the soft earth. Police officers hurried about. PC Woods led a small team to the back of the fire-blackened shed. An energetic officer cut down weeds by the pond. Another prodded the silt with a pole. Careful and slow and thorough.

Even at this early hour, word had spread through the village. A small crowd assembled by a hawthorn bush shaded by a stand of ash trees. Fenella took each person in, capturing every detail. In an unfashionable green tracksuit complete with a matching striped headband, a fat man with a greedy face watched. His left hand clutched a pork-pie, his jaw working hard between bites. A stooped woman wearing a peach headscarf popped a stick of gum in her mouth and chewed. Then there was the young man in a white t-shirt with his arms wrapped around the shoulder of a twenty-something woman in a lime floral dress. Leaning against a tree trunk, a twig-thin woman with wild honey eyes prodded a scab on her chin.

They were quiet; that's what Fenella would remember most; as quiet as a midnight vigil. Two uniformed officers kept watch of the silent throng.

It occurred to Fenella she might have been reckless in ordering the search with nowt but her gut to go on. Was the madhouse of officers crawling over the overgrown property a waste of time? Had she got it wrong? The weight of it all suddenly pressed down, and she worked her jaw, grinding her teeth and massaging the knot of tension in her neck.

"If there is anything there, guv, the team will find it." Dexter leaned against the dry-stone wall, eyes never leaving the scene. "Reckon that pond holds dark secrets. They'll find something buried in the deep."

As the energetic officer continued to cut back the weeds, the shape of the pond became visible. It resembled an eye socket. Curved and dark and still. The stink of pond mud shimmered in the air—the whiff of a million dead things.

Fenella sucked in a breath through her teeth. "My

money's on PC Woods and the shed, but I'd not bet against that pond."

An officer trundled a cart loaded with green waders, nets and poles of all sizes. The wind whistled a haunting song shaking the branches of the trees. Overhead, a buzzard soared from the hills, gliding above the treetops. Fenella eyed the bird and thought of the missing woman, Ann Crombie, and she thought of the crimes that had taken place in Borrans Wood and she thought of the cold dank pond water. Lost in sad thoughts she dabbed her eyes with a tissue. Was a pile of rotting bones the very best she could expect?

Dexter sighed. "Guv, couldn't sleep last night for all the thinking and went to the hospital this morning. Nothing new on Kate Owen but she had a visitor." He paused as the officer with the pole edged around the pond and began prodding in a new spot. "Vicar Bill Kemp."

"Is she a member of his church?"

"Kate is a wild one, guv. Not the Sunday-school type."

Fenella turned her gaze from the activity to Dexter. "Might be doing his duty as a priest. Still, we'd best have another chat with him."

The officer with the pole was shouting. Two other officers hurried to his side. Fenella wanted to jog over to find out what the fuss was about but knew better than to poke her nose in. Her gaze drifted to the shed. PC Woods, shovel in hand, stooped to dig. Sergeant Waller barked orders. Another officer unrolled a mat and kneeled down to search in the long grass. A gust howled, stirring up a clump of dead leaves.

Whenever she turned to watch the crowd, their numbers

grew. They clustered behind blue and white police tape hastily strung between two ash trees. The hunched old woman in the peach headscarf shoved her way to the front. She pulled out a stick of gum and chewed, licking her lips as she watched. PC Sid Fenwick joined the officers. The dark circles around his hooded eyes were now midnight black. But never once did anyone try to break through the line. That soothed Fenella's nerves. Word hadn't spread to the press. Yet.

"Over here." The shout, from the officer with the pole by the pond, caused a flurry of activity.

Fenella leaned on the wall, holding her breath. It was all she could do not to clamber over the lichen-smeared stones and dash across the bindweeds to the pond.

Dexter rubbed his hands. "Think we should nip in and have a closer look, guv?"

"Nah, Sergeant Waller will blow a gasket if we inter-fere." She resigned herself to keeping her nose out. "We best wait. It's not our place to tell them what to do."

The officer with the pole put on a pair of wading boots and then made slow progress into the murky pond wa-ter. Another officer joined, wading out with careful steps. Fenella urged them on under her breath. She wasn't sure how long she watched before the shouting began.

"They've got something, guv, and it ain't a fish." Dex-ter's voice crackled with excitement. He pushed off the wall and paced.

The officers tugged at something under the water. They struggled.

Wrestling.

Pulling.

259

Heaving.

When the arm surfaced Fenella ran to the gate. A slick sheen of pond slime covered it, a pale green radiance under the brightening sun. The officers were tugging and pulling and grappling and hauling. She was about to enter the garden gate when the head emerged covered in glistening pondweed. She stopped, clapping a hand over her mouth.

"It's a mannequin, guv." Dexter huffed in disgust. "A bleedin' shop doll."

The officer raised the mannequin's head, its glass eyes peering skyward.

Everyone started yelling. Fenella at the officers to get a move on. Sergeant Waller telling her to keep off his patch. Dexter hustling along the garden path and telling Sergeant Waller to mind his tongue. And the crowd murmured at the madness of police officers squabbling. And they murmured at something else, too. Superintendent Jeffery, in full uniform, strode along the trail. Mrs Soper, Dawn Margot, the camerawoman and sound engineer hurried to keep up. Jones huffed at the back, late and carrying a large paper cup of coffee.

Fenella and Dexter retreated. Sergeant Waller cursed under his breath and strode off in the opposite direction. Neither wanted Jeffery to catch them in a dust-up.

Dawn Margot pointed to a hawthorn bush for a camera shot. Jeffery struck a pose. A tilt of the head. A wolfish smile. Forcing her carnivorous grin wider at Dawn Margot's urging. Eyes staring off into the distance. *Click. Click. Click.* More poses. More shots.

Fenella couldn't stand it. Even if she wanted to, she could no longer poke her nose in where it wasn't wanted.

"Going back to the village to have a coffee, want to join me?"

"No thanks, guv." Dexter lowered his voice. "Got a bet with Jones that Jeffery will steal the show and turn it into a fiasco. The lad thinks otherwise. Losing money is a good way for him to learn."

56

When the call that started the craziness came through, Fenella was sipping coffee and staring out the café window. Her elbows rested on the table and she was feeling pleased with herself for not ordering a giant scone. Her mobile phone rang with an enthusiastic tinkle—Dexter.

"News, guv. Big news."

He fell silent for a full minute and she strained her ears for the minutest detail. In the background, almost drowned out by excited chatter, she made out the voice of PC Woods. "Do what it takes Woods is what they call me." More voices. Sergeant Waller laughing and she picked out the word *rigour*. And then came the voice of Superintendent Jeffery, exaggerated and precise and full of importance, calling everyone together and making an announcement.

Dexter came back on the line. "A grave, guv. Behind the shed. PC Woods found it. Still digging."

Fenella jerked to her feet, phone glued to her ear, heading for the door, breaking into a run.

Exhilaration.

Revulsion.

Relief.

57

When Fenella arrived at Bede Thatch, the crowd had doubled in size. They mumbled in a wild chorus of excitement above the hiss of the breeze. They sensed from the swagger of the police officers something was up. Spades and shovels and poles and nets. It was obvious they'd found a body. Another corpse in that cursed house in Borrans Wood.

Then she saw them and a shard of ice slithered down her spine. Journalists. A huge rat pack of the buggers. They massed by the stone wall of Bede Thatch. The BBC were there. Everything live on breakfast telly. Cameras, lighting, microphones.

Fenella stared for a long while. *No way did they show up out of the blue.* Bewildered, she came to the grim conclusion that Jeffery had informed the press. *Might even have had them on standby.* Then she saw Tess Allen, the press communication officer, working the rat pack—nodding and smiling and shaking hands. *No accident, then.* It was a staged event to make Jeffery look good. *Didn't the boss say Chief Constable Rae might show up?*

Fenella turned back to face the crowd but a movement out of the corner of her eye caused her gaze to drift to the hills beyond Borrans Wood. On the crest of the trail, a sole figure in a pea-green duffle coat scurried. Rat fast. She couldn't tell from this distance, but she was sure Rodney Rawlings was cursing.

"This way, boss." Jones met her at the gate and pointed to the shed. "The grave is behind the burnt out shack."

58

Fenella stepped to the edge of the grave. She took in the narrowness of the plot, its depth and its length—less than five feet. The photograph of Helen Grimes with her aunt outside of Buckingham Palace flashed through her mind. Helen was less than five feet tall, her aunt much shorter. That made Ann Crombie no taller than a child. She stared at the deformed skeleton and her stomach flip-flopped.

Rib bones gleamed through the dark soil, bleached white. Fragments of brown cloth were visible, the remains of a sheet used to wrap the corpse. A dryness caught in her throat the instant she caught a glimpse of the pelvis. Wide. Very wide. Her gaze moved to the feet. They were still buried in soil but she made out a rag doll, brass key, faded brown leather cover of a bible, and blue vase. She edged around the pit, peering at the ragged brown cloth which covered the skull. The jaw was visible, projecting out through a tear. She edged further and took in the wall on the opposite side. An oversized crucifix, rusted with age, poked from the soil.

As she processed the scene, Fenella struggled to control the hollowness in her stomach. The bedroom in Bede Thatch had a huge crucifix on the wall. Coincidence? She searched the crucifix in the grave for details, checking them off against the cross in Bede Thatch—the agonised face of Christ, the twisted crown of thorns, the life-sized nails through the wrists. Coincidence dwindled to none. It was an exact copy in every detail, except the flakes of rust.

She stepped back, hands on hips, mind working through a blizzard of thoughts. She was about to say something when Superintendent Jeffery appeared and Mrs Soper waved everyone out of camera shot. Jeffery and Jeffery alone would claim the glory for the find. Her crowning moment, everyone in Cumbria watching on the telly, including, presumably, Chief Constable Rae.

Drawing back to the garden gate, Fenella gathered her team—Dexter, Jones and PC Woods.

"Do what it takes Woods is what they call me, ma'am." PC Woods had repeated that phrase so many times in the past hour it came out like a song. "You can count on me to do what it takes. Ace Woods has a nose like a bloodhound, always gets the job done."

Fenella didn't mind his boast, her attention was on Jeffery and the shed and the grave. A small grave. A child's grave with a deformed skeleton with bleached bones.

"It's her, isn't it?" This was Jones. "It's Ann Crombie. We've found her."

"I found her." PC Woods rocked back and forth. "Takes uniform to get the job done. We're the ones with street smarts. Wonder if I'll be asked to speak on the telly." He ran a hand through his hair. "They always speak with the person who found the body."

Ignoring him, Fenella's gaze bounced from Jeffery to the shed and the grave. Jeffery was jabbing and pointing and smiling her wolfish smile. Uniformed officers stood back. Someone had brought flasks of tea, and they were sipping from paper cups, relaxing.

Jones took out his phone. "Dr MacKay is on his way, boss. Here in five minutes." He put his phone away and pointed at the shed. "The person who set the shed on fire is the fiend who dug the grave. Let's hope forensics finds enough for us to nail the person. Must have been a man to dig that deep."

"Or a gang of folk, lad." This was Dexter, staring in the direction of the gravesite and shaking his head. "Saw a movie a while ago where an entire village turned on a lass. The local vicar led the mob. Cunning as foxes are village folk when they get upset."

Fenella massaged her neck and turned to the crowd. Their voices had fallen silent. Astounded. Transfixed. Resolute in their desire to see what would happen next. She recognised some of the faces. Miss Fish, rouge cheeks, pink lipstick, coin flat eyes, stood between a gaggle of white-haired men. On the far side and standing alone in the shade of an ash tree, Vicar Kemp tapped a finger on his oversized forehead. He saw her watching and stepped back into the shadows.

"It don't make no sense, guv." Dexter stared toward the shed; his face twisted in shock. "This whole case is lunacy. It don't smell good."

"Aye." Fenella understood what he meant but kept her eye on the crowd, taking in each face, committing them to memory. Something didn't sit right.

PC Woods, still grinning from ear to ear, couldn't help himself. "I suppose Ann Crombie was attacked in her house and the body dragged out here to be buried. Not that I'm a detective, mind you. She must have been terrified. Cruel brutality dished out on a completely helpless old lady and the monster had the cheek to bury her in her own yard. Astounding. Turns my stomach. But I did what it takes, ma'am. I found her."

And he was right in so many ways. There were a dozen reasons for delight. They had found the grave. They had found the body and forensics would soon find more clues. Still, an unsettling thought whirled at the back of Fenella's mind. Tiny at first and growing. A shadow of unease whose shape had not yet formed into words.

Dexter rubbed a hand over his neck. "A small grave, guv. Dug deep. Child-sized. I dunno, it smells like fish gone bad."

And now Fenella realised what was bothering her. Bothering Dexter, too. The shape and depth of the grave were wrong. Dexter was right. She would have mulled it over but for the arrival of Dr MacKay. "What trouble have you got for me this time Fenella?"

"A strange one that has me baffled." Fenella pointed at the shed.

Dr MacKay smiled. "I heard your people found a skeleton." His voice filled with enthusiasm. The man loved working with the dead. Obsessive. "Buried at the bottom of the garden. Man or woman?"

"Difficult for me to say. Wide pelvis." Fenella shrugged. "That is why we need you. Bones are tricky."

Dr MacKay glanced toward the shed. "Ah, I see the boss is here with the movies. Must be a biggie as she is wearing her official costume. Excuse me whilst I strut my stuff in front of the TV."

He hurried along the path to the shed with surprising speed. Jeffery greeted him with a wave and invited him onto her stage. The camera rolled. Dawn Margot shoved a microphone under his mouth. Fenella was too far away to hear what they were talking about.

With great fanfare, Dr MacKay bowed, grinning at the camera, then suited up, hood over his head, and skipped to the edge of the grave. He circled it twice, clockwise, his protective white suit catching the light so he gleamed like a ghost. He walked around the other way and then placed his hands on his hips. He stood still for a long while, a phantom hovering over a grave. Then he clambered down into the soft soil, vanishing like a ghost.

In that same instant, Fenella realised what else was bothering her. The grave site was pristine as though someone had made a promise to themselves to lay the bones to rest in a peaceful place. Her mouth dropped wide in startled horror. She staggered against the low stone wall, legs buckling in shock. It couldn't be, could it?

"Guv, you alright?" Dexter was at her side, steadying her with his arm.

"Oh God." Fenella clutched her head. "This is all wrong."

Before Dexter spoke again, an angry shout came from the grave. Dr MacKay dashed, phantom fast, back to Superintendent Jeffery. He tore off his protective hood and was shouting, giving a blow-by-blow account of what he'd found, arms waving and jabbing and pointing at Jeffery as if it were all her fault. "I'm no gold-braided officer of the law skilled in the art of policing but I can tell you her name. It is Bobo, and she was the beloved pet of the circus performer who built Bede Thatch. If I am not mistaken, Superintendent Jeffery, you have dug up the bones of an orangutan."

59

Fenella paced her small office in the Port St Giles police station, door closed, window open wide. The call from the duty sergeant, Len Moreland, requesting she return to the station did not come as a surprise. A restless wind howled through the room. The cord from the blind *clacked-clacked* against the glass. A few hours before, she had been wondering where in the garden of Bede Thatch they would find Ann Crombie's bones. Now she waited for another call she knew was coming. The tap on the door from Mrs Soper to go straight to Superintendent Jeffery's office.

What level of hades had she stepped in?

She wandered to her desk, took a gulp of lukewarm tea and flipped open the file on Bella Timbol. She was still reading an hour later, her mug of tea cold and the wind gusting through the open window.

Footsteps came from beyond the closed door. Voices travelled up from the courtyard. Fenella was oblivious to the world. She turned another page and read on, all the while thinking about the bones in the grave, Ann Crombie, Bella Timbol and Bobo the orangutan.

A siren sounded from the courtyard shattering her thoughts like splinters of glass. Frustrated, she paced to the window. The breeze pounded her face, warm with the hint of rain. Her team had scattered. PC Beth Finn was gathering information from the villagers. Jones was looking into the woman in the morgue's finances. Dexter and PC Woods remained at Bede Thatch. They had so many leads to follow and loose ends to tie up that the slow pace was fraying her nerves.

She should be there now, Ambleside, asking questions of the crowd gathered at Bede Thatch. She wanted to speak to Vicar Kemp about parishioners who might have a grudge against women. She wanted to be anywhere but waiting in her poky office for a knock on the door from Mrs Soper.

Then it came.

A knock.

The door opened.

PC Fay Bright, the family liaison officer, poked her head into the room. "Bede Thatch. It's not your fault, ma'am."

Before Fenella replied she was gone.

Her phone rang—Dexter.

"Guv, has the big boss called you in yet?"

"Nah."

There was a pause. "Want me to join you, guv? I can be at the station within the hour. I don't think you should take the—"

"Nope, you and the rest stay well away, got that?" No way would Fenella let the flack fall on her team. She ordered the dig. They found monkey bones. As simple as that. The blame lay squarely on her shoulders. She tilted her neck from side to side. "No point us both getting roasted like a pig on a spit."

"They'll continue the search until nightfall, guv." His words came out as though his throat was dry and the shock of the morning was still frozen in his windpipe. "Ain't found anything so far."

She imagined him with his mouth still gaped at the orangutan find and stifled a grin. "If anything is in that garden, Sergeant Waller and his team will find it." She fired off her words to boost his morale and her own. "I've confidence in him."

But she hated to admit the grim promise of finding Ann Crombie buried in the soft soil of the garden had faded to less than a hope. It would take a miracle now. Had she let her obsession with that overgrown garden lead her down a dead end?

Dexter cleared his throat. "If Ann Crombie ain't buried in the garden, she might be in the house. Under the floor-boards or stuffed in a wall." He paused and she could hear the puzzled hesitation in his voice. "Except the cottage has stone floors and the walls are solid brick. Still, it might be worth another look. We'll need another search warrant for the house."

Fenella imagined chaotic scenes as they searched the house. Camera's flashing. Journalists shouting. Villagers gathered close, the mumble of their voices like wasps about to sting. This time Jeffery would stay well clear. "I'm not Jeffery's favourite person right now, but I'll put in the request, see if I can ride out the boss's objections."

There was nothing from Dexter for a moment. "Jeffery ran straight to her bunker from Bede Thatch, guv. They say she is holed up in her office and on the phone. It don't bode well."

Fenella had heard the same rumour. What stench was Jeffery planning to unleash to deflect attention from her being at the centre of the Bede Thatch Fiasco beamed across the nation by the BBC? They didn't call her Teflon Jeffery for nowt.

A vein convulsed in Fenella's neck. "It will give us a breather, eh?"

"We need it, guv. I hear Jeffery had a chat with Chief Constable Rae and it weren't pretty. Crap hitting the fan and all that. No way for Jeffery to duck this one."

Another siren screamed from the courtyard. Tyres screeched as a patrol car sped away. It was none of Fenella's business but she couldn't help herself. "How much did you win from Jones?"

Dexter laughed. "He were screaming like a baby when he opened his wallet. Never seen so much dust between notes. I've donated the winnings to the Port St Giles Food Bank." His voice became serious. "Guess the boss thought a press conference at the grave site would explode her career into the stratosphere. But the news headlines will blast her with more stink than a broken sewer pipe. Feel sorry for Tess Allen, she'll get covered in it too. It's like a train wreck you can see about to happen. We'll have to jump fast to get out of the way. A moving target is hard to hit."

Fenella hung up. Dexter was right. Well, she wasn't about to wait for the fan to change direction and fling its vile load at her. When Mrs Soper visited, she'd be out. She slung her handbag over her shoulder. Time to visit the hospital and have a word with Kate Owen.

60

Kate's first conscious thought was for Skye. Was her daughter safe and well? She smelled fresh sheets and antiseptic, the strong tang of disinfectant and the sweet scent of vanilla. She tried her best to look around, and what she saw terrified her. A white tile ceiling, soulless cream walls and a shadow she could not make out. It was the beeping instruments out of her sight that scared her the most.

She was in a hospital room.

In a hospital bed.

Beep-beep-beep.

Then she sensed the tubes in her arms and snaking up her nose and freaked out. *Jesus Christ.* She tried to sit up, but a headache throbbed and every muscle ached.

Beep-beep-beep.

"Been waiting for you, luv. Are you awake?"

Kate tried to lift her head, but the effort was too much. Neither hands nor feet would move. She lay there helpless, blinking at the woman with shoulder-length grey hair smiling at her.

"I'm Fenella, Detective Inspector Sallow." She looked around. "You've got a posh ground floor room with French doors looking out on the gardens. Fancy, eh?"

The detective sat at the side of the bed, and a memory of that same face urging her to stay awake emerged from deep within Kate's brain cells. This was the woman in the woods who found her. This was the woman who helped.

The automatic air freshener spat out a hiss of vanilla scent.

Again, Kate tried to move. The pain was torrential. Even too sharp an inhale of breath sent lightning forks through her chest. With a slow movement of her jaw, she opened her mouth expecting more agony. When none came, she spoke. "Are you the one who saved me?"

"It was a team effort. You did the hard work."

"Can't move. Why?"

"The doctor says you've had a brutal shock. Not to worry, though, you are very strong and will do well. Do you remember what happened?"

Kate turned her head, gaze settling on the door. Faint footsteps hurried along the hall and she made out the mumble of voices. She did not speak.

"Don't worry, you are safe here." The detective winked. "We've put a police officer outside the door so no one can come in to hurt you."

Kate swallowed. "My daughter, is Skye here?"

The detective's eyes shifted, and she leaned forward to adjust the pillow. "I'll not beat about the bush. We've no idea where the lass is."

"Moved out." Kate let out a huge cough. It blasted her ribs with murderous pain. With great effort, she went on. "Carlisle."

"Your daughter has moved to Carlisle?"

"Yes."

"Is that where her dad lives?" The detective's gaze sharpened. "Has Skye moved in with her dad?"

Kate felt feverish, and the question sickened her. She'd struggled so hard to bring Skye up the right way without the help of her dad. Never once did that violent man lift a finger to contribute, except for the night Skye was conceived. And now her baby had moved in with a middle-aged car salesman. Obese, no doubt. A heart-crushing abomination.

Kate's jaw opened and closed then opened. "She has moved in with her boyfriend." Her voice came out unmistakable and clear. She didn't want to say anything else. *Christ*, how she wanted to keep this secret to herself, but she couldn't. It was driving her berserk. She wanted the police to track down Skye and bring her to her bedside. "Skye has run off with an older man who sells used cars. She is still at school. I don't approve."

The detective said nothing.

Kate wanted to swear. How had she made such a terrible mess of things? In the end, Skye leaving home came as no shock. It had simmered below the surface for years. She knew the day would come, had tried to push it off, to believe they'd be a family with Ken Ashworth as the dad. Not happening now. Or ever. Never.

The detective broke into her sorrowful thoughts. "Tell me about the places you've worked."

"I've been at the pub in the village for years."

"And before that?"

"Why?"

"Sometimes old workmates bear a grudge. We'd like to speak with them."

Kate told her and when she finished sighed. "Not much

of a resume is it?"

Fenella said nothing.

"Might go back to college when I'm well. There are loads of mature students these days." Kate's voice brightened. "Something to do with computers. I hear it pays well and I..."

A glob of phlegm formed in her throat and she couldn't go on. She let loose a giant cough which racked her body and sent thundering pain through her ribs. She'd never experienced such agony. It twisted its ragged knife and twisted again. She went limp and felt totally useless.

The detective took her hand. "The medics have done a brilliant job. You will soon be on the mend. And don't worry, we'll track down Skye. I'm sure she'll come running once we tell her what has happened." The detective stopped and stared with the saddest eyes Kate had ever seen. "Tell me what happened, pet. Why were you in Borrans Wood in your nightdress?"

Kate recalled the night with vivid clarity—her fermenting rage fuelled by ale and gin; the smirk on Mrs Fowler's face as the woman told her about Skye falling for a balding car salesman; she even recalled her lunatic decision to leave the house in the dead of night to seek out the pub landlord. *What the hell was I thinking?*

She blinked and said nothing.

From the hallway came the clatter of feet and the squeal of the wheels of a trolley. Someone shouted *Goddammit.* Someone else howled in pain. What was going on in the hallway beyond the closed door? Kate tilted her head to hear better but a shard of pain stopped her.

The detective leaned forward. "I'm here for you. I'm

278

listening. What happened?"

The formidable gaze of the detective set off a windstorm of acid in Kate's stomach. She didn't want the woman to know she'd been at the ale and the gin bottle all night long. Most of all, she didn't want the detective to know she was drunk when she left the house and made a wrong turn on her way to argue with the pub landlord about losing her job. She couldn't explain why she'd turned the wrong way and ended up in Borrans Wood. She thought about Ken in his bright clothes and skinny blue jeans and she wanted to cry. She couldn't reveal what happened last night. She just couldn't.

She swallowed. "I don't know."

"The doctor says you were drinking."

"I don't remember."

"Ale and gin and some food, baked beans. Do you remember that?"

"It's a blur."

"Who were you meeting in the woods?"

"I wasn't meeting anyone."

"What were you doing there?"

"I got lost in the dark."

"Where were you going?"

"I remember being at home and then I was here."

"Why were you drinking?"

"Hard day."

"Because of Skye?"

"Because of life."

"Still, ale and half a bottle of gin is a lot to put away."

"It was on hand. I must have overdone it." Oh God, she couldn't admit the truth. She just couldn't. "I don't know why I left the house. I didn't know where I was going. I don't know what happened."

"Do you have a boyfriend?"

"Why?"

"What's his name?"

"I. . . er. . . don't have a boyfriend."

The detective's eyebrows drew into a frown, then her face morphed to an earnest expression and she spoke in the soft reverence of a priest. "What do you recall of last night when you left home?"

"Nothing."

"Were you followed?"

"Maybe."

"Man or woman?"

"I can't say."

"One person or many?"

"My memory feels like it's been hacked and the brain cells taken away. I don't recall anything. Nothing."

The detective carried on as if she didn't hear the reply. "Did you recognise the person who followed you?"

"I don't know that I was followed."

"Were you followed by your boyfriend?"

"I'm a single mam."

"Was the person known to you?"

"No."

"Who was it?"

"Last night is a blank."

The detective paused for a long moment, then spoke in a motherly voice. "Please think about it. We will keep you safe. Now, what is the name of your boyfriend?"

Kate closed her eyes and tried to look like she was thinking. When they opened, she had her plan. "I'm single with a child to raise. Oh God, why am I always ruining everything? I've done that my entire life. Now my daughter has gone and I'm in the hospital and trying to understand why. It sounds so ridiculous that it has me in a kind of shock. Like a blast from a bomb which blinds you for an instant. I can't think. Is this normal? "

"Aye, pet. That's normal."

"I'm so sorry your visit has been a complete waste of time. I don't remember anything. I saw no one. Nothing."

The detective was silent for a long while. "Miss Owen, never feel bad about wasting my time. I came here hoping for answers but more importantly, to see how you were doing with my own eyes. I get reports but there's nowt like meeting a person face to face. We'll get to the bottom of what happened. Police officers are everywhere."

The detective stood and Kate saw a flicker of something moving in the woman's eyes. "Is there anyone I should notify?"

"Tell Ken."

"Ken?" The detective's lips quirked at the corners. "What is his surname?"

"Ashworth. He lives in the village. Tell him I'm fine. He'll be worried sick. He loves me."

61

When Fenella returned to the Port St Giles police station, she walked through the public reception area in hopes of a chat and an update on any station gossip.

The flooring was worn and in need of repair. Grey and white linoleum matched the plastic chairs bolted to the floor. Beige paint peeled from the walls and the room smelled of sweat, stale coffee and disinfectant. A man in a blue t-shirt and stained jeans sprawled across two chairs with his eyes closed. His long grey hair and shaggy beard reminded her of a wizard. She'd seen him in the town market begging. He let out a snore and turned so his back was to the counter, passed gas and sighed. A foul stench wafted on an invisible cloud.

The duty sergeant waved Fenella to the counter. "It's all over the news media, ma'am."

She'd worked with Len Moreland for years, even babysat his bairns when they were small. If anything was happening in the station, he knew about it. He'd tell her the latest on Superintendent Jeffery.

She massaged her neck. "Are you talking about Bede Thatch?"

"Yes, ma'am."

He beckoned her closer and tapped on his keyboard then turned the screen—the *Westmorland News* website. Fenella leaned in to read the headline: POLICE *MONKEY BUSINESS COSTS TAXPAYERS BIG TIME.*

Underneath was a grim photo of Superintendent Jeffery. She stood by the shed in Bede Thatch looking panicked and shocked and confused.

Fenella read the screen:

Outraged Ambleside villagers woke to an army of police marching through their streets. The officers swarmed in the garden of a quaint cottage known by locals as Bede Thatch and began to dig. They were searching for the body of a missing local woman, unnamed.

Rodney Rawlings was ruthless. His paragraphs dripped with rage. Each word was executed with the expert precision of a man about to wield a knife. Fenella read on:

A shiver of excitement crackled through the onlookers. It turned to stunned shock with the discovery of a shallow grave. PC Woods, a stout officer from Port St Giles, was ordered to dig. Within ten minutes a fearful cry escaped his throat. "Bones. I've found bones."

Fenella paused. Len was glued to the screen; his eyes bright. *It's like he's watching a blockbuster show on the telly and he can't drag his eyes from the screen.* She, too, was eager to read on:

Superintendent Jeffery, who was on site, called an instant press conference. Her smug face soured into a disgusted snarl when the pathologist relayed his find. "Monkey bones" belonging to Bobo, an orangutan buried years ago by its owner. Superintendent Jeffery claimed...

Fenella straightened and massaged her neck. "Prefer it

when Rodney Rawlings is on our side."

Len clicked his teeth. "He's like an assassin with a pen. What'd you do to upset him?"

Fenella changed the subject. "Any news on Jeffery?"

"Still in her office." Len picked up a pen and jabbed it at the ceiling. "The whole station is holding its breath. God only knows what monstrous pile of doom will come our way as a result of this. Politicians. Board members. London. Everyone's been calling Jeffery's office. Mrs Soper says it's mayhem."

Fenella said nothing.

The homeless man let out another blast of gas. Long and slow and bubbly.

Len waved a hand in front of his nose. "I fear the worst, ma'am. The station's at an all-time low. There'll be a shake-up for sure. A new broom and all that." He gazed at Fenella with sad eyes. "Jeffery's ruined but she won't go down without sinking the ship. Take my advice, ma'am, and get a union official to join you when you are called to the dragon's lair. Don't go in there alone, and when you do go in, say nothing. This one is heading for the cold case files."

62

Fenella strolled to the canteen for a mug of black coffee and wandered back to her office. She sniffed the sharp tang of the Cumbria Constabulary brew hoping it would keep her alert. She sent a text message to Jones to have a word with Ken Ashworth and for a while listened to the sounds of the station settling down for the evening—a siren blasted on its way to a call, the hum of a vacuum cleaner, a woman laughing from the hallway. But now, as she read, she heard nothing, seeing only black words and grim photographs. A jumble like scattered puzzle pieces.

She went over the details of each death, intrigue singing a lullaby of hope into the dark recesses of her mind. The woman in the morgue first. Then Bella Timbol. Last, she reviewed the notes on Kate Owen. She read and reread, each time picking at a loose thread and puzzling over what it meant. Then she focused on connecting the dots into a meaningful shape. But her mind kept going back to Bobo's bones and Jeffery's news conference fiasco.

After an hour of getting nowhere, she glanced at her phone. Nothing from Dexter or Jones or PC Beth Finn or PC Woods. She turned to her computer and scoured the headlines. Nowt but Bobo and Jeffery's stunned photograph. Everywhere.

She twirled a finger around a lock of hair, flicked off the news sites and returned to the files. Her phone rang—Dexter.

"Guv, I spoke with Helen Grimes and she told me her aunt had a pension from her deceased husband, paid in once a quarter. She didn't know the exact amount, but said it was large as he worked as a banker on Wall Street. I reckon it tallies with the payments we saw coming from America." He paused and there was something about the way that he did so that made Fenella instantly alert. "Bede Thatch belongs to Helen Grimes, guv. She bought it as a gift for her aunt to live in. Now she is asking when she can move in."

That surprised Fenella. She thought about it for a moment. "Superintendent Jeffery's call."

"I know guv. Mrs Grimes has been in touch with her. Guess she'll get the green light soon given the find in her..."

His words fell away into a silent void. The frantic search of the garden of Bede Thatch and the humiliating find of Bobo's bones hung like a bad stink in everyone's nostrils. Fenella tried not to let the failure take over her mind but feared she'd already succumbed. How had she got it so wrong?

A shout came from the courtyard below followed by a burst of laughter. The growl of a car engine screamed to life and a moment later came the screech of tyres. Life carried on at the Port St Giles police station despite the shroud of gloom.

Dexter was still talking. "Guv, I'm hearing news from

the station and it ain't good. Jeffery is in a corner and swinging to get out. Your neck is on the line. I'm going with you when you enter her office."

He hung up before Fenella replied. She stared at her phone for a long while wondering whether to send a text message or call him back. In the end, she did neither. Even if she ordered him away, he'd show up.

She needed a new plan and fretted for several minutes still convinced the key to the deaths lay inside the walls of the isolated cottage or buried deep in the overgrown garden. She pulled out her phone and gazed at the image of the handwriting scrawled on the back of the Giles Rare Books Store till receipt—*Mail Benny Label. Okay?*

Maybe the answer lay in those scrawled words. Or maybe not. Maybe it was another dead-end track. At any rate, there were more questions and no answers. She forced herself back to the files. Within fifteen minutes her mind settled on a single question. One she'd asked before without an answer. Why was Bella Timbol killed in the laundry room at Grange Hall? What was she doing there? PC Beth Finn had suggested fraud. Fenella considered that for a long while. *Fraud, eh?*

She glanced at the clock on her phone, saw it was after five and wondered if she should make the call. *No, this kind of thing is best done in person.*

63

Even though the blinds shut out all daylight, Fenella made out the furnishings of the room—oak bookcases lining the walls and a round table littered with handwritten pages. The smoky seasoning of cigars and pine and cedar wood hung in the air. An orange glow from a banker's lamp cast shadows across Professor Lee Coben's face.

His bare feet rested on the cherry wood desk, and he wore a red shirt open at the collar and brown cord trousers. He read from a report bound in grey leather and grunted with contentment.

Fenella hesitated, eyes adjusting to the gloom and trying to banish the name *Robot Drone* from her brain cells. A dull lecture on balancing the ledger was not what she came to his private study for, and she planned to keep her chat heartbeat brief.

Professor Coben looked up, rose and came toward her, his hand extended. "Come in, Inspector Sallow." A tremendous smile stretched from ear to ear on his hairless egg-shaped face. "Delighted to see you."

When she heard the metallic grate in his voice, she wanted to run. The glint of his teeth unnerved her. *He thinks I'm here about his work as a civilian advisor and is looking forward to a four-hour chat.* "I can tell you are busy and won't take much of your time." Fenella nodded at the huge grey report. "Busy days, eh?"

"Oh this?" He waved the file. "I'm reading about a case where thousands went missing from a care home in Carlisle. Insane, isn't it? Criminal accounting is everywhere, and I'm doing my best to thwart it. Many people don't know that life itself is captured in the accounting ledger. It is through the careful review of digits and accurate reconciliation that we can breathe. Our world would be in chaos without it. Even the Babylonians kept accurate books. I'm pondering a research paper on the issue, tossing it over in my mind."

His voice, monotonous and robotic was already grating her nerves.

Fenella snatched a furtive glance at the door. "I'll not stay long."

"Nonsense." He waved her to a chair and returned to his side of the desk. "Are you here to discuss my input into your strategic plan? I've the whole evening free and have written extensive notes which we can go over."

There was no point beating about the bush. She tried not to sound too happy. "Nah, Superintendent Jeffery shelved it. Her priorities have changed."

"I see..." He stood and walked across the room to the bookshelf, stared at it for a moment and went to the window. "We have a wonderful view from here."

Fenella wasn't sure what he was looking at. Unless he had X-ray vision, there was nowt to see but shuttered blinds. She set her handbag on the desk, folded her arms and waited. She was good at the wait.

Professor Coben turned. "You are not here about my

civilian advisor role?"

"Nope."

"We are not, as it were, on the meter, then?"

"Professor Coben, I'm here to pick your brains on a case I'm working on."

He ran a hand over his chin, stroking it as though it held a beard. "Ah, so we are on the meter?"

"Think of my visit like a bite of cheese in the supermarket."

"Cheese?"

"They give you a free nibble in the hopes you'll get hooked and buy a big slab. I won't take up much of your time, only a nibble."

He laughed and for the first time sounded almost human. "Very well Inspector, but please report back my cooperation to Superintendent Jeffery. It is she who holds the purse strings, isn't it?"

Fenella said nothing and fought the urge to tell him to sit down. She wanted her eyes on his face as he replied to her questions. She didn't know why, but it struck her as important.

He turned back to the window, his gaze on the drawn blinds. "Fire away."

"Come and sit, it's no fun speaking to a shadow."

His left hand flew upward, grasped the cord on the blinds and twisted. Brilliant sunlight flooded the room, harsh and flickering with a late afternoon bonfire glow.

"Much better, don't you think, Inspector Sallow?" He returned to the desk and settled himself down. "Now, your cheese?"

Fenella decided to take her time and warm him up with

some general questions. "Didn't realise the university had a campus in Ambleside."

Professor Coben spread his hands on the desk. "It began with Charlotte Mason's cottage. She called it her House of Education and opened it over a hundred years ago."

"Ah, so the buildings are around the same age as Bede Thatch?"

"Pardon?"

"Bede Thatch, you've heard of it?"

Professor Coben's left hand dipped below the desk and a drawer opened and closed. When his hand reappeared, it clutched a blue handkerchief with white petals stitched in the corners. "A terrible business."

"Did you know the woman who lived in the cottage?"

"Ann Crombie?"

"Aye, were you and she friends?"

He folded the handkerchief twice, then wiped his bottom lip. "Why do you ask?"

Fenella watched, riveted. "We are trying to build a picture of the woman's life. Did you know her?"

His face paled two shades to the colour of an eggshell. Two dark pinpricks stared at her. Wary. "This is insane, I thought you had accounting questions and now you switch bait and ask about Ann Crombie."

"I'm just ticking a box." Fenella flashed a smile. "So, you did know her?"

"She was an important local artist, a visionary in many ways. I'm horrified at the savage nature of her death. Beheaded, isn't that so?"

Fenella said nothing.

A clock chimed in some distant room.

The colour was coming back to Professor Coben's face and so was the drone in his voice. "Ann Crombie was a wonderful artist and I wish she'd survived to reach her full potential." His eyebrows furrowed. "She had an imagination very few are blessed to possess. A creative genius who came out late in her life. Alas, it never got to fully blossom."

Fenella saw a look of admiration on his face. He was an Ann Crombie worshipper. "Tell me, did you view her latest creation?"

"No, no. But I bid for one which recently came on the market, lost out to a medical man; a pathologist."

"I hear it sold for a pretty penny. You'd have had to use your savings, eh?"

He sighed, picked up the handkerchief and again dabbed his lower lip. "I found Ann's work fascinating and wanted an original for my own pleasure. I'd even marked out a spot on the wall. I'm a big fan of local history and preserving the natural landscape. Ann shared my concerns for the countryside and captured them in her paintings. Not a day goes by when I don't walk in the campus nature reserve and reflect on Ann's work." He paused, clearing his throat and looking longingly at the cigar box on his desk. "The nature reserve is gorgeous at dawn and dusk with a quiet smoke. That is where I first met Ann. I found her painting by a brook. There is a trail that leads from the nature reserve to Borrans Wood and Bede Thatch."

"Do you know if she had a boyfriend?"

He glanced around the room with the nervous twitch of a cigarette smoker. His hand went to the cigar box. "Ann's boyfriend?"

"I want to know his name."

He glanced at Fenella and he glanced at the cigar box and his hand dropped to the desk. He sighed. "I don't know."

"But you must have seen or heard something?"

"My interest is in the landscape and old buildings, not so good on the relationship side." Again his eyes slid to the cigar box. "Did you know Bede Thatch is nowhere near the oldest building in the village? They knocked up Bridge House in the 17th century. It spans the river Rothay. Old Gabriel still lives there."

"Who is he?"

"I wouldn't have known myself except I'm an accountant and Old Gabriel was a notorious gambler."

"Was? I thought you said he still lives there."

Professor Coben grinned. "Old Gabriel lost his hand in a game of dice, then gambled away his soul in a card game. He became a monk soon after and died begging God for his soul back." His gaze went back to the window. "At night, in Bridge House, you can sometimes hear the click of rolling dice and the wail of Old Gabriel. Some even say it is Old Gabriel that wanders Borrans Wood at night muttering in a strange tongue as a church bell tolls. The monk with no face. The monk who warns of coming death."

"Oh aye, and for a minute there you had me." Fenella took a heartbeat to ask her next question. "When was the last time you visited Bede Thatch?"

"Not since the insane death of Ann. Before that, once or twice a month on my walk through Borrans Wood. It's a long walk, stretches the legs. Would you like a cup of tea? I have some rather fine custard creams."

Fenella thought his behaviour eccentric but nodded and

he rose and left the room. His answers gave her plenty to mull over. He didn't strike her as a crackpot, just weird in the strange way of academics. Still, she sent a text message to Jones to run a background check, and another to Dexter to see if he'd heard anything odd about the professor on the grapevine. Then she opened the lid of the cigar box, peered inside and closed the lid.

So this is where he keeps his hoard of marijuana.

Professor Coben returned with a stainless-steel teapot, two mugs and a plate filled with custard creams. He was humming to himself, mouthing an unspoken song. He placed the food on his desk and returned to his chair.

"Nicked them from Rigg Cottage, that's the Student Union. I sneak a few away when I get the munchies. You won't tell anyone, will you?"

They slurped their tea and ate the custard creams in silence for a few minutes. Fenella decided to stick to the original reason for her visit. *Focus on fraud at Grange Hall.* She placed her mug on the desk. "Don't suppose you knew Bella Timbol?"

"Of course, she is a huge donor to the university. My job here is a result of Timbol family generosity." He stuffed a whole biscuit into his mouth and munched for several long seconds. "I've had nightmares she'd pull her funding and I'd be out on the dole. To be unemployed isn't easy these days, the market for academics has dried up. That's why I do a spot of consulting on the side. If this job goes, I've still got some income."

Fenella eyed the last biscuit and took it. "You've made quite an impression on Superintendent Jeffery, congratulations. The police can always use fraud experts."

No harm in buttering him up a bit, he looked the type to enjoy it, and she wanted to loosen his tongue, get him speaking freely.

He jabbed a finger at the ceiling, eggy face bright and pompous. "Theft from our elderly community is on the rise, I need not tell you that. Care homes are notorious for bad accounting practices which leave them open to..."

He spoke for ten minutes without drawing a breath before Fenella raised a hand. "I'm interested in Grange Hall Care Home."

"Grange Hall?" He put the mug to his lips and gave it a violent tilt. "Yeah, I've seen the place. Posh."

There was something he was hiding. "How familiar are you with it?"

"Is this off the record?"

"Aye."

"Senior management called me in to audit the books."

Bingo! Fenella felt like she was on the right path now. "Were they concerned about fraud?"

He shrugged. "The Board brought me in as a hygiene check."

"Hygiene check?"

"To assess if they are doing things by the book." He spoke with an air of great importance. "Well-run financial operations welcome the independent audit of their books." His gaze drifted off into the distance and the drone returned to his voice. "In 1922 when Westminster..."

The way he blathered was maddening. He drew out his words, syllable by syllable. Unhurried and slow. Fenella wanted to know if he had found any evidence of someone cooking the books. She didn't want a lecture on the history of audit. She let him run on for thirty seconds more.

"... passed an act of parliament in the summer of 1952—"

"What did you find?"

His eyes slid back to the present. "Find?"

"At Grange Hall Care home."

"I was getting to that."

"You were in 1952."

"Was I?"

"Yes."

"I'll get straight to the point, then." He sniffed. "Grange Hall Care Home?"

"Yes?"

"In Westpond, Port St Giles?"

"Aye."

He wrinkled his nose. "I found nothing illicit and gave them a clean bill of health."

64

Fenella stared at Professor Lee Coben for a full thirty seconds.

"Nothing at all?"

"Not a whiff of corruption. Not a digit out of place. In fact, I was so concerned at how clean their books were that I urged them to bring in an independent firm to check my work. It's not unheard of for academics to get it wrong. They brought in Henry, Harvey and Clark from Carlisle. Have you heard of them?"

"Nah. What did they find?"

"Same as me. Nothing. I commended the Grange Hall Board for their proactive approach in bringing me in. They responded with a contract to audit their business every other year. A win-win, don't you think?"

That gave Fenella much to think about. Her visit had been a waste of time. She was about to stand when a soft knock sounded on the door.

A twig-thin woman with wild honey eyes hovered in the doorway. She reeked of weed and scratched her neck then picked at a scab on her chin, flicking it into the room.

Professor Coben stood. "Ellie, this is Detective Inspector Sallow."

The woman shuffled back out the door, slamming it shut.

Professor Coben sighed and eased back into his seat. "Ellie is one of my research students."

"Oh aye?" Fenella sniffed. "The lass is as high as a kite."

"I take what help comes my way and am grateful for it." Professor Coben smiled. "When Ellie is not at one of those crazy all-night raves, drinking and smoking and injecting, she is a genius. I had her research the controversy over Adam Humphrey's will."

"The circus man who built Bede Thatch?"

He nodded. "Mr Humphrey stated Bede Thatch was to remain in its original state and all redecoration was to be in the original style. Inside, the furniture is rather old-fashioned. There is even a huge oak Victorian wardrobe large enough to hide a very fat man, an iron-framed bed and a giant crucifix on the wall. All originals. It's like visiting a museum."

He fell silent, the faraway look returning to his eyes. Once again, Fenella became aware of the savoury shroud which cloaked the room.

Professor Coben sighed. "Mr Humphrey was religious and sinful in equal measure. What man makes his home with a female orangutan?"

Fenella didn't know. Neither did she feel it was her place to respond. She changed direction. "Tell me about Mr Humphrey."

"He was quite a character, enjoyed his drink, and parties, and went to regular confessional with the priest each Monday morning." Professor Coben picked up the handkerchief and placed it back in the drawer. "Adam Humphrey went quite mad when Bobo died, and insisted on having the local priest conduct the burial. After, he let the garden go and festered in mourning. There were reports of terrible screams late at night. The local bobby visited on occasion but didn't make an official report. A complete mental breakdown is what we might call it today, back then locals said he'd gone monkey mad. And worst of all, after Mr Humphrey's death, his young daughter was left penniless and evicted from the house."

"He had a daughter?"

"Quite late in life, although he never married and there are no records of the mother's name or the child's birthdate on parish records. She looked nothing like him, dark and hairy and short, even for a girl. I've read his occasional diary; the child appears with no explanation of where she came from. Ellie, my research assistant has been trying to track down more details, alas, without much success." He leaned back in his chair and frowned. "Mr Humphrey used to dress the poor girl in monk's robes and make her march up and down the trail on Sunday carrying a cross. He said it was penance for man's sins. Like I said, he went quite mad after Bobo's death."

Fenella gave a furtive glance at the door. She didn't think he had much more to say and wanted to be on her way. But she had one final question. "What happened to the bairn?"

"Ended up in a care home, got fostered out a few times but she was too wild a thing for ordinary carers."

Fenella took out her notebook and began to write. "Is she still alive?"

"Oh yes, I've interviewed Thea Humphrey many times. She's a bit rough around the gills, but once you see through the grizzle, she's all human. Must be in her sixties now and lives in a council flat in Barrow-in-Furness."

65

Kate awoke with a start to the smell of antiseptic and a distinct lemony scent. The fitful dream had terrified her. Something to do with a medieval dungeon slowly filling with the giant weeping tears of a bright red balloon. She had drifted off while staring at the white-tiled ceiling and supposed the cracks between the tiles, which reminded her of a castle wall, had triggered the nightmare.

She lay quite still for several minutes waiting for the images to fade and listening to the endless *beep-beep* of a medical device. Far out in the hallway came the mumble of frantic voices and the *clack-clack-clack* of trolley wheels clattering between wards.

The drugs made her head foggy, but she sensed pain waiting to strike the moment she moved, so she kept her eyes shut and focused on her breaths.

A soft sigh from the foot of the bed startled her and for a moment she was back in Borrans Wood, in the dead of night with only her coat and negligée and hiding between the trembling brambles, staring at the figure in the skinny blue jeans. The blue jeans danced and shimmered and twirled, then they raced toward the shivering brambles.

Her eyes snapped open.

She wasn't in Borrans Wood.

She was in a hospital room with a police officer outside to stop anyone coming in who might hurt her.

The sigh came again but the urge to jerk her neck to look was stifled by the fear of more pain. A thin spark of dread began to crawl from her stomach. *Oh Jesus God, not that detective woman again.* If she was back so soon, it was with bad news. And the only news Kate cared about was Skye. *Sweet Jesus, please let her be well.*

"Awake now?"

The voice came from far down beyond the foot of the bed. Kate struggled to turn her head to get a better look. A dark shadow stood by the open French doors. It wasn't the woman detective. Nor a nurse. She blinked, clearing the haze from her mind.

It was a man.

The figure tiptoed toward the bed; feet as quiet as a cat stalking a mouse. "Been waiting for you, Sweetmeat."

She eased her head to the left and saw Ken Ashworth standing at the foot of the bed. He held a single flower stem in his left hand. A rose with soft white petals. It caught the thin ceiling light so the petals glowed with a ghostly luminance.

And his face, dear Lord, was as pale as bleached bone. Even his spiked black hair appeared greyish. Only the gold stud in his nose retained its gleam.

He raised a finger to his lips. "Had to sneak around the back to get in. There is a policeman at the front." He flashed an impish grin. The grin she found irresistible. "This is for you."

An unbelievable thrill surged through Kate. Her entire

body trembled. Her heart pumped blood with tremendous speed. The urge to weep almost overcame her. Ken was here to see her. *Oh God, I must look a mess, shrivelled and curled on the bed.* Somehow she struggled up on her elbows ignoring the agony which screamed in her tendons.

Ken placed the rose on the bed and bent to kiss her. When he straightened, he ran a hand through his hair. "You look terrible."

"I'm bulletproof."

He cast a nervous glance at the door and lowered his voice. "It happened in Borrans Wood?"

"I don't remember."

"Nothing at all?"

"Not a thing."

"That is for the best." He smiled and kissed her again on the forehead. "It's a miracle, Sweetmeat, a bloody miracle. I think it is very good that you don't remember a thing."

"You think so?"

He watched her closely. "I'm sorry about what happened, Sweetmeat, but some things are just meant to be."

A breeze hissed through the room, rattling the blinds and blowing the rose so it tumbled off the bed to the hard tile floor.

Ken picked it up, placing it on the bedside table. "Hope this isn't a stupid question, but are you feeling better?"

"Lots of pain if I move too much." She remembered the wart on her chin and touched it. "Pure agony."

Ken watched her closely. "And you don't remember what happened?"

"They've pumped me full of drugs."

He frowned. "Maybe when they wear off something will come back."

She looked at him and gave *her smile.* "I don't think so."

"Good. Very good. Yes, yes, let's agree that is for the best. Anyway, memory can play tricks on you, make you see things which are not there." He snatched a glance at the door. "What have you told the police?"

"I feel like hell, Ken."

Sweat pimpled his forehead. "Did you speak with them?"

"Why?"

He placed a hand on her right cheek and then stroked her throat. "A detective came to speak with me."

"A woman?"

"A bloke. Detective Constable Jones."

Kate hated all the talk about the police and wanted Ken to kiss her again. "I spoke with a woman, Detective Inspector Sallow. Sharp as a tack. She asked about you."

"Me?"

She brushed his hand away from her throat. "You are a dangerous man, Ken." She wished she hadn't said it, but it was true. When Ken became enraged he'd do anything, say anything. "Why can't you be more like..."

"Who?"

Frustrated, Kate blurted out the first name that came into her head. "Liam Brampton."

Ken laughed. It wasn't pleasant. "Even the circus would reject that freak of nature as too weird to show in public."

"You are obsessive, Ken. And compulsive. When you get a thing in your head there is no shaking it. It's like it is set in stone. You do what you want to do. You take big risks. And here you are in my hospital room. What if you get caught?"

"They'll never take me alive." He flashed his impish grin. "Didn't you want to see me?"

She did, but she wasn't going to let him know that. "Liam Brampton would have been a nicer surprise."

"What are you telling me?" Ken's eyes were small and mean.

"Is it wrong to want a man's love?" She said it to provoke him, felt a momentary flash of pleasure then regretted her words and tried to correct them. "That's all a woman like me wants."

"I'll kill him."

"You don't own me." Kate fought back tears. "Can't even put a ring on my finger."

Ken's lips stretched into a strange grin. "Look at us, at it like an old couple. Let's not argue." He touched his gold nose stud and then rubbed his hands. "What did you tell that woman detective?"

Kate stared at him and felt her heart thump. She flashed *her smile.* "I told her you'd want to know I was in here."

"Yes, yes, yes." Ken's words came out so fast white foam bubbled from the corner of his lips. "But the buggers are always pointing the finger of blame, that is why I came to see you..." He turned to glance at the French windows. "...through the back door."

Kate's eyes fluttered shut. She saw herself as she once was. Young and fresh and moving into her cottage in Ambleside. Full of hope for a better future and Skye just a child. At the kitchen table, now. Long dark winter evenings with Skye tucked in bed and a candle flickering as she picked up a pencil to sketch. Nights upon nights she had spent swimming in black and white, the soft scratch on paper, creating images, pouring love onto the page. Creation flowed from her mind back then and she realised all she wanted to do was to capture the world through her art. Then, Ken appeared, like the shadow of St Mary's steeple, stretching across the kitchen table. Slow at first, just a flicker of dark. Then you blinked and it was midnight. She couldn't recall the last time she picked up a pencil to draw; hadn't noticed the dust settling on the cover of her sketchbook.

Kate exhaled, letting the images pass before she opened her eyes. "I thought you came to see how I was doing."

"I couldn't stop thinking about you, Sweetmeat."

Kate thought of Ken marrying Millie and she thought of them moving into a posh new house and she thought of herself as an old woman, alone, eating from a can of cold baked beans in a glum council flat.

"Liar." She surprised herself with the word. "You are a bloody liar."

"Don't get upset, Sweetmeat." He raised his hands in surrender and cast a nervous glance at the door. At any moment a police officer or nurse might walk in. He flashed another smile, showing all his teeth and the spit in between. "What we have is special. We'll never let them take it away, will we?"

"What the hell do we have?" The question sent a jolt of pain through her ribs. She stifled a gasp. No way would she let him see her in agony if she could help it. "You are marrying Millie and want me to be your bit of rough on the side. Talk about having your cake and eating it."

Urgent voices came from outside the door—more clacking and clattering of a trolley wheeling along the hallway. Nurses and doctors racing to another emergency. She wanted Ken to say he loved her, that he'd marry her and they'd live happily ever after. And she'd tell him the past did not matter, she'd stand by her man.

Ken puffed out his lower lip and cleared his throat. "You and me, Sweetmeat. We live by our own rules. To hell with what society says, you and me will always be. We are like iron forged in the hellfire of life. I've got your back Sweetmeat and you've got mine. That detective asked me where I was the night Ann Crombie was killed. Then he asked me about Bella Timbol. He just kept asking me questions about those two women like he was suspicious. Gave me the chills. The thing is, I don't have an iron-clad alibi, so I thought of you, Sweetmeat."

So that is what this is about. He's here to save his own hide. A cloud of misery shrouded Kate. Why couldn't he just tell her he loved her and then everything would be alright? She closed her eyes and focused on her breathing.

Ken was still speaking. "You'll back me up, won't you, Sweetmeat? You'll tell them I was with you."

Kate kept her eyes shut.

"Sweetmeat?"

Kate said nothing.

"Chicken Drumsticks, you'll help your Ken, won't you?"

Still, Kate did not speak. Nor did she open her eyes.

Shallow breaths.

In-out.

In-out.

Ken's voice changed. "It's Liam Brampton, isn't it? What aren't you telling me? I'll smash his face in." A growl came from deep within his throat. "You are mine, Kate. Me and you forever."

Kate sensed the chill in the air, sensed him glaring at her, and saw in her mind's eye the whiteness in his clenched fists. She opened her eyes and for the first time, saw him for what he was. Mutton dressed up as lamb in his designer clothes and wilting rose stem and eyes wide with fear. Spiked hair and gold stud and soiled teenager tight jeans. Fake to the rotten core.

She kept her eyes on his clenched fists. "If I scream, the police officer will come in here and arrest you."

"For Christ's sake, don't be a complete fool." He spoke in a restrained tone, higher than his earlier sweet whisper, not high enough to be a shout. Spit and foam dribbled from his mouth. "I did it for you Kate, need you. We need each other. Everything I've done is for us."

Kate remained perfectly still.

His eyes bore into her, two balls of hellfire. She was certain he would lash out if there wasn't a policeman on the other side of the door. Teacher or not, she'd seen it before in men like him.

"Chicken Drumsticks, it's me, your Ken. You love me. We are special."

Kate bit her lip. She didn't want to say it. "Let your wife Millie lie for you."

Ken groaned. "The buggers got to her before I had a chance. She already told them I wasn't with her and she has started to act funny since she spoke with them."

Kate perked up. "Funny?"

"Strange. Distant, like she doesn't trust me." He blinked. "What will they think if she changes her story? Tell them, Kate. Tell them I was with you. You are the only woman in the world I can trust."

Kate said nothing.

"I'm desperate Kate, I need an alibi otherwise they'll haul me down the station and God only knows when I'll get out. You know what the bloody police are like. When they get a bite, they don't let go. Question after bloody question, prying into my private life. And the courts, my God, once you are in the dock there is no end to the misery the judge and jury will inflict. A court case will ruin me, and, whatever the outcome, the police will put me on some terrible list. When they ask, tell them I was with you."

"You want me to lie?"

"Yes."

"But you were not with me the night Ann Crombie was murdered, were you?"

"Tell them anyway."

"Where were you?"

"Bloody hell, just tell them I was with you."

"I can't do it."

"Yes you can, Chicken Drumsticks."

"Don't call me that."

"Sweetmeat, we are a team."

"I won't lie for you."

He stared at her for a moment, his face flushed in shock. "I'm Ken Ashworth, the man you love so hard you'll do anything for, won't you, Sweetmeat?"

"Not that."

"Come on, Kate. I'm a decent man. An art teacher."

"I can't lie to the police, not after what has happened."

"But I'll be an old man when I get out. I want a family, want to pass on my genes to the next generation before it is too late." He watched her for several moments, breathing hard. "Okay, okay, forget Millie. You and me forever. I only ever wanted you. I've been such a fool. Tell the police I was with you and then we'll make a fresh start." He flashed his impish grin. "I've been looking at engagement rings. Giant diamonds. We'll take a trip to London to pick one out. You'll stand by your man, won't you, Sweetmeat?"

Kate could only think of three words. "Sling your hook." Then more words came, fast and furious and freeing. "You've got ten seconds to leave the way you came or I start screaming."

Ken Ashworth glared at her for a full eight seconds, turned and fled.

66

Fenella's first glimpse of the block of flats came through a curtain of fog. It blew in loose swirls over the carpark, shrouding the building in a mysterious glow. Through the mist, it looked like an ancient ruin. She studied the building, gaze settling on the third floor. Thea Humphrey lived on that level.

Darkness filled every window and filled her with doubt. Was seven on a Thursday morning too early? She hadn't called ahead to keep the element of surprise. Now she thought that might have been a mistake.

She strode through the lobby scrawled with graffiti despite the CCTV. It smelled of stale tobacco, cannabis, urine, sweat and the sharp tang of cheap bleach.

"Lift is out of order, you'll have to take the stairs." A wizened man in a flat cap stepped from the shadows. Late sixties at a guess. A bent stem pipe dangled between his lips. He sucked and exhaled a plume of smoke. "The council wallop us with sky-high rents but ain't got the money to fix them. Sweet Jesus, help me, they don't clean the place neither. It's a bleedin' scandal. You'll read about it in the newspaper one day, mark my words."

"Oh aye." Fenella squeezed out a breath and sucked in

a sip of the foul air. "Lived here long?"

"Who's asking?"

"The police, luv." She flashed her warrant card.

His eyes went from the photo to her face and back to the photo. "You sure that's you?"

Fenella had taken it a while ago and needed to get it updated. "Cheeky sod."

"Aye, well we get all sorts here." He jabbed the pipe at the graffiti-stained walls. "Used to be spotless when I first moved in. A bleedin' paradise. But they've rented the place to families with teenagers. Like a pack of attack dogs on the rampage. Which floor, eh?"

He paused, and she sensed him waiting for the bigwig from the police to tell him who she was visiting and why.

"And you are?" Fenella never felt the need to share, especially when she was on police business.

"Jim Baker, from flat nineteen and chair of the Residents Committee."

Fenella took out her notebook and wrote as she considered her next step. He would know if anything unusual went on at the flats—strange people coming and going. She regarded him on the sly. He looked bored and eager for some excitement.

"Mr Baker, I'm investigating a murder."

She waited for a shocked expression to cross his face.

"Sweet Jesus, help me." His mouth hung open for several heartbeats, then he sucked on the pipe and jetted smoke through his nostrils. "Not here. Not in my block of flats, else word would have come my way. The worst we've had here is an overdosed druggie. She lived. May I ask where this grim and unspeakable deed took place? Not that I intend to go and take a peep. No, no, no."

Fenella could see him on the bus to Ambleside with his packed lunch and a flask of tea. A day trip to a murder site. Later, he'd have stories to tell his retired friends. She handed him her business card and lowered her voice. "I can't give any details at the moment. As the chairman of the Residents Committee, please keep this to yourself. It wouldn't do to frighten the wider community."

He hid his disappointment well, took the card and stared at it in the same way he'd stared at her warrant card. "Is there anything else I can help you with?"

"Have you noticed any strange comings and goings in the past few weeks?"

He shrugged. "Nowt comes to mind, but I'll give it a think and call if I remember something. Oh, and you'll want to speak with Thea Humphrey, she has a keen ear. Third floor, number thirty-three."

Fenella made a show of writing down the details. A pretence. She already had them. "Righto, I'll have a chat with her next."

Her phone buzzed. A text message from Dexter:

Guv, the top brass has summoned Jeffery to Carlisle. I hear she won't be back today. I've rounded up the team for the briefing at nine.

She let out a sigh of relief, hellfire over Bobo's bones wasn't coming today. Then she remembered the search warrant for the dwellings at Bede Thatch. She'd made the request and not got a reply. Tomorrow she'd be in Jeffery's office and no matter what happened, she'd bring up the request.

Jim Baker took another long drag on the pipe, exhaled

a plume and coughed. Phlegm rattled in his chest. "There is one thing, Inspector. Not sure it is worth your trouble."

"Go on, I'm listening."

"A couple of weeks ago a reporter came snooping about. A posh woman. I caught her sneaking around the carpark and looking up at the third floor. She said she was from the *Westmorland News* and was writing an article on the outrageous conditions we have to put up with in this block of flats. But..."

"But what?"

"The lass was kind of edgy like she didn't like being seen." He sucked his pipe. Smoke oozed from between his teeth. "I suppose she was one of those undercover reporters. Although for the life of me, I don't know why you'd go undercover. Anyone can see the conditions here are bad."

Whatever the reporter was researching, Fenella doubted it had anything to do with the living conditions in the block of flats. "Did she leave a card?"

"Nope."

"What about a name?"

"Sweet Jesus, help me." He closed his eyes for a moment. "Bella. Yes, her name was Bella Timbol."

Fenella kept her mouth shut for fear her rising excitement would give too much away. She breathed in and out then handled her phone, scrolled and showed him a picture of Bella Timbol. "That her?"

He squinted. "My eyes aren't what they used to be. It could be her. Thing is, I thought I saw her again last week. She was outside in the carpark staring up at the third floor with a pair of binoculars. Late at night. She wore a hoodie, and it was another foggy one so I couldn't be sure it was her. But she had binoculars, alright. A big bloody pair."

Fenella had him go over his answer again and again. She had him close his eyes while puffing on his pipe, asking over and over for the details of what he'd seen. She asked him the time, the height of the woman and the colour of the hoodie. She asked him about the CCTV camera (broken) and whether he saw the woman's car (no). By the third time, she was confident he'd told her the entire story.

"That will be all, Mr Baker. An officer will stop by later to take a formal statement."

As Fenella strode toward the stairwell, she was beginning to see the case in a whole new light. *I'm on to your secret Bella Timbol.*

67

Thea Humphrey leaned against her doorframe glancing both ways along the unlit hallway. All in pink. Slippers. Bath robe. Lipstick. Late sixties pushing seventy. There was a flatness to her face. Nose. Eyes. Forehead. Only the mouth jutted out in a chimpanzee leer. And she was short and dark with a tangle of white hair which curled tight on her head and grew in thin wisps across her upper lip and clung in clumps from her chin. Her amber eyes glowed with an animalistic gleam. She held a mobile phone in her left hand.

"You the lady from the police?" Thea raised the phone. "Jim sent me a text. The walls have ears. This way, please."

They walked through a dark hall. Thea shuffled with bandy legs, hips rocking from side to side. They entered an immaculate kitchen which smelled of fresh coffee and peanuts. A window cloaked in thick net curtains let in a drizzle of foggy light. Pinned to the wall were dozens of photographs. A mass of images from floor to ceiling. One monstrous snapshot faded yellow with age, showed a much younger Thea standing next to an elderly man.

Fenella pointed. "That your dad, Adam Humphrey?"

Thea grunted in a way that might have been yes or no,

her gaze on her mobile phone. When she looked up, her amber eyes seemed to glow. "Says here you dug up the grounds of Bede Thatch and found Bobo's bones. What's all that about?"

"I'm the lead detective. Mind if we sit?"

They settled around a scrubbed pine table with a large blue China bowl filled with raw peanuts in their shells. Thea placed her phone on the table and reached a hand into the bowl. The nuts rattled in her firm grip. She placed three peanuts next to her phone.

Fenella wondered whether they were breakfast. She pictured the woman tossing her head back and crunching the nuts in their shells, crumbs tumbling down her hairy chin. But she knew better than to say anything.

The lights were off and a faint babble came from another room—a voice, in earnest conversation, although the words were unintelligible.

"Are you here alone?" Fenella thought the voice might have come from a neighbour's flat, the walls in these places were paper thin. "How about you turn the light on?"

Thea didn't respond at first, her fingers toyed with the peanuts. "I live alone, twenty years now in this bleedin' hellhole. The lights burn electricity and hurt my eyes. You asked about Adam Humphrey?"

There was something about the way she said his name that struck Fenella as odd. "You called your dad by his first name?"

"Don't you?"

"No, pet, he was always Dad to me. Tell me about him."

"Adam toured with an enormous circus, the world over.

317

Made quite a name for himself." Thea spoke the words like she didn't want to say them; like it was best if they didn't come out, like the past was something best left there. She snatched up a peanut, cracked open the shell and placed two round pale nuts by her phone. "He's long dead, why are you asking about him?"

"Hikers found a body in Borrans Wood. I'm gathering background information. Anything you tell me might help."

"A woman's body?"

"What makes you say that?"

Thea picked up a shelled peanut, rolled it in her hand and placed it back by the phone. "It is always a woman, isn't it?"

Fenella didn't see the point in denying it. "Aye, and she lived in Bede Thatch where you grew up."

A faint babble came through the wall. Like a shout or a moan. It wasn't from another flat. It sounded too close. Fenella glanced around. "Visitors?"

"Only people I let in are Jim Baker and my carers."

Fenella listened for a moment, heard nothing more and continued. "What can you tell me about your dad?"

Thea shrugged. "Adam became renowned for his Dr Doolittle act. Called himself Dr Santini the great primatologist—that is a person who studies monkeys. Not that he had any scientific training. He was a showman who fell in love with his pet the same as a cat owner falls in love with their tabby. He treated Bobo like a human." She paused and stared at the bowl of peanuts. "The orangutan ate better than me."

"Oh aye?" Fenella wanted to hear more about Bobo but she feared they'd veer off track. Still, she had time. The team briefing wasn't until nine. "And why was that?"

"Bobo had brains."

"Eh?"

"Adam fed Bobo the finest foods because he said the ape was a genius." She laughed. It didn't sound right. All warped and twisted. "I dined once he and Bobo were finished. It was I who ate the scraps."

Fenella said nothing.

Thea took a deep breath. "Adam became famous because of his showmanship. He'd ask the audience for a question and Bobo answered. Never wrong, either."

"The monkey spoke?" Fenella couldn't help herself; the words came out before she got them in the right order. She knew orangutans were apes, but it was too late now, she had to keep moving forward. "In English?"

Thea's eyes flashed with a flicker of excitement. The woman was enjoying her moment in the limelight, talking to the police about the man who trained an orangutan to talk.

Thea lowered her voice. "Here's how it worked."

Fenella pictured Thea dressed in sequins on the stage with the spotlight on full beam. If her dad was a showman, so was she.

Thea continued. "Someone in the audience would ask a question, and Bobo would give the answer."

"Any question?"

"Only mathematics. Addition, subtraction, division and multiplication." She paused. "Bobo gave the answer on her fingers."

Fenella thought it must have been some trick and wanted to know the secret. "How'd Bobo figure out the

319

answer?"

Again Thea shrugged. "When I came along, they'd both retired from the circus. Adam spoke much about his exploits but never revealed his performance secrets. But ask me anything else, not too many take an interest in what I have to say. Even the social worker didn't believe me when I said it was I and not Bobo who slept in the cage. In those days they laughed at you and told you to stop telling lies." Her voice dropped to a sinister whisper. "I used to dream about locking the social worker in a cage and running away with the key. Yeah, I'd like to see her in a bleedin' cage eating raw peanuts and bananas in their skin."

Fenella thought she was getting to the heart of the matter now. She had touched a raw nerve. She wanted to know about Thea's childhood and she wanted to know about Bede Thatch and she wanted to know if the woman could tell her anything that would help in the murders of Ann Crombie and Bella Timbol.

"Did you live in Bede Thatch your entire childhood?"

"Until I went into care when Adam died. That's where I learned to read and write and use a knife and fork. Adam wasn't big on school. The Bible and Bobo and his wild flings with women I had to call 'Aunty' were the sum of my education."

"Did you ever find out your mam's name?"

"Never bothered to look. I figured if she dumped me with Adam, she didn't want me. By the time he died, he'd gone as mad as a hatter, started calling me Bobo, and forced me to dress in monk's robes and carry a cross up and down the trail on Sundays to atone for his sins. I didn't know any better." Thea grimaced. "The care home system was my saviour."

The voice babbling from the other room grew louder. Female, young, girlish; and zealous, although the words remained unclear. Fenella pictured a nun on her knees in prayer. Except, Thea said she lived alone. There was no one else in the flat, was there?

Fenella glanced at the wall where she thought the sound came from. "You said you live alone?"

"That's right."

"I thought I heard voices."

"This place is full of ghosts."

Fenella went back to her original line of questions. She wanted the names of Thea's friends who still lived in Ambleside. There might be a link to Ann Crombie or Bella Timbol. A long shot, but so was most police work.

"When were you last in Ambleside?"

"Haven't been back since the day I left."

"Not once?"

"Never."

"And your friends from the village, do you keep in touch?"

Thea laughed. "What friends? My only friends were the birds and the bees. Nah, my link to the village is in the past and that is where I want it to stay. Too many ghosts."

Fenella leaned back in her chair. She'd heard nothing that would help. An overwhelming sense of distress slithered around her stomach and her enthusiasm drained away. Another dead end.

It was a girl's scream, loud and terrible which jerked her upright in her chair.

"Help me. Help me. Sweet Jesus, help me."

68

The voice came from beyond the wall, in another room of the flat.

"Help me. Help me. Sweet Jesus, help me."

Thea jerked to her feet, snatched her phone, two shelled peanuts and marched from the room, bandy gait rocking from side to side.

Fenella followed to a living room that smelled of floral air freshener. It had mauve wallpaper filled with peacocks, beige carpet and a flat-screen telly in the corner next to a replica bar. A huge cage rested by the net-curtained window.

"Help me. Help me. Sweet Jesus, help me."

"What's with the shouting?" Thea marched to the cage and gave the blue-throated parrot a peanut. "Can't you see I'm speaking to a police officer?"

She fed the bird another peanut and turned to Fenella. "She's quite a talker. Had her for years and not a peep until Jim Baker trained her to speak. Now she won't shut up. I've not had my breakfast yet, fancy a bacon butty and a mug of tea?"

69

They'd finished their bacon sandwiches and were sipping from steaming mugs of tea, strong and sweet, when Fenella saw it. Amongst the collage of photos on the wall was a cluster of smiling women in neat nurse-like uniforms. Thea followed her gaze.

"My wall of carers. Nice to have someone to chat with in the mornings. They all work for Care Bright Agency and usually show up around nine, and the district nurse with my injection about ten." She pointed at the photos. "I remember them all, even those that didn't stay with me long. Those two, Marge and Jen, have been with me for five years."

The smiling face in a yellowing photo, half hidden by Marge and Jen, caught Fenella's gaze. She walked to the wall, peeled off the photo and waved it at Thea. "Who is this?"

"Zoe Haynes, another one who was always asking about my life. She left seven years ago. Went to Australia with her boyfriend."

But Fenella wasn't listening. She was looking at the black tattoo of a castle on the left arm of the lass in the photo, certain the face staring back belonged to the woman in the morgue.

70

The Port St Giles town hall clock chimed the nine o'clock hour and in the briefing room the focus was on Zoe Haynes.

Fenella paced by the whiteboard, staring at the blown-up image of Zoe's smiling face. Jones had worked some computer magic. Thea Humphrey's blue-throated parrot stared from the cage in the background. The peacocks on the mauve wallpaper were clear. And so was the logo on the care worker uniform, and the ink-black tattoo on Zoe's arm.

In the hallway, the duty sergeant, Len Moreland, was talking to trainee officers. Fragments of his words carried through the door. Sharp slabs of motivational sounds.

Fenella turned to face her team. "Zoe lived in Barrow-in-Furness, worked for the Care Bright Agency as a home care worker. Ten years in the job. Then, according to Thea Humphrey, about seven years ago, she left for Australia with her boyfriend and was never seen again."

Dexter rocked from foot to foot by the door. Jones sipped tea, laptop on his lap. PC Woods was shaking his head. PC Beth Finn sat next to Jones and was already writing in her notebook.

Fenella continued. "Except Zoe Haynes wasn't in the

326

Land Down Under, was she? She was living in Bede Thatch having taken on the identity of Ann Crombie."

Dexter stopped rocking and cleared his throat. "It is like she was living the life of Cinderella. From rags to riches and the good life in Bede Thatch."

Fenella nodded. "Aye, and we all know what happened when the clock struck midnight."

The team were transfixed like bairns at story time, fascinated by what came next.

Fenella continued. "And now Zoe's corpse is in the hospital morgue and we are left to make sense of the pumpkin. What is going on?"

"Are we sure it is the same woman?" This was Jones, laptop now open and staring at PC Woods. He lowered his voice. "Might not be Zoe Haynes. We should be extra careful after the pile of monkey bones."

PC Woods groaned. "It wasn't my fault. I only followed orders. They said 'dig' and I dug. How was I to know what I'd find?"

PC Beth Finn raised a hand. "We are checking medical records, dental records and I've been on the line to the Foreign Office to see if Zoe Haynes emigrated, ma'am. I called a friend in the Passport Office." She looked around with a broad smile. "This is unofficial, Zoe has never applied for a passport. They don't have her details on record."

Fenella clapped. "Perfect. I couldn't have done any better."

Jones glared at PC Beth Finn, and not for the first time Fenella wondered about his on-and-off relationship with the uniformed officer. She was curious and fascinated that it had lasted at all. They both had their heads so deep in the job that it was hard to see how they kept it going. Still, she wanted to poke about in their private business and find out what was going on. *Like a pig in a trough.* At times her nosy gene drew her so far off track she wanted to scream. *Focus Fen. Focus.*

Jones tapped a finger on the laptop. "We should wait for medical or dental confirmation before jumping to any conclusions. That is Cumbria Police best practice and we are a team that follows protocol, aren't we, boss?"

He was right, of course. They should wait, but no way would Fenella do that. She was about to say so when Dexter piped up.

"It's her, lad. Zoe Haynes is the lass in the morgue, a tenner says so."

Jones spoke before Fenella could remind the team such bets were against police protocol. Not that she would have bothered to moan much. She loved the banter between her team. A bit of crackle and spit lifted everyone's game. And somewhere in the back of her mind she was placing the same bet.

"Done." Jones sat up straight and drained his cup.

PC Beth Finn raised a hand. "Me too. I'm in. It is her."

"Hey, I'm with you two." PC Woods was still shaking his head but grinning now. "Already counting my winnings."

Fenella clapped and waited several seconds for everyone's attention. "This is a briefing room, not a bookies madhouse. All bets are off. Whatever we find, the ales on me. Food too. Tonight at seven, Sailors Arms. Who will join me?"

Cheers erupted.

TELL-TALE BONES

PC Woods licked his lips. "I'll have double of everything if you are paying, ma'am."

Everyone laughed.

The team needed time to relax and chill out in each other's company. And the Zoe Haynes breakthrough deserved a celebration although they were a long way from understanding what it all meant.

Ahead lay a tidal wave of trouble—Jeffery's rage over Bobo's bones, the bigwigs in Carlisle, the salivating press and the killer who might strike again. Fenella pushed that future into a small compartment at the back of her mind. Tonight they'd have some fun.

She waited for the team to settle. The choices she had to make now centred around Zoe Haynes. "What else do we know about Zoe?"

Dexter cleared his throat. "The lass was a member of the Barrow-in-Furness Artists League, guv, and she used to act a little, amateur dramatics. I found her profile on social media. She was handy with the paintbrush. Found quite a few of her landscapes online and they ain't bad." He glanced around the room, eyes blazing. What came next was important. Very important. "Paintings of the Cumbria countryside with foxes prancing about the place."

Once again clapping broke out with everyone talking at once. A tremble of excitement bloomed in Fenella's chest. *So, Zoe Haynes was an artist, eh? Like Ann Crombie whose home she lived in.* A chink of fog had cleared. They were a step closer to puzzling it out.

Dexter turned to Jones, wagging a finger. "That dead woman in the morgue is her, lad. It's Zoe Haynes on the slab."

Fenella was still working it out. A little at a time. Gathering the pieces and putting them together. "Right, let's assume Zoe Haynes took on Ann Crombie's identity. Three questions. First, what happened to Ann Crombie? Second, who killed Zoe and Bella Timbol? Third, why?"

Now theories hurled through the air like stones fired from a slingshot. It was Jones who came up with the best idea. "Zoe must have been working with someone, boss. Didn't Thea Humphrey say she went to Australia with her boyfriend? I reckon the boyfriend *is* the someone else."

"Go on." Fenella leaned forward, her face a ball of concentration.

Jones went on. "Here is what happened. The boyfriend and Zoe had a tiff about money. Not a small argument, a monster blow-out. After years on easy street in Bede Thatch with no one noticing, he got greedy. We saw regular cash payments going out of Ann Crombie's bank account. That was Zoe Haynes and her boyfriend's spending money."

Again he paused and looked around to see if everyone was following. Fenella nodded for him to go on.

Jones straightened his back. He'd reclaimed the throne of teacher's pet. "I reckon the boyfriend wanted more. They'd been living on the same amount for years. We can see that in the regular cash withdrawals from her bank statement. Prices go up and he wanted a bit of lush. They fought in Borrans Wood. He clobbered her. She fell and he killed her with a violent blow to her head. Then, in a blind rage, he hacked at her head with an axe. I reckon he is local."

"And ain't right in his head, lad." This was Dexter. "Do we have the boyfriend's name?"

Fenella tried to shake it free from her memory of the earlier meeting with Thea Humphrey. Then she realised she'd not asked for the boyfriend's name. A mistake. She made a mental note to correct that. "Don't have his name, but I'll double-check with Thea."

"I'll make a list of eligible men, guv." Dexter was writing in his notebook. "Might have another chat with the vicar. He seems to have a handle on what's going on in the village."

Fenella clapped again. Things were going well and, at last, they were on track. "Let's play with your theory. Why did Zoe's boyfriend kill Bella Timbol?"

"She was a reporter, boss." Jones rocked from foot to foot. "Reckon Bella found out Zoe's real identity. She must have been penning a story to sell to the press."

A murmur of agreement came from the group. Reporters went after stories like a dog at a bone. The more unique the better. And Bella Timbol was an ex-columnist for the *Westmorland News*. It all made sense.

Fenella tucked a loose strand of hair behind her ear. "Tell me again how this worked?"

Jones jabbed a finger at the image of Zoe Haynes. "First, she and her boyfriend did away with Ann Crombie. Second, since Zoe and Ann were artists, I reckon they met on the circuit. Art is a small world." He bit his lower lip. "Now, Zoe was a home care worker and we all know the pay is peanuts. So, she and her boyfriend found out Ann Crombie had a wad of cash and planned to move to an isolated house. They killed her, moved in, kept a low profile and withdrew regular wads of cash. It is all in her bank statement, boss. Regular withdrawals of cash and everything else paid via electronic transfer."

"What about the body, lad?" This was Dexter. "What did they do with the body of Ann Crombie?"

Jones didn't miss a beat. "Buried deep in the woods."

PC Woods was now on his feet. "Yes, yes, yes. The buggers knew we might come looking and removed Bobo's headstone so we'd dig in the wrong place. The boyfriend must have had a good laugh, but he'll not ridicule us when we get permission to dig up Borrans Wood."

Again more clapping and cheering and pumping of fists.

"But why did Zoe's boyfriend kill her in Borrans Wood and leave the body where it would be found?" This was PC Beth Finn. "Why did he snatch up her negligée, leaving her exposed?"

Silence.

And something else stirred at the back of Fenella's mind. She waited, tilting her neck from side to side as a new question formed. Bella Timbol was a respected law-abiding member of Ambleside society. Why didn't she come to the police if she found out Ann Crombie was a fake? Why didn't Bella knock on Thea Humphrey's front door? And what reporter watches a block of council flats in the dead of night with a pair of binoculars?

Fenella scowled. "Let's put a hold on searching Borrans Wood until we have gathered more information. Any CCTV or video images of Zoe in Ambleside?"

"Nowt, guv." Dexter rubbed his neck. "Not a dickie bird. Anyone else find anything?"

Jones glared at his laptop. "Nothing from the Port St Giles Building Society."

Fenella wondered if Zoe had known where the CCTV

cameras were and had avoided them. *Don't think daft. Zoe was a carer, not a Russian spy.* She made a mental note to contact Giles Rare Books Store to see if they had a shop video. "What about snapshots of Zoe with locals?"

A shake of heads.

Fenella waited thirty seconds and then asked again. "Has anyone seen an actual photo of Zoe in Ambleside?"

The silence lasted a full ten seconds before the knock on the door.

Len Moreland, the duty sergeant, popped his head in. "A Miss Millie Williams is here to see you, ma'am. Says she wants to speak with the senior detective about the murder of Ann Crombie."

71

Maybe it was because she dressed like a Paris fashion model. Maybe it was because she looked like one too. Maybe it was a tinge of green envy at never having had such good looks. Whatever, Fenella wasn't sure what to make of her first impression of Miss Millie Williams, and all she could do after settling down in a chair in the interview room was to sip from her mug of tea whilst Dexter opened his notebook.

There were no windows in the room. Only one door, a thick iron slab with a small metal flap. It creaked when it opened and clanked when it closed. The still air held the sweat of past visitors. A line of ceiling bulbs shone down with a harsh glare; bright rays of white light where nothing could hide.

Miss Williams was twig thin with a shaggy mane of brunette shoulder-length hair. She wore a leopard print blouse too tight on top. Two gold hooped earrings jangled and her eyes were cornflower blue. She watched with a startled expression below her lush eyelashes. A giant cluster of diamonds mounted on an engagement ring glistened on her ring finger. Her expensive French perfume clashed with the faint scent of disinfectant. She sat quiet and expectant as though going over in her mind what she intended to say.

Sometimes Fenella tried to guess what would come out of an interviewee's mouth. Not this time. She regarded the woman, unable to get a good read. "You are Miss Williams?" She kept a formal tone. "Miss Millie Williams?"

"Uh-huh, but please call me Millie."

Dexter wrote in his notebook, his pen making scratching sounds on the paper. He grunted and looked up. Millie fluttered her eyelashes, picked up her mug of tea and slurped. Long and sensuous and slow. Fenella smiled. She'd got her first read on the woman. *A good looker and crafty with it.*

A knock sounded on the door. It creaked open. Jones poked his head in. "Can I have a word when you are finished, boss?" He spoke the words in whispered reverence, his eyes greedily taking Millie in.

Behind him, PC Woods watched with a gluttonous stare as the scowling face of PC Beth Finn looked on. Word had spread around the station that they had a *good looker* in. Fenella pictured drool dripping down the chins of Jones and PC Woods and waved them away without a word.

The door clanked shut.

"Now, Millie." Fenella relaxed her tone; she knew exactly how to handle this woman. "You have some information for us about the recent death of Ann Crombie?"

"Are you the senior detective?" Millie gazed at Dexter, eyes pleading it to be him then turned back to Fenella. "I want to speak with the person in charge."

"Aye, pet. I'm Detective Inspector Fenella Sallow."

Millie's eyebrows shot up and then her eyes narrowed. "I shouldn't have come here. I was hoping to speak with a. . . man."

Dexter gave a lopsided grin. "One hundred per cent red

bloodied male here, ma'am. You can tell me and the guv anything."

Millie flashed a sexy smile and fluttered her eyelashes. "Are you sure?"

Fenella sensed this would take longer than average if she didn't put her foot down. *A bit of shock treatment, eh?* "Now, Sunshine, you've come all the way from Ambleside to knock on the police's door. It must be important. I want to hear it and I want to hear it all and I'll be furious with you if I find out later I haven't heard the very last drop."

Millie held the mug between her hands, her eyes downcast. "I don't want to get anyone in trouble."

Ah pet, that's why you are here. You do. "I'm waiting, luv. And I'm not a patient woman."

Fenella enjoyed playing the part of the formidable detective, although she wondered if she'd been too extreme with the lass. There was a delicate balance between going in too hard and not going in harsh enough. Now she waited for Dexter to play his good cop role.

"Here lass, take another sip of that tea." Dexter smiled again. Big and broad and friendly. "And take your time. Me and the guv are here to help. Ain't none of us pointing fingers. We just want to hear what you have to say." He picked up his pen and again smiled. "We can't do our job without the public. You will be a great help, won't you?"

Millie took a gulp, this time without the sensuous slurping act. She placed the mug down and looked at Dexter with her startled gaze. "Are you sure what I tell you won't get out?"

Dexter's friendly smile began to break. He'd had enough, too. "There'd be hell to pay if everything the public told us leaked out. The big boss upstairs would go ballistic. Now, please go ahead or we'll nick you for wasting police time."

Millie did not answer at once. She picked up the mug then put it back down and turned to face Fenella. "It's my boyfriend. He's been acting strange."

"I'm not with you, luv." Fenella kept her voice light and low, like the hush of a summer breeze. "What is the bloke's name?"

"Ken Ashworth."

Fenella pretended to write something in her notebook. Someday she'd be caught out, but she needed time to think. Wasn't that the same Ken Ashworth Kate Owen had mentioned? Two men with the same name in the village of Ambleside wasn't plausible. "And what do you want to tell us about him?"

Millie swallowed. "He wanted me to tell the police he was with me the night Ann Crombie was killed."

"And was he?"

"I've no idea where he was, but he wasn't with me." Millie's right hand twiddled with the engagement ring. "That is the truth and what I told Detective Constable Jones. He said to let him know if I thought of anything else."

"And you've thought of something else?" Fenella tapped a finger on the table.

"I came to the station because I didn't want to speak over the phone. Ken's been acting weird since the death in the woods."

Fenella waited a heartbeat. "And you think Ken Ashworth might know something about what happened to Ann Crombie?"

Millie let out a soft sob. "He started to get up in the middle of the night when I was sleeping and crept from the house. In the morning, he'd be by my side as if nothing happened. I tried to ask him about it, but he denied it, said I was mad. I didn't push it. He gets nasty when he is angry."

"Has he ever hit you?"

She looked at her hands. "I don't want to get him in trouble."

"Then why did you come here?"

Millie pouted and said nothing.

Fenella lowered her voice. "How long has this creeping about at night been going on?"

Millie looked up. "Recent. A month at most and that's what has got me worried. Ken is a planner. He watches and waits and gets to know your routine. That's how we met. He pounced when I was at the supermarket in Barrow-in-Furness, told me about his lush teaching job and that he lived in Ambleside. The rest is history. And now Ann Crombie is dead and Ken's been sneaking out of the house at night. It might be nothing, but I couldn't live with myself if I didn't tell you."

Fenella watched her for a long moment but saw nowt but the flash of self-interest in Millie's eyes. Whatever the lass came to the police station to tell them was for her benefit and her benefit alone. "You have no idea where he went on his nighttime wanderings?"

She shook her head, her startled expression looking genuine.

But Fenella didn't believe her. "What about another woman?"

Millie let out a miserable moan but said nothing.

Fenella slapped a hand on the table. "Is Ken Ashworth seeing another woman?"

Millie's eyes were wide now, and for the first time, Fenella thought she was startled. "He told me he'd finished with her. He told me he wasn't seeing Kate Owen anymore." She was speaking fast and wild between huge sobbing gasps. "I followed him last week to make sure it was true. I trust him, but wanted to see for myself."

"Where did he go?" Fenella wanted to know and she wanted to know now and she wanted to know if they'd stumbled across a significant breakthrough.

Millie kept her eyes on her engagement ring. "I know what you are thinking, but I'm not a nosy parker. I have a right to know, don't I?"

Fenella repeated the question. "Where did he go?"

"On the trail that leads to Borrans Wood. I think he sensed someone was behind him because he dashed into a stand of trees and I lost him in the dark." Millie sniffed. "So, you see he wasn't going to see Kate, he was up to something else and now Ann Crombie is dead and Kate Owen is in the hospital. I feel terrible, but I swear I came to you as soon as I figured it out. Ken has a temper on him and will kill me if he learns I've spoken with you."

Fenella thought about the wicked way two women had already died. Yet, there was something in Millie's words that didn't ring true. "You said Ken is your boyfriend?"

"That's right."

Fenella glanced at the giant cluster of diamonds on Millie's ring finger. Something wasn't right with the picture. *How could Ken afford those monsters on a teacher's pay?*

"Are you engaged to Ken?"

Millie blinked. "Yes."

"Don't lie to me, pet. Unless you want to sleep behind bars. I want the truth. Now."

"Look, I told Ken I was pregnant with twins and he proposed. I'm not. The truth is I don't want kids. Never did. I don't know why I told him that." Millie spoke in a hysterical rush. "I suppose it is because he is a teacher, and, well, that's not a bad lark, is it? I mean, all those holidays and he has a nice house in the village. I fancied a bit of that lifestyle, don't want to marry him now. I'm not getting wed to a cheating fiend. Ken is a bloody liar. I could never marry a man like that. A marriage without trust is no marriage at all."

And once again Fenella had the distinct sense the woman was lying. "Is that the truth?"

"Yes."

"I don't believe you." Fenella stood, taking her time, eyes fixed on Millie's startled face. "I'm arresting you for—"

"No. Please, I'll tell you everything." Millie's gaze dropped to her ring finger.

Fenella sat and waited and tried not to let the edge of her lips quirk.

"Okay, okay." Millie's voice fell an octave. "Once I call it off with Ken, I'm marrying Rupert, the pub landlord. This is his ring." She looked up, her face tightening. "I know what you are thinking, but I'm not a gold digger. Is there anything wrong with wanting a better life, for dreaming of something more? I love Rupert and he loves me. He is going to buy a cottage in the village because I don't want to live above an alehouse."

72

Fenella would later remember it as the hour from hell. It started in confusion and ended in chaos. She blamed herself for the mess.

A fog hung low over the village of Ambleside. A swirl of thick mist blew in from Lake Windermere. It clung to the trees and the hedges and the stone-walled cottages. Soft and still so when you looked the land vanished in a tunnel of murk. Fenella puffed out a breath as she pulled her Morris Minor to the curb.

"Ain't surprising people get killed on these lanes, guv." Dexter looked toward Ken Ashworth's cottage. "Can't even see the front gate. Hope this is the right place. Imagine what it would be like at night?"

They were definitely outside the right place, well, according to the satnav. It beeped and told them they had arrived at their destination. Fenella cut the engine. "Can't be far. I want to hear what Ken Ashworth has to say for himself before we haul him in."

Her phone rang. She stared at the flashing icon on the screen for a moment before she realised it was Jones. She swiped on the speakerphone.

"Boss, I've got through to Ken Ashworth's workplace."

"He's an art teacher, right?" Fenella recalled that much from when she met Ken outside Bede Thatch. The bright-coloured shirt and punk-style hair lodged in her memory. "Teaches in the school in Troutbeck Bridge, eh?"

"That's right, boss." Jones sounded a touch upset. He wanted to be the hero with all the details. "He's been there for seven years. Well, I spoke with Mrs Masters, she is the headteacher."

He stopped and Fenella understood. He wanted a few words of praise for his effort so far. *If that is what it takes to keep him sweet.*

She smiled. "Schools out for the holiday. How did you track her down?"

"I called her at home. She said she wasn't surprised to hear from me because complaints about Ken Ashworth have poured in over the past few days. She sounded over-whelmed."

"Oh aye?" Fenella's interest level shot through the roof. "Did she say who the complaints were from?"

Fenella's question hung in the empty air for two heart-beats. Dexter grunted but did not speak. They wanted the answer and they wanted it now and they could tell by the tone in Jones's voice they'd get a nasty shock.

Dexter couldn't control himself any longer. "What is it, lad? What did Mrs Masters have to say about who complained?"

Jones answered in a high-pitched excited voice. Two words. "Ann Crombie."

Footsteps scurried past the car. A shadow hurried into the gloom. From high in an unseen tree came the caw of a raven. Fenella never thought a simple background check on Ken Ashworth would have revealed such a direct link. "Did Mrs Masters give you details of the complaints?"

There was a long pause before Jones replied. "She said she couldn't share the contents without a written request."

Fenella thumped the dashboard. "Oh that is hilarious. You told her we are in the middle of a murder investigation?"

"Yes, boss. She was adamant. Said any requests had to go through the school's lawyer, Zeeb and Lacy in Barrow-in-Furness. I've put in a request."

"Nice job, pet." Fenella tilted her neck from side to side. "Did she give a clue about the nature of the complaints?"

"Mrs Masters said she didn't want a horde of reporters baying at the school gates but it wasn't a criminal matter. And here is the thing, boss, Ken Ashworth is no longer working at the school. He left two weeks ago."

73

Thick fog swirled around the car. Fenella dropped her phone in her handbag, mind shuffling through the questions she had for Ken Ashworth.

"There is someone at his door, guv." Dexter pointed.

Through a brief gap in the fog a figure was visible. A woman bent forward and peeped through the letterbox. She wore a Macintosh coat, grey, and so long it covered her ankles. The woman straightened and crept to the side of the house.

Fenella dropped her voice. "Let's keep her in sight."

They eased the car doors shut and followed with silent footsteps. The woman scrambled through a low hedge, approached the back of the house in a cat-like crouch and peered in a window.

The sour growl of a car engine broke the stillness. A sudden cough and splutter as it made its way along the lane. Fenella and Dexter would have watched unnoticed if the woman hadn't spun around. The car gave a final cough before its growl faded.

The sight of the red-faced woman transfixed Fenella for a heartbeat. "Miss Fish, what are you doing?"

"I. . . er. . . all seems to be in order here." Miss Fish's face bloomed a deeper crimson, flat coin eyes wide. "One must be ever vigilant to the risk of fire."

"Can't sniff no smoke." This was Dexter. "Can't see no flames, either. What you up to, lass?"

"I'm the chief fire warden and came here to perform my duty as—"

"Don't give us no blarney, lass." Dexter wagged a finger. "Or we'll sort it out at the station. We'll have to send for a car with them blue flashing lights and screaming siren. The neighbours will come running. But it is up to you Miss Fish."

"Oh dear. . ." Miss Fish's voice echoed in the fog. She staggered back two paces. "Goodness me, what must you think?"

Another car trundled along the lane erupting a foul grumble into the dense air. Pistons pumping; tyres squealing; headlights cutting through the gloom.

Fenella touched Miss Fish's arm, fascinated and sad. If this was what she thought it was, it would ruin Miss Fish when it got out. She fought back that thought. There had to be another explanation. "Why don't me and you have a little chat?"

Miss Fish looked everywhere but at Fenella's face.

Fenella took Miss Fish by the arm and led her along the garden path and stopped close to the shed, shaded by the broad leaves of an ancient oak tree. The single window of the shed watched with a blank stare. Branches creaked in the slight breeze.

Miss Fish sighed. "I don't know what to tell you."

Fenella knew exactly what she wanted to hear. She kept her gaze on Miss Fish's face. "Now, pet. I already know what this is about, but I want it in your own words. The truth."

Miss Fish offered no resistance. A trip in a police car to the station terrified her more than the naked truth. "I've been such a fool. It started about a month ago and quite by accident. I happened to be undressing by the bedroom window. The setting sun splashed such a wonderful glow over the garden that I did away with my usual practice of drawing the curtains. I was admiring the rhododendron bushes when I saw him leaning on the garden gate, watching my bedroom window. He held a pair of binoculars in his right hand."

"Go on, pet. I'm listening." Fenella's voice came out as soft as fog and swirled away into nothing. Anticipation and curiosity and the need to know it all. *Like a pig in a trough.* "Tell me now and tell me it all."

Mrs Fish bowed her head, gaze on her twitching hands. "A strange madness seized me, for I hurried from the bedroom window to turn the lights on. Then I returned and continued to undress while he raised the binoculars to his eyes. He came back the following night and we've played our little game twice a week since then."

"So, this man was the *beefy* bloke you complained to PC Sid Fenwick about?" Fenella hated to admit she was right with her guess. "The bloke looking into your bedroom window at night?"

Miss Fish raised her head, locking Fenella in a fierce gaze. "You should know we have never spoken to each other. It was our little secret. I've never told another living soul about Ken Ashworth."

74

It was shock, Fenella told herself, that caused the hollowness in the pit of her stomach. Ken Ashworth, the art
teacher, was the village Peeping Tom. And Miss May Fish
had egged him on. But there was more, she knew it, much
more.

Miss Fish was speaking freely now, telling it all. "Since
Ann Crombie's death. . . Oh dear, I don't know what you
will think, but. . . Mr Ashworth has missed our regular. . . rendezvous. Twice. I came here to see if he was
alright. This fog is so thick, I never thought anyone would
spot me. I was about to knock again when you came. He
sleeps late when school is out."

Fenella looked at Miss Fish's long grey macintosh but-
toned tight at the top and she looked at Miss Fish's bare
legs which vanished into a pair of hiking boots and she
looked at the pink lipstick on Miss Fish's face, freshly applied and glistening. Miss Fish had done herself up to knock
on Ken Ashworth's door. What was the woman wearing
under the grey coat? She squeezed her eyes tight for a
heartbeat. When she opened them, she said nothing.

Miss Fish sniffed. "I'll never live this down, will I, Inspector Sallow? If I crawl under a rock and hide for twenty

years, I will always be the woman in the village who—"

"You are not the only one, luv, are you?"

"I don't know what you mean?"

"Aye, pet you do."

Miss Fish nodded. "I had my suspicions."

Fenella pushed harder. "Come off it. You knew Ken was watching other women, didn't you?"

Miss Fish whimpered. "Please... I don't know. Oh heavens, what must you think?"

Fenella didn't let up. "Ken Ashworth is the village secret, isn't he?"

Again Miss Fish whimpered. "Yes."

"Who are the other women?"

"I don't know."

"Ah, but you followed him, didn't you?" Fenella pictured the scene. A moonlight night, dark with the hiss of the breeze in the trees. "One night after you'd finished undressing for Ken, you grabbed your grey Macintosh, slipped on your hiking boots and followed him. Boots and Mac and nowt else underneath."

Miss Fish opened and closed her mouth. Then she opened it again. "Only once. A woman knows when a man is cheating on her, and like you, I assumed there must be others. Yes, I knew about his girlfriends, Kate Owen and Millie Williams, but I wanted to know who else he was watching. Older women, I suspected. I wanted to set eyes on the competition."

Fenella folded her arms. "And?"

"I... followed him on the trail, keeping close to the trees so he wouldn't see me. He walked fast almost a trot, eager to get to his next watch post, I suppose. It began to thunder and the worst of it was the wind picked up so rain fell in great sheets. What with the dark and the low clouds and the rain, I lost him in the murk. I hurried home, a drowned rat, and took a long hot bath."

A fox screamed from its den. Another car clattered along the lane. A gust shook the trees, skittering leaves and clattering branches and sending trembling swirls of fog in demented dances.

Once again Fenella gazed at the dark bedroom windows. "But you knew where he was going, didn't you, Miss Fish?"

"I couldn't be sure, but he trotted toward Borrans Wood. The only cottage in that area is Bede Thatch."

75

Less than ten seconds after Fenella sent Miss Fish home, telling her not to leave the village, her mobile phone pinged, but she ignored it and walked over to where Dexter was waiting.

"Heard every word of it, guv." He rubbed his hands. "I can see Miss Fish standing by her window weeping tonight, like one of those maestro paintings on the wall in them high-class art galleries. A shocking story. This village has more secrets than a Russian spy. Wonder what else it is hiding from us?"

Fenella wanted to pick over what she had heard, strip it down to the bare bones and bounce ideas off Dexter. She got the firm sense he wanted to do that too. *He's worse than me. Two pigs in a trough, eh? And feasting on every last sordid bite.* But they were still outside Ken Ashworth's house and both wanted to speak with the man.

"No point gnawing over Miss Fish now. There'll be plenty of time once we've nabbed Mr Ashworth." She looked up at the dark windows of the house. "Reckon he is at home?"

"Aye, guv. He'll be tucked up in bed and sound asleep after his nighttime activities." Dexter grinned. "It'll be a shame to shatter his dreams."

76

When they knocked, no one answered.

"Could kick it in, guv."

Fenella had lost count of how many places she'd entered with Dexter, feet first or his broad shoulder splintering wood. There'd be reports to write and forms to fill in if they forced their way in. She pictured another fiasco like Bobo's bones and became suddenly cautious. She bent forward and peered through the letterbox as she'd seen Miss Fish do.

"Mr Ashworth, this is Detective Inspector Fenella Sallow. I need you to come to the door and let us in."

She stood back and looked up at the house. A gust lifted a pile of dead leaves sending them in a filthy swirl.

"He's hiding, guv." Dexter rubbed his hands. "Knows the game is up."

The last thing Fenella wanted was a foot chase in billowing fog across the countryside. They would take Ken Ashworth in quietly. "Go round the back in case he does a runner."

Dexter was gone before the words came out of her mouth. She reached for the door handle.

It turned.

She pushed.

The door creaked open a crack.

Fenella listened and on hearing nothing unusual, shoved the door wide. Solid wood. Thick and heavy. It let out a deep moan.

"Mr Ashworth, this is the police. Please come to the door if you are able."

A full thirty seconds passed.

Nothing.

She massaged the knot forming in her neck, remaining on the threshold. Butterflies flitted in her gut; a rapid beat of startled wings scattering in every direction. Always the same alertness when she stepped across a threshold into the unknown. Always the same fear something nasty would lurch from the dark.

She moved into the hallway.

It smelled of aftershave—sweet and exotic. Expensive. Out of a glass bottle. From Paris, no doubt. Fenella once again listened but heard only the click of a wall clock.

"Mr Ashworth, this is the police. Show yourself."

Tick-tock.

Tick-tock.

Fenella searched for the light switch and turned it on. Soft amber rays from ceiling spotlights gave the hallway a warm glow. She took in the shoe rack with three pairs of tan cowboy boots, all polished to a mirror shine. A brown monk's robe hung on the coat hook, crumpled and soiled through use. The cream rug on the floor, deep shagpile, looked new. Shoved against the wall was a large cardboard box filled with brown cloth sacks. Above the box hung a framed poster of a Henri Michaux artwork, a jumble of black squiggles on a cream canvas. She studied it for a full thirty seconds trying to make out what it was.

Her phone buzzed again and this time she glanced at the screen. A message from Helen Grimes:

I've been given the all-clear to move into Bede Thatch. I've left the hotel and will spend my first night in the place. I can't wait. It will help me feel closer to my aunt. Vicar Kemp has been in contact, said he'd say a prayer for the place. So nice of him. Any news on Aunt Ann?

Fenella sent a quick reply:

Will update you later.

She tucked her phone in her handbag and used another full minute to walk through to the back of the house, open the door to the garden and let Dexter in.

She spoke in a hushed tone. "He's not downstairs unless he's hiding."

They searched the living room and the kitchen and the hallway again. Careful and cautious and slow. Each time calling for Ken Ashworth and listening for a reply.

At the bottom of the stairs, Dexter looked up. "He must be up there and sound asleep, guv. Bet the bugger's dreaming about the women he watched last night. It would be champion to wake him while he is wandering about the village in his dreams and reliving his greatest peeps. I want to see his miserable face when I have him in me iron-clad grip."

Fenella took the steps two at a time, hand pressed against the wall to steady herself. She paused on the landing to flick on the lights. Three doors.

One to her left.

One to her right.

One straight ahead.

She took the door on her left. It led to a small bathroom. Sink, toilet, bath with built-in shower and a medicine cabinet. She opened the cabinet door. Pills and potions and aftershave made in Paris.

The door on the right led to a box bedroom—an executive swivel chair and a desk littered with teaching materials. The thick mauve curtains were pulled shut. This was the room where Ken Ashworth did his school work, marked and graded essays.

The final door led to the master bedroom. All black, it smelled of aftershave, heavy and thick and sweet as if someone had splashed bottles of the stuff around the room. There was a huge waterbed with black silk sheets, a mirror on the ceiling and a night table with a pile of magazines which all featured bare-chested women smiling into the camera while half twisting and bending over.

Fenella's gaze settled on the black binoculars, the type and model popular with birdwatchers.

From the gap between the bed and the wall came the soft buzz of flies. A black cloud rose as they approached.

"Flies don't get that big overnight, guv." Dexter covered his nose. "What they've been feasting on has been dead for a while."

Fenella stepped forward and noticed three things all at once. First, the pale face of a man. His empty eyes stared at her, his face crawling with flies. A scruffy rabbit foot poked out through his lips as if shoved in after death to make some hideous point. Second, the pool of blood, dark and hardened and smeared across a brass tin, lid open, white rose petals inside. Third, the man's wheat gold smock. It stretched tight over his bloated gut and came short just above his bare knees. Fenella stepped closer. He was wearing only the smock. No clothes underneath. And his head was six inches away from the rest of his body.

"I know the lad." Dexter rubbed the back of his neck. "He's a local artist. Liam Brampton."

77

The town clock rang out. Eight long chimes. The start of a cool evening where fog clung low over the town. A shroud so thick it dulled the evening to night. Despite the discovery of Liam Brampton's body in Ken Ashworth's bedroom. Despite the fevered activity of the scene-of-crime officers crawling all over his house. Despite the fact that Ken Ashworth had vanished without a trace and was presumed to be on the run. And despite the certainty that by morning the mob would be baying for her blood with Superintendent Jeffery at the head of the pack, Fenella kept her word.

She'd promised her team a meal at the Sailors Arms pub in Port St Giles and they'd already agreed on tonight.

The team sat around an ancient oak table. Hardwood floors, frosted glass windows and worn red leather seating—originals, tattered and worn by time and in need of replacement. Three men sat at the bar, chatting and telling stories of the old days. All retired police officers. Fenella knew each of their names. The pub was a favourite watering hole for old-timers of the Cumbria Police fraternity and a hidey-hole where working officers relaxed in peace.

"Can't eat no more, guv." Dexter pushed his plate away. "I've attacked it twice, but I'm stuffed."

Fenella, too, was stuffed, warm and contented. The sure hellfire of tomorrow seemed a long way away.

PC Beth Finn wiped her lips with a serviette. "This was absolutely the best meal I've had in ages. When you live on your own, it's the microwave or the curry house. Thanks, ma'am."

PC Woods waved a fork. "Steak and kidney pie with beefeater chips and green peas, all washed down with six pints of ale. Delicious." He forked a monster wedge of chips into his mouth and eyed Dexter's plate. "You sure you've finished? You've left a chunk of pie, mind if I nab it?"

His fork moved to Dexter's plate and the slab of crust was between his lips. He swallowed and gave a contented burp.

Dexter shook his head. "Cor blimey, don't your lass feed you at home?"

PC Woods flashed a boozy smile. "Me thinks I've room for one more round before the dessert mission begins." He stabbed his fork at a pea. "When the boss says she'll feed you, you don't miss a beat, do you? Been making room for this feast all day."

"I wondered why you only ate four jam doughnuts for your lunch." This was Jones, sipping from a glass of red wine. "And there was me thinking you were going down with something."

Everyone laughed. PC Woods was the station expert on putting food away. Some said he was obsessed with it. His relentless gastronomical abuse bulged in a thick layer of pudge around his waistline.

The bulldog-faced barman wandered over, slapped Dexter on the back and shook PC Beth Finn's hand. He was a retired desk sergeant and had run the pub for years. He turned to Fenella. "Bakewell tart with custard good enough for your team? It is in the oven and will take a little while."

The idea of more food seemed impossible a few moments ago, but Bakewell tart? Fenella laughed. "Genius idea. I've always got room for Bakewell."

"Big bowls." This was PC Woods. He raised his fork, slurring as he spoke. "Squire, bring us big bowls slopping with custard."

Fenella pointed at Jones. "I'll leave it to you to drive him home tonight. And make sure to tell his wife that the girls are having a bingo night next Friday. I expect her to join us."

The landlord, still at the table, ran a hand over his bulldog-shaped face. "Hear you had a spot of bother in Ambleside today. Must have given you quite a fright after the death in Borrans Wood?"

Fenella was loathe to discuss it but she sensed the pub landlord had a good idea of what had gone on. "The victim was a local artist, a Mr Liam Brampton. He lives in the village. Know him?"

The Bulldog shook his head. "Not ringing any bells. What about the bloke on the run? Hope you catch the psychotic monster. Got a name you want me to keep an eye out for?"

Fenella was aware her entire team watched. They'd agreed not to discuss the case tonight, but to refuse to answer would be churlish. By the morning the full story would be all over the newspapers and she'd be in Superintendent Jeffery's office. "He is a local teacher, Mr Ken Ashworth."

That provoked a curious response from Bulldog. He

pivoted on his heels and flapped his arms like the bird-man of Alcatraz. When he staggered from side to side and rolled his eyes, Fenella understood. "Know Mr Ashworth, do you?"

Bulldog's arms stopped flapping. "I walk the Ambleside trails with PC Sid Fenwick a couple of times a month. Birdwatching. I've encountered Ken Ashworth a few times. The man has a reputation for crashing about the woods at night like a drunken duck." He began to flap his arms again and staggered back two paces. "Last time I saw him was a week ago, skulking near the path that led to Bede Thatch, a can of ale in one hand and a pair of expensive binoculars slung around his neck. The poser! I'm yet to see him point those field glasses in the direction of anything feathered."

He turned and walked away.

Fenella's gazed bounced around her team, taking in the expression on each face. They wanted to talk about the case now their bellies were full and booze sloshed in their bloodstream. Although Dexter, like Fenella, had drunk only orange juice.

"Okay," Fenella raised her hands. "I didn't bring it up, and neither did any of you, but since it is hovering over us, have at it."

PC Beth Finn was the first to respond. "I think Mr Ashworth has fled south, ma'am. Birmingham or London to lie low."

"He'll not do that, lass." This was Dexter. "The bugger's got no contacts down south. He's running west and already on a boat floating to Ireland."

Jones gulped a mouthful of wine. "France, boss. He took the boat from Dover and is lying low in a château."

PC Woods, munching through the remains on Dexter's plate, looked up. "Wherever he is, it is nowhere we'll find him, ma'am. Might as well be on the moon. But if I were him, I'd stay near and wait for my chance to strike again. I'm no detective, but every victim was a member of the Ambleside Village Artists. That's a long list to strangle and knife your way through. The man is an evil genius, that's why we can't puzzle him out. Who's next for a dose of his insane butchery?" He shrugged. "God only knows cos we don't."

Fenella wanted to pursue some more theories, narrow things down, take action, but it was well after eight o'clock. Was there anything they could do other than wait for news in the morning?

She was still considering this question ten minutes later, the soft bubble of pub voices and clink of glass replacing the chat of her team. The barman dragged a rag across the counter then pulled two pints of ale. Two uniformed women officers ambled through the front door and sat at the bar. A man with a walking stick shuffled in a few moments later. He raised his cap at the pub landlord and joined the two officers at the bar.

The idea of returning to the station to review the case files flared and died in Fenella's mind. Ploughing through reports again at the end of a death-filled day didn't fill her with any desire. But the thought nibbled and gnawed and she couldn't let it go. She glanced at the frosted windows. Condensation clung to the glass, droplets streaking like a mother's tears.

I have to do something.

No way could she sit and wait for the hand of fate in

the morning. But what could she do?

She stifled back the bitter frustration forming in her gut and reached for her handbag.

A distraction might help.

She pulled out her copy of *Northworder*. "Talking of puzzles, here is one I've not been able to work out. While we wait for dessert, let's see who can claim the Word Master Champion's crown."

PC Woods lolled back in his chair and let out a soft snore. PC Beth Finn's brow crinkled in concentration but Jones spoke. "Go on, boss." He was always up for a challenge and came top in his postgraduate art class and did his undergraduate work at Cambridge. "What is the clue?"

Dexter joined in the fun. "I ain't no boffin head like the lad, but I'll give it a go."

"Me too." This was PC Beth Finn.

PC Woods continued to snore.

Fenella read aloud. "Five across, eight letters. The first letter begins with 'A': Steamed marmalade pudding is twice as nice for Napier's gran."

Jones opened his mouth then closed it, lips a straight line.

Dexter laughed. "Ain't got a clue, have you lad?"

Jones shrugged. "I can't even make a wild guess, but there is something about that clue that makes it compulsive. Marmalade pudding and Napier's gran?" He was silent for a long while, then puffed out his cheeks and let the air out slow. "Nope, nothing is coming to mind."

PC Beth Finn placed a hand on his arm. "It doesn't matter, really it doesn't. I've no idea either."

Dexter rubbed his hands. "Listen lad, it don't make

no sense except we are in a pub enjoying food paid for by the guv. Now, marmalade pudding is a dessert made by my gran, and what is pudding without a dollop of custard? And I likes a drop of custard with me pudding, but after a big meal I've got to have the appetite. That is what my gran always said before a meal and I reckon Napier's gran said the same thing. That's your eight letters, lad. I reckon the answer is appetite."

Fenella could have kissed him. She stood, slung her handbag over her shoulder and pointed at PC Woods. "We'll leave sleeping beauty here. The rest of you, with me."

78

An hour later, Fenella and her team arrived in the village of Ambleside. They made their way through the fog and across the moonlit trail, headed for Bede Thatch.

"We'll need to keep a low profile." Fenella's legs ached, and her heart pounded her chest. She hadn't explained her hunch in all its gory detail, wasn't sure it made sense. But Dexter's answer to the crossword had firmed up her hope. She forced herself on, helpless in the dual clutch of fear and curiosity. If she were wrong it would be agony, and she'd look absurd. But if she were right, she'd save a life. Either way, she had the appetite to take the risk.

Uphill they climbed, on a dirt track with the night air heavy with the tang of Lake Windermere. "This ain't nowt like walking the trails in the day, guv." Dexter huffed. "It's dark, and the fog makes it hard bleedin' work."

They were all breathing hard. It was easy to turn an ankle or trip over a root in the dark. A shadow scurried across the path, keeping close to the ground. A fox on the search for its next kill.

Jones grunted; the glow of his phone firefly bright. "What can we do without a search warrant, boss?"

Fenella said nothing.

Jones continued. "Want to call for backup, boss?" He kept his voice soft but everyone picked up the nervous tremble in his deep tones. "I have the station on speed dial."

"Nah." Fenella understood his concern. They were stepping into the unknown. Borrans Wood lay ahead shrouded in the dark of a foggy night. Legends and myths and ghosts haunted those ancient trees. A place where pandemonium reigned. "Let's wait until we are sure. For now we watch and listen."

Fenella was certain of only one thing—that word of Helen Grimes staying in the isolated cottage would have spread throughout the village. And again she thought of the strange handwritten note on the back of the Giles Rare Books Store receipt:

Mail Benny Label. Okay?

Yes, she was certain Benny was in the killer's sights. Helen Benedicta Grimes alone in Bede Thatch. Bait on a fisherman's hook. It wasn't a flawless plan. Only much later, would she realise how right she was about that.

"Helen Grimes might have changed her mind, ma'am." PC Beth Finn puffed hard. "With all this fog, she might be in the hotel. I wouldn't blame her."

Fenella hadn't called ahead; didn't want to frighten Helen Grimes with her concerns. Were they already too late? She grimaced. "No harm in a quick check."

They crested the ridge which led down to the woods. The moon shrank behind black clouds throwing the landscape into midnight blue. Dark and shadows. Mist hovered in ethereal swirls. A barn owl blared its hunting call. Then came deep silence. An eerie quiet. It hung over the landscape as though the night was holding its breath, watching and waiting for what was to come.

The curtain of fog cleared. In the distance, a solitary light flickered in the window of Bede Thatch. A lamp.

"Wonder if the electric is out, guv." This was Dexter. "I hear it ain't reliable in these parts. Might be a line down in all this fog. Why else would the lass light a lamp?"

Fenella stopped, placed her hands on her hips, caught her breath and stared at Bede Thatch. The light seemed to sweep from left to right across the window pane, its bright glow like the pupil of some hideous eye. And what was that shadow behind it? The flutter of a curtain? Helen Grimes settling down at the table to read verses from the Good Book? Or was it like that night when she and Dexter staked out the bungalow of a frail old woman and caught a burglar creeping about her bedroom, sack over shoulder and stocking mask pulled down distorting their face?

The fog surged and swirled in giant plumes. Bede Thatch became a blur. The light vanished. Fenella wanted a second long look at that window. Tonight nature didn't agree. The fog thickened and deepened and sank to the ground. It clung to their faces and suffocated all sound. They trudged on, picking up the pace, Fenella's sixth sense flashing with alarm.

They came to a stand of larch trees which shimmered in the slight breeze. They stopped and clustered in a semi-circle, peering through the bluish gloom toward the stone wall which surrounded the garden of Bede Thatch.

Nothing moved.

No crunch of hurried feet.

No high-pitched yell of voices.

Not even the hoot of a hungry owl or snarl of a disturbed

fox.

Everything was quiet.

Deadly still.

"Ain't nowt going on, guv." Dexter's voice broke the unbearable silence. "Bet Helen Grimes is in bed and reading the Good Book. Ain't that what former nuns do of a night?"

"With a cup of cocoa." This was PC Beth Finn.

"And listening to classical music through her phone." Jones couldn't help himself, he had to join in. "Beethoven and Brahms mixed in with Gregorian Chants."

Fenella said nothing. Was Helen Grimes enjoying the solitude of her first night? Were they wasting their time? Doubts multiplied like bacteria in a Petri dish. *I should call it off, tell them to go home, get some sleep and we'll reconvene at the station in the morning.*

Then she thought about the note scrawled on the back of the till receipt: *Mail Benny Label. Okay?* Something nasty was going down tonight. Her gut was right. She knew it. A tragedy would happen if she didn't prevent it.

She waved Jones and PC Beth Finn closer. "Go around the back and wait. If anyone comes out that way, nab them."

She watched them pick their way through the gloom and vanish into the fog. That's when she heard it. A cracking of twigs followed by a sharp metallic jangle. She held up her hand, ears like lungs breathing in all sounds, shuffling them, sorting them, extracting their meaning from the ambient noises of night.

It came again. Loud and sharp and shrill.

"That ain't no bird tweeting, guv." Dexter kept his voice

low.

A brassy timbre echoed in metallic cascades.

"Sounds like a bell, guv." Dexter sucked in a breath, chest rasping with the intake of murky air. "But who'd be ringing one of those in the dead of night?"

Fenella thought of the curse Bella Timbol had said hung over the place—the curse of Borrans Wood where a church bell tolled even though there was no church in the woods. A sullen metal thud to warn of death carried by a monk-like figure who never spoke and had no face.

She said nothing.

They became so still they might have been stone sentries placed to guard the entrance of a great Pharaoh's tomb. A full sixty seconds passed before the sound came again. And this time, ears attuned, they caught every vibrant tone.

Dexter raised his hand, finger pointed at the garden gate. "Look, guv."

Fog pressed cold palms against Fenella's face, blurring her vision with its thick fingers. She blinked, and it seemed the world had gone haywire. She tried to make sense of what she was seeing. Her brain cells drew a blank. Dexter grunted, but no words came out. He, too, was dumbstruck.

79

A shadow detached itself from the darkness. A flicker at first and with it came the ring of a hand bell. It clattered once, twice, thrice. Then came a strange chanting. Deep and guttural and in words that weren't English.

"Pater Noster qui es in caelis..."

The moon broke through the clouds splashing shafts of golden light across the treetops. It was the robes Fenella saw first, shimmering through the fog. Then the high forehead and watchful eyes like two raisins in dough bread.

Vicar Bill Kemp, enrobed in the vestments of Holy Communion, carried a giant crucifix. He held it high above his head with his left hand, a giant hand bell in the right. He turned and Fenella could see he was grinning.

Thin lips.

Perfect teeth.

Brilliant white in the yellow moonlight.

80

Shadows moved behind the vicar.

People.

Lots of people.

And they swayed from side to side like zombies in a grotesque death dance. Fenella tried to make sense of it all, but in the dark and murk with the hand bell ringing and mumbling voices her brain cells refused to fire.

Again the handbell rang out, followed by the droning voice. "Et dimitte nobis debita nostra..."

Fenella raced through deep banks of fog to the gate and burst into the garden. Dexter, puffing hard, ran two paces behind. They reached the ghost of a flowerbed trembling with brambles when a babble of voices joined in with a single solemn word—"Amen."

Vicar Kemp turned.

He was grinning, his white teeth glinting in the moonlight. He waved at them. "Your presence is most welcome." He spoke in the smooth tones of a late-night radio jazz presenter, his eyes watchful. "Tonight our mission is a complete success."

In a flash of white moonlight, other faces became visible. Villagers. Most names were unknown to Fenella. A fat man in an unfashionable green tracksuit stood next to a stooped woman with a peach headscarf tied tight around her small head. A young couple, him in a white t-shirt, her in a lime figure-hugging dress, held hands near the front.

And then there were the faces whose names she now recognised. PC Sid Fenwick, out of uniform, swayed from side to side, his face moonlight pale, beard a black smudge, hooded eyes two pools of dark. Miss May Fish hung at the back between a gaggle of white-haired men. She wore a black velvet ballgown with a high neckline.

Vicar Kemp was still speaking, eyes bright. "Detectives, it is the Lord's hand that has guided you here. It is His works we are all commanded to do. Tonight we finish the job."

He thumped the crucifix three times on the soft soil and rang the handbell. The shadows behind him parted. People were making a gap, stepping aside. A short woman wearing a pink sundress and black knee-high boots danced to the front. Her frizzy brown curls blew wild in the breeze. If Fenella didn't know better, she'd have pegged her as a miniature Medusa replete with snakes in her hair.

Mrs Helen Grimes raised both hands. "Sweet Jesus, I was telling the vicar we should have invited you." Her gaze bounced from Fenella to Dexter in astonishment. "I told everyone how you made me feel at ease at the morgue, and how I prayed you would give me an update on my missing aunt. And now you are here."

"Aye, luv. Here we are." Fenella glanced around, perplexed. "Seems half the village is here with us. What's going on?"

Helen laughed. "Thank God for Vicar Kemp." She

grabbed the vicar's arm, pulling him close. "He's a miracle worker."

Vicar Kemp's smile widened. Big and broad and Hollywood bright. When he spoke it was in the sing-song voice of a contented man. "Helen asked if I would bless the cottage grounds on the occasion of her first night here. After the exhumation of Bobo and the discovery of the body in Borrans Wood, it seemed the right thing to do." He turned to face the flickering shadows of the crowd. "I saw fit to invite my congregation. Quite a turnout, eh? It is not every day the niece of our beloved Ann Crombie stays overnight in our village." He turned to Helen and flashed his dazzling smile. "Your Aunt wrote to me before I moved to the village, promised to be a patron of our church."

Helen patted his arm. "I intend to spend my summers in the village from now on. I can see what Aunt Ann loved about..."

Fenella tuned out and recalled her first meeting with Vicar Kemp. He had complained about the number of blessings he had to perform. Tonight he'd pulled out all the stops—an enormous parade with half the village. A grandiose performance to woo Helen Grimes to donate to his church. And the former nun seemed agreeable to the idea. A small miracle.

Fenella stepped away from the crowd and made her way to the overgrown pond to watch the rest of the ceremony seated on a bench.

She sucked in the damp smells of the pond and decided she was too tired to think. She sent a text to PC Beth Finn and Jones telling them to enter the garden and meet her at the pond.

Dexter arrived, slumped on the bench, pulled a hand-kerchief from his pocket and dabbed at his brow. "Bede Thatch is a never-ending Russian doll, each one filled with an even bigger surprise."

81

The midnight chimes of Market Hall clock echoed across Ambleside. At Bede Thatch, the last of the visitors were making their way back across the trail. Fenella clutched her handbag, thankful nothing bad had happened.

"Time to go." She nodded at her team and tried to sound cheerful, tried to hide the ghosts haunting her that she'd got it all wrong, tried to shove the dread roiling in her stomach away. "The walk will seem far shorter on the way back."

Jones and PC Beth Finn hurried along the garden path. It'd been a long night piled on a long day piled on an even longer week. She didn't blame them for wanting to get home. Tonight she'd soak in the bath and, later, fall into a deep sleep swathed in dreams free from the grotesque horrors of the past few days.

Dexter stayed by her side, shaking his head and glancing at the cottage. "Strange, guv. When I was younger, I'd have believed the worst of it was over."

"And now?"

Dexter rubbed his neck. "Same as you, guv. I'd place my hand on the bible and swear it isn't over. Not by a long shot. I reckon Mr Ashworth is one of those compulsive types, won't give up until he has his way."

Fenella was about to reply when Helen Grimes appeared. She'd seen the vicar off at the garden gate and now hurried back to the overgrown pond. "Thank you so much for coming to the ceremony. I thought you had news of my aunt, but that was not the purpose of your visit, was it?"

"No, luv." There was no point hiding the fact they'd not got a whiff of what happened to Ann Crombie. "When we have news, I'll tell you what I can."

"I'll hold fast to that promise, Inspector Sallow. I'm bereft at the loss." Helen tapped the side of her head and offered a weak smile. "At least I have wonderful memories of Aunt Ann. They remain vivid in here. I can almost touch my aunt, but my heart won't find peace until I lay a bouquet of white roses at her final resting place. Now, if you'll forgive me, I'll turn in."

Helen Grimes turned away and was almost at the front door of Bede Thatch when a shout rang out. It came from beyond the garden gate. From Borrans Wood.

82

Vicar Kemp, shrouded in fog, hustled along the garden path, still enrobed in the fine garments of the earlier blessing. Despite the late hour, he moved with electric speed.

Fenella thought of his unpublished romance manuscripts and she thought of his romance books covered in brown butcher paper and she thought of the smell of fine cigars in his study. She knew why he'd returned even though he'd not said a word yet.

The vicar had expensive tastes and was a perfectionist. That's why he was back. He wanted to make sure his ducks were in a row.

He slowed when he saw the detectives and eased to a dignified walk when he spotted Helen Grimes.

Helen returned to the detectives; by the pond, they watched and waited.

The vicar flashed a bright smile, his eyes receding deep beneath his domed forehead. "Helen, I've been thinking about an exciting new committee I'd like you to chair. I should have mentioned it earlier, but with the prayer and the blessings and the crowds it clean went out of my head." He smiled again with glittering teeth. "I'd like you to be the chairwoman of the Cleric's Transportation Fund. So important the clergy have reliable transportation, don't you think?"

Helen did not hesitate in her reply. "I'd love to. Now, what exactly does it..."

Fenella's mind drifted to the till receipt—*Mail Benny Label. Okay?* It still bothered her. Tightening her grip on her handbag, she knew what she must do. She cast a sly glance at the vicar and Helen. They were engaged in animated conversation. Next, she gave a slight nod to Dexter. He got the message and nodded back.

With silent steps she moved away and hurried through the billowing fog to the front door of Bede Thatch.

83

The key was to get inside, look around and get out before Vicar Kemp and Helen finished talking.

At the door to Bede Thatch, Fenella glanced back through the fog. Dexter stood a step or two apart from the former nun and the man of the cloth. Although she couldn't be certain, she thought Dexter gazed in her direction. He'd delay them and give her fair warning if they finished their chat before she was done.

With care, she reached into her handbag, took out her mobile phone and swiped up the volume so she'd hear the warning ping. She was ready now, but reluctant to admit she didn't know what she was looking for.

A quick nosy about. Like a pig in a trough.

Tugging the handle, the door opened with a creak.

Damp and dark were her first twin sensations. The bare brick walls of the front room smelled of mould with a faint whiff of the pond. Gone was the stink of rotting fish and the hungry buzz of flies. A shaft of moonlight shone through the curtainless window. Enough for her to make out the untidy clutter. Paint cans and brushes and tins of solvent lay scattered around an easel. Sparse furniture— worn green canvas sofa, and against the wall, a round pine table with a single chair. Nothing much had changed from her first visit.

Fenella moved to the centre of the room and looked around. Nothing caught her eye. She padded to the door on the far side. It led to the bedroom. Opening it with a gentle heave, she stepped inside.

Moonlight shone through the bedroom window making strange dappled shadows. She blinked and saw the giant crucifix above the bed with Christ's face twisted in agony. Same dresser with the cracked mirror. Same rush-seated chair. Same iron framed bed. Same silence as deep as a pond. She placed her hands on her hips.

Nothing has changed.

As she crossed the room, mindful the clock was ticking, her gaze fell on the oak wardrobe. Tall and broad and deep. It squatted against the wall like a hideous coffin. She'd not want furniture that looked like that in her bedroom. It would remind her the end was soon nigh. Who wants to dwell on that as they close their eyes to sleep?

She glanced at her phone. Nothing from Dexter. Her gaze went back to the wardrobe. The angle of moonlight through the window shifted and something shifted in the room. Not a physical movement. Or the faint rasp of sound. But a feeling. It triggered the hairs on the back of her neck. An uneasy tingle.

Something about the wardrobe wasn't right.

Fenella shook her phone and the small torch came on. Moving it left to right, she scanned the front of the wardrobe. For a heartbeat, she didn't know why her breathing picked up or why the skin on her arms pimpled. Then she saw the crack between the wardrobe doors.

She took two steps closer to get a better view. The gap between the doors was less than an inch. Not more than a slither.

Her phone buzzed—Dexter's warning shot.

If not for her curiosity, she might have turned and hurried back to the front door. But she listened to the silence of the room for two heartbeats. Then she spoke. "Come out now, luv. There is no point hiding."

With a high-pitched squeal, the wardrobe doors flew open.

Ken Ashworth stood inside the wardrobe, bright shirt crumpled, skinny blue jeans stained, foaming at the lips like a rabid dog. It was his eyes Fenella would always remember. Wild and savage and as soulless as a demon.

"You have no right to be here." Ken ran a hand through his spiked black hair and then twiddled with his gold nose stud. He clenched his fists. "No right whatsoever. You must have a search warrant to enter this place. Bede Thatch is private property."

Fenella took a step forward. "There are times when you have to break the rules to keep the rule of law, Sunshine. Now come out and we'll have a chat about it at the police station."

It happened so fast; Fenella did not have time to react. Ken Ashworth leapt out, knocking her aside, his intent to escape through the door. He made it to the threshold before bouncing off the solid wall of Dexter. The two men struggled, twisting and turning. Knees and elbows and fists and feet. Fenella entered the fray, swinging her handbag and striking Ken on the side of his head. He staggered back. Dexter's fist landed on his jaw. Ken screamed, crumpling to the floor.

Dexter pounced, pinning Ken flat on his stomach, his knee in the centre of Ken's back. He twisted Ken's arm in a painful lock. "Ain't no point struggling Mr Peeping Tom, it will only make the pain worse."

84

For Fenella, the real heartbreak began after the truth came out, on that following hellish day.

It was seven in the morning when she parked in the Port St Giles Cottage Hospital. Wind swirled leaves across the empty tarmac. They swished against the car with the soft rustle of a small animal burrowing for cover. Last night's events would soon reach Kate Owen's ears. Fenella wanted to be the first to tell her of Ken Ashworth's capture. Break it to her with care before the news media went berserk. Who wants to learn their loved one is the village Peeping Tom? And there was something else too. Her gaze settled on the hospital entrance.

Two women waited by the automatic glass doors. A police officer, PC Fay Bright, and a teen in a scruffy peach jacket which clashed with her blue streaked hair. Skye Owen hung her head, shuffling from foot to foot.

Fenella watched the lass for a long while, then tilted her neck from side to side to ease the growing tension. Teenagers weren't easy at the best of times. Today would not be the best of times.

Her phone pinged. A text message from Jeffery. Congratulatory. Ken Ashworth caught lurking in the bedroom of Bede Thatch was a big deal. Chief Constable Rae and other bigwigs from Carlisle would arrive at noon for a debriefing. Then a press conference at Town Hall with Jeffery at the helm. Afterwards, a joyous meeting in the conference room where platitudes would be handed out. All recorded by Dawn Margot, the documentary reporter and her film crew, presumably.

Fenella pushed the upcoming media circus to the back of her mind and hustled from the car to the hospital entrance.

"I'm detective inspector Sallow." She kept her tone brisk, taking the lass in. "And you must be Skye?"

"I didn't want to come here." Skye pouted and folded her arms. "But PC Bright made me."

Fenella held Skye's gaze and didn't mince her words. "Pet, you will speak with your mam. You will tell her everything and then PC Fay Bright will take you to the station. Later today, you and I will have a long chat."

"I can't see her. Not now." Skye's voice trembled. "Not after what I've done."

Fenella wasn't in the mood to argue. She took Skye by the arm leading her through the hospital lobby. They paused outside the florists.

Fenella released her grip. "Tell me about your dad."

"What is there to tell?" Skye's voice broke. "He ran off when I was small."

Fenella hustled Skye into the flower shop, PC Fay Bright a step behind. The shop assistant looked up from a magazine then went back to reading.

Fenella stopped at a row of pre-wrapped bouquets. "For your mam."

"What?" Skye stared, bewildered.

"Flowers."

"Oh."

"They'll cheer her up, luv." Fenella pointed. "White roses?"

Skye sniffed. "I don't have any money."

Fenella picked up a bouquet of sunflowers and sweet peas. "She'll like these. Nice smell."

Skye shrugged. "Suppose."

"What else?" Fenella didn't wait for a reply, grabbed a large box of Belgian chocolates, paid and they left the store.

They walked a few steps then Fenella stopped and held out the two gifts. Skye took the bouquet and tucked the box of chocolates under her arm; eyes cast down. "I can't do this."

"Aye, you can, luv. Your mam needs to know the truth. She needs to hear it from your lips."

They walked through the hospital corridors without another word, their footfalls striking the concrete floor with a harsh slap. Misery lay ahead for mother and daughter. More misery than either of them had ever known.

85

From the moment Fenella entered the hospital room, she knew how it would end. Time stood still; like a toothache at midnight when the medicine cabinet is empty of pills. A hellish warp of slow motion where each nerve pinching pulse throbs in an endless void.

Kate Owen leaned against a pillow, childlike and plump, her hair rumpled. She read a comic, her lips twisted in a huge grin, and did not look up.

"I've brought your daughter to see you." Fenella moved close to the bed, pushing Skye ahead of her. "She has things to tell you."

Kate put the comic down. Her grin drained away. Mother and daughter looked at one another.

Fenella stepped to the edge of the room where PC Fay Bright waited. For a long minute there was silence broken only by Skye's heavy breathing.

Then Skye spoke. "I hate hospitals." She sank into a chair at the bedside, placing the flowers and chocolates on the bedside cabinet. "They spook me, Mam."

Kate exhaled a sharp breath. "I should never have brought you with me to Ambleside."

"Don't, Mam." Skye folded her arms. "Don't put yourself down. Not now. Not after all that has happened."

Kate touched her daughter's cheek. "You need to do more with your hair. Why don't you grow it a little and let it return to its natural colour? You had beautiful long hair when you were small. You'll catch a man with a good job if you let it grow a little."

Skye made a face, picked up the bunch of flowers and sniffed. "Are you getting better?"

"I don't know. The doctor says it is serious. Something to do with my liver. They have given me pills, never been so tired."

"I don't like you here." Skye pouted. "You don't look well and this place smells of death. Hospitals make you sick, you are better off at home. Do you want me to bring your sketchbook?"

"I've given it up."

"You should try it again. Practice makes perfect."

Kate leaned over to kiss her daughter's cheek. "Who is he, Skye? Who is the man that has stolen my baby from the cradle?"

"Please, Mam, don't."

Kate sighed. "I hear he is a used car salesman."

Skye's head drooped. "Who told you that?"

Kate tried not to shout but she couldn't help herself. "Throw him back. Sling your hook again and catch a rich one. A man in a profession. A man you can stand by."

Skye shrugged. "They've arrested Ken and are holding him at the police station. They say he is a—"

Fenella cleared her throat. "Last night we arrested Mr Ken Ashworth at Bede Thatch cottage. He is helping us with our inquiries."

Kate puffed up her cheeks and closed her eyes. One second, two, three. . . ten. She exhaled a long slow breath. Her eyes opened. She turned to Skye. "Will you come and visit me again? Without police company, if you can."

"It's Ken, Mam, that's why I'm here." Skye's voice rose to a screech. "The police have got Ken."

Kate reached out to hold Skye's hand. "Whatever he's done, we will get through this together." She hesitated, gaze darting from Fenella to PC Fay Bright. "Will he be released soon, Inspector Sallow?"

Fenella said nothing.

Skye gulped back a sob. "Oh Mam, can't you see?"

"What is it Skye?" Kate looked at her daughter with tenderness. "What don't I see?"

"Ken doesn't love you." Skye shook free from her mam's grip. "He found me a bedsit in Carlisle and comes to see me when he can. I've moved in with him."

Kate became very still. "Please be sweet, don't lie to your mother. You always were a child that told big lies. When you were six it got so bad the teacher washed out your mouth with carbolic soap, do you remember? You even lied to me about what had happened, but I already knew. I spoke about it with your teacher in advance."

Skye lifted her chin. "You want me to say I'm coming home. I'm sorry, Mam, but I'm all grown up now. Sixteen next month and a woman. I've left school and Ken got me a job in a tinning factory. It does not pay all the rent but Ken helps out. He stays with me most nights and told me he loves me. I cook him cottage pie, kippers and everything."

Kate's hands flew to her face. "That man is poison. You must leave that devil before it is too late. I want you to come back home. I want us to be a family."

Skye leaned forward, her voice dropping to a whisper. "I'm in love, Mam. I'm so in love. You are going to be a grandmother; I'm having his child."

Kate slapped Skye so hard that she tumbled from the chair. "You filthy—"

"Stop that." Fenella stepped forward before more unsavoury words tumbled from Kate's lips. "Skye, PC Bright will take you to the station now. Your mam needs her rest."

Skye sprang to her feet, strode to the door and let out a bitter laugh. "You never liked him, but I do. I'll look out for him, have his back. I don't care what the police say about him, I'll be there when Ken gets out. I'll stand by my man."

86

Finally, the door clicked shut.

Only then, as Fenella's heart skittered, did the tension in her neck loosen. She kneaded both sides with firm hands, horrified at seeing such a heartbreaking scene.

Kate Owen lay on the bed, gaunt and pale, tubes snaking from her arm, chest heaving.

In. Out.

In. Out.

Shallow breaths of life.

The lass looked worn out. Frail, like she'd not last long. She needed rest and medical help and the arms of her family around her. Questions so soon might send her on a downward spiral. Fenella would not want a detective firing questions at her as she lay half dead in bed and reeling in shock from her daughter's news. Should she come back tomorrow or the day after when the lass had regained her strength?

Fenella sucked in a long slow breath and her hands fell from massaging her neck. How would Kate find the strength to face the torture of the coming days? There would be endless questions from the police, social workers, psychiatrists, neighbours. Each picking over the ruins of her family life. Each pulling apart Kate's role as a mother. It was only a matter of time before the news media picked up the scent. Soon, the dam would burst.

In. Out.

In. Out.

Kate's breath. Hard and heavy.

And again Fenella considered. Did Kate have the presence of mind to answer her most pressing questions right now? Before the onslaught began. Before the sheer hell of it wore Kate Owen down to a numb nub and the news media rat pack feasted on the bones. She pondered the issue. Stay and risk the lass suffer a mental breakdown, or come back later to give Kate time to rest?

Fenella eased into the bedside chair. Better to get the questions in ahead of the pack. Then she'd go back to the police station and kick off the formal interviews with Ken Ashworth and Skye Owen. Today she'd peel away the lies to get at the pungent truth.

"Kate?" Fenella waited a heartbeat. "Are you up for a chat?"

Kate stared off into the distance, her face twisted in anguish from the barrage of painful truths unleashed by her daughter.

Fenella picked up the box of chocolates, lifted the lid and offered it to her. "Teenagers, eh? Not easy. You love them with all your heart and then they do something silly that pierces it. Not on purpose. Not with spite. They don't think. I know. I've had five."

Kate's hand stretched out on automatic. "My problem is that I'm too trusting of men." She chose a hazelnut swirl, then dropped it back into the box. "It is not Skye's fault.

I won't blame her. She is young and naïve. An innocent child."

Fenella said nothing.

Kate squeezed her eyes shut for a heartbeat. "I want you to put that bloated leach, Ken Ashworth, away for the rest of his life. The world will be a better place without him roaming free. I will do anything, say anything to help you do that."

Fenella leaned in. "You don't mean that, do you, pet?"

"If you nail Ken for what he has done, it will be the best news of my life." Kate gazed with sad eyes. "Forgive me, I sound terrible, like a right miserable old—"

"You've had a shock, luv. Shock makes you say things you later regret."

"It's not shock. I'm not in shock. I've been through too much for shock to mean anything to me." Kate's voice came out clear, crisp, firm. "You've no idea what Ken has done to my life. He's ruined my family, plundered me both physically and emotionally and now he is doing the same with my daughter. I want him to go down. I want him behind bars for a very long time. Do you understand?"

"Oh, come off it, pet. It is the drugs talking. They have clouded your head."

"I'm fine." Kate touched the wart on her chin. "See, I'm still here, still whole. Apart from my liver, I'm as clear-headed as I ever was."

"That's what I thought, luv." Fenella closed the choco-late box lid, placing it on the bedside cabinet. "The doctor said as much, said you passed out from too much drink, said there were no signs of an attack."

Kate flicked a stray strand of hair from her face. "What

is this about?"

"When Skye told you she was seeing Ken, you took it well."

"What do you mean?"

"You already knew, didn't you?"

"No."

"You sure?"

"Yes."

"Don't lie to me. I'm a detective and spend my days talking to people to get at the truth. You knew about your daughter and Ken, didn't you?"

The sound of Kate's breathing changed. She hung her head. "Not about the baby. I didn't know about the baby, I swear."

Fenella let that hang in the air for a heartbeat. "How long have you known?"

"Months."

"How many?"

"Two."

"Liar."

Kate shrank back against her pillow and ran her fingers through her lank hair. "Almost a year."

"You sure?"

"Yes."

"I believe you."

Kate sighed. "It's disgusting to think I let that roach into my life. Sickening, that I let Ken stay, and now he is taunting me through my own daughter. But please don't judge me. I'm a single working mam with a rebellious teen. Sometimes I can't think straight and want to scream. My God, the terrible strain of all that has happened is killing me. Killing my liver. If I'd brought up Skye in a proper family with a real man rather than a cockroach, this would not have happened."

"You are not the first to be taken in, luv. It happens all the time and all over the world. Lying. Cheating. Stealing. It's why the police are so busy."

Kate let out a short puff of breath. "The bones didn't roll my way with Skye's dad either. He abandoned us when she was small."

It was a story Fenella knew well—love turned to flames of rage when a bloke vanishes after getting a lass pregnant. She looked straight at Kate. "Tell me about Bart Owen?"

A flash of surprise crossed Kate's face, and she studied Fenella for a long moment. "I can see you have done your homework. Bart ran off without leaving me with so much as a ten pound note. I had to face the bills and the landlady and his so-called friends whom he owed money."

Fenella tapped the chocolate box lid. "Sounds like Bart was a bad penny."

Kate laughed. "I was so young. Why did I believe his story about inheriting money from his great-aunt? He told me she had a jewellery box so large it took two grown men to move it. A treasure trove, that's how Bart described it. All his when his aunt kicked the bucket, along with the house."

"He lied to you, then?"

Kate snorted. "When I told Bart I was with child, he promised we'd get wed before the baby was born. A posh wedding with hundreds of guests in a fancy hotel in Carlisle." Her voice became sorrowful. "Everything Bart told me was a pack of lies. There was no great-aunt. There was no treasure trove. We were married on the cheap in the registry office in Barrow-in-Furness. I had to go to work to pay for the rent on our bedsit."

A knock clattered on the door. Dexter entered the room. He nodded at Kate but she didn't seem to notice. Her eyes were in a faraway place.

"Sometimes I dream of another life where I never met Bart." A smile kissed Kate's lips. "Where Skye has a good father, a rich gentleman who'll pay for her college and take me on expensive holidays. There are mornings when I stay in bed holding on to that dream with all my strength."

"Aye, pet. I'd dream the same thing if I was in your shoes."

Kate came back to the present and blinked. "But I wake up. We have to, don't we? I was just a naïve girl exploited by an older man. Nothing new in that. The cycle has repeated itself since time began. If it weren't so tragic I'd laugh, but joy doesn't pay the bills."

They fell silent for a moment. A medical device beeped.

"Working as a barmaid can't be easy." Fenella kept her voice soft. "Rent, food, heating, all on a basic pay and tips."

"It is very hard. The pub landlord keeps half the tips and when he is not counting his money he is trying to touch my—"

Fenella interrupted. She needed Kate to stay on track. "And Bart never helped out?"

Anger flashed across Kate's face. "He wouldn't lift a finger other than to shove food in his mouth. When he ran off, I knew it was over."

She stopped, chest heaving in wild jerks, her breathing

hard and heavy.

Fenella wanted to keep her talking. Every word helped fill in the puzzle. Every sentence clarified things in her mind. "You never divorced Bart, why is that?"

Another flash crossed Kate's face. Not anger this time. Surprise. "My God, you've a nose on you."

"I'm a detective, luv, we do nowt but nose about in other folks' business." Fenella knew she was pinching a raw nerve, watched for signs of tears and seeing none, kept the pressure on. "Are you still in love with him?"

Kate sniffed. "Bart said he'd take care of me, provide for me. But he only wanted one thing and when it wasn't offered freely, he took it with his fists."

Fenella's voice filled with concern. "Is that how you became pregnant with Skye?"

87

Kate gazed at the bouquet of sunflowers and sweet peas. "I love Skye, but she was my hook to Bart's future riches. An insurance policy which was supposed to pay out when his aunt died. I wanted Skye, and I wanted Bart until I found out he was a rat."

Again Fenella asked the question. "But you never divorced him?"

"All that legal stuff makes my head spin."

Fenella kept her face blank, hiding her eagerness for the answer to her next question. "Has he contacted you in the past few days?"

Kate's eyes glistened and her face twisted in a scowl of raw pain. "If he did, it would be for money and I've had no luck with that."

"So, you haven't seen him since the day he ran out on you?"

"What do you think?"

"That you killed Bart Owen and hid the body in some place we'd never look."

Ashen-faced, Kate swallowed. "You can't prove that."

"No, pet I can't." Fenella raised both hands, palms out. "But a lad like Bart Owen doesn't run off without a trace.

Yes, he might leave town, but wherever he surfaces, you can guarantee there'll be a trail of petty crime leading to his door. Yet, we found nothing. I've got no proof, just my gut."

Kate slumped against the pillow. "He was a very bad man, Inspector Sallow. There wasn't a week when he wasn't caught up in some dodgy scheme. My love for him turned to hate when I saw what was behind the curtain. That man made a fool of me, and I won't stand for that. Not from anyone."

"So you killed him?"

Kate let out a bitter laugh. "Look, Bart was a man of broken promises whom the world doesn't miss. It won't miss Ken when you put him away for murder."

"I never said anything about Ken Ashworth and murder."

"But you—"

Fenella raised a hand. "I said Mr Ken Ashworth was helping us with our inquiries. It is you who mentioned murder."

Silence, except the thrum of a medical instrument, and, thought Fenella, the cogs whirring in Kate's brain. A sweep of golden sunlight swept through the French windows.

Kate turned to gaze at the curtains and the lawned garden beyond. "I'd like to rest now. Please leave."

Fenella did not move. "Kippers. We found a plate of rotten kippers in Bede Thatch next to a tub of sour yoghurt. What were they doing there, stinking out the place like that? All the windows and doors were shut. There were so many flies I heard their buzz before I saw them. Too many flies. Big and black and bloated. You put them there."

Kate swallowed. "I don't know what you are talking about."

Fenella kept her voice low. "The stench would drive anyone with half a nose to throw those kippers out. But the woman who lived in the cottage didn't throw them out. Why? Because you put them in her art studio sometime after she died. You hacked off her head in rage and put rotten kippers and festering yoghurt in her house. As for the flies, you worked on a maggot farm, didn't you?"

"You can't think I..." Kate's stared from the bed in innocent shock. Crimson splotches spread across her cheeks. "You've got it wrong, I'm a single mam for God's sake. I've a family to protect. Can't you see I'm the victim here?"

Fenella leaned forward; gaze fixed on Kate's face. "Blackmail, that was your motive."

Kate sank back against the pillow, eyes wide. "Get out."

Fenella did not move. "Where did you meet Zoe Haynes?"

Kate touched the wart on her chin. "Who?"

"The woman pretending to be Ann Crombie and living the good life as an artist in Bede Thatch." Fenella paused for a heartbeat. "The woman you blackmailed."

"No. It isn't true." Kate's voice trembled. "It's Ken you want to focus on. You've seen what type of man he is. There were times when I thought he might strike me, kill me in a rage. And you found him at Bede Thatch, didn't you? What was he doing there? Please focus on him. The man is a ball of spite. Ask him all your questions."

The door opened. A nurse looked in, smiled and left.

Fenella took out her mobile phone, swiped and read the screen. "Mail Benny Label. Okay?" She held Kate's gaze.

"Do you know what it means?"

Kate shifted her weight. "Your guess is as good as mine."

"I found it inside a puzzle book in Ann Crombie's bedroom. A handful of words scrawled on the back of a book receipt. It puzzled me. Aren't you intrigued?"

Kate looked baffled. "Notes written on scraps of paper? I write things down so I won't forget. Maybe she did the same."

"That is what I thought, and it kept niggling me. Why was it written on the back of a Giles Rare Books Store receipt? Why was it placed between the pages of *North-worder*? I knew it meant something. But what?"

Kate laughed. "Could it be a message from the other side?"

"That's exactly what it is."

Kate blinked. "No way. It is a scrap of paper, nothing more. There is no secret in that."

"The key was those blank pages in the copy of *North-worder* I found in the bedroom of Bede Thatch. As I flipped through the pages, I noticed the crossword and sudoku sections were blank. Only the word searches, anagrams and mazes were partially complete. That told me a lot, but not enough. It was not until you killed Liam Brampton that I understood the message on the back of that till receipt. You killed him, didn't you?"

"How dare you say a wicked thing like that about me and that...creep!"

"I'm sorry, pet, but it says right here on this till receipt that you killed him."

Kate scoffed. "You've lost it Inspector Sallow. It is you

who should be lying on the hospital bed."

Fenella's lips quirked at the corners. "Zoe Haynes loved puzzles, that's why she flourished wearing the mask of Ann Crombie. It was a challenge for her. A giant puzzle she almost pulled off. But you spotted her and blackmailed her and got a wad of cool hard cash paid like clockwork each month to keep your lips sealed."

"What has this got to do with the till receipt?" Kate tilted her chin in a show of arrogance, but her voice came out weasel thin. "Where does it say I'm the killer?"

Once again, Fenella turned her phone around and pointed at the screen. Kate stared at it, squinted and blinked. "You've lost me."

"I didn't get it until I remembered Zoe Haynes loved puzzles." Fenella paused to glance at the phone's screen and then turned it again so Kate could see. "She went to Giles Rare Books each month to load up on puzzle books and spent twenty-five pounds each time."

"Okay, the woman loved puzzles and plopped down a wad of cash, so what?" Kate squinted at the phone. "I still don't understand what this has got to do with me."

Fenella smiled. "Zoe Haynes left behind a list of the people who knew or might know her real identity. It was her insurance policy in case anything nasty happened to her. She left it where the police would find it."

"Rubbish!"

"No, Sunshine. Not rubbish but fact. Take the first word, 'Mail', that is Liam spelled backwards. 'Benny' is the nickname of Helen Grimes, the real Ann Crombie's niece. You can see the word 'label' spells Bella. That's Bella Timbol the woman you killed in Grange Hall Care Home and a fellow member of Ambleside Village Artists. You killed them all except Helen Grimes who I feared would be next."

Kate's jaw dropped. If any words came out, they were unintelligible.

Fenella continued. "Now take the last word, 'Okay'. An interesting word. I don't need to tell you what it means, but did you know it is the most frequently used word on the planet? Every language has borrowed the word or knows of it. You can use it anywhere and they'll understand. I reckon Zoe knew this and used it to point the finger at you. Okay is often shortened to 'OK', which reversed is 'KO' and stands for Kate Owen."

"Jesus Christ!" Kate was hyperventilating, clutching at her chest, gasping for air. "You witch. This can't be happening. All I did was ask Zoe to up her regular payment by a few hundred quid. I needed the money to help pay my bills."

"And she agreed?" Fenella kept her voice low.

Kate shook her head. "The sow snorted, folded her arms and told me it was over. Her art was selling, and she wanted the world to know who she really was. Zoe's success with those bloody foxes meant she didn't want to wear the mask of Ann Crombie anymore. She planned to go public and confess what she'd done."

"When?" Fenella kept her question short, trying not to disturb Kate's flow.

"Soon. Very soon." Kate trembled. "Zoe laughed when she told me she wasn't going to toss any more coins my way. A big belly laugh like I was a joke. Just like Bart laughed when I told him not to touch me. Just like Ken laughed when I asked him to marry me. Just like Skye laughed just now."

Again Kate stopped, face exploding in crimson.

"Go on Kate." Fenella hissed the words through her teeth. "You have to let it out. You have to tell me what happened. I want to know it all."

Kate let out a vicious laugh. "Zoe said she was doing me a kindness. I argued with her, told her it was madness and that we had a sweet deal, but she said she was ready to pay the price, reckoned it would cause demand for her work to skyrocket. She wanted her real name attributed to her paintings. She wanted the world to know that she was a great artist, wanted to tell the truth about what she had done."

"So you killed her?"

"She said she was going to tell the police about me. Tell them what I'd done." Kate stared with wide-eyed innocence. "I'm a single mam with my family to protect. I had to do something."

403

88

Dexter leaned against the wall, phone in hand, recording the conversation.

Kate seemed to come up out of her dream. "Who is he?"

"He is with me." Fenella touched Kate's arm. "It's time to get the full story. Go on, let it out, I'm listening."

Kate's eyes glazed over and she spoke as if to herself. "I dared not wait long. When Zoe made up her mind to do a thing, she did it. I noticed her decisiveness when we first met at the Barrow-in-Furness Artists League. I considered myself a sketchbook artist back then. Zoe longed to work with landscape paintings. And she made her wish come true, even though she started as a care worker."

Again she stopped, her breaths fast and shallow. Fenella didn't want to disturb the flow. A wrong word and it would be over. She waited, heart skittering in her throat.

Kate's face scrunched in a ball of hate. "I knew what I must do and waited until nightfall. I have a key to Bede Thatch but Zoe never locked the door, so I didn't need it. I crept inside with a field mouse in my pocket. Zoe had a soft spot for mice. I knew where she would go when she found it. I rattled around her room until she stirred, leaving as her head rose from the pillow."

Kate paused and inhaled a deep breath as though sucking back the words. As though they belonged inside where no one could see them.

"Keep going." Fenella felt her heart pounding against her chest, and whispered now, light and as soft as warm air. "Keep telling."

Kate exhaled. "Once Zoe was in the woods, the rest was easy. I used to work in the back room of a butcher shop. Thought I might be the owner's wife one day and volunteered to slaughter live chickens. Lots of clucking and feathers but it is easy once you get the hang of it. It is all in the swing of the blade, but I was rusty that first time and made a right mess."

Fenella had heard enough and changed direction. "And the kippers?"

"Yeah, I put them in Bede Thatch."

"When?"

Kate's eyes turned inward. "Locals always dress up in fancy clothes for the Ambleside Village Artists Walkabout. I wore a monk's outfit on Saturday morning. I didn't plan it, it just happened."

"You keep a monk's robe in your wardrobe?"

"I... er... hired it from a fancy dress shop in Port St Giles."

"Sunshine, don't lie to me. You got it from Ken Ashworth's cottage. We found one hanging in the hallway of his house."

Kate's eyes narrowed. "He liked to dress up sometimes when we were alone, but I swear I didn't plan to go back to Bede Thatch on purpose. It was a spur-of-the-moment thing."

"What about the maggots?" Fenella sniffed. "Are you telling me you just happened upon a box of maggots ready to turn into flies?"

Kate picked at the wart on her chin. "Bella Timbol was by the garden gate chatting with Miss Fish. Neither saw me enter Bede Thatch." Her lips twisted into a nasty grin. "Zoe kicked up such a pong about coming clean, I thought I'd leave her a little dollop of stink as a farewell present."

"So you did plan it?"

Kate's eyes gleamed, but she said nothing.

Fenella rubbed the bridge of her nose to ease the tension behind her eyes. She had to ask the question which had sickened her at the very start. "Why did you cut off her head and leave her breasts exposed?"

Kate glanced down at her flat chest and again said nothing.

Fenella's gut heaved. "Tell me about Bella Timbol."

"The snooty cow was on our trail. Reckon that was another reason Zoe wanted to come out." Kate chuckled in an unpleasant way. "When I saw Bella outside Bede Thatch last Saturday morning, it made me mad. I knew she was there because she knew something was off. The cow was looking for clues. Well, I knew her game and sent an anonymous note that I had information about the real Ann Crombie. I told her to destroy the note and meet me at Grange Hall Care Home. The dozy cow took the bait, even dressed as a nurse."

"Tell me about that." Fenella leaned forward; eyes fixed on Kate. "Tell me what happened at Grange Hall."

"There is a path at the back of the home that leads to

the cellar where they do the laundry. No CCTV cameras. I know. I worked there as a cleaner a while back." Kate licked her lips. "I waited. Finished the job in record time. Not even a scream. A clean swing of the meat cleaver. Easy when you get the hang of it."

Her words were a salutary reminder of what Fenella was dealing with—a cold-blooded killer who saw nothing beyond her own twisted needs. Fenella held her revulsion in check, clear where the last puzzle piece fit. "What happened to the real Ann Crombie?"

Kate twisted the wart on her chin. "I thought you lot would find her when you searched the garden of Bede Thatch."

"But we didn't. Can you help?"

Kate rolled her eyes. "The old fart was long gone before I got on the scene. I never caught a whiff of her." Her lips twisted into an evil grin and she spoke as though keeping a secret. "Have you dredged the lake?"

Fenella couldn't ignore the intensity which boiled in her gut. She felt responsible for finding out what had happened to Ann Crombie. She wanted to tell Helen Grimes the truth, give her the chance to bury her aunt. *Rest in peace.* It was personal. It had been since the start. But she gestured as though the question was not important.

"I'm more interested in what happened to Liam Brampton. I hear he had some talent and might have gone on to greater things."

Kate glared; lips sealed.

Fenella held Kate's gaze. "Here is what I think happened—you got drunk after you killed him, tried to knock it from your brain cells with booze. Then, tanked-up and out of your head, you ended up in Borrans Wood and passed out. That is how you ended up in the hospital, eh?"

Kate sneered. "The creep figured out Zoe Haynes wasn't the real Ann Crombie. When Zoe died, he knew it had something to do with me."

"Oh come off it, luv. How would he know that?"

"Zoe went to Port St Giles once a month. We'd meet up in a café to exchange payment. Zoe paid the bill, always twenty pounds plus a five pound tip. Then she'd give me my money. Liam saw us once, by chance. He was waiting in the café the next month, and the month after that. We changed café, but within a couple of months, he was back, watching."

Kate's energy seemed to sag and her voice faded.

"Keep going, Kate." Fenella kept her voice a whisper. "I'm listening."

Kate closed her eyes. "Last week Liam approached me in the pub, asked if I would pose for him. I said yes because I wanted to know what he was up to. But I killed Zoe the night before we were due to meet, panicked and called it off. I didn't want him asking questions about her death. Not when it was so close and raw. I needed time to settle my nerves."

Fenella raised her voice. "When did Mr Liam Brampton tell you he suspected you?"

"What? No, no—no, no, no. That is not what happened. He was too sly a man for a direct approach. After I killed Zoe, Liam started following me and I *knew* that he knew what I had done."

"He never accused you?"

She shook her head. "He wanted me to pose for him,

so I arranged to meet him at Ken's place. I have a key." Kate's features were skeletal sharp, eyes sunk into her skull. "Not an easy kill. Fat men have more blood."

Fenella changed the subject. "And the white rose petals?"

"You noticed them?"

"Aye, and you put them by the bodies."

"A little of something sweet to cover the stink those people left in my life."

Fenella knew the answer, but she asked anyway. "Why did you kill Liam Brampton in Mr Ashworth's house?"

"Ken tormented me; I want him to rot behind prison bars for what he has done to my family. I want him to pay with his life." Kate covered her face and began to sob. "I wanted to be the teacher's wife but he wouldn't marry me."

89

It was four o'clock the following afternoon and Fenella had a promise to keep. She wore a blue ankle-length floral dress, hooped gold earrings and her grey hair swept into a bun. She hoped she hadn't overdressed.

From the moment she entered the lobby of Grange Hall Care Home, her mouth watered at the sweet scent of baked goods. On Friday the residents enjoyed High Tea. Fresh baked cakes and cream scones, Earl Grey and Darjeeling tea. Local jams in stone pots—blackberry, damson and redcurrant. She'd promised to meet with Mr Kuck to talk about his time with the police.

She glanced around the empty lobby. Sunlight shone through the huge windows. It splashed on the peacock-patterned wallpaper and glittered off the polished hardwood floor. It was her second visit within a week and despite all that had happened the place still reminded her of a posh hotel.

A soft Irish voice called out. "Ah, there you are Inspector Sallow." Miss Kim Jennings, the general manager, appeared from nowhere. She wore a mauve velvet dress with a string of white pearls around her neck and a huge glittering smile. "Mr Kuck said you were coming; right fierce he was about it. I told him not to get his hopes up. This way."

They entered through a walnut panel which Fenella only now realised served as a door. It led to a dining room with round tables covered in white tablecloths. Waiters in black served from silver platters filled with cakes and pastries. The tinkle of a piano drifted across the room. The pianist, in a white tuxedo, swayed as he played *Fly Me to the Moon.* Fenella swallowed a gasp. Vicar Bill Kemp seemed to be in a trance as his fingers danced across the keys.

Miss Jennings lowered her voice. "No mobile phones in the dining room, the pings and rings disturb the atmosphere. Please turn your phone off now."

Fenella did so, trying not to stare at the vicar. The man was good. Very good. And he swayed as if he and the music were one.

Miss Jennings pointed to a table near the window. "Oh look, there is Mr Kuck."

He wore a black tuxedo, and a cream shirt with a black bow tie. He gulped from a cup of tea and then stuffed a cream scone into his mouth. Two elderly women sat next to him, one grey-haired and the other with a blue rinse. He appeared to listen, nodding and sipping and munching as the woman with the blue rinse spoke.

Miss Jennings touched Fenella's arm and pointed. "Mr Kuck is in our memory care unit, along with his two friends—Mrs Sparks and Miss Zest."

Mrs Sparks was broad with a plum-shaped face and a mop of blue-rinsed hair which sprang from her head like bed coils. Miss Zest was thin and frail and her eyes seemed too large for her small head.

Miss Jennings continued. "I've only been here a week, but I've heard the three of them have been with us for years. They are good friends, but you've got to watch them. Crafty devils. Mr Kuck is the talker. Mrs Sparks says a word or two. Never heard Miss Zest speak." She lowered her voice and tapped the side of her head. "Too far gone."

Fenella's Uncle Glen had lost his memory. A slow decline at first. Then it sped up, and he entered a tunnel of endless misery. In the end, she took each day as it came, grateful for the hours when he had clarity.

She gazed at the three elderly people around the table. "How is Mr Kuck doing today?"

"Grand." Miss Jennings touched her pearl necklace. "I'm not sentimental, can't be in this business, but I like to think Mr Kuck's tales keep those two ladies going. Like music, I suppose, stimulates the brain cells."

Fenella thought about Uncle Glen. About his confusion. About his distress. About her tears. She pulled out a tissue from her handbag and dabbed her eyes. "Mr Kuck wanted to talk about his time on the police force. Do you think he'll remember any stories? I don't want to embarrass him."

Miss Jennings laughed. "Talks about his time in the police as if it were yesterday. All day. Every day. Take my advice—grab a slice of cake or a scone. The damson jam is to die for. If he starts to talk about coconuts, feel free to close your eyes."

Miss Jennings led her to the table and withdrew. A waiter appeared and poured a cup of tea.

"What pastry would Madame like?"

Fenella recognised the voice, mouth dropping in shock

to see PC Sid Fenwick dressed as a server.

"I'm part of the volunteer crew, ma'am." PC Sid Fenwick kept his voice low but his black beard moved with a slow twitch, his hooded eyes watchful. "The vicarage at Ambleside supply staff for High Tea every other month. Vicar Kemp's doing and I like to do my part for the community. Liam Brampton used to help out as a server. Shame he won't be doing that anymore. I considered him a friend."

"Sorry?"

"We worked together in the abattoir. He kept the place spotless. No other cleaner had his eye for grime. We used to call him a genius, the Mad Mop Professor. He liked that. When you work in a low-paid job, the comradery helps." Again his beard twitched. "That's what I do when I'm not the part-time village bobby or serving here. I'm part of the nighttime cleaning crew."

Fenella gave a nod of understanding and turned her mind to the food. *A slice of Victoria sponge cake or a large soft scone?* She thought of the giant scone she'd denied herself on the day she waited in the café in Ambleside. The day they'd dug up Bobo's bones. "I'll have a slice of cake... and two scones. Save you running to and fro. Oh, and rustle up two pots of that damson jam and a pot of clotted cream. Please."

PC Sid Fenwick's eyes widened, but he said nothing, bowed and walked away.

Mr Kuck tinkled a spoon against his cup. "Ladies, have I ever regaled you with the curious story of the stolen coconut?"

Mrs Sparks smiled. Miss Zest smiled. Fenella wondered whether either woman knew where they were. She wondered if Mr Kuck recognised her. It didn't matter. She wanted to hear the tale. *Like a pig in a trough.*

She flashed a friendly smile. "Let's have it, then. And don't miss anything out. Did it happen when you were in uniform or when you were working as a detective?"

Mr Kuck blinked and stared at her. "We met earlier this week when I snatched the orderly's keys, didn't we?"

"Aye, and don't do it again."

He flashed a sly grin. "Gives me something to do."

There was a question on Fenella's mind that remained unanswered. She smiled at Mr Kuck. "Do you remember the new nurse?"

"Who?"

"The woman you told me about when we first met in the lobby. You said she had a big secret." There was no doubt in Fenella's mind that the nurse was Bella Timbol. She leaned forward. "What did the new nurse tell you?"

He squeezed his eyes shut. "New nurse? The old brain cells come and go. I don't remember what I said. I don't remember her. I forget a lot these days."

"Not to worry." Fenella tried to hide her disappointment. "I must have got it wrong, but I didn't forget about your invite to High Tea."

Mr Kuck grinned. "Thank you for visiting. Not many do. They put you away when you are old. My memory comes and goes these days. It frightens folk who don't understand, scares the hell out of me. I mean, one minute it is as bright as the sun, the next faded to dark. Today has been a good day, so far."

"Well, hurry up with the story before you forget." Fenella waved him on with a shooing motion. "And it better be a good one."

PC Sid Fenwick returned with Fenella's cake, scones, clotted cream and two pots of damson jam.

Mrs Sparks pointed at Fenella's plate, a greedy gleam in her eyes. "Is all that for you?"

"Aye. I've had a tough week in the trenches and it is Friday and I reckon it is going to be a long story."

Miss Zest waved at PC Sid Fenwick and jabbed a finger at Fenella's plate. It was clear what she wanted, but she did not speak.

"Me too," added Mrs Sparks. "We ladies must stick together."

PC Sid Fenwick nodded and left the table.

Fenella took a bite of Victoria cake. *Moist. Buttery. Sweet.* She turned to Mr Kuck. "You'd best start with your tale before the sun sets and they ring the bell for bedtime. Tell me about your time in the police."

Mr Kuck licked his lips, chortled with contentment and began. Fenella smothered a scone with clotted cream and damson jam. Mr Kuck told the story of the stolen coconut and he told the story of a missing child who turned up alive and well six months later on a narrowboat and he talked about his many encounters with poachers.

Fenella ate and sipped tea and said nothing. Mrs Sparks mumbled a few words and laughed at the right places in Mr Kuck's story. But Miss Zest's blank gaze stirred something deep and sorrowful in Fenella. It stirred something else, too. She waved PC Sid Fenwick over, whispered in his ear, then took a huge bite of scone slathered in clotted cream and damson jam.

The vicar played the final notes of *Fly Me to the Moon*

then he mopped his huge forehead with a handkerchief and sipped from a glass of red wine. A few people clapped, including Fenella, to show their appreciation.

Mr Kuck continued his tales. Mrs Sparks burst out in a fit of laughter, this time ahead of the punchline. Undeterred, Mr Kuck continued and acted out a struggle with a poacher. A physical hand-to-hand battle which saw the poacher behind bars and another medal pinned to Mr Kuck's chest. Mrs Sparks clapped. Miss Zest clapped. Fenella clapped too.

Mr Kuck talked with such steady ease, his voice low and soothing, that Fenella almost missed when Dexter entered the room. She waved and held her breath, hoping she'd not made a big mistake.

At Dexter's side, holding his arm, Helen Grimes glanced in their direction. A new melody tinkled from the piano—the vicar's rendition of the theme song from *The Wizard of Oz*. Each note tinged with sadness. Each chord filled with hope.

Fenella wasn't sure how long Helen Grimes screamed. A second or two. Maybe more. Whenever she looked back on the next few moments, the wail stretched for an eternity. Not an American accent. Not a British one either. A universal sound, the same in every language. A roar of pure joy from deep within the soul.

Helen Grimes dashed across the dining room. Miss Zest rose to her feet, blinked, seemed confused, and then opened her arms. The two women hugged.

"Helen?" Miss Zest repeated the question, her eyes alive and glistening.

"Yes, it's me." Helen Grimes was hugging and kissing

Miss Zest. "Aunt Ann it's me, your niece."

90

The sun was setting when Fenella climbed out of her car at her cottage on Cleaton Bluff. Clouds scurried in from the sea carried by a warm gusting breeze. On the porch, Nan eased back and forth in a rocking chair, her head down in a book. Eduardo ambled through the front door and held out an ale bottle.

Fenella folded the events of the past few days into a tight parcel and shoved it to the back of her mind. Friday night was here. The end of the work week. Time to start the weekend. Her children and her grandbairns would arrive in the morning. Family time.

Eduardo placed the ale bottle on a table next to Nan. She looked up. "You greedy bugger." Then she glanced across the yard to Fenella's car. "Fen's home. Is that for me?"

"Ah. . . yes. . . yes." Eduardo made a little bow.

"Well, get one for Fen. And yourself, seeing as it is the weekend. Only one, mind you."

Eduardo didn't go back into the house. He walked across the yard, took Fenella's arm and held her there. "Hard week?"

He looked at her, eyes soft, but did not ask about what

she'd seen. He never asked about the details of her job. Knew about her work-home life switch. Loved her all the more for it.

"Aye." That was about all she'd say on the matter. "Now where is that ale?"

They walked arm in arm back to the porch. Eduardo kissed her on the lips then wandered to the kitchen. Fenella sat by her mam. They'd chat until the dying light faded to dark, and when the moon came up, they'd eat dinner right here on the front porch and drink another beer.

Author's Note

Thank you for reading this book. The village of Ambleside is a very popular tourist destination rich in natural beauty and cultural heritage. As a writer, I've created a fictionalised version of the village. Borrans Park with its open green space, park benches, views across Lake Windermere and ancient Roman road, was the inspiration for Borrans Wood and Bede Thatch.

The name of the village pub is not mentioned but there are many delightful watering holes in Ambleside. I leave it to the visitor to guess which is the local where Liam drank and Kate worked.

There are other loose ends to tie up and questions to be answered, of course. A bit like a *Northworder* puzzle where the solution exists and is hinted at in the text but the diligent reader is left to figure it out.

If you ever visit St Mary's church, you might just catch a glimpse of a stooped woman wearing a peach headscarf and kneeling in a pew. If you do, offer her a stick of gum and five minutes of your time.

There are many more Detective Inspector Fenella Sallow stories in the series. I hope you enjoy them all.

Best wishes,
NC Lewis

WANT MORE?

If you would like to receive news about new books in the series and other works, please use the QR code to join my reader mailing list.